The Strongholder

I0637514

Steve Pillinger

Book Three of
The Mindrulers
series

Cover design by Cathy Helms, Avalon Graphics LLC.

ISBN: 978-0-6399077-5-8

Although some of the characters in this book were inspired by real people, they remain entirely fictitious, and any identification made with actual persons is the reader's interpretation, not the author's intention.

Note also that the theological speculations in this book represent the characters' attempts to understand the situation in which they find themselves, and do not necessarily reflect the beliefs of the author.

Readers may notice in this book that pronouns referring to God are not spelled with capitals (he, him, his, etc.). This does not imply any disrespect for God. It simply follows the example of most English versions of the Bible.

To my family
who played the game,
inspired the story, read the drafts,
and kept me writing.
This is your book!

Other titles in this series:
The Mindruler (2017)
The Restorers (2019)

Praise for this book:

"A stunning end to a riveting series. Highly recommended." – Fiona Veitch Smith, CWA Historical Dagger shortlisted author for *The Jazz Files*, UK.

"I found The Strongholder deeply engrossing and very moving too. The best of the three books in *The Mindrulers* series, leading to a very satisfying finale." – Adriana, South Africa.

"Steve Pillinger has woven together a great adventure filled with tender, moving moments, unforgettable characters, spiritually powerful scenes, and a great finale to the Restorers' saga! This novel (and the series) stays with you!" – Sean, UK.

"*The Strongholder* brings everything together from the previous two books in an epic climax! As always with Pillinger's writing, the many threads of the plot are so delicately intertwined that you're on tenterhooks to see how they will all come together in the end! I was glued to it right to the last word." – John, UK.

"Pillinger's gifted story telling and dynamic world building shine in this exciting conclusion to his *The Mindrulers* series." – Chris, USA.

"Packed with excitement and unexpected twists and turns, *The Strongholder* is an epic and riveting finale to *The Mindrulers* series. Thoroughly enjoyable." – Sophie, South Africa.

Praise for The Mindruler:

"The rich setting and world-building of this novel drew me in and enticed me to keep reading from the beginning. ... I would recommend this book for readers who enjoy vivid world-building and portal fantasy with a bit of grit." – Bridgett Powers, USA.

"One thing I really like is the characters. They're not the usual flat and stereotypical heroes – they feel real, flawed and quirky, like they could be your own grandmother, over-enthusiastic friend or rebellious cousin." – Jennifer, UK.

Praise for The Restorers:

"I loved the first novel, *The Mindruler,* but this novel takes the story to even greater heights! It is the best adventure I've read—with great moments of spiritual truth and reality, and a tantalizing finish (complete with a twist)."
– Caleb, UK.

"There were times when I cringed, times when I yelled, and times when my heart sang while reading *The Restorers*. ... I recommend this book for Christians who enjoy a large-scale fantasy where God is not relegated to the position of a bit-player on the world stage." – Christine, USA.

"Kudos to Steve Pillinger! He's given us an even more amazing sequel! I can't wait to see what book three holds, but I know I want this series to be more than a trilogy! Get the first two and enjoy them fully!" – Stan, USA.

Table of Contents

Acknowledgments

This book has taken shape over many years, with helpful input from many people. Those who have been there from the beginning are my family, and many of the characters and events took shape during the happy hours we spent playing the 'Family Game'. You know that this story is yours as much as mine.

Then there are my 'beta testers' — the intrepid band of friends who read my half-baked drafts and made constructive comments. Thank you for your perseverance!

Among these special mention must be made of the Beardlings, my fellow-writers in Thame, Oxfordshire. Andrew and Victor, you so often put your fingers on the exact issue that needed correcting; our sessions of coffee, laughter and helpful criticism have improved the story immeasurably.

To Fiona Veitch Smith, whose penetrating and insightful critique tightened the story and removed many rough edges — I can only say a deeply heartfelt thank you!

Last, in pride of place, is my wife. She ruthlessly slashed excess verbiage, transforming my writing style. The movie-like 'scenes' she pictured provided seminal ideas that enriched the plot time and again. It is no cliché to say that this book could not have been written without her.

Who's Who

Ademu	Agent of the Selmian Renegade Royalty.
Alanya	Dûrian name of Lannie Catterick, Restorer (Dûrion) and website designer (UK).
Barilu Dantorida (**Bari**)	Cousin and best friend of Konnaru Galenida (Konnar) during their childhood in Selmion.
Barkt	Men's Overseer of the Olbizân teméyn plantation in Barazhân. Husband of Felhis.
Belyeru (**Mindbender**)	The Strongholder's Chief Mindbender.
Bishop Harlon	Dûrian Head of State and Hearth (Church), reinstated after the death of Shambor.
Bishop Mâron	Dûrian Bishop Suffragan, replacing Shambor: responsible for the day-to-day running of the state under Bishop Harlon. *On Earth:* Father Martin, Vicar of the Round Church of Leston.
Brakhól	Grûzhack child tortured by the Selmians to become their Child of Despair, who was rescued in *The Restorers*.
Cârinor don Danneret (**Cârin, Câr**)	Surviving member of the twins: former rebel soldiers who joined the Restorers in *The Mindruler*. His brother Shîrin (Shîr) was killed in Shambor's ambush in *The Restorers*.
Children of Despair	*See* **Gorelenye**.
Danîsha ('Neesh)	Dûrian name of Denise Thompson, Restorer (Dûrion) and retired teacher (UK).
Dorbians	Intelligent wolf-like species living to the far north of Dûrion, whose Legion commanded by Gwargif came to the Restorers' aid in Book 2, *The Restorers*.
Edoru (**Prince**)	Selmian aristocrat and member of the Privy Council of the Renegade Royalty.
Estaron don Geldor	Dûrian Bishop Suffragan's Secretary: formerly to Shambor, now to Bishop Mâron.
Father Martin	Earthly name of Bishop Mâron, former Kindler of Sûrilane and Vicar of the Round Church of Leston in Oxfordshire.

Felhis	Women's Overseer of the Olbizân teméyn plantation in Barazhân. Wife of Barkt.
Frengor	'Visionary' or head of the Travelling Order of Lightist priests, who support the Restorers.
Garset (Lord Marshal)	Commander of the Dûrian army under Bishops Harlon and Mâron.
Gedoriu	Major-domo in the Strongholder's palace, Orselm.
Gelmion	Dûrian name of Gil Denbigh, former mindbent slave of Bishop Shambor (Dûrion); and university lecturer (UK).
Gil Denbigh	English name of Gelmion.
Gorelenye	Children of Despair, whose innate telepathic abilities are refined by torture to cripple enemies by broadcasting intense negative emotions.
Grûzhack	Tall, technically advanced race living in the Hidden Magistry of Barazhân in the Tallisor Mountains — the only source of the drug *teméyn*.
Gwargif	*Hrarkhez* or High Commander of the Dorbian Legion.
Harlon	*See **Bishop Harlon**.*
Ilinu	Stonemason and agent of the Selmian Renegade Royalty.
Jomel	Former prostitute in the Temple of Gadesh, rescued by the Restorers in *The Mindruler*. Cousin of Perrely.
Kastenu (Prince)	Selmian printer and member of the Privy Council of the Selmian Renegade Royalty.
Konnaru Galenida (**Konnar**)	Cousin and best friend of Barilu Dantorida (Bari) during their childhood in Selmion.
Lannie Catterick	English name of Alanya.
Lingetu	The Strongholder's chief spy.
Mâron	*See **Bishop Mâron**.*
Mistil Na-ReyDerid	Wife of Tal Gha-Derid. Mother of Shakhere and Brakhól.
'Neesh	Nickname of Danîsha (Denise Thompson) used by the Restorers.
Nist	Head of the network smuggling goods and supplies through Grûzhack army lines to the Galeronden people in the Tallissôr Mountains.

Nomariu Tarenida a KariLanta (Prince)	Heir of the Selmian Renegade Royalty and rightful King of Selmion.
One, the	Short for the One Creator God: All-powerful God in whom Lightists believe.
Ongaret	Travelling priest, personal assistant to Frengor.
Otaru	Personal steward to the Governor of Selmion.
Pastenu	Steward to Prince Sindetu Lenorida.
Perrely	Young Dûrian girl of noble family, Jomel's cousin, who joined the Restorers in *The Mindruler*. Shiván's sweetheart.
Prince Orrénne	Son of the One Creator God.
Shakhere	Grûzhack army scout.
Shambor (Bishop / Mindruler)	Former Bishop Suffragan and de facto ruler of Dûrion, as well as Mindruler and head of the Cult of Gadesh, until his timely death in *The Restorers*.
Shiván	Dûrian name of Steve Harston, Overguardian (Dûrion); *Hrarborgh* (Father of Warriors) to the Dorbians; and university student (UK). Perrely's sweetheart.
Sindetu Lenorida (Prince)	Prince Regent of the Selmian Renegade Royalty. Head of the Privy Council.
Strongholder, The	Chief Initiate of the Cult of Gadesh, Ruler of Mindrulers and Lord of Selmion.
Tal Gha-Derid	Docent of the Grûzhack Seminary for History and Culture in Kharzil, Barazhân. Father of Shakhere and Brakhól.
Tindoru (Prince)	Haulier and member of the Privy Council of the Selmian Renegade Royalty.

Maps of Dûrion, Selmion and the Dûrai Area

Key to Map symbols and shadings

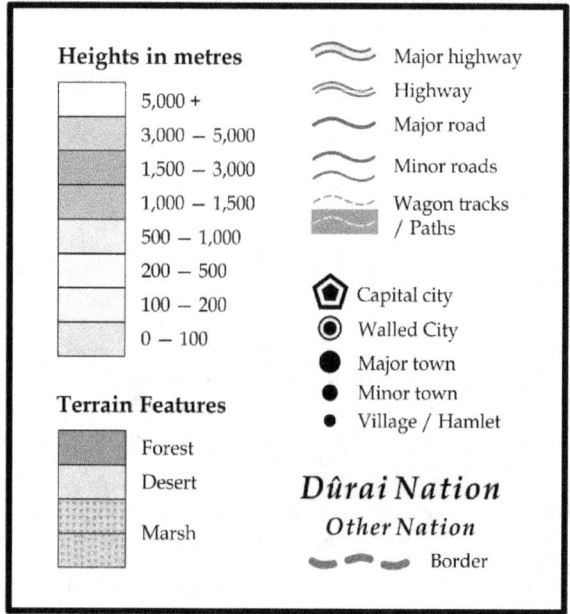

Note: The **Dûrai Nations** are Dûrion, Selmion, Thrinar, Marûvin, Pandiar and the city-state of Calardane.

The primary Dûrian unit of distance is the *aldor* (plural *aldoret*), which is equivalent to approximately one and a quarter kilometers or three quarters of a mile.

Map 1:
The Dûrai Area

Map 2:
Central & Eastern Dûrion

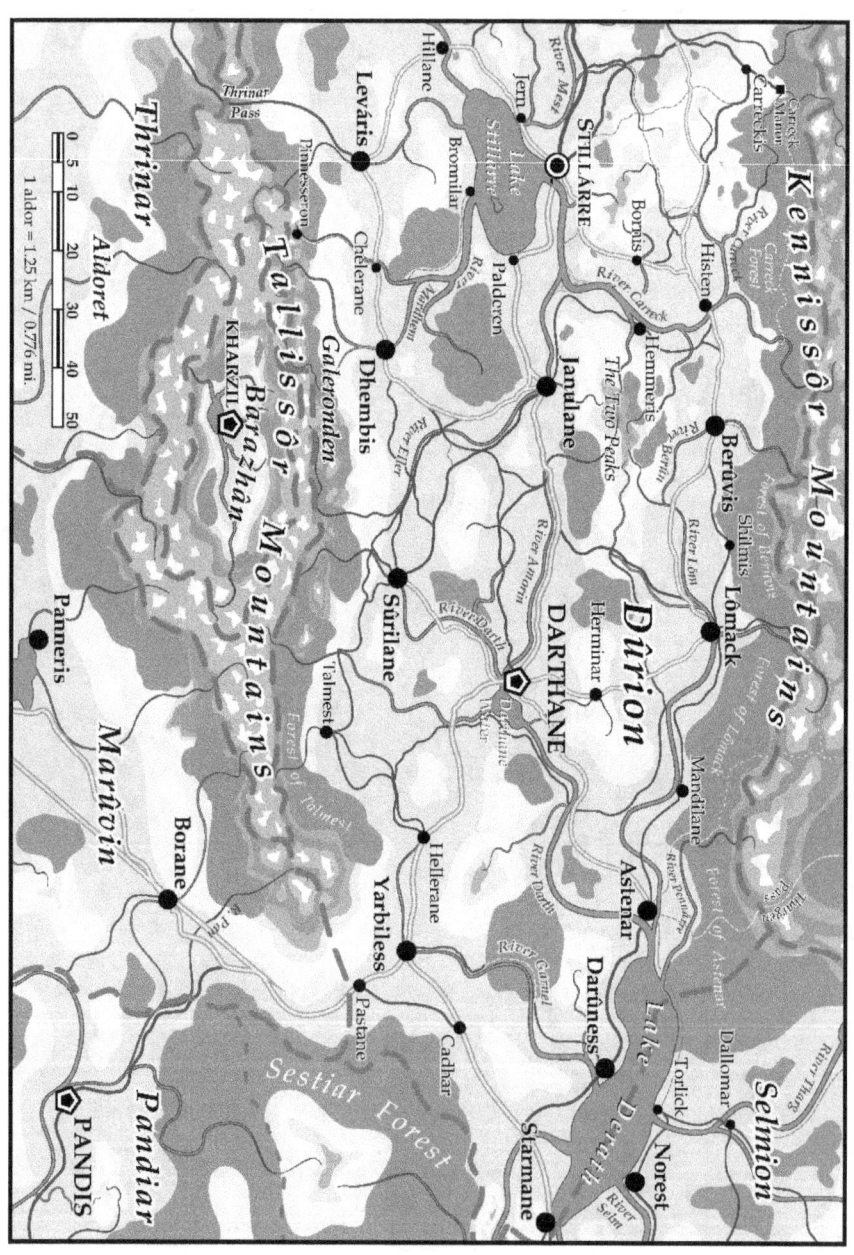

The Story So Far...

In the land of **Dûrion** on a distant planet, the majority of the population worship **the One Creator God**. But the country has suffered for years under the growing abuses of **Shambor**, supposedly their Bishop. In fact Shambor is the **Mindruler** of a network of subordinate **Mindbenders** who keep people in subjection through groups of telepathically-controlled spies and 'Bishop's Guards'.

In book 1 of this series, **The Mindruler**, we see how the One brings four ordinary English people to Dûrion to challenge the power of Shambor. Steve (known locally as **Shivàn**), **Lannie (Alanya)**, Denise **(Danîsha)** and **Gil (Gelmion)** find themselves in this alien place, where they gradually make friends and learn the language. They discover that the Dûrians' beliefs are surprisingly similar to the Christian faith on Earth; and in time all except Gil, who does not believe in God, come to accept their new, daunting rôle as the **Restorers of the Way**, long prophesied in the Dûrian scriptures.

Among those the Restorers meet is **Gwargif**, the strange, wolf-like emissary of a far northern people, the **Dorbians**. Gwargif tells them how their priests received a message from the Shining One instructing them to find and support his 'Warriors of Light' in distant Dûrion. Gwargif has no doubt that these are the Restorers of the Way. He returns to his homeland to summon the five-thousand strong Dorbian Legion to support their cause.

Meanwhile Gil, the agnostic, decides to leave the others and make his own way in Dûrion. This leads inevitably to his capture and enslavement by a Mindbender. The other Restorers set out to rescue him together with some Dûrian friends, including Shivàn's sweetheart **Perrely** (a young noblewoman with unconventional ideas). They succeed at last by killing Gil's Mindbender – much to the displeasure of the Mindruler. Shambor now turns all his attention and considerable resources to the task of eliminating these troublemakers...

In book 2, **The Restorers**, the four are on the run, narrowly slipping through the dragnet Shambor throws out. Little do they realise, however, that Gil, presenting himself as a believer, is still mindbent: now by none other than Shambor himself. The Mindruler follows their every move through Gil, and cunningly leads them from one trap into another.

But the stakes are raised when the Restorers find the **Ambon of Sûrilane**, the long-lost national emblem of the Dûrians' faith in the One. When raised up, the Ambon summons many believers to their cause.

Among them is **Garset**, an army captain who places his company of four hundred One-fearing soldiers at their disposal.

Another development that seriously hinders Shambor is the war that breaks out in the south, largely thanks to actions taken by the Restorers. The tall, fearsome **Grûzhack** come pouring out of their mountain fastness of **Barazhân** with their fire weapons, and Shambor's forces are stretched thin as he attempts to hold them back.

Nevertheless Shambor allows the Restorers to summon thousands to their cause through the Ambon, leading them with Gil's help into a well-planned ambush. In a massive battle, Shambor uses **Brakhól**, a tortured 'Child of Despair' and strong natural telepath, to deluge the Restorers' army with soul-destroying emotions of pain and hopelessness. The army falls apart and thousands of lives are lost. Perrely, Danisha and Lannie are captured and taken to Shambor in **Darthane**, the capital. The only gleam of hope is that after rescuing the child Brakhól, Shiván manages to escape with him and a small band of companions. Garset joins him later with a few others.

Hopelessly outnumbered, Shivan and Garset lead their remnant to Darthane. There, when they're on the brink of defeat, Gwargif and the wolf-like Dorbian Legion come pouring in from the north to their aid. Though Shambor's forces are driven back into the city, the high stone walls keep the Restorers' army out. Then, as they sing songs of praise, the Dorbians' deep, resonant voices join in, and the One brings the city walls crashing down as he did for Joshua in the Bible.

They enter the city in triumph: but Mindruler Shambor is ready for them. He almost succeeds in snatching victory from defeat when they approach, mindbending Garset and preparing to do the same with Shiván. But Shambor doesn't know that Perrely, Lannie and Danîsha have escaped during the earthquake when the walls fell. At the last moment Danisha confronts him like an Old Testament prophet, her God-given words penetrating the brokenness in Shambor's psyche and driving him over the edge of sanity. In unendurable mental conflict he throws himself out of a high window, finally ending his reign of terror in Dûrion.

Peace! For a few months at least, as winter puts an end to warfare.

But come spring, Dûrion will face the wrath of the **Strongholder**, Ruler of Mindrulers and Shambor's superior in the eastern nation of **Selmion**. And in the south the Grûzhack are preparing a new offensive...

Two superpowers, both seeking to snatch away the battered nation's new-found freedom.

The Restorers' mission is far from complete.

The Strongholder

Prologue: *Winter of Content*

BISHOP SHAMBOR WAS DEAD; *and Dûrion was alive again.*

In the Winter of Content that followed Shambor's death, old Bishop Harlon resumed the reins of government amid nationwide rejoicing, appointing Kindler Mâron of Sûrilane as his new Bishop Suffragan. The Mindbenders and their reign of terror were over. The infamous Bishop's Guard was disbanded, its few surviving members in the care of the Travelling Order. The old Dûrian clan structure blossomed once more, and village Elders were reinstated across the country. Young people flocked to join the renewed Dûrian army under Lord Marshal Garset — renowned for his part in the War of Restoration.

But most revered in the people's eyes were the Restorers of the Way — the One's emissaries whom he had sent from a distant sky to overthrow Shambor's tyranny: Lady Alanya *Atémban*, Restorer of Hearing, who had used her bess — her shell of Thrinar — to overhear the Usurper's plans; Lady Danîsha *Atémbellar*, Restorer of Song, who had frozen the Bishop's Guard in their tracks with the God-given music of her seven-stringed bellaril; and especially, of course, Lord Shiván *Aténnelor*, the Overguardian, wielder of the Blade of Darthane, who with the One's wisdom had devised the brilliant strategies that led to Shambor's downfall.

Little was said of the fourth Restorer, Gelmion, the supposed *Atémbis* or Restorer of Sight with his two-handled glass, the Blaise. The other Restorers had used the blaise to good effect in the war; but Gelmion was a traitor. He, with Shambor, had set up the disastrous Ambush of Stillárre where thousands of good men and women had been slaughtered. It was only by the Restorers' mercy that Gelmion had not been executed. He now lived as a virtual recluse in the private apartments of the Cathedral.

But the other Restorers were far from inactive. Together with the Bishops they were rebuilding the nation after the ravages of war and Shambor's oppression: removing all traces of the Mindbenders' evil Cult of Gadesh; finding healing for the many innocent victims of mindbending; redistributing the wealth hoarded by Shambor's greedy barons; rooting out graft and incompetence. Lady Alanya heard difficult legal cases and discerned the rights of the matter; Lady Danîsha played her bellaril and declared the One's truth in song—often accompanying the young Grûzhack child Brakhól, whose singing had to be heard to be believed. Lord Shiván inspired the people with his stirring speeches, while he and Marshal Garset continued to guard the nation from outside perils.

In Darthane, of course, Lord Shiván and Lady Perrely en Nelláy a GarMadin were the most sought-after guests at banquets, and the question on all lips was when they would be betrothed…

But looming behind the joy was the dark backdrop that no one mentioned—the ever-growing menace of the two superpowers. In the south the fearsome Grûzhack military had left their mountain fastness and with their fire-weapons had captured the Dûrian towns of Dhembis and Leváris. And in the east the Strongholder, Lord of Selmion and Ruler of Mindrulers, had dispatched his armies to subjugate Dûrion once again to the evil Cult of Gadesh. He would exact terrible vengeance for the killing of his instrument, Shambor.

The citizens of Dûrion lived in the moment, enjoying their freedom while they could.

Chapter 1: *The man in white*

DESPITE THE EARLY SPRING SUNSHINE, there was still a nip of winter in the air as Shiván and Danîsha trotted their two-humped Dûrian camel-horses towards the south-eastern Dûrian town of Yarbiless. Flanking them on either side was an escort of ten blue-caped cavalrymen. Danîsha's bellaril was slung over her shoulder; and perched in front of Shiván was Brakhól. In the absence of Perrely, Shiván was glad to be riding with the Grûzhack child. Brakhól's pale, ridged face and down-turned eyes belied a happy nature, which, with his amazing ability to broadcast his happiness, made a joy of any journey.

It was at Garset's request that they were making this one. He and the army had laid siege to Starmane, the easternmost town of Dûrion, which had been captured by the Strongholder's forces from Selmion. It was vital that they not be allowed to break out of that narrow bottleneck between the Shinára Hills and Lake Derath: if they did, the whole of eastern Dûrion—and the capital, Darthane—would lie open to the ravages of the dreaded Selmian cavalry.

Shiván, being in overall charge of military strategy, had remained in Darthane to keep an eye on both the Selmian and Grûzhack fronts. But now Garset's forces were in trouble. The Selmians had brought Children of Despair into Starmane, and their cries of agony when tortured drained all hope from mens' hearts, breaking the army's morale, causing some to desert and sapping the courage of all. Exactly the same, in fact, as when Brakhól had been used as a Child of Despair in Shambor's Ambush last year.

Only now he was their Child of Hope, the antidote to despair. Garset's request—relayed via Lannie and the bess—was not for Shiván or Danîsha: it was for Brakhól.

"When will I sing for the soldiers?" the child asked again. Shiván laughed. That was about the tenth time in two days.

"Soon," 'Neesh replied. "You'll sing songs about the Prince for them. You like singing about the Prince, don't you?"

"Yes!" A burst of happiness accompanied the enthusiastic response, bringing smiles even to the most hardened faces among their escort.

3

Shiván's thoughts went back to that incredible day a couple of months ago when Brakhól had met the Prince. The two of them had gone for a walk in the Bishop's Park, and the boy had been full of questions about the One and his Son, Prince Orrénne. When he understood that the great Prince of all the skies wanted to be friends with *him*, Brakhól, and he only needed to ask—he had done so, and an explosion of joy had shaken the whole of Darthane. The city had basked for days in the happiness radiating from the Grú-zhack child as he discovered the boundless love of the One Creator God.

Brakhól loved to sing, and 'Neesh had taught him songs about the Prince on the bellaril. Simple as the songs were, when Brakhól and the bellaril sang together all work stopped as the music of God's love poured into thirsty hearts.

That was why they were travelling now to Starmane. Brakhól *had to* turn the tide and prevent the Selmians from breaking out. Shiván thanked the One for the hundredth time that the southern nations of Marûvin and Pandiar, which were also controlled by the Strongholder, had very little between them in the way of an army. The Strongholder had summoned what troops they had, but several Dûrian companies and a squadron of cavalry were holding them at bay in Pastane, just south of Yarbiless.

The horses crested a rise, and there ahead on a dry, grassy plain was Yarbiless itself, its sand-coloured, brown-tiled buildings spanning the River Garnel. Shiván's heart sank at the thought of the festivities they'd be subjected to yet again. The Restorers had not yet visited eastern Dûrion, and he and 'Neesh were greeted as conquering heroes in every little town and village, forced to listen to speeches of welcome, suffer being draped with coloured ribbons, offered sumptuous banquets, and (Shiván, at least) numerous hands in marriage by the parents of moon-eyed young ladies. Their frequent refusal of these offerings in their haste to reach Starmane had not always been well received.

Shiván shook his head as he remembered the succession of yearning feminine eyes he'd been subjected to. This despite the fact that everyone in Dûrion knew where his heart lay. Over winter the story of his love for Perrely, and what she had suffered for him at Shambor's hands, had been told in every inn and hostel from Starmane to Varlez.

4

Perrely. Pain wrung his heart at the thought of her. She loved him, he knew; but she remained unshakeable in her conviction that the One intended her to remain single, wholly devoted to his Son, Prince Orrénne. Yet for Shiván, leaving her now in Darthane had torn an aching gap in his heart that no simpering beauty could fill.

He sighed. He firmly believed God would show Perrely otherwise one day; until then he just had to endure the pain.

* * *

"Ney li silmend, Aténnelor – Light stay with you, Overguardian." Lieutenant Cârin don Danneret of the re-formed Dûrian army threw Shiván a quick hand-on-heart salute.

Three days had passed since Shiván had reached Starmane with Danîsha and Brakhól. Great days, in which Brakhól had sung and the tide had turned. Their grip on the occupied town had tightened, and Garset wanted to weaken the defence just a little more before launching an all-out assault to recapture it.

On the point of entering his tent, Shiván turned and grinned at Cârin. The slim rebel scout – now dressed in the green infantry cape of his former enemies – was like a brother to him. He completed the Dûrian goodnight: *"Illi ristend.* – And keep you."

Cârin lingered. "You acquitted yourself well today. The troopers can't stop talking about your exploits."

Shiván cocked an eye at the half-smile on Câr's face. "And I bet you helped them along with a few well-placed exaggerations."

The lieutenant gave an elaborate shrug. "Just boosting your reputation, Hero! After Shambor, this country needs leaders it can look up to."

Shiván grinned. "Well, *I've* been telling everyone that any good swordplay I displayed was thanks to your training over the winter."

"Good thinking. Adds humility to your reputation."

"Hah! If I listen to you any more my head won't fit into my helmet. *Ney li silmend."*

"Illi ristend." They clasped hands and raised them in the Dûrian high handshake.

Shiván ducked into the tent. He was glad his status as Overguardian gave him a tent to himself, even if it was in the centre of the camp. He yawned and started preparing himself for bed. It had been a long day, and the extended celebration this evening hadn't helped. But he couldn't blame Garset's troops: until his arrival with Danîsha and Brakhól they'd had a thin time of it. Only Gwargif's Dorbian Legion had prevented the Selmians breaking out of Starmane—though initially they had been the ones in need of support, losing many of their wolf-like warriors to Selmian archers as they circled close to the town to keep the Selmian cavalry penned in.

But all that would change now they had Brakhól.

He straightened his long night-shirt and knelt down in front of a small basin that contained salty water. The dagger strapped to his thigh was uncomfortable, but both Garset and Cârin insisted he should wear it, even at night. Taking a short stick with a frayed end, he brushed his teeth. The stick was getting soft—he'd have to replace it soon. After spitting the water out, he climbed on to his bedding and pulled the thick blanket over him to keep out the chill.

His muttered prayer faded into silence as he fell asleep.

* * *

The man in white was just another shadow in the darkness that surrounded the camp. No light fell on his hooded face as he smiled.

Not far away a Dûrian sentry leant on his spear, staring away into the grey ranks of tents. He yawned noisily, and the man in white sensed his thoughts. *That was some celebration tonight! Went on a bit long, though. Just my bad luck to be on guard duty. But after today I can tell them back home that I fought alongside Shiván* Aténnelor, *the Overguardian! The way he wielded the Blade of Darthane... and those amazing kicks and punches in between... Light help any Selmians who tangled with him! Not that the Light did help them. We sent 'em scuttling back into Starmane before they knew what hit 'em...*

The man in white stifled a contemptuous snort. Let the fool gloat while he could. Yes, the Dûrians now seemed to have everything going for them. To combat the Children of Despair, Shiván had brought with him the first and greatest Child, the Grûzhack boy, stolen from that lunatic Shambor dom Beldet. The Dûrians affected to call the Grûzhack brat their 'Child of Hope'.

He was the reason they had been dancing round their campfires tonight while the older female Restorer—one of their foreign leaders—played the bellaril and the Child sang. The bellaril alone was a devastating weapon, but fortunately he had not been close enough to be affected by it. The singing was bad enough, broadcasting waves of nauseating emotion that left him choking on his own bile. He hadn't been able to start his mission until that obscene racket had stopped.

Then, of course, there were the Dorbians: the ongoing scourge of the Selmian cavalry. From the start those savage, wolf-like beasts had prowled the perimeter of Starmane, their powerful feral scent sending any camel-horse that dared show itself bolting back to safety. The Selmians were hemmed into the small town between the hills and the lake, with the cavalry—their pride and joy—reduced to mere foot soldiers!

But the man in white smiled. That was all about to change.

* * *

Shiván jerked awake. What was that? Something had disturbed him. He glanced round the tent, but saw nothing. It was still dark outside, and there were no sounds of movement in the camp. He sighed and let his head sink back down. Soon he drifted off again.

But this time he was restless. He kept half-waking, thinking someone was in the tent, hearing whispers and the distant drone of someone reciting poetry. Annoyed, he tried to get back to sleep.

Suddenly he opened his eyes to find a young man in white bending over him. "Greetings, Shiván *Aténnelor*." The young man smiled, though his eyes were like ice.

Shiván tried to jump up, to reach for the dagger on his thigh, but he couldn't move. His visitor continued to speak, now in a foreign language, those intense, unnerving eyes boring into him and pinning him to his bed.

Then the intruder smiled again, and Shiván's blood ran cold.

"Farewell, Shiván *Nistállenor*!"

Unable to speak or move, Shiván felt a grey mist descend over his mind.

Chapter 2: *Stumbling block*

SHIVÁN WOKE TREMBLING from the worst nightmare he'd had since his last bout of depression several years ago. It had been amazingly vivid. That young man with the piercing grey eyes bending over him in the tent… He shuddered at the memory.

The white-robed stranger had been talking in a foreign language, hadn't he? But he'd greeted him in Dûrian, using his title — *Aténnelor*. He'd also said farewell in Dûrian, using a different title. What was it? *Nistállenor*, that was it. He hadn't come across the word before. He'd have to ask Cârin.

Anyway, it was only a dream, the One be praised!

Feeling a call of nature coming on, Shiván got up and stumbled outside. He glanced around as he did the necessary. The individual tents were just beginning to show up in the grey pre-dawn light. The camp would start waking soon; he had another half-hour of sleep at most.

A hollow, drumming sound caught his attention. Looking frontwards he was appalled to see that he was wetting his own tent. How embarrassing! The orderlies would see the damp patch when they came to clean up. He shook his head as he rearranged his night-shirt and ducked back inside. It was many years since he'd done anything as stupid as that. He collapsed on the bedding and closed his eyes…

"*Shiván, wake up! Shiván!*"

Cârin was shaking him. He sat up groggily. "What time is it?"

"Time to put your armour on, you lazy so-and-so! You've missed the dawnmeal. The troops are all drawn up, and Garset's just waiting for your Hero-ship so he can order the attack!"

"Okay, okay… Wait!"

"Shiván, we can't wait!"

"I have a question."

"Leave it till later! Get your breastplate on…" Cârpulled him upright and grabbed the pliable, interwoven strips of metal that formed a Dûrian soldier's breastplate.

Shiván's eyes were unfocused. "What's a *Nistállenor*?"

"What?"

"A *Nistállenor*."

8

"Shiván, pay attention! *Hold* the breastplate while I buckle it at the back."

"What *is* it?"

With a sharp tug Cârin tightened the second strap. "It's what you're being right now! A stumbling block, a nuisance, a hindrance! Now will you *please* concentrate? Your helmet — your greaves — "

Shiván walked out in a daze. A *stumbling block*? "No, not *that* way," Câr exclaimed, pulling him towards the assembled troops. "Holy Flame, what's wrong with you?"

The moment they engaged the enemy a Selmian infantryman charged Shiván . He swept the Blade of Darthane down in a devastating arc to strike the sword from his hand — only to find that he'd missed completely. Leaping clumsily aside he just managed to evade the soldier's thrust. Bringing the Blade up in a convulsive reaction, he barely countered the return swing. For a moment he stood stunned. *What's going on?*

"Shiván! Behind you!" Cârin's urgent shout broke through the fog enveloping his mind. He whirled round. A cavalryman was almost upon him with lance extended. He launched into his famous 'sword-kick', as it had been dubbed, when he used his martial arts to kick a weapon out of the enemy's hand.

He missed, and landed ignominiously on his back. Cârin appeared above him, sword whirling in a blur as he struck the lance aside. Nearby Dûrian troopers tackled the cavalryman while Shiván stumbled to his feet. His mind was in a daze.

"*Shiván!* Get it together, for the One's sake! You can't fall asleep on the battlefield!"

"I don't... Something's not..."

"*Watch it!*" Cârin leapt in to block a charging swordsman, whose weapon sliced Câr's sword arm. A streak of red appeared. He smoothly switched sword and shield and continued fighting with his left hand.

Shiván lunged at a cavalryman coming up behind them, and the Blade grazed the horse's neck — which was not where he'd been aiming. The animal screamed and reared up, hooves flashing. Shiván leapt out of the way and cannoned into Cârin's opponent. They both fell to the ground, and with a quick stroke Câr finished his enemy off.

"Shiván, what is *wrong* with you?" he hissed, his eyes like twin daggers as Shiván again struggled to his feet. Again the nearby Dûrian troopers came to their rescue, several throwing disbelieving glances at Shiván.

"I *don't know!*" Shiván snapped back, anguish and frustration roiling within him. The Blade—only yesterday an extension of his arm that flowed smoothly from one target to the next—felt today like an awkward lump of metal in his hands. He even seemed to have forgotten his martial arts, which he'd practised for years.

"*Aténnelor!*" Garset appeared nearby on horseback. The man in white's substitute title leapt to Shiván's mind: *Nistállenor*. No longer the Overguardian; just a stumbling block. "Will you lead the advance on the right flank? They're faltering, and we need a strong man in front."

Then you don't need me, Shiván thought dismally. He managed a nod to Garset, who smiled warmly and rode off to deal with other matters.

"Well, that's just wonderful, isn't it?" Câr exclaimed when Garset was out of earshot. "A heroic charge just when you'll probably lead them the wrong way! Well, I'm coming with you, and so are *you*—" he slapped a nearby trooper's shoulder "—and you—and you!" He fixed the three troopers with a stern glare. "The Overguardian is out of sorts today, and you are now his personal guard under my command. You will not allow an enemy near him. Got it?" They nodded, eyes wide. "Then to the right flank we go!" He flourished his sword in that direction, and they set off at a brisk trot, Shiván running blindly in their midst, his mind engulfed in shame.

On the right flank he did little better. With his "guards'" help he somehow he held his own, and they made inroads into the enemy lines; but he was painfully aware that Cârin was watching over him like a father with an idiot child. It was only his reputation, not his prowess in the battle, that was spurring those behind him to greater effort.

After one of his guards was felled by a back sweep Shiván should have blocked, he couldn't take any more. He turned and strode off the battlefield with Cârin behind him.

"Shiván, what's the matter with you?" Câr stormed at him when they were halfway to the tents and out of earshot. "Have you forgotten everything I taught you? You haven't been *concentrating*. A bad night is no excuse!"

Shiván turned and faced his honorary brother. "Câr, I'm not making excuses. I don't *know* what's wrong, okay? Maybe I just need a break…" A familiar knot of darkness, the prelude to depression, was forming within him. He could *not* give in to it.

Cârin surveyed him, eyebrows raised and arms akimbo. "Oh, the great Shiván needs a break! Apparently no one told him there are no breaks on the battlefield!"

"It's either that, or get more people killed protecting me from my own mistakes!" he snapped. "Câr, I'm sorry. I must sort this out myself. You go back and fight for us both."

Cârin stared at him for a long moment his eyes smouldering. Then he bowed stiffly. "As my Lord Overguardian commands." He turned and marched back to the battle.

Shiván sighed and walked on towards the tents. He *had* to think positively. At least he hadn't gone totally to pieces out there…

* * *

The sun was shining on the wide, grassy plain around Starmane, and there was a feeling of spring in the air. Danîsha sat on a low stool outside her tent in the centre of the Dûrian camp, playing an ancient children's game with Brakhól. They had to take an occasional break from singing. The six-year-old Grûzhack boy squatted on the ground in front of her. "*Am… sen… dôr…*" they intoned in unison, hands behind their backs; then up came Brakhól's right hand, clenched in a fist, while Danîsha brought hers out with her fingers waving in a rippling motion. Brakhól's cry of "*Gabil!* — Rock!" clashed with Danîsha's "*Elár!* — Water!"

"Rock beats water!" Brakhól cried with a bubbling laugh, sending waves of happiness wafting across the battlefield.

The despair from those poor Selmian children in Starmane could be felt, but only as a minor counterpoint in the background. Garset had said last night that Brakhól's joy probably strengthened the enemy soldiers as well — at least, those who were not mindbent; but even so, with his help the Dûrians and their Dorbian allies were preventing the Selmian cavalry from breaking through.

Danîsha sighed. The winter in Darthane had been so full of joy. But then as spring approached, grim reality had reasserted itself: the reality of two powerful nations looming over them, eager for conquest — Selmion in the east, the Grûzhack in the south and west.

11

The Selmians moved first, their cavalry capturing Starmane... And so peace and joy had faded away.

Of all that Brakhól was blissfully unaware, Light be praised. Out came his hand, palm upward: "Paper!" Danîsha matched it with flicking fingers: "Fire!" Before he could protest she darted her hand on to his, tickling his palm. The game dissolved in giggles.

Brakhól insisted on another chance, so they started again. But the child's transparent enjoyment reawakened an uneasy feeling that had troubled Danîsha from the start of this trip. Were they right to use Brakhól in this way? Where was the line between using and abusing? The Selmians had savagely abused him, treating him as a mere weapon of war and torturing him to produce the despair that unmanned their enemies. Were they, the Dûrians, now doing the same in reverse?

Nonsense. Once again she refuted her own argument. It arose out of the western notion back on Earth that 'children' right up to their mid-teens should not be required to do any meaningful work. Burdening them with such responsibility was considered 'abuse'. Yet in many cultures children worked alongside adults. Had she not done that herself on the farm where she grew up? Her parents loved her and had given her freedom to play as well. But it had given her a sense of pride, of belonging and being responsible, which children nowadays lacked. One day Brakhól would need to learn how to handle his own powerful gift... And that day would come only too soon.

The sound of approaching footsteps made her look up. To her surprise Shiván appeared in full battle gear from between the tents. She jumped up. "Shiván, what's happened? Are you alright?"

"*Shibán!*" Brakhól ran to him, his arms wide. Shiván scooped him up and tossed him in the air, as he usually did, and the child gave a whoop of delight. But as he came down Shiván fumbled the catch, and Brakhól slipped through his fingers, hitting the ground hard. The wail he let out sent a shaft of agony across the plain. Danîsha and Shiván both gasped, and there was a roar from the battlefield.

In that instant the darkness broadcast by the Selmian Children of Despair hit them in full force. Shiván stood slack-jawed, and Danîsha sat down suddenly, overwhelmed by a flood of hopelessness. The Dûrian army would crumble. The Selmians would break through. They would all drown in a sea of despair...

Forcing the dark images from her mind, Danîsha reached out with difficulty for Brakhól, lifted him and hugged him to her, crooning a gentle song. The agony eased. Slowly the despair lifted. 'Neesh murmured, "Boy beats ground!" and tapped Brakhól's nose with the tip of her finger. He gave a gurgling laugh, and suddenly the world was right again.

"Whew! Sorry, 'Neesh," Shiván muttered.

Brakhól's smile faded as he looked up at Shiván. "Why did you drop me?" The emotional equilibrium wobbled.

"I'm very sorry, Brakhól," Shiván said hastily. "I didn't *mean* to drop you. I would never try to hurt you."

"It's okay!" The sun shone again. "Orrénne will help you never to drop me again."

"That's right, Prince Orrénne will help me."

"Let's sing *Prince Loves Me!*" Brakhól cried.

Danîsha was anxious to know what had brought Shiván back from the battlefield, but Brakhól's emotional stability took priority. With a rueful glance at the Overguardian, Danîsha reached for her bellaril and began playing the boy's favourite song. They did it a dozen times every day; but Brakhól never tired of it. He sang with gusto, and Danîsha and Shiván joined in. Once again happiness wafted across the plain.

They finished, and Danîsha started a game of hand-clapping and knee-slapping. Shiván sat down beside them. As soon as she found a moment Danîsha asked, "Why have you left the battle?"

Shiván looked confused, started to say something, then abruptly glanced to his left and right. "Who's there?" he demanded.

Danîsha felt her face crease in a frown. What was wrong with the young *Aténnelor* today? He wasn't usually this slow on the uptake. She told Brakhól to wait, and reached into her tunic pocket. "Don't be silly," she said to Shiván. "No one's there. Someone's trying to contact us from Darthane, that's all. Probably Lannie."

That feeling of being watched was how the *blaise*—Gil's two-handled lens—affected you when someone was trying to get in touch. The blaise only gave sight, like a silent movie; Lannie's shell provided sound. Danîsha didn't know how they could have come this far without the 'instruments' the One had given them. It had seemed like magic, at first; but she'd come to accept that they were like the physical objects in the Bible that had acted as conduits of divine power: Moses' staff; the hem of Jesus' garment; Samson's hair; the Ark of the Covenant…

She lifted the bess out of her pocket, still wrapped in its protective cloth. Garset had given it to her at the dawnmeal in case of just such an event. She unfolded the cloth, revealing the shiny turquoise shell. Taking it in both hands she held it against her ear. "Lannie?"

She repeated the name a couple of times before an echoey voice sounded in the shell. "Danîsha! At last. Some important news. Can you hear me?"

"Yes, loud and clear. What news?"

"The Grûzhack are leaving Dhembis. Our scouts have reported large numbers heading for Lestack."

"What!"

"What is it, 'Neesh?" Shiván exclaimed. She ignored him, trying to take in what she was hearing. Then Brakhól started plucking at her tunic. "Is Lannie alright?" he asked anxiously.

"Give me the bess," Shiván demanded. She did so reluctantly, and turned her attention to reassuring Brakhól.

"They're heading towards the city?" Shiván exclaimed, and Danîsha glanced sharply at him. Lannie had said Lestack to her, a village near Sûrilane, and quite a distance from Darthane. But still, the news was not good. The weak point of this campaign against the Selmians, which they had recognised all along, was that it assumed the Grûzhack would be content for a while yet with the enclave they had carved for themselves around the southern Dûrian cities of Dhembis and Leváris. Whereas the Selmians were clearly not content to remain in Starmane. Hence the decision to throw all they had against the menace from the east. But if the Grûzhack were on the move now as well…

"Okay, Lannie, thanks for letting us know. We'll organise something. Tell Perrely not to worry." There was a pause. "Yes, I know, but we can't let the grass grow under our feet. Thanks. I'll get back to you."

He removed the shell from his ear and sat staring into space.

"Shiván!" Danîsha finally caught his attention. "What did Lannie tell you? Say it in English because of you-know-who."

"Um… The young man's people are heading towards… our capital city."

Danîsha frowned, but quickly put back her smile as she continued playing with Brakhól. "That's not what Lannie said to me."

"Oh yes, that's what she said. Perrely..., um, that is, the city is in danger. We have to do something."

Danîsha shot an anxious glance at the young man, who sat staring with clouded eyes at the surrounding tents, turning the bess over in his hands. Much as he loved Perrely, it wasn't like him to put her before the city and country. "Let's not overreact, Shiván. Lannie told me the... other enemy were heading towards Lestack. It'll be some time before they're any threat to the capital."

As if she hadn't spoken he said musingly, "The army must stay here. Splitting up won't help anyone. But they're also needed in Darthane..."

"Shiván, no —"

Suddenly he turned to her, urgency in his face. "We have to go back — you, me, and... himself."

Danîsha's eyes widened, and she couldn't keep the shock out her voice. "But Shiván — He's so badly needed here! You felt it just now — what it's like when he's not blocking out those Children of Despair. In any case, we discussed this at the Bishop's Council. He *might* make a good defence against his own people — but we can't be sure. He might also strengthen them. And if we bring him too close and they realise he's one of theirs, they may go all out to rescue him. What then? What will they do with him? And in any case, I don't think Lannie was saying there's any immediate danger to Darthane."

"'Neesh, we can't leave the city unprotected! There's only half a legion there — not enough to prevent the Grû-... his people laying siege. And they have cannon, remember? The new wall won't last long. We discussed that at the Council, too. We have to prevent them achieving... what did Garset call it? — 'full enclosure'. Maybe the young guy won't have any effect, but maybe he will. He could save hundreds of lives in the city!"

Danîsha had seldom seen him so set on his own plan. "But surely we can wait a day or two?" she pleaded. "Garset was saying that if we keep wearing the Selmians down, we can try to retake Starmane. Then we can spare troops to send back to Darthane."

"Darthane!" Brakhól exclaimed. "We're going home? I want to go home again!"

Danîsha did her best to deflect that one positively while Shiván sat clutching the bess and staring at the ground. At one point he put the bess down and buried his face in his hands. Danîsha frowned. *What was up with him today?* She had never seen Shiván like this, one moment unreasonably stubborn, the next racked by indecision. She fingered the small wooden comb in her pocket, as she did in times of stress. It had belonged to Teynel, the young Dûrian girl killed in the Manor massacre, who had taken to Danîsha as an adoptive grandmother.

"Can't we at least contact Lannie again, to be sure of our facts?" She held out her hand for the bess.

He stood up abruptly, apparently without hearing her. "Let's get packed."

"Shiván—"

"Don't worry, 'Neesh, call it one of my crazy ideas—you've seen them work before."

"Aren't you at least going to discuss it with Garset?"

"Yes, yes, I will. He'll see that we need to get back to Darthane as soon as possible."

"But Shiván, we're not even sure—"

"Trust me! Remember how I got us all into Stillárre when every gate was manned against us? How I killed Dhelgor against the odds and set you free—then rescued Jomel? How I diverted Shambor's soldiers to the Grûzhack fort? How I pulled things together after the Ambush, and linked up with the Dorbians, and we sang the walls of Darthane down? This is the same. It'll turn out well, you'll see!"

Danîsha shook her head, racked by doubt herself. Which Shiván should she trust? The super-confident one before her now, or the one who a moment ago had buried his face in his hands? Her fingers rubbed hard on Teynel's comb.

Maybe she should give him the benefit of the doubt. He *had* done crazy things before, and they had worked, rescuing the Restorers from any number of predicaments. He had shown himself worthy many times of the title Overguardian.

She sighed. "Well, Brakhól will be glad."

He shot her a brilliant grin. "So will we all!" He turned and hurried towards his tent, still holding Lannie's shell.

"Don't forget to give Garset the bess!" she called after him.

She told Brakhól they were returning to Darthane. The child jumped up and down shouting, "Home! We're going home!" The blast of joy suffused the battlefield.

But we've only been here three days, and Starmane hasn't been recaptured yet, Danîsha thought. *Is this really the right thing?*

Chapter 3: *Disastrous withdrawal*

SHIVÁN, DANÎSHA AND BRAKHÓL reached Yarbiless on the second evening, accompanied by the two armed escorts Garset had provided. In this, the main town of south-eastern Dûrion, they could hardly avoid staying overnight with the Town Elder. He of course feasted and toasted and paraded them before the excited citizens — despite having done so only a few days earlier on the outward journey. But now at last the razzmatazz was over, and Shiván was able to relax on a comfortable bed.

The parting with Garset had not been easy. Shiván cringed inwardly, recalling the disbelief on the Lord Marshal's face at the news that they were leaving so soon with Brakhól. Garset had repeated all Danîsha's arguments with increasing urgency, emphasising over and again how much Brakhól had already strengthened them, and that he'd actually put victory within their grasp. But Shiván had made his decision, and his foggy brain was not up to the task of either rational argument or diplomatic soothing; he'd simply insisted they had to leave. It hadn't gone down well — either with Garset or Danîsha. Or Cârin. As they rode off they'd passed the lieutenant, who'd simply watched with an unfathomable expression.

But here in Yarbiless the Town Elder had told them the Dûrian troops in the nearby village of Pastane were successfully holding off the Strongholder's Pandian and Marûvian forces. And that was without Brakhól's help. So it really wasn't a problem taking the child back to Darthane. It was the seven-foot-tall Grûzhack who were the real threat now, advancing on the capital with their cannon and muskets...

Eventually the jumbled thoughts faded, and Shiván fell into a troubled sleep. He tossed and turned, dreaming of Perrely. She was on the new wall of Darthane, encouraging the troops as they fired futile arrows at the cannon of the besieging Grûzhack. Enemy warriors bristling with swords and muskets swarmed up siege ladders, and one fired directly at Perrely... But still she stood, blood pouring from her chest. She grabbed a bow from a dead archer and loosed a wild shot at her assailant. Then the wall trembled under a huge cannon blast. It buckled inwards, and gradually began to collapse. Perrely tumbled off the edge of the battlement, and began an agonisingly slow fall towards inevitable death on the jumbled masonry below...

"Overguardian! Are you all right? Overguardian...!"

Shiván jerked awake. The Town Elder was peering anxiously at him from the door. "I'm sorry to disturb, but you were crying out. Is there anything...?"

"No, no. I'm fine," Shiván croaked. "I appreciate your concern. It was just a... bad dream."

"Oh, that's all right, then. You'll be okay now...?"

"Yes, of course. My apologies for waking you."

"Not at all, not at all." With an encouraging smile the man left.

Shiván wiped his face with his hands. He was covered in perspiration. And full of anxiety about the Grûzhack advance Lannie had reported. They were approaching Darthane! Where Perrely was. That was far more serious than any trouble in distant Starmane. The Restorers needed every resource available to them to counter this threat. He knew 'Neesh and Garset wouldn't approve... But Perrely took precedence – and after all, he was the Overguardian.

Climbing out of bed he turned up the lamp and went to a nearby writing table where sheets of paper, a quill pen and a bottle of black ink had thoughtfully been set out. His Dûrian handwriting left much to be desired, but he could make himself understood in the flowing script. Penmanship with Mâron's secretary Estaron and swordsmanship with Cârin had helped fill the long winter days. He began writing...

Half a page later he read the result. Yes, it would do. Perrely – and Darthane – would now get the support she needed. He sanded the letter from the recessed sand tray in the desk, then hunted in his pouch for the Overguardian's seal Bishop Mâron had had made for him. His fingers couldn't find it. He felt the bar of sealing wax, a firestick, a pot of fireclay... and a long, smooth oval object. The bess! Oh dear. He should have returned that to Garset. At last – *there* was the metal seal. And something else – his old King James Bible which he'd found at Carreck Manor, where they'd first stayed in Dûrion, and carried all across the country with him.

Shiván paused as his hand felt the smooth tortoiseshell of the ancient book's cover. When had he last read it? David and the Old

Testament kings—the good ones—had turned to God before taking any important action. Shouldn't he do the same now? He hesitated. But he was just in the middle of sending off this letter. He'd do that, then read his Bible.

Taking the items he needed from the pouch, he smeared a joint on the bamboo-like firestick with the clay, then briskly snapped it. Both sides of the stick burst into flame. He threw one into the empty fireplace, then bent over the folded letter and melted the green sealing wax so that it dripped into a puddle spanning the top edge of the letter where it overlapped the bottom half. Then he quickly pressed the Overguardian's metal seal into the soft green wax. He removed it, and smiled at the perfect image that appeared: an ambon with the long rod widening into a road at the bottom, and hands underneath holding it. The Overguardian's crest, which he'd designed himself.

There could now be no mistake about who had sent this instruction.

Pulling a robe over his night-shirt, Shiván went down to the Town Elder's front door. As expected, one of Garset's escorts was on duty there. Shiván handed him the sealed letter. "As soon as it's light, find a town messenger and tell him to deliver this post-haste to Marshal Garset at Starmane. It must arrive today, without fail. Is that understood?"

"Yessir."

"Good man."

Later that morning Shiván and his party resumed their journey to Darthane, bidding farewell to the Town Elder and local dignitaries. "Overguardian, we are so grateful for your protection from the Selmians!" the Elder exclaimed. Shiván clapped him on the shoulder. "Never fear, friend, our forces are keeping the Strongholder at bay both in the east at Starmane, and in the south with our garrison at Pastane. Everything will be fine!"

Danîsha's eyes shot daggers at him as they trotted off. Shiván adjusted his shoulder pouch, and felt the outline of his Bible. He hadn't read it yet. He would, when they reached Darthane.

* * *

In the early evening of a difficult and heartbreaking day, when they had lost many men to despair and had only just managed to contain the Selmians within Starmane (thanks to the Dorbians), Garset received a sealed letter brought in by a messenger from Yarbiless on a sweat-lathered camel-horse. He examined the seal, sitting on a stool outside his tent. The Overguardian! What did Shiván want now?

He broke the seal and started reading... and fury rose within him. The words were poorly formed and littered with spelling mistakes, but their meaning was clear. *Lord Marshal Garset, I urgently require you to request Warrior High Commander Gwargif to return forthwith to Darthane with the Dorbian Legion, for the defence of the city. He may not be able to read this letter, but I believe he will recognise my seal. In the name of the One Creator God and his Son Prince Orrénne* – *Shiván* Aténnelor.

It was unbelievable. Shiván had deprived them of Brakhól, and now with a stroke of the pen he was removing the Dorbians as well. Why not sign a death sentence for every Dûrian soldier fighting at Starmane? Garset found he was breathing heavily. He closed his eyes and tried to relax, to regain some perspective.

This had to be referred to higher authority. The Bishop's Council had entrusted Shiván with the overall administration of military policy; but they would never approve an order like this. He went into his tent to fetch the bess and contact Alanya in Darthane. She had a level head on her shoulders.

A few minutes later he came out, breathing heavily again. The bess wasn't there. Shiván had used it to speak to Alanya the other day; he must have taken it with him.

That left only one hope: that Gwargif would see this letter for what it was. The Dorbians were not part of the Dûrian chain of command. They served freely. He stood and grimly made his way over to their section of the camp.

The grey, shaggy Dorbian leader was sitting with his officers at the outer edge of the large marquee that had been erected for them — somewhat like a cave, open all along one side, and lower at the front than the back. Many wolf-like figures were lying together in groups within. Some whimpered or snarled as others tended their wounds. The legion had taken a battering today. Did Shiván have any idea it was only thanks to the Dorbians that his army still survived?

Gwargif greeted Garset cordially, and they walked away from the tent for a private conversation. Gwargif padded along regally on all fours, and when Garset seated himself on a rock Gwargif sat down beside him, their heads at about the same height.

The Lord Marshal did not believe in beating about the bush. He showed Gwargif the letter, with the Overguardian's seal, and told him what it said. The Dorbian's intelligent eyes held Garset's gaze for a moment, then he turned and stared across the grassy plain towards Starmane.

"Commander, this is one order that *must* be ignored," Garset said in an intense undertone. "Some madness has overtaken the Overguardian. He's not himself." When this brought no response, Garset's outrage overflowed. "He cannot be allowed simply to throw away the eastern half of the country!"

After a lengthy silence, Gwargif turned and looked at him steadily. "Shiván *Hrarborgh* is Father of Warriors. He orders — Dorbi obey." He rose and returned to the marquee, where he began issuing instructions.

Early next morning, while Garset and his men watched helplessly, four thousand Dorbians trotted out of the camp and away down the western road.

* * *

Chief Mindbender Belyeru smiled at the mental image of the Strongholder, relaxing back in Orselm in his royal white outfit. "*Yes, your Supremacy. Beyond expectations.*"

"*The Grûzhack* gorelenyu *has gone, I hear.*"

"*It has. And this morning the Overguardian withdrew the Dorbians as well.*"

A delighted peal of youthful laughter filled the Selmian Mindbender's thoughts.

* * *

Being a military officer to the core, Garset was incapable of mutiny. After the inevitable breakout of the Selmian cavalry from Starmane that morning, he endured seeing his men deserting or being slaughtered under the dark pall of despair for as long as he could. Then he sounded the retreat.

They fell back first to Cadhar, fighting rearguard actions all the way. In the distance they could see the Strongholder's forces fanning out in all directions from Starmane. With bile in his throat Garset dispatched messengers to Darûness, Tallerane, Astenar, and Galmanest, warning those towns to prepare as best they could.

When they reached Yarbiless after abandoning Cadhar, Garset was confronted by an indignant Town Elder who declared, "But the Overguardian was just here! He said everything would be fine!"

Garset sent a messenger to recall the garrison at Pastane. The Marûvians and Pandians would now be free to join their Selmian masters in the conquest of eastern Dûrion.

They dug in at Yarbiless while the townsfolk hastily packed themselves and their more precious belongings into carriages, wagons and handcarts. A general exodus began to Darthane.

Garset knew that he and whatever was left of his army would soon be following.

Chapter 4: *Bleak future*

342 NF / Twenty-two years ago

THE SUN WAS SHINING, home-schooling was done for the day, and Barilu Dantorida was ready for an afternoon's fun with his cousin and best friend, Konnaru Galenida. Konnar's school would have closed now, too, and they'd arranged to meet just outside the Orselm city walls — almost in the country — and make their way to their secret hideout.

In Bari's shoulder pouch as he walked down the dusty road was a stoppered flask of chass that his mother had packed, along with a bag of their favourite *sherili* cakes. He and Konnar had celebrated their eleventh birthdays together a couple of days ago, and these were the last of the spoils. They would enjoy them before he told Konnar — But he didn't want to think about that now.

Suddenly Bari heard shouts and cries of pain up ahead. Shrilling over them was Konnar's familiar high-pitched voice. His heart sinking, Bari's long legs broke into a run, the pouch bouncing against his back. By the time he arrived five older boys were writhing on the ground by the side of the road, clutching their heads, while Konnar screamed at them. His friend's narrow, normally pale face was red with fury, his angular arms waving about, fists clenched. *"Hurt me 'cos I'm a f-f-freak, will you? I'll sh-show you how a freak h-hurts! There! Like th-that! And that!"* The boys on the ground yelled with each onslaught of pain.

"Konnar! Stop!" Bari cried. *"Stop!"* He grabbed his friend's shoulder. Konnar whirled round and punched Bari on the cheek. "Ow!" He staggered back.

"Bari!" Horror filled Konnar's pinched features. "I'm s-s-sorry! I didn't s-see —"

"It's okay." Bari touched his cheek. He'd have a rich bruise there. He turned to the five bullies, scrambling up off the ground. "Get out of here! And leave Konnar alone!"

The boys slunk off, muttering and clutching their heads.

Bari turned back to Konnar. His friend was still panting, his colour slowly returning to normal, though his yellow-brown hair stuck up wildly. He dropped his eyes, shamefaced, under Bari's level stare. "Konnar, you know you shouldn't do that! If it happens too often, their parents will start believing them when they say *you* gave them a headache. You'll get into big trouble, and the school may send you to a Mindbender!" Here in Selmion that threat hung over everyone. He was just thankful Konnar's outburst had taken place on a deserted stretch of the road.

"I c-c-couldn't help it!" Konnar's voice rose and his eyes glistened with tears. "They f-followed me, and g-grabbed me, and started p-p-p-pushing me around and c-calling me a *f-f-freak!*" Bari shook his head, knowing how painful that word was to his friend. It was what Konnar's father had often called him before he abandoned the family. "I t-tried to l-l-laugh about it like you said, but D-D-Dilaru started s-s-s-singing 'Frea-eak, frea-eak, frea-eak,' and they all j-j-joined in, then Shenu p-p-punched my arm—*hard*—and I c-couldn't take any more, Bari. I *couldn't!*"

"Maybe next time you should run away. You can run faster than anyone. They'd never catch you."

"R-run away? Th-then they'll m-m-mock me even more!"

"That's better than ending up with a Mindbender. But anyway. Let's forget all that now and have some fun!" He put an arm over his friend's shoulder and they started walking towards the hill where their hideout was. Bari's times with Konnar were too precious to be spoilt by something like this. Bari's parents didn't send him to a normal school—they said the priests taught lies—and for the same reason he wasn't allowed to make friends among the neighbourhood kids. Cousin Konnar was the one exception, and as long as he and Konnar could be friends he didn't need any others. He pushed aside the thought that being friends with Konnar would become a lot harder soon.

* * *

Konnar didn't know how to handle Dilaru's gang. They never tried anything when Bari was with him, of course. But then Bari was... He glanced at his friend, who was telling him something funny his father had said. Bari was... Bari. He was tall, he was strong, he didn't stutter, his black hair never seemed out of place; and there was a strength in his face and in the gaze of his pale blue eyes that made people think twice about crossing him. Konnar wished he was like that.

Yes, when Bari told Konnar to laugh off the bullies—or run away from them—it sounded the most normal and natural thing to do. But Konnar knew he could never carry it off. Which meant he would always fall back on his 'gift': though that was dangerous. Very dangerous. As Bari said, he could be handed over to a Mindbender... A shudder ran through him. He'd heard stories about what the Mindbenders did to you. That was a hundred times worse.

But at least there was Bari. He needed to be with Bari as often as he could. As long as the two of them were together, he was okay. He only wished Bari wasn't home-schooled.

He laughed as Bari reached the end of his father's joke. He could feel, without mindreading him, that Bari wanted to turn Konnar's thoughts away from his problems at school and just enjoy the afternoon. Bari was always kind. Well, Konnar was more than happy to forget Dilaru's ugly gang. But there was a sadness in Bari's mind today that he couldn't account for.

They entered a squalid little village with its wattle and daub huts and the stink of human waste. Across the fields to the east stood a forbidding grey building—the local Mindbender's mansion. Konnar suppressed another shudder. He was glad they weren't headed *there*. They walked through the village, ignoring the wide-eyed stares of the usual crowd of little kids, and carried on towards the patch of woodland beyond, with the rocky crown of a small hill sticking out like a bald head in the middle of it.

As Bari talked about this and that, Konnar continued to be aware of the strange undercurrent of sadness in his friend's aura. In due course Bari would share it with him, Konnar knew, because they had no secrets from each other.

"Race you to the cave!" Bari cried, leaping off along the woodland path. Despite Bari's longer legs Konnar caught up with him easily, then pulled into the lead. As always he was the first to reach their private place. Pushing aside the bushes that hid the entrance, he plunged into the small cave on the side of the hill that rose up out of the trees. A moment later Bari cannoned into him, then wrestled him to the sandy floor shouting, "You beat me again!"

They mock-wrestled for a while, then sat up panting. "Chass and sherili cakes?" Bari asked, grinning.

Konnar looked round the cave. Their table—a board resting on several bricks—was at the back, with Bari's leather wallet and some precious sheets of paper tucked under it; beside it was the bookshelf with the five story books Bari's mother had donated; and the rusty lamp stood in pride of place on its tall stool. But the vertical open box that acted as cupboard was empty. "*What* ch-chass and sherili c-c-cakes?"

"These!" Bari said, opening his shoulder pouch which he'd dropped on the floor before their wrestling match. "Oh."

He started chuckling, and held the open pouch towards Konnar. Inside was a gourd flask, its stopper off, resting in a pale pink mush that filled the bottom of the pouch. A sickly smell of sherili berries mixed with chass arose from it.

"Yuk!" Konnar began to giggle, which set Bari off again, and soon they were wiping tears from their eyes.

"Oh well, maybe next time," Bari sighed, still smiling.

"W-won't Uncle D-Dantoru be a-angry about the p-p-pouch?"

"Dad? No. Mum will try to be cross, but she'll be laughing too much."

Konnar nodded. He tried not to envy Bari's happy family. "S-so. What shall we d-d-do now?"

"We could read *The Boy Prince* again."

Konnar was silent for a moment. Bari had something he needed to share with him, but he was putting it off—and that worried Konnar. It wasn't like Bari to pretend.

"W-w-what is it you w-w-w-want to t-tell me?"

The smile faded from Bari's face. He looked at Konnar for a long moment. Finally he asked softly, "Did you read my mind?"

"No! I'd *n-n-never* do th-that!" Konnar exclaimed. "Never! How often have I t-t-told you? We've been f-f-f-friends since we were little k-k-kids, and I have *n-never* m-mindread you. I never will!"

"Okay, okay! Sorry, of course I believe you. It's just that— It would be so easy for you. I'm glad you don't use your gift on me, Konnar."

Konnar looked down at the floor of the cave. "You kn-know what happens when I m-mindread my f-friends. I l-lose them. That's why I haven't g-g-got any. Except you."

"I know. I want to stay friends, Konnar."

"The th-thing is — I never *n-need* to mindread y-y-you. I need to m-mindread the others, b-because I know they're l-l-lying to me, or only p-p-pretending to like me, or h-hiding things f-from me. B-but you n-n-never do that."

Bari nodded, then looked away towards the cave entrance. "About that thing I need to tell you, Konnar... You won't like it." He heaved a deep sigh, and Konnar's heart sank.

Bari spoke, and his words were like nails hammered into Konnar's flesh. He felt his eyes filling, and the tears ran unchecked down his cheeks as Bari slowly killed him. "We're going away, Konnar. Dad, Mum and me. We'll be living a long way from Orselm. A very long way. I don't know where, they wouldn't tell me. But we'll come back once a year. We'll be able to see each other then."

There was a long silence as Konnar stared at Bari, the hurt slowly seeping into every fibre of his being. Bari swallowed and looked away.

"Why?" Konnar whispered.

Bari's eyes were moist now. "I don't know. I think... a Mindbender is trying to find us, and we have to escape. I heard Dad saying something to Mum, and that's what it sounded like."

"When?"

A tear trickled over the spreading bruise on Bari's cheek where Konnar had hit him.

"Soon."

"W-will we b-be able to s-s-see each other b-b-b-before then?"

"Yes. I'll bring more chass and sherili cakes." Bari's weak smile quickly faded.

The two friends sat together, staring silently into a bleak future.

Chapter 5: *Dire consequences*

GIL WAS SITTING on a balcony of the Cathedral in the early evening. From here he could see the Southgate, where the highway from Yarbiless entered the city. It had been a bright day for March—for *Emmerand*, he reminded himself; but now the shadows were lengthening and flowing ever further from the bright western horizon.

He didn't have a book to read, and that was a pain. Since learning to read Dûrian with Estaron over the winter, he'd devoured every book with half an ounce of interest in the Cathedral library. It was all he had to occupy himself. But now the only books left were endless tomes of theological speculation, dry legal volumes, and economic records with lists of commodities bought and sold.

A growing upsurge of noise at the Southgate caught his attention. Four riders were attempting to enter, hampered by a clamouring crowd reaching out to touch them. There was a small figure clinging on behind the second rider—and a familiar, slightly cloying wash of emotion passed over him.

Brakhól was back.

And with him, obviously, Shiván and Danîsha. They were back early. Things must be going well.

Yes, 'Neesh had been summoned to the battle front with Brakhól, and it was Shiván who got to go with them for protection. Not Gil, though he had more expertise with the longsword than Shiván with the Blade.

The fact was, he'd never been fully accepted since his betrayal last year, when he'd led the Restorers into Shambor's devastating ambush near Stillárre. Added to which, his paralysis from the mindlock following Shambor's death had dragged on a long time. Even after regaining movement, it had been well into the new year before he'd felt able to start relating to his former friends—and then mainly to Shivan and Father Martin (or Bishop Mâron, as he now was—the new Bishop Suffragan).

He was out of place here, unsure of where he stood, but with nowhere else to go.

And they were equally unsure about what to do with him. Everyone knew that to have risen so high in Shambor's favour, he had to have co-operated along the way. He'd been more than a mindbent slave. So here he was—the only 'Restorer' not on the Bishop's Council. There was no rôle for him. He was surplus to requirements.

The only way he could fit in was if he 'opened himself to the Light' — or 'met the Prince' — or 'was lightened' — or 'regenerated' — or any of the other clichés they had for the special experience that made one a Lightist. It wouldn't change what he'd done; but it would make him more acceptable. He knew that everyone's eyes were on him, waiting for that to happen. One thing was for sure, though: if he ever 'opened himself to the Light', it would be a simple, logical decision. There was no way he'd 'have an experience' just to satisfy expectations.

* * *

344 NF / Twenty years ago

Konnar and Bari were together again for a couple of precious weeks while Bari's parents paid their annual visit to Orselm. They had found a house not far from Konnar's, and Konnar was to stay with them for the whole period. It was heaven after a long, bleak year during which only the thought of this time with Bari had kept him going.

Now thirteen, Konnar grinned at the little kids who scampered out of their path in the village they had to pass through to reach their secret hideout. He couldn't wait to tell Bari all that had happened, and to let their imaginations run riot about the glorious future they would share together.

As they approached the end of the village a couple of small boys in tattered loincloths burst out from between two of the huts. The second, larger one caught the first and hurled him to the ground, pummelling him with his fists. "Give it back, give it back!" The first boy was clutching something to his chest and screaming at the top of his voice. Bari immediately hurried towards them, and Konnar followed, glancing around as he did so. No adults or older kids in sight—they would all be working in the local Mindbender's fields.

"Stop that!" Bari shouted. The boy on top jumped up, startled, and Bari grabbed his arm firmly before he could run away. Konnar pulled the other boy to his feet and held him tight. A circle of younger kids gathered round.

"Now then! What are you fighting about?" Bari said, turning his stern glare from one boy to the other. Both were staring at them with wide eyes. Konnar hid a smile. The half robes he and Bari wore — though poor by city standards — gave them status in the villages.

The two boys gazed at them fearfully and said nothing.

"Come now. You!" Bari turned to the smaller boy with the object clasped to his chest. "Show me what you're holding."

The boy shook his head. Bari continued to stare at him. Konnar slipped gently into the boy's mind and eased his possessiveness. The kid slowly moved his hands down from his chest and opened them to show the slightly battered red-orange sphere of a *miléss* fruit.

"That's mine!" the other boy exclaimed, and made a lunge to grab it. But Konnar had already seen his intention, and swivelled his captive out of reach while Bari jerked the attacker back and tightened his hold.

"It's yours? So you had it, and your friend here took it away from you?"

"Yes."

Konnar's prisoner started to speak, but Konnar gently silenced him.

"Where did you get this fruit?" Bari asked the other boy softly. Good question. No one in this village could afford a *miléss*.

"I found it."

"He's lying!" the boy holding the *miléss* burst out.

"Where did you find it?"

"In the road. It fell off a wagon." Bari glanced at Konnar. Konnar shook his head very slightly. He allowed the boy with the fruit to speak.

"No, it didn't! My Dad was given it by the lady at the great house. He helped her in the garden!"

Bari eyed him, and he fell silent. "You say it fell off a wagon?" he asked the other boy.

"Yes."

"Did the wagon go through this village?"

The boy in Bari's hands squirmed, but Bari had too good a grip on him. There was some murmuring now among the children watching. Konnar caught the words "no wagon…". He mentally prodded Bari's captive. "*No!*" he squealed.

"It didn't go through the village? Then where was it?"

"On the highway!"

There were jeers from the spectators. No kid from this village would go anywhere near the highway.

"Nobody believes you. You're lying, aren't you?"

"No!" Konnar gave his mind the tiniest jolt of pain. "*Ow!* Yes!" Bari shot Konnar a dark look. Konnar pulled an apologetic face. That way was quicker, but… Bari had his own method of doing things.

He was now pronouncing judgment. "You're a thief and a liar. That fruit is not yours, and these good people here —" Bari's hand swept round to indicate the circle of kids in their tattered rags " — will make sure you never get it. Am I right?" He looked expectantly at the children, eyebrows raised.

"Yes! We will!" the smaller kids chorused, eyeing the convicted felon with glee. Bari let him go, and he darted away as the spectators gave chase.

Konnar laughed. "He's f-f-faster. He'll e-escape. But th-th-that one —" he pointed at the boy with the fruit, who was scuttling off in the opposite direction " — will m-m-m-make sure he never f-f-finds the *miléss* again. You p-p-passed a good s-sentence!"

As they walked on towards their cave in the wood beyond the village Bari exclaimed, "We make a great team, Konnar! I couldn't have got the truth out of those kids without you. After we finish school we'll do that kind of thing all the time. Only it won't be little kids any more: we'll get rid of the Mindbenders, and make Selmion a country where people don't have to be afraid any more. Won't that be great?"

Konnar nodded and smiled. "Yeah, it w-will." As long as it was with Bari it would be great. He couldn't see them getting rid of the Mindbenders, but if Bari believed it, that was enough for him.

Once they reached the cave Konnar opened the shoulder pouch he'd been carrying and brought out a flask of chass and a bag of the little cakes made with red sherili berries which Aunt Wirilai had packed for them. "At l-l-least it's not a m-m-mush when I c-c-carry the p-pouch!"

Bari punched him lightly on the arm as he was taking the stopper off the flask, and warm chass sloshed over Bari's shift. He yelped and Konnar laughed. "S-s-serve you right!"

There was silence for a while as they shared the flask and munched the sherili cakes, sitting at the mouth of the cave and looking out between the bushes at the woodland beyond.

Konnar sighed. "I w-w-wish it was a-always like th-this."

"Me too."

"I c-can only do g-g-good things when I'm with y-y-you, B-Bari. If o-only we c-could always be t-t-t-together."

"Yeah. At home I haven't got anyone I can do stuff with like we did today. The boys there just mock me or stay away from me."

Konnar nodded. He knew all about *that*.

"But the two of us would make great rulers together, Konnar! Just think how we could change Selmion. I would make a list of all the wrongs that needed to be put right, and you would help track down the wrongdoers with your mind powers and get the truth out of them. Which would show us *more* wrongs to be put right! And as we did that more and more, we would establish what Dad calls 'good governance' — with everything done properly, and justice for everyone, and no one needing to be afraid any more!"

Bari's enthusiasm was contagious. "Yes!" Konnar said. "And I c-could p-p-punish the wr-wrongdoers so that they d-d-don't do it again. M-maybe we c-could k-k-keep a few M-Mindbenders j-j-just to help with th-that."

Bari frowned. "We don't want to keep any Mindbenders, Konnar. And we'd only want a little bit of punishment, because my Dad says good governance is based on justice and mercy, not vengeance. Remember when we were kids and Dilaru's gang attacked you? If I hadn't stopped you, you would have given them such bad headaches that their parents would have complained, and you might have been sent to a Mindbender. Punishing people too much is as bad as not punishing them at all."

Konnar dropped his head. "Yeah, I s-s-suppose so." He hated it when Bari criticised him. But Bari was usually right, and when they did things his way they always turned out better.

His thoughts went back to Bari's idea of ruling together, which had fired his imagination. "But I c-c-can help you f-find out things, and p-p-put wrongs right—and p-p-people will l-like that! Then m-m-maybe we can c-create such good g-g-g-gov— g-govance—"

"Governance."

"Yes—that we'd c-c-conquer the whole w-w-w-world!"

Bari hesitated. "Well, maybe we wouldn't want to go that far, but we could start with Selmion—and maybe Dûrion."

"Y-yes, and s-s-see what h-happens after that. B-but w-w-we'd need to h-have a w-war to b-become rulers. Where would we g-g-get the s-soldiers?"

Bari thought for a moment. "Maybe we could first go round the country telling people about good governance, and they would get so excited that they would join us and start a revo-… revolution. Like Prince Orrénne did, and everyone followed him, and he could easily have become king—only he chose not to."

"Yeah, we c-c-could d-do that. W-w-when shall we s-s-start?"

Bari laughed. "As soon as we finish school! Then I'll come back to Selmion, and we'll go round telling people about good governance!"

The smile faded from Bari's face, and Konnar felt his own grin falter and vanish.

It would be a long, long time before they finished school.

* * *

Present day

Shiván walked rapidly up the stairs to the third floor of the Cathedral where the living quarters were. He couldn't wait to see Perrely. Danîsha was behind him with Brakhól. He crested the stairs, turned into the passage—and there she was, hurrying towards him with a radiant smile lighting up her face. For a moment it looked as though she would run straight into his arms, but she pulled up at the last minute, and they clasped hands in the Dûrian high handshake.

"Shiván! You're back!" She glanced behind him. "And Danîsha—and Brakhól. It's so good to see you again."

"Perrely!" Brakhól ran to her for a hug. Shiván envied the little tyke. Danîsha and Perrely kissed each other on the cheek. "Good to see you well," 'Neesh declared. As usual, Perrely was wearing a green high-necked tunic with long sleeves to hide the scars of Shambor's torture.

"You're back early," Perrely said. "I hope everything's all right in Starmane?"

"Oh, fine," Shiván assured her. "Garset has things under control. They'll keep those Selmians bottled up."

There was loud snort from Danîsha. She apologised, shot a searing glare at Shiván, then took Brakhól by the hand. "Excuse me, he can't wait to see Jomel." "Jomil!" the child exclaimed, and went charging down the passage. Danîsha hurried after him.

Perrely stared after her, puzzled. "What's Danîsha upset about?"

Shiván shifted his feet and coughed. "Oh, er, she didn't want to come back so soon... But let's go somewhere comfortable to talk, shall we?"

They went to a reclining room off the passage with a thick blue floor-cover, four matching recliners, and several occasional tables. They stretched out facing each other on two of the recliners. Shiván gazed intently at the woman he loved, provoking a smile in response. He had to protect Perrely, whatever happened.

"Tell me about the Grûzhack advance on Darthane. How close are they to the city?"

Perrely frowned. "What Grûzhack advance on Darthane?"

A premonition of disaster touched Shiván's heart. "The one Lannie told me about. She told me with the bess that the Grûzhack had left Dhembis. That they were headed this way."

Perrely's face cleared. "Oh! No, they haven't come anywhere near Darthane. They're camped outside Lestack. It's Sûrilane we're worried about, but they haven't started moving in that direction yet."

Shiván stared at Perrely and felt the blood draining from his face. He'd got it wrong! The Grûzhack were not advancing on Darthane. But that meant —

"Shiván!" Perrely exclaimed. "That's not why you came back, is it? Because you thought the Grûzhack were about to attack Darthane?"

A sickish feeling engulfed Shiván. "Yes," he muttered. "That *is* why I came back."

"Shiván, Alanya was just letting you know that the Grûzhack had left Dhembis!" He cringed at the growing alarm in her voice. "It didn't warrant taking Brakhól away from Starmane. The

Council hasn't even decided yet whether we can risk using Bra-khól against his own people!"

They were both sitting upright now. Perrely was staring wide-eyed at Shiván, and he couldn't meet her gaze. "What about Garset?" she said. "He did he agree that it was okay for you to take Brakhól... didn't he?"

"No," he said softly. He stared at the floor, chaotic feelings tumbling and clashing within him. His hands gripped the recliner on either side of his legs, the knuckles white.

"Garset didn't agree?" It wasn't a shout, but it might as well have been.

He looked up at the horrified mask of her face as despair crashed in on him. How could he tell her—now—that he'd also recalled the Dorbians, leaving Garset at the mercy of the Selmian cavalry, as well as their Children of Despair?

"Shiván, what have you *done?*"

* * *

Lannie was dressed for riding in a tunic of supple tan leather with dark brown boots and leggings. Leaning against the wall behind her recliner was her shortbow and a quiver of twelve arrows. She'd wanted to learn the Dûrian longbow, but didn't have the strength for it. Several afternoons in the week she would ride out to the park on the other side of Darthane Water, where she could practise her horsemanship and archery. Over the winter she had become quite proficient at both, and took pride in being able to hit the bull's eye at a gallop six times out of ten. She wanted to get her average up to eight. God knows she might need it in the days to come.

But right now she was caught in a discussion with Danîsha and Perrely about what was ailing Shiván. She stood up and glanced out of the window in the third floor reclining room. The afternoon was half gone. She'd have to get away soon.

"It must be some kind of outside influence," Perrely was saying, her eyes red-rimmed. "You know Shiván. He may do things in... unusual ways sometimes, but he always has a plan. This was an impulsive, spur-of-the-moment action—and that's not like him!"

Lannie thought it was very like him, in certain circumstances—such as being head-over-heels in love with Perrely. But she didn't say so. "What do you mean, outside influence?"

"I don't know… a curse, or… or mindbending."

"Mindbending! How on earth could he have been mindbent?"

'Neesh chipped in. "It might have happened at Starmane. There were Selmian Mindbenders there, working on those poor Children of Despair."

"Nonsense! He never went out of the Dûrian camp, did he? When he wasn't fighting, I mean."

"No, but—"

"So a Mindbender would have had to enter the Dûrian camp avoiding the guards, find Shiván's tent, mindbend him, then slip out again unseen. Even at night, that's very unlikely. Mindbenders are ordinary flesh-and-blood people. They can't make themselves invisible. And last I heard they can't mindbend anyone from a distance."

"Maybe the Selmian Mindbenders have powers we don't know about. They're directly controlled by the Strongholder."

"Maybe. And maybe Shiván just thought he could do what he liked because he's the Overguardian. I'm sorry, Perrely," she added, as tears flooded the girl's eyes, "but he wasn't listening properly when I talked to him with the bess, and he obviously jumped to the wrong conclusion. Then he took drastic action because he thought you were in danger. Men have done crazier things for love."

"But you don't understand, Alanya. He's not himself any more!" Perrely exclaimed, her scarred hands clasping and unclasping in her lap. "Something's happened to him, I can tell. He doesn't look me in the eye. He's disappeared into his apartment and won't open for anyone, not even me. When I met him and Danîsha in the passage yesterday evening, he tried to pretend everything was fine in Starmane—though he knew perfectly well they would be struggling without Brakhól. That's not the Shiván I know!"

"Sounds a lot like a man with a guilty conscience, though." At the shock on Perrely's face and the dawning anger on Danîsha's she added quickly, "I'm sorry, that was unkind. But honestly, Perrely, I've listened to many former mindbent slaves since Shambor died, because of my gift of perceiving truth. Shiván doesn't sound at all like them. I'm quite sure he hasn't been mindbent. But he's very aware that he's made some foolish decisions, and I don't think you need look any further for an explanation of his behaviour."

She stood up. "And now I must hurry if I want to have time in the park before sunset. Try not to worry about Shiván, Perrely. He just needs time to get over these mistakes, especially the blow to his masculine pride. I'll see you both at the daymeal."

She picked up her bow and quiver and left the reclining room, slinging them over her shoulder as she hurried down the passage. She might just manage an hour in the park.

* * *

"But Shiván, *why* did you think you had to rush back to Darthane with Brakhól?" There was pain in Bishop Mâron's kindly eyes.

Mâron, Shiván and old Bishop Harlon were reclining comfortably in the Bishop's solar, the cheerful sun-filled room on the top floor of the Cathedral which had been built in the space formerly occupied by Shambor's torture chambers. Somehow during the past twelve hours Shiván had managed to regain a little emotional equilibrium, but this question brought despair flooding in again and his eyes dropped. This was the man he still thought of as Father Martin, the English vicar who'd been instrumental in bringing them all to Dûrion last year. A man he deeply respected, whom he'd now failed completely. As well as Bishop Harlon, the father of his people, whose face was furrowed with lines of concern.

He forced himself to look up again. "I— I somehow thought Darthane was about to be attacked by the Grûzhack. I'm sorry— I know that's not what Alanya told me. I just... got it wrong."

Bishop Harlon's anxious frown deepened. "That's so unlike you, Shiván," he murmured.

"I know." Shiván found himself unable to maintain eye-contact.

Mâron sighed. "So now Garset is back where he was, with only the Dorbians able to withstand the Selmian Children of Despair." He glanced at Harlon. "Alanya needs to contact him as soon as possible to find out how he's managing."

Shiván's heart clenched. *How can I tell them?* But he had to. "Um... about that..."

They looked at him. "I'm sorry, but... Garset doesn't have the bess. I accidentally... brought it with me."

Both bishops froze in shock. Misery eating like acid into his heart, Shiván forced himself to continue. "And I— I was so worried about the Grûzhack attacking Darthane— that on the way back I... I sent a message to Gwargif. I summoned him—"

His voice faltered at the horror dawning on their faces.

"...back to Darthane," he finished in a small voice, burying his head in his hands.

Silence.

"Oh, Shiván." Harlon's voice, laden with sorrow.

A deep sigh from Mâron. "So eastern Dûrion is lost."

Silence.

Finally, "We need to think about this, Shiván. Let's meet again tomorrow."

After a brief glance at their stricken faces, Shiván nodded and stumbled out of the solar.

* * *

The next day the Dorbians arrived outside the city wall, sniffing the breeze for any sign of the enemy they'd been summoned to fight. Gwargif confirmed that the Overguardian had sent for them. Regretfully, Bishop Harlon asked them to turn back and support Garset as soon as they were fed and rested: and Shiván was summoned to meet with the two bishops.

They gathered again in the solar. After a minimum of small talk Mâron began.

"We've given careful consideration to the three 'mistakes' you told us about, Shiván, and we've reached a conclusion: One misjudgment could have been a simple error. We all make them. But these three things together—all out of character for you—seem to indicate that there must be some other factor involved."

Shiván frowned. Harlon's kindly old eyes were sharp as he asked, "Did anything else happen while you were in Starmane? Anything unusual?"

Shiván thought a bit, then shrugged. "I lost my ability to fight."

"What do you mean?"

"On the fourth day—just before Alanya contacted us on the bess—I went out to battle as usual, but I seemed to have forgotten all my swordsmanship—and my martial arts. Instead of being an example to the troops, Lieutenant Cârin and a few others had to protect me. Eventually my carelessness got one them badly injured. So I left the battlefield."

Mâron's eyebrows were high. "Our elite swordsman and martial arts practitioner just walked out of the battle?"

Shiván nodded. He remained silent, strangely reluctant to share with them his bizarre dream about the man in white.

The bishops exchanged a glance. "Shiván," Mâron said carefully, "all of this points to the involvement of a Mindbender. You haven't actually been mindbent — we would have detected that — but it may be some kind of curse. Unfortunately we have no way of knowing what the curse was, or how long its effects will last, but obviously you have not been yourself recently. Would you agree?"

The word *Nistállenor* echoed derisively in Shiván's mind. He gave a dejected nod.

There was a wealth of sympathy in Harlon's face. "We, and everyone on the Council, and all who know you, will pray continually for your recovery. But meanwhile —" he paused, and Mâron stepped in, his voice sad but firm.

"We feel you need to take time now to rest and recover. Pray, spend time with Perrely. Practice your fighting skills if you like, but…"

"I'm suspended as Overguardian?" Shiván asked, his voice unsteady as the full meaning of *Nistállenor* bit home.

"No, not as Overguardian," Mâron said. "That is your calling, and that you will always be. But in the meantime — until we know the curse's effects have ended — we feel it would not be wise for you to make military decisions. You will still be welcome on the Council, but…"

He paused, and finished in English. "…As a non-voting member."

Shiván felt himself sinking into a dark pit. If only this was a nightmare, soon to fade in the carefree light of his student house in London! But it was real. The despair that had blighted his teenage years rose rose up to reclaim him, and all his defences — his faith in God, his carefully cultivated optimism — were lost in the black mist that filled his mind.

* * *

Next day the refugees began straggling in; and in the days that followed the trickle grew to a flood. They came from Galmanest, Astenar, Hellerane, and a dozen other towns and villages to the south and east, and told tales of the Selmians spreading like a grey and tan sea across all of south-eastern Dûrion — but heading always westward. Other refugees arrived from the south-west, from Sûrilane, Morlis, Cristane and Colmenar. The Grûzhack were moving eastward. The paths of the two superpowers would intersect at Darthane.

Then one evening Garset and the Dûrian army reached the southgate. The citizens of Darthane stared in shock at the tattered remains of the proud force that had set out just over two weeks ago. The Lord Marshal of Dûrion and his senior officers walked silently up the hill to the Cathedral. Garset's face was a grim mask, his eyes sunk in deep shadows, his gold-edged green infantry cape torn and smeared with blood and dirt.

Many of the wealthier spectators saw the writing on the wall and hurried home to pack.

* * *

Tears dimmed Bishop Harlon's eyes as he heard Garset's report. When the Lord Marshal had finished he nodded without speaking and clasped his shoulder. After a moment he said, "Go and rest, my friend. The Council will meet at the first hour tomorrow." He glanced at Mâron, standing beside him. The Bishop Suffragan bowed and left with Garset. Harlon knew he would inform the Council members.

The Bishop of Dûrion made his way slowly to his private chapel in the Cathedral, feeling his age. He closed the door and locked it, then bent his knees to the soft floor covering. The pain he felt was too deep for words. For a long while he knelt in silence before the One Creator God, in the posture of total humility and entreaty. Then he looked up towards the wooden ambon on the wall, and the agony of his heart spoke out.

"Oh Father, have you reinstated me only to see my people defeated once more? In answer to prayer you brought the Restorers. In your name they challenged the Strongholder by removing Shambor, his tool. Did we achieve that only to be crushed by two powerful nations fighting over us like dogs over a bone? Where are *you* in this, Father? What is *your* intention?"

He fell silent again. Then he murmured, "Yet you are King over all nations, and you rule in the Light. These are your people, and this is your beloved city, and this Cathedral stands as a beacon of *your* radiance to all the lands.

"I am only your servant. Show me, show us, your way."

The hours of the night passed, and in the silence a stillness settled over the Bishop's heart. A passage from the Book echoed softly in his mind: *The shepherd leads the sheep to a safe meadow, where no enemy can enter and every thirst is quenched.*

As the first light of dawn touched the windows of the chapel he murmured, "If this is from You, Father, let it be confirmed by the unanimous approval of the Council."

He struggled slowly to his feet, his knees clicking, every limb aching. Prayer was never easy.

* * *

The Bishop's Council met in the dining chamber of the Bishop's reception suite. There were eight seated round the polished *shey*-nut table: Bishops Harlon and Mâron; Shiván *Aténnelor*, the Overguardian; Alanya *Atémban,* Restorer of Hearing; Danîsha *Atémbellar*, Restorer of Song; Perrely *Nem Sûriac*, Lady of Prayer; and Garset, the Lord Marshal. Estaron, Mâron's secretary, was taking notes at his sloping writing table to one side. Though formerly employed by Shambor, Estaron had not been mindbent; and he knew more about the day-to-day running of the country than anyone alive.

Garset was giving his report. Danîsha was glad he'd freshened up, so he looked less like a walking announcement of defeat. His face was still drawn, but there was a stubborn glint in the deep-set green eyes. Danîsha's heart was a lump of lead within her as she listened to his report, delivered in a dispassionate monotone. News in last night was that the Selmians had captured Hellerane.

There were gasps of disbelief around the table. "That's only a day's journey from Darthane!" Perrely exclaimed.

"Yes, and they would be here already if it were not for the Dorbians." Garset's gaze drifted to Shiván, who dropped his eyes. "Gwargif and his warriors are patrolling ahead of the Selmians, out of bowshot, but terrorising the horses sufficiently to slow their advance."

He took a breath before continuing. "Meanwhile to the south-west, the Grûzhack have attacked Sûrilane. Before that happened I sent my last company of veterans there to mount whatever defence they could. They may hold the Grûzhack for a day or so, but only until they bring up their fire weapons. After that they have orders to abandon the town." He turned to Bishop Mâron. "It's a good thing you had the Ambon moved to Darthane well in advance, your Serenity."

Mâron nodded. "It may yet come in useful."

Garset inclined his head. "It may, though I think all would agree that we do not want to summon thousands of ordinary people to be slaughtered, as happened last year."

There was a general nodding of heads round the table. Except Shiván's, Danîsha noticed. His head was already lowered. He appeared to be examining the grain of the wood in minute detail.

"Therefore, your Radiance," Garset addressed Bishop Harlon as head of the Council, "Darthane is threatened from both the east and the west, and we have no means of withstanding either attack for any length of time."

He fell silent, and no one else ventured to speak. Danîsha shook her head. Was this what their glorious overthrow of Shambor had brought them to? To be destroyed by both the Grûzhack and the Selmians?

"We all know what has to be done, don't we?" Lannie said softly. "There's no point waiting here to be caught between the whip and the *grûn*'s backside. Let the superpowers fight over Darthane—but not over us. We must abandon the city."

A deathly hush followed. They had known it would come to this. But hearing it spoken out loud carried a chilling ring of finality. To abandon Darthane, proud capital of Dûrion since records began! It was only one step up from total defeat.

"But what message will this send to those of our people already suffering under foreign rule?" Mâron said, his eyes haunted. "They'll lose hope when they hear Darthane has fallen."

"They'll lose even more hope if their leaders die in a death-or-glory attempt to defend it."

"And what about everyone living here, and those still coming in from other towns?" Danîsha said. Her heart clenched at the thought of all the misery that would flow from this decision.

"If we go, many of them will follow," Perrely said. "It's mainly the poorer people left in the city now. They have no horses or carriages, like the rich merchants who've been getting out for days already. I think some will go to relatives in the country; and I suppose some will be foolish enough to stay. But many will follow us." She turned to Garset. "I assume we'd go to Stillárre?"

The Lord Marshal nodded. "It's our only other walled city. And it's protected to the east by the River Carreck, to the south by Lake Stillárre, and to the north by the Hills of Géris."

Perrely nodded. "But it's also a hundred *aldoret* away — at least four days on foot. How will families with young children manage that? And how will you protect such a huge crowd if we're attacked?"

"I don't know, my lady. But what is the alternative?"

Perrely stared at him, distress in her eyes.

"This is one of those times when our trust in the Creator God has to be very practical," Bishop Harlon said quietly. The old man had aged in the months since Shambor's passing. Yet he was deeply loved as head of state; and the Restorers had learnt the value of his quiet wisdom — so often backed by prayer. Seeing the weariness in his face now, Danîsha guessed that he had not spent the night sleeping.

"We have a decision to make," Harlon continued. "Do we stay and find the One's will here in Darthane? Or do we abandon this beloved city and move to Stillárre, where we can oppose the growing darkness a little longer? With so much at stake we must all be in agreement."

He turned to Mâron. "Bishop Suffragan?"

Mâron sighed, his eyes troubled. "It's a drastic and unprecedented step. But... no. We can't stay."

"Lord Marshal?"

"We cannot defend Darthane. We must leave."

"*Atémban*, this was your proposal. I assume you are in favour of leaving?"

"I think it's the only option," Lannie said.

He turned to Danîsha. "*Atémbellar?*"

She felt the tears running down her cheeks. In her pocket she fingered Teynel's comb. But there was really no alternative. "Yes, we must go."

"*Nem Sûriac* — Lady of Prayer?"

Perrely could only nod.

Harlon's eyes were moist. "I, too, see no alternative. It is decided, then. We will abandon Darthane."

Danîsha glanced sadly at Shiván. He sat silent, his face set in a mould of despair. His opinion was not consulted. He'd been broken by some dark influence, and was now set aside as no longer fit for use. _One Creator God, please heal him._

Chapter 6: *The grey mist*

346 NF / Eighteen years ago

"THE ACADEMY OF LAW! Oh, Bari, how wonderful!"

His mother came round the dining table and kissed his cheek. Bari grinned to cover a blush.

"That's very good news, son," his father said quietly. "The Astenar Academy is a prestigious institution. It can't be often they invite someone as young as you."

Bari cleared his throat. "The Senior Kindler said fifteen was the youngest anyone had been invited. Ever."

"Oh, Bari," his mother repeated, her eyes shining. He busied himself with his midmeal. She continued, almost breathlessly, "You'll become an advocate — or even an arbiter!"

His father nodded. "It will also be excellent preparation for… the future we all pray for."

The three of them exchanged glances. This was the subject they seldom talked about openly.

"Well," Dad continued, smiling, "it means you'll have your work cut out for the next five years. Can't give them any reason to withdraw the invitation!"

"I know. There are lots of people who'd like to make me slip up so they can take my place."

"Oh, Bari!"

It always amazed him how many different meanings his mother could infuse into those two simple words. This definitely wasn't congratulations.

"Not *all* the students in the school can be that bad," she continued on a well-worn theme. "You should go out more, get to know them. Other mothers *sympathise* with me: they say, 'He's a bit of a loner, isn't he?' This is not like Selmion: you really should make more friends. You *need* friends to get on in life here. Doesn't he, Dantoru?"

His father just nodded. He never allowed himself to be drawn any further into this particular debate.

"I do have friends — sort-of."

"Who? You never mention any."

"Lormenet. Gilliston… Haldet."

"Oh, not *them*."

Bari nodded glumly. Only them. He focused on the last of his mother's casserole. Dad cleared his throat, warning Mum off. The unspoken conclusion every time was that Bari had been spoiled for all other friendships by the one he no longer had. With Konnar.

The agony of that trip to Orselm last year hadn't faded. He'd gone with his father to Konnar's house full of eager anticipation – only to find it empty and closed up. They'd returned every day – but Konnar and his mother had left, and none of the neighbours knew where they'd gone. Bari had wept silently within himself all the way home to Dûrion. Then he'd closed his heart. He would not leave himself open to such pain again.

Konnar was gone and Bari had no friends.

When the midmeal was over Bari left the house and took the woodland shortcut back to school – hoping to avoid those three dropouts he'd called friends to keep his mother happy. No such luck.

"Hey, Estaron!" Lormenet's voice boomed out behind him. With a sigh he acknowledged his Dûrian name and slowed to let them catch up. The Mighty Misfits were never apart: walking with looming muscleman Lormenet was Gilliston, the aristocratic dandy, and the short, ferret-faced schemer, Haldet.

"So," Gilliston proclaimed, coming alongside Bari on the narrow path. "The Selmian foreigner has made good! Astenar Academy, no less!" He clapped him on the shoulder.

"Estaron," Lormenet's bass rumbled from behind, "will you share some of all the money you're going to make with us?"

Bari's lips compressed. "Okay, let's just accept that I got an invitation from the Academy. Can we leave it at that?"

Haldet's reedy tenor chirped out from the rear. "Ah, but there's a question of national importance still to be answered! When you're an arbiter, Estaron, with a big fat income, will you still pay Dûrian taxes, or will those go to the Strongholder?"

Estaron stopped. Lormenet and Haldet almost bumped into him. He fixed Haldet with a long level stare, which he then turned on Lormenet and Gilliston. They knew that stare, and the danger of ignoring it.

"I think you three had better go on ahead," he murmured.

"Of course! Our Selmian friend needs to be alone," Gilliston explained graciously to the other two. "We understand! Quite natural in the circumstances. We'll meet again!"

With unctuous smiles and hands raised in farewell the three went on down the path. Estaron stared after them with smouldering eyes. So much for his Dûrian friends.

He heaved a shuddering sigh. Where was Konnar now? Was he even still alive? What wonderful dreams they'd had, of 'good governance'! He smiled despite himself. He'd been sailing close to the wind there, he knew; one careless word on *that* subject, and Konnar would have discovered his secret — the one his family seldom talked about, that no one here in Dûrion knew and only a handful in Selmion were aware of. He'd never told his parents that Konnar could actually mindread people; if they'd realised that, they certainly wouldn't have allowed the friendship to continue. They wouldn't have shared Bari's trust that his best friend would *never* mindread him.

With Konnar gone the annual visits to Orselm had become meaningless. He no longer viewed Selmion through rose-tinted spectacles, and hated its squalid poverty under the Strongholder's rule. Haldet's insulting comment about paying taxes came to mind, and the revulsion he'd always felt for that little creep deepened. No. He had no friends in Dûrion. He didn't want any.

Yet in the meantime, for better or worse, his future was here. At least it was a bright one.

He hadn't seen Konnar for three years. If he ever came across him again, would he even recognise him?

Forget it. Much as he disliked the name, he was Estaron now. The 'Bari' chapter of his life was closed.

* * *

Present day

The great procession straggled to a halt in the shade of the Forest of Gend, not far from Janulane. The exodus stretched as far as the eye could see back towards Darthane — though they were a long way from the city now. Perrely watched as people settled themselves down in groups all along the grassy verge of the broad highway and began taking food from their bags. A great rumble of conversation filled the air. But many heads still turned to look back towards the city they'd left — the only home many had known; perhaps still the home of loved ones separated by this great upheaval. Perrely's heart went out to them. She herself had lost home and family. She knew that ache that never really went away.

Her prediction at the Council meeting had been fulfilled. Many had followed the Bishops to Stillárre. But many others had left on their own, more slipping away each day to join relatives and clan members elsewhere in the country. And there had been a surprising number who had elected to stay, despite the appalling prospect of falling under Grûzhack or Selmian rule.

To be abandoning Darthane to the enemy... Perrely still could not take it in. *Darthane!* The great walled city of their people that had stood for generations, crowned by the glorious Cathedral that soared skyward, proclaiming the splendour of the One Creator God. The Jewel of Dûrion. To think of that destroyed — or worse, defiled by the worship of an alien god...! She felt sick at the very idea.

But she knew there had been no option. She looked south across the highway, where the remnant of the army stood on guard. Better that these, at least, had survived than that all had died trying to defend Darthane.

Beyond the army were the Dorbians, ranging up and down the column and further afield. The One be praised for them. They had caught several Grûzhack scouts already, preventing news of the exodus from reaching the enemy commanders.

A groan interrupted Perrely's thoughts. Nearby, Mâron was helping Bishop Harlon down from his horse, and the elderly bishop was obviously feeling the effects of the day's journey. Secretary Estaron eased Harlon's red-and-gold robe of office off his arms and shoulders; he only wore it to encourage the thousands who followed on this long, dangerous walk to Stillárre. His robe and the Ambon of Sûrilane, carried beside him, were the twin symbols of their nation, and lifted the hearts of those who followed.

Mâron helped Harlon on to the folding chair that was his only concession to comfort. Estaron folded his robe and laid it on the ground beside the gold-and-silver Ambon. The others in the vanguard settled themselves around the old man: Bishop Mâron and his wife Shindorel; Gelmion, Alanya, Danîsha and Brakhól, Garset, Cârin, Jomel, Estaron. And Shiván. Perrely watched sadly as the Overguardian slumped to the ground with a heavy sigh beside Cârin. He avoided her as often as not these days. At least Cârin could cheer him a little with his lighthearted banter. Perrely sat down beside Jomel, carefully straightening her long tunic over her legs and then tucking her scarred hands inside her sleeves.

Alanya was checking the surrounding countryside with the blaise, as she did several times an hour. "All clear," she announced, and there were several sighs of relief. Her eye passed impersonally over Gelmion. She had taken over his instrument when he was incapacitated by the mindlock, and had not returned it.

That relationship had come to a bitter end. Both Alanya and Gelmion looked older, Perrely thought: Gelmion thinner, with deep circles under his eyes; Alanya with wrinkles on her brow and around her mouth that hadn't been there before. But she'd found a new poise and self-awareness, a confidence in her rôle of 'restoring hearing' by discerning the truth (though she hadn't initially seen the truth about Shiván). Perrely wished Gelmion could discover his true rôle, and Shivan regain his. The Restorers were crippled now, with two of them out of action.

"Any news of the Selmians?" Lannie asked Garset.

"Nothing new," Garset replied. "Going by past performance, they'll be advancing on a wide front from Hellerane. Their progress will be quicker without the Dorbians hindering them; but they won't take any risks. They're liable to reach Darthane about the same time as the Grûzhack."

A gloomy silence fell at the thought of two foreign powers fighting over the capital city. Perrely was grateful Brakhól was with them; it was his spontaneous joy, broadcast on a wide waveband, that helped keep everyone going on this heartbreaking tramp to Stillárre.

There was a burst of laughter, and Perrely turned her attention to the other side of the Bishop's circle, where Gelmion, Shiván and Cârin were sitting with a group of Dûrians.

"No word of a lie," Cârin declared. " 'That old geezer's not the Bishop,' he said. 'Bishop's got a red robe and all!' Just then Estaron helped his Radiance into his robe and up on to the horse. You should have seen the feller's face. *'Keldon hallár!'* he said, and shot off through the crowd!"

Perrely smiled amid the laughter that followed, and was pleased to see Shiván grinning, too. He spoke up now, continuing the story. "Yes, and then he ran straight into Garset, and he said... that..., he said…" The light died in Shiván's face as he stammered to a halt. Perrely's heart went cold.

Cârin jumped in smoothly. " — He said, 'He *is* the Bishop, y'Lordship, I never said otherwise!' and dashed off. Garset stared after him, scratching his head."

There was some muted laughter in the group. Everyone avoided looking at Shiván. He got up, stumbling over the long sheath of the Blade of Darthane attached to his belt, and walked into the forest as if to relieve himself.

Perrely's heart ached for him, and she felt a renewed stab of alarm. Shiván had been doing that more often recently — starting to speak, then forgetting what he was going to say. At the Cathedral he'd blundered into a reclining room once, stared around as though surprised to be there, then left just as suddenly.

Were the effects of the curse, or whatever was afflicting him, getting *worse*?

Perrely decided that as soon as they were settled in Stillárre she'd have a long talk with Frengor about it. The Visionary of the Travelling Order had visited many lands, and might have a better idea of what was wrong with him. And how to treat it.

* * *

Shiván walked alone as the exodus resumed its journey to Stillárre. The black tide of depression threatened to overwhelm him. How tempting it was to give up the tremendous effort of fighting the grey mist in his mind that prevented such normal things as *thinking* and *planning* and *talking*. How much easier it would be just to sit down now at the side of the road and go no further. He knew that temptation oh so well from years gone by.

But he couldn't add that burden to his friends; he couldn't become even more of a stumbling block — a *nistállenor* — than he was already. Whoever that man in white had been in his dream at Starmane, and whatever he'd done to him, its effects were real — and devastating.

Shouldn't he tell someone about it? *No!* The same powerful aversion reared up in him every time he thought of sharing that experience.

Was this a curse that he was prevented from telling anyone about? Was he mindbent, despite the bishops' assurance to the contrary? He didn't know. But ever since that night the grey mist had fogged his thoughts, confused his logic, made his every decision random and self-defeating.

He knew nothing any more.

No. That wasn't true. He knew one thing.

A verse from his ancient King James Bible echoed softly in his mind: "Yea, though I walk through the valley of the shadow of death, I will fear no evil: for *thou* art with me…"

He knew that one thing. He knew that even now, in this black despair, God was with him.

He walked on, clasping the Bible in his pocket and repeating silently to himself over and over, "I will fear no evil: for *you* are with me. You are with me. I will fear no evil."

Chapter 7: *Overwhelmed by song*

JOMEL AND PERRELY found places in the third row of seats in the ancient Stillárre Hearth. The Bishop's party had the privilege of being seated first; otherwise they might not have got in, given the large crowd of excited citizens outside. The exodus from Darthane had only arrived yesterday, but the Bishops had arranged the thanksgiving hearthtime for this morning, as it was Anderil — the One's Day.

A voice spoke on Jomel's other side. "May I sit here?"

She looked up. Oh no. Gelmion. He was smartly dressed in a dark blue tunic and matching leggings. The priests at the Travellers' Domicile, where the Bishop's party was staying, had gone to some trouble to find suitable clothing for the dusty, travel-stained celebrities.

"I suppose so." She moved up to allow space between them. She eyed him as he took his seat. His hair, though overgrown after the journey and the chaotic weeks preceding it, had clearly been washed and carefully brushed. Unlike Shiván's unruly tangle in the front row. Gelmion was still an attractive man in an uncouth, foreign kind of way; but not to her. The darkness in his *shiláy* was obvious — he didn't fit in.

Looking around the Hearth, Jomel saw that the ambon on the wall above the empty altar had been replaced by the gleaming gold and silver of the national emblem — the Ambon of Sûrilane. It looked beautiful against the fresh white paint of the wall. The whole interior of the Hearth had been redecorated since she'd last seen it many months ago: the walls and roof repainted, the windows re-glazed, and the wooden seats varnished and upholstered in a dark green fabric matching the thick, newly-laid floor-cover.

Jomel had mixed feelings about being back in Stillárre. On the one hand, the city had been her home for many years — ever since her family had moved here from Selmion, where she'd spent her childhood. On the other hand, it held many painful memories. Her last image of the city was of that dreadful moment, which she'd thought was her last, when she'd been propelled on to the steps of the Temple of Gadesh before a screaming mob, expecting any moment to be thrown to them and trampled to death. Then Shiván and the Restorers had arrived out of nowhere and whisked her away to safety—a miracle, if ever there was one. After that she'd never wanted to come back here.

Yet she remembered her surprise this morning on entering the city square and seeing an open space between the buildings on one side, littered with rubble. It was occupied now by the flotsam of the great exodus from Darthane—poorly dressed people and the makeshift lean-to's they'd spent the night in. It had taken her a moment to realise that this was where the Temple of Gadesh had stood: her home and torture chamber for so many months. Now it was gone, torn down following Bishop Harlon's first edict after returning to office: the edict banning the Cult of Gadesh from Dûrian soil.

The days when the Temple had dominated the city square seemed like a different era now: the era of Shambor and the brutal reign of the Mindbenders. She shivered; dear Creator God, don't let those times return.

The Kindler of Stillárre—as always, a benevolent white-haired old man—came to the front of the Hearth, accompanied by Secretary Estaron. They conferred together for a moment, then Estaron moved the Kindler's chair closer to the lectern and adjusted the position of both—for the Bishop, presumably.

Jomel's lips quirked. Estaron was the indispensable organiser who made sure everything ran smoothly. She couldn't imagine Dûrion surviving a moment without him. It would be his job, she knew, to find homes and work for many of the Darthane refugees in the weeks to come, as well as food and shelter for the Dorbians, who for the moment were camping outside the city to allay the inhabitants' fears. She didn't envy Estaron the challenges he faced.

By now the Hearth was full to overflowing—and as Jomel glanced around she realised that most of those who were seated must either be exiled Darthane merchants or local dignitaries, to judge by their expensive clothing and self-important postures. The back of the Hearth was crammed with standing figures; and there would be many more out in the square, crowding close to hear as much as they could.

At last the Kindler came to the lectern and raised a hand for silence. In a slightly shaky voice he declared how delighted the people of Stillárre were to welcome the Bishop of Dûrion and the people of Darthane to their city; and without further ado he invited Bishop Harlon to open the hearthtime.

Bishop Harlon thanked the Kindler and the people of Stillárre for their welcome. "We come as unexpected guests," he said, "without clan ties or hospitality-gifts; yet you have taken us willingly into your homes, and for that we will forever be in your debt."

Then, like a father calmly discussing a family crisis with his adult children, the Bishop explained to the people of Stillárre the impossible choice he and his Council had faced in Darthane. How, threatened by superior forces from both east and west, there had been no option but to abandon the city.

"And in fact," he continued, "three days ago one of our army scouts arrived with news. He told us –" The old man's voice quavered. "He told us that Darthane has fallen. The city has been taken by the Grûzhack."

A deathly hush filled the Hearth. Then a low, inarticulate moan spread through the building and into the square outside. What the Bishop had announced, Jomel knew, was already common knowledge in Stillárre. But the public declaration of this incalculable loss moved many to tears.

After a pause Bishop Harlon continued. "Nevertheless, by the One's gift we and many of the people of Darthane have escaped destruction. We were not attacked on the way here; we are tired from a long walk, but alive! That is cause for rejoicing. We cannot help mourning the loss of Darthane; but soon the Grûzhack will be defending the city against the Selmians. And while our enemies fight each other, we can build up our strength here in Stillárre, and look to the One to preserve us in the days to come. So let us rejoice in the One Creator God, our Fortress and our Defender, and trust in his immeasurably great power over the forces of darkness!"

During the thunder of applause (and cheering from outside) that followed, the Bishop retired to the Kindlers' chair; and Danîsha went forward with young Brakhól to the musicians' seats on the left, carrying her bellaril. Jomel glanced at Perrely, and they shared a warm, anticipatory smile. The people of Stillárre were about to experience something they would remember for the rest of their lives.

Danîsha sat and took the bellaril in her hands, and Brakhól perched on the chair beside her, looking small in the wide space at the front of the Hearth. Danîsha struck a chord and rich harmony filled the sanctuary. A breathless silence fell. Then a glorious melody broke out, a paean of praise to the One Creator God — and Brakhól's pure, angelic voice filled the Hearth and poured out to those beyond.

* * *

Four Grûzhack scouts watched Stillárre's Westgate from a small copse on a hill only a couple of hundred paces away. Dressed in mottled black, brown and green, no one saw or heard the watchers. Hunched down to hide their seven-foot height, they were a seamless continuity with the light and shade of the trees. Like all Grûzhack they had pasty white faces, their brows heavily ridged, their eyes slanted downward, giving them a permanently melancholy expression.

They had come up from the south, slipping past towns and villages, to investigate the flatlanders' second city.

Down below, on the road that passed through the Westgate, a steady stream of people dressed in their best clothes was entering Stillárre. Very few were leaving. From inside the city, carried on the breeze, they could hear the sound of a large crowd.

The scouts' leader, Shakhere, turned and murmured to the others, "Something special is happening today." His voice was little more than a breath on the breeze. He stared contemptuously at the unguarded gate. The flatlanders were not expecting enemies to come from this direction. In any case their army was so small they probably did not have the men to guard every entrance; and their tame wolves were patrolling elsewhere.

The scouts watched and waited — which was their job.

Then, without warning, the music hit them. Someone started singing: it was distant but clear, and Shakhere reared back as the song scorched his soul. He found tears streaming down his cheeks — and turning thunderstruck to his companions, he saw that they were similarly afflicted. Stirred to the depths of his being, Shakhere felt his heart probed and laid bare, vulnerable, open and unprotected.

There was an electrifying familiarity to that singing. He stood transfixed, unable to move, unable to think, gripped by a deep, unbearable longing.

For a long moment he remained frozen. Then with an inarticulate cry he leaped out of the copse. His companions followed, army discipline forgotten. They ran like the wind through the unguarded Westgate into the city, scattering terrified civilians. They charged down streets and alleyways into the market square, bowling pedestrians over and leaving a growing scream of terror behind them.

Shakhere knew only one thing: he had to be *there* at the source of that incredible singing.

* * *

Shiván, like everyone else inside and outside the Hearth, was caught up in the music. When Danîsha and Brakhól praised the One together in song, it was as if heaven opened. His present troubles faded away, and his heart rejoiced in the everlasting, unshakeable truth of the God who cared.

He didn't notice the disturbance at first. Only when people inside the building cried out did he turn to look—and saw four seven-foot, demonic figures bursting into the packed Hearth like an unstoppable cannon shot. They were already halfway down the aisle before Danîsha stopped playing. Sheer momentum carried them on, until they stumbled to a halt before Danîsha, Brakhól and the Bishop, who with the rest the congregation had leapt to their feet. The Grûzhack dwarfed the five-foot Dûrians—and even Danîsha, who was roughly his own height at five foot six.

While terrified worshippers yelled and struggled to get out, Garset, Cârin and other soldiers in the Hearth battled their way forward to protect the Bishops and Restorers. "They're Grûzhack warriors!" someone shouted, increasing the panic.

But the warriors only had eyes for the child. Even as Garset and his soldiers reached and grabbed hold of them, one of the Grûzhack cried out, "*Brakhól!*"

Everyone froze. The boy stared with wide eyes at the contorted features of his countryman. Firmly held by Cârin, the warrior poured out a guttural volley of Grûzhack.

In the silence that followed Brakhól said in a small voice, "Shakhere?"

Twisting himself in Cârin's grip the warrior turned to the Bishop. In heavily-accented Dûrian he said, "Dis my brudder."

With a cry of delight Brakhól ran and threw his arms around the Grûzhack. Câr lost his grip, and the warrior tumbled to the ground with Brakhól laughing on top. Shivan blinked to see the other warriors sagging in their captors' grasp, eyes riveted on the child, fresh tears running down their cheeks. Brakhól sat grinning on his brother's chest, pummelling him and rattling off quick-fire bursts of Grûzhack.

When the child calmed down a little, the warrior Shakhere sat up and enfolded him in a long embrace. Brakhól chattered away happily, but the warrior's face was filled with dazed wonder, his eyes brimming. The Dûrians watched silently. No one could doubt the genuineness of what they were witnessing.

At last Shakhere stood and set Brakhól on the ground. The boy grabbed his hand and stood looking up at him. Shakhere turned to the other warriors. They talked for a moment, faces sombre. Shakhere bent down to Brakhól and said a few words. The boy stared at him, uncomprehending. Then the warriors turned to face the Bishop and knelt before him, heads down, exposing their necks. And waited.

Lannie left her front-row seat and joined the group at the front. Shiván and the other members of the Bishop's party followed. By now the centre of the Hearth was empty, with people huddled against the walls and struggling to get out of the packed doorway. Outside the hubbub was growing.

Lannie looked at the kneeling Grûzhack, then at Garset. "Are they doing obeisance? Switching sides?"

Garset shook his head. "They think they've disgraced themselves. They're inviting us to execute them."

Lannie's voice clashed with Danîsha's.

"No!"

"We can't do that!"

Garset shrugged. "If we don't, they'll find some way to do it themselves."

"Perhaps not." Bishop Mâron looked thoughtfully at the four prostrate figures. "All of them seem strongly affected by Brakhól. If we pardon them, *he* may give them a reason to stay alive."

"You could be right, Mâron," Bishop Harlon said. "In any case, we cannot kill them in cold blood. We must either keep or release them."

"With respect, your Radiance," Garset said, "I do not believe they will accept either of those options. By kneeling before you these scouts have shown their determination to follow the Grûzhack code of honour. Even if we removed their weapons, they would find some way of killing themselves—as the few Grûzhack we have captured have always done. In any case we cannot spare any troopers to guard them."

Brakhól had been looking anxiously from one speaker to the next. Now he ran over and seized Shivan's hand. "Shakhere won't die, will he?"

Silence fell as everyone felt the child's distress. Heartened by his trust, Shivan took the boy's hand. "I— don't think he should." He turned to Harlon and Garset. "We *have* to find a way round this."

They nodded, and moved away from the kneeling scouts to continue the discussion in private.

After a moment of silence Lannie said quietly "Your Radiance, I think Bishop Mâron had the right idea. Brakhól is the key. He's apparently the brother of this warrior Shakhere; and he's had a deep effect on them all. We've heard how hard and ruthless the Grûzhack are, even towards themselves. Yet these four have been *weeping* in our presence. Have you ever seen that before, Garset?"

The Lord Marshal shook his head. "No, *Atémban*."

"I think everyone would agree it was Brakhól who caused those tears. There is more going on here than the Grûzhack code of honour. Why don't we let Brakhól tell the warriors that they can stay with *him*?"

There was a silence. Then Danîsha exclaimed, "Lannie, that's perfect! If they're accepting Brakhól's invitation, they'll stay alive for *his* sake."

"And since it will be by their own choice, they won't need to be guarded," Mâron added.

Garset's eyebrows were raised, and murmuring broke out among those near enough to hear. But the Bishop smiled. "*Atémban, bar tarrathi.*—Restorer of Hearing, you have found the way. Let the child be our spokesman."

Shivan couldn't avoid the bitter thought that in times past he would have been the one to make such a suggestion.

Lannie came and stood in front of Brakhól. "Brakhól, you don't want Shakhere to die, do you?"

A vehement shake of the head.

"Would you like him to stay with you?"

"Yes!" There was a sunburst of joy. The four warriors quivered.

"Can his friends stay, too?"

"Yes!"

"Will you tell him that in your language — in Grûzhack?"

"Yes!"

Brakhól ran to his kneeling brother. "Shakhere! Shakhere!" He clutched the warrior's shoulders. Shakhere raised his head and stared bemused into the small face. He started to say something in Grûzhack, but Brakhól overrode him. "*Tisikht darj lhuftad igged! Ergizept ghân!*"

The stream of forceful Grûzhack widened Shakhere's eyes. The other warriors lifted their heads to stare at Brakhól. Shakhere looked at the Bishop, who nodded.

"*… Nakhimân dey?*" The child's final demand rang out. A lengthy silence followed. Brakhól's expression changed from challenging to pleading. "Shakhere?"

The warrior slowly stood. His three comrades followed suit. Shakhere bowed to the Bishop.

"Beeshop give Shakhere to Brakhól? Also udder friend?" He indicated his comrades.

After a moment's hesitation Harlon responded, "I do."

"Den us no more warrior. Us guard for Brakhól."

The Bishop smiled. "That is good. Guard him well."

Without a trace of humour Shakhere replied, "Us die for Brakhól."

Chapter 8: *New departures*

346 NF / Eighteen years ago

So. Expelled from school. Again.

Konnar pondered the latest crisis as he walked along the country lane. He was fifteen now, and he'd been in a different school every year—sometimes twice a year—since that unforgettable day when he discovered he'd missed Bari's visit.

He couldn't blame Bari or his parents for not finding them. Two weeks earlier he'd gone and locked his whole class in their classroom overnight—along with the temple priest teaching them—placing in their minds a powerful inhibition against opening the doors or windows. He'd had enough of them being so high-and-mighty with him when he knew all the smutty little secrets in their minds. Especially the priest.

So he and his mother had had to leave in a hurry and stay with Grandma in Asilindora for four weeks to let the uproar die down. And of course it had to be just *then* that Bari and his family had come for their annual visit. When he realised he'd missed seeing Bari he'd been totally devastated, and all hope had died within him.

After that he'd kept getting into trouble, and Mum had kept moving to save him being handed over to the Mindbenders. He felt a twinge of remorse. It had been hard on her. But it had been hard on him, too. Without Bari there was no way he could avoid resorting to his 'gift' when people started their nonsense. First, thinking he was a pushover and taking advantage of him; then, calling him a freak when he retaliated the only way he knew how; then ganging up on him and forcing him to resort to his greater powers. Then— expelling him.

If only Bari's family hadn't moved all those years ago. With Bari around permanently he could have learnt to react differently when people started their nonsense. Together they could have starting bringing about that 'good governance' Bari used to talk about...

Yeah. If only.

His gloomy meditations were cut short by a shout from behind.

"Hey, freak!"

He turned round. Three burly young men from the senior class were bearing down on him. Oh, right. These were the big brothers of three of those he'd punished in the episode that led to his expulsion.

The leader was a muscular member of the boxing team. He was at least an arm's length taller than Konnar, and about the same amount wider all round.

"You think that's it, now that you're expelled, freak? My brother has a broken arm thanks to you, and you think you're just gonna walk away? Well, I don't think so!"

He lunged towards Konnar, the other two coming up to cut off any escape.

Konnar was dimly aware of a carriage approaching along the road behind the leader. Anything he did would be witnessed... What the heck. He and Mum would soon be out of here.

The boxing hulk loomed up and Konnar said "*Stop.*"

The hulk stopped so suddenly he almost fell over. Shock spread over his face.

Konnar turned to face the two behind him. "*Stop.*" They did so. Confusion warred with amazement as they stared at him.

"*Now. Each of you go and fetch a stick from those trees.*" He nodded towards a small copse in the nearby field. "*A big, thick one. Quickly!*"

Shock turned to horror as they left at a stumbling run towards the trees.

Konnar had to concentrate on maintaining control, but in his peripheral vision he saw that the carriage had come to a standstill a short distance away. Someone was looking out of the window — enjoying this little local drama, no doubt.

The three arrived back armed with stout branches.

"*Now start hitting each other. Hard.*"

After a short moment of paralysis they began laying into each other. Cracks, thuds and yelps wafted over the fields. Konnar watched critically. From time to time he mind-shouted, "*Hit harder!*" He saw with satisfaction that the other two ganged up on the boxing hulk, who was definitely getting the worst of it. The cries became more pain-laden and blood began to flow.

"*I think that's enough, don't you?*"

Konnar spun round, thunderstruck. Someone was mind-speaking *him!*

A portly gentleman in a violet and white robe had climbed out of the nearby carriage. *"Better stop them before they do any serious damage. And make them forget what happened."*

Konnar stared at the man, whose friendly, deeply-lined face wore a half-smile.

Numbly he did as the man suggested. *"Stop fighting. Go home now and forget what happened."*

The three combatants dropped their sticks and stared around for a moment, dazed. Then without taking any notice of Konnar and his violet-robed companion they started limping back down the lane, arguing loudly among themselves about whose idea it was to come here, who had started the fight, and why.

The tall man looked at Konnar. His smile broadened. *"I think you and I need to talk. Can I offer you some refreshment at my home?"* His lips still had not moved. He pointed invitingly towards the carriage. In a daze, Konnar climbed in.

Once the vehicle was under way the man turned to Konnar with a smile. "Did you know that you are absolutely extraordinary?" he said out loud. He had a warm, deep voice to match his smile.

"W-w-what?" Konnar stammered.

"Absolutely extraordinary. Never have I seen such a virtuoso display of subtle control by a completely untrained mind." The man's eyes gleamed with enthusiasm as Konnar gaped at him. "Not only multi-targeted mindspeech, but instant command, effortless override of powerful intentions, detailed remote bodily control, and memory erasure. All without prior mental subjection or chemical facilitation. *That*, my dear young man, is unprecedented in one so young—and utterly inconceivable, if I hadn't seen it with my own eyes, in one with no training whatsoever. I'm right, aren't I: you have not had any training in these mental techniques?"

Konnar could only nod dumbly.

The man shook his head. "Just imagine what you could be with training!" he murmured. Then he seemed to shake himself. "But that's jumping ahead a little. Here's my house: we'll have refreshments and talk some more."

Konnar blinked as he looked out of the window at the great grey manor house they were pulling up to. He'd hardly noticed the long, winding drive and extensive gardens they'd already passed through.

As if in a dream he followed his host past the intricately carved front door into the house. They entered a reclining room that was luxurious beyond Konnar's imagination with green leather recliners, matching thick floor-cover, a dozen glittering light trees, tapestries with finely-woven equestrian scenes, and other pieces of furniture and decoration he couldn't even put a name to.

"Do take a seat," the man said, pointing to a recliner. He settled himself on one elbow on another recliner, and Konnar followed suit. "What can I offer you?"

Offer him? Oh, refreshments. Ummm… "Ch-chass and sh-sherili c-c-cakes?"

With a quirk of the lips his host snapped his fingers, and a servant who had followed them in hurried off.

"You do realise what heights you could rise to?" the man said earnestly, leaning towards Konnar. "With your powers—trained— you would outshine any other adept of the mental arts practising today. I mean that."

Konnar swallowed, his mind whirling. It was almost too much to take in. He didn't know which 'adepts of the mental arts' this man was referring to, but he was *praising* him for the very things others rejected him for. The things that made them call him a freak.

"Such success would not come instantly." His host's gaze grew stern. "It would require discipline and perseverance. You would have to work hard. Would you be willing to do that?"

Konnar found himself nodding eagerly. "Y-yes, I w-w-would."

The man smiled. "Well, it would be worth it. I believe you would soon achieve power and influence beyond your years."

The servant arrived with a tray holding a silver chass service and a silver plate of the largest sherili cakes Konnar had ever seen.

"Do help yourself." Konnar did so. "By the way—forgive my rudeness in leaving this so late—but what is your name?"

Konnar already had a mouthful of sherili cake. Spraying crumbs he said, "Konnaru Galenida."

The man smiled. "Thank you. I am Faranu Nilestida, the Mindbender of this area."

Konnar sprayed more crumbs.

* * *

Present day

Lannie was in a pale blue mood as she walked down Bishop's Avenue in Stillárre, a broad thoroughfare boasting merchants' houses, high-class tailor shops and other establishments that catered to the wealthy elite. Four days had passed since that sensational moment when the Grûzhack scouts had burst into the Hearth, and the city was still simmering. The scouts had been given lodgings in the underground crypt of the Travelling Order's Domicile, and they'd barely stirred from there. Feeling against them was running high.

The Domicile also housed the Bishop's government-in-exile, so it was getting pretty full these days.

She glanced up at the spring sky. It was a beautiful day. Small white clouds were drifting across the clear blue. There was a nip in the air, a gentle reminder that summer was not quite here yet. Yet, as often happened these days, she'd fallen prey to a quietly oppressive melancholy.

She was returning to the Domicile after resolving a dispute between a Stillárre merchant and a farmer who supplied him with grain. The farmer claimed a higher price had been agreed last time than was written on the merchant's bill of purchase — which he said was not the one he had signed. The merchant was a shifty individual who couldn't meet Lannie's eyes. Yet there was an earnestness about his protests that made her think twice. Supporting the farmer's statement was a husky young farmhand, who declared loudly and repeatedly that his master was speaking the truth. Lannie suddenly barked at him, *"How much was offered?"* His startled, unrehearsed answer settled the case.

Yes, finding the truth in cases like that was rewarding. She was grateful to God for the gift he had given her. Yet there was an emptiness in her inner life that it couldn't satisfy.

She glanced into the window of an aristocratic clothier's shop as she walked by. There was a mannequin draped in the latest feminine style of tunic and culottes in a delicate shade of salmon; and it turned her thoughts to her old life on Earth. The faces of friends and family flashed on her mind's eye, and she longed to see and speak to them again. Her brother and rather stuffy parents.

Her colleagues at work. The school friends she met from time to time.

And especially her ex-fiancé, Matt... She found herself seriously missing his strong but kindly face, the quirk of his eyebrows, his quick, no-nonsense responses when she contradicted him. If Father Martin—Bishop Mâron—was right, then if she ever *did* get back to England, no time would have passed at all: she'd pick up the strings of her life just where she'd dropped them eight months ago. And this time she'd make sure she found Matt and put things right.

Lannie often wondered what she had seen in Gil. How could she ever have been attracted to such a self-seeking opportunist? She should have been warned early on, when he'd shared with her the sordid story of his impending disgrace at the University of London. Eager for the professor's chair, he'd plagiarised a junior colleague's work to improve his prospects—and had been found out. She, dazzled by his intellect like a silly young girl, had ignored her natural distaste and sympathised.

Well, that was over now. The One had enabled her to discern the truth about people, and there was little danger that she'd be taken in like that again. She still struggled to forgive Gil—both for deceiving her, and for his betrayal of them all last year. She, too, had been mindbent by Shambor—but she had not co-operated.

"Thinking of home, *Atémban*?"

Lannie jumped. Frengor had joined her. She smiled at the Visionary of the Travelling Order in his purple robe. Frengor was short, bearded and thickset, his kindly face wrinkled like a walnut, every crease lighting up when he grinned—which was often. He, too, discerned more truth than most people.

"Yes, I was thinking of home... and a few other sad things," she said. "But I'm sure you'll cheer me up."

Frengor's smile widened. "Well, I'll certainly try! Let me see now... Have you heard Brother Ongaret's latest? You know his dry sense of humour. When you all arrived last week Ongaret was organising your accommodation in the Domicile, and he conducted Secretary Estaron to a large room. Estaron was delighted until he noticed the four beds. He said that wouldn't do, he couldn't share with others. He spoke about all the work he'd have resettling people, how he'd need privacy and plenty of space for the books and papers he'd brought. Ongaret looked at him for a moment, then took him to an old storeroom. It had shelves and a desk, and various other stuff stacked up high in a corner. Estaron said that would be fine, but where would he sleep? 'Up there,' Ongaret said, pointing to the pile in the corner. On the very top was an old bedstead!"

Lannie laughed. "What happened? Did he accept it?"

"Oh yes. Ongaret had all the junk removed and installed another bed. Estaron smiles now when he sees Ongaret."

"Well, that's something! You hardly ever catch Estaron smiling."

"True. He has a reserved manner, but he's a good man."

"That's what I've always felt."

They were passing a group of townsmen who were muttering and casting black looks at them. One voice now rose above the others: "Cursed Grûzhack!"

Frengor rounded on them immediately. "Oh? And you, my friends, are *not* cursed? I'm glad to hear it. Because it means you're eager to obey the Prince's command not to judge others in case you yourselves are judged. Am I right?"

The men stared at him sullenly. After a moment they turned and wandered off, still muttering.

Frengor sighed as they resumed their journey. "That's going to be a problem. Many in this city have had friends and kinfolk who have died at the hands of the Grûzhack. Shakhere and company will not be able to stay here for long."

Lannie nodded. "The real problem is, what will happen to Brakhól? He's thrilled to be with his brother again, but he's found happiness and stability with us. It'll tear him apart to be separated either way."

"Yes, that's a hard one…" Frengor was silent for a moment. "But tell me, do you know how Brakhól got separated from his family in the first place? Shakhere must have shed some light on that."

Lannie nodded. "It's a fascinating story. We had trouble understanding Shakhere's broken Dûrian, but we managed to work out most of it. It seems that their parents worked in the *teméyn* trade. As you know, that only grows in the Grûzhack country—in Barazhân. They transported the processed drug in wagon convoys from the high mountains of Barazhân to the surrounding nations. They were going to Marûvin one time when thieves attacked the convoy. Their wagon was in front, and their father tried to escape by putting on speed down the narrow, winding road. They'd almost reached the plain and the highway to Marûvis, when the wagon went out of control and crashed into a gully.

"Shakhere said both their parents were killed, but later— Anyway, I'll come to that. Shakhere had a broken arm. Brakhól was unhurt, but screaming his head off. And you know what happens when Brakhól is upset..."

"I do," Frengor said feelingly. "I was there, at the Ambush last year. I take it that frightened off the thieves?"

"Yes, it did, but it also attracted a Mindbender and his party. They were on the highway en route to Selmion, and Brakhól's broadcasts brought them rushing up. They grabbed Brakhól, and Shakhere with his broken arm couldn't stop them."

Frengor shook his head. "So that's how the Strongholder found a child with powerful mindspeech to train as his first Child of Despair. What happened to Shakhere afterwards?"

"The Mindbender's slaves beat him up and left him beside the highway. Later a Dûrian merchant found him. He took Shakhere to his home, and he and his wife looked after him for about six months. This was before the war."

"Still, very noble of them. So that's how he learnt Dûrian."

"Right. Then he left them and returned to Barazhân. At that point his story got confused. He said he went back to his parents. But earlier he'd told us they were killed in the wagon crash."

"Grandparents, maybe?"

"Yes... Or extended family. We asked him what he meant, but he just shrugged. Anyway, he'd already had some military training, so he was drafted into the army. Because he knew a little Dûrian, they made him a scout. Recently he and his group were sent to investigate Stillárre—and the rest you know."

"Amazing." They walked in silence for a few moments. Then Frengor turned to Lannie with a grin. "Well, one thing we can be sure of: God had a special purpose in bringing Shakhere and Brakhól together *here*, with you. It'll be fascinating to find out what that is!"

* * *

Danîsha and Shiván made their way carefully down the steep ladder. At the bottom the crypt stretched out, dim and echoey. Light spilled out of the partitioned enclosure further along where Shakhere and the Grûzhack scouts were staying. Danîsha shivered, remembering the time when she and the other Restorers had taken refuge from Shambor's forces in this hidden vault under the Domicile.

"Mâra! Shibán!" Brakhól came running up to them. He grabbed their hands, and began dragging them towards the enclosure. "Come! Shakhere wants to talk to you!"

The Grûzhack scouts had been staying in the crypt for nine days now. Their meals were brought down to them. They'd remained there partly because they preferred to keep to themselves; and partly because of the growing antipathy towards them in the city. Danîsha was sorry for the four young men. They were prisoners in all but name.

She and Shiván entered the enclosure, where Shakhere and his three companions were seated at a table. Danîsha checked her memory for their names. To the right of Shakhere was Ganid, an albino with white hair and pink eyes; then Migezh, the very thin one; then Dellikh, who had a cast in his left eye.

"Sit," Shakhere told them. There were no other chairs, so the two Restorers found spaces on the beds facing the Grûzhack. Their lowly position was emphasised by the scouts' seven-foot-something stature. Danîsha felt towered-over. Brakhól scrambled on to his brother's lap.

"Shibán," Shakhere announced. "Stillárre people not like us. Is better for you we leave."

Shiván nodded. "Yes. I, um, I think you're right, Shakhere. We're glad you... er... that you..."

Danîsha leapt quickly into the breach. " — That you've been with us. It's been good for Brakhól. Will you go back to the Grûzhack army?" Poor Shivvie. Put him under the slightest strain these days, and words failed him. She did so hope the One would heal him soon. They had prayed. They had read his King James Bible with him. They had fasted. God *would* put him right.

While Shakhere translated for his comrades, Danîsha waited apprehensively for his response. If they returned to the army, would they report what they'd learnt about the city—which, though limited, might give valuable information to their military leaders?

She breathed a silent sigh of relief as Shakhere said, "Not go army. Not warriors now. Go back home." Then he dropped the bombshell. "With Brakhól."

"You want to take Brakhól?" she blurted out. She'd known that was a likely outcome; they all had. But hearing it stated so matter-of-factly was a shock.

The child was looking up at Shakhere with a puzzled expression.

"Is my brudder. We go back to parents," he said in a tone of finality. He turned to Shiván. "You tell Warriormaster send soldiers, take us to Hillane." It was the nearest town south of Stillárre controlled by the Grûzhack. "We go night time past guards, we come to my country. You fix to happen soon. We not wait long."

He stood, putting Brakhól down beside him. The other three scouts rose also. The audience was over.

But not for Brakhól. His small face was troubled, and there was a heaviness in the air. He ran to Danîsha and seized her hand. "'Neesh, you'll come too?" he asked anxiously. He turned to Shivvie. "And Shibán?"

"*Dakhileyn shezik* ghân, *Brakhól*," his brother said roughly.

The child turned and poured out a torrent of high-pitched Grûzhack. Shakhere replied angrily, sending Brakhól into a fully-fledged temper tantrum such as Danîsha hadn't seen for a long time. He screamed at his brother, threw a pillow at him, ran over and began pummelling him.

By then all four scouts had collapsed in their chairs, clasping their heads and groaning. Shiván and Danîsha weren't feeling too good themselves—nor, probably, was most of Stillárre—but they pulled Brakhól away from Shakhere, and Danîsha gathered her remaining strength to tell him off severely for losing his temper. The child burst into tears and threw his arms around her.

As she cradled the boy's head against her shoulder, his distress squeezing her heart, the tears ran down Danîsha's cheeks. She found herself thinking of the old proverb, 'Laugh and the world laughs with you; cry, and you cry alone.' That didn't apply to Brakhól. When his feelings ran high—positive or negative—they were broadcast far and wide. There would hardly be a dry eye in the city right now.

Footsteps clattered on the ladder down to the crypt, voices calling out to know what had happened.

Danîsha met Shiván's appalled glance. What were they going to do about Shakhere and Brakhól?

* * *

Shiván sat on the floor beside the altar in the Stillárre Hearth, hugging his knees as he stared up at the Ambon of Sûrilane on the wall above him. Over the past nine days he had come here often to think and pray. He found a peacefulness under the great Ambon that eased his despair and cleared his mind.

The golden rod and silver circle gleamed in the late afternoon sunlight streaming in from the open front door. This was the instrument the One had used to bring the Restorers to Dûrion, and to summon his people to the battle against darkness. He remembered how ordinary Dûrians had flocked to it during the war against Shambor; how when raised aloft those compelling trumpet calls would ring out, which no one who loved the One Creator God and his Son Prince Orrénne could ignore.

He himself might have lost the plot in recent months, but God hadn't. He was still calling them to be his agents in overthrowing the dark power of mindbending and restoring his Way in this world. For the first time in a long while there was peace in Shiván's heart and clarity in his thoughts as he pledged himself afresh to that task. Despite having more reason than ever before to slide down into his old nemesis, depression, God had kept him from that; and he poured out his heartfelt thanks.

Then he turned to his other standby in times of trouble, his old King James Bible. He'd been reading it a lot since his present trouble had begun. Hope and confidence sprang up renewed as he read its undying message of God's unshakeable, never-ending love for those he had created.

After a while his mind went back to Brakhól's outburst an hour ago, and the uproar it had caused in the city — which was only now settling down. There would be a lot of soothing to be done tomorrow. But what was the best solution for Brakhól in the long term? It tore Shiván's heart to think of sending him away. They *couldn't* hand that special child with his incredible gift over to a pack of Grûzhack warriors! Yet Shakhere had a far stronger claim on him than they did…

Shiván puzzled and prayed over it; and gradually an idea took shape.

* * *

The mood the next morning in the Domicile's Fraternity Room was grim. The six Council members present for this emergency session had gravitated towards one end of the large circular table. Frengor, co-opted to the Council since their arrival in Stillárre, was seated on Bishop Harlon's right. Bishop Mâron, Estaron and Garset were not there: they had gone with an escort of troops to reassure the large crowd that had gathered in the market square.

Shivan was eager to share his thoughts about the dilemma to be discussed; he curbed his impatience as he waited for people to settle so that Harlon could open the proceedings.

Finally the Bishop cleared his throat, and all eyes turned to him.

"Friends, we're facing a serious dilemma. It's obvious from yesterday's events that the Grûzhack scouts must leave Stillárre as soon as possible. People have taken Brakhól to their hearts because of his wholehearted delight in the One—but they have not accepted the scouts. They will be even more angry when they learn it was the scouts who provoked him last night. Yet, how can we abandon this vulnerable child to Shakhere and his comrades—a group of rough, teenage soldiers? Brakhól needs special care and protection. He is still recovering from the Strongholder's abuse." He looked around the group.

"Yes," Lannie added, "and the Strongholder won't be sitting idle: he'll be doing all he can to get his Child of Despair back. There may be spies in Stillárre already, waiting for a chance to kidnap him. He'll be safer in Barazhân. There's no future for him here in Dûrion."

Harlon nodded. "Very true. The boy would be devastated to be parted from his brother now. Yet, he would also be devastated to be parted from us." Harlon paused, and Shiván seized the opening.

"Your Radiance, there seems to be only one solution to this problem." All the Council members except Frengor looked at him in surprise, which quickly turned to doubt: they were wondering,

Shiván knew, what fresh idiocy he was about to propose. He steeled himself. "The Restorers — or some of us — must go with Brakhól and the scouts to Barazhân."

Lannie snorted and looked up at the ceiling; Perrely and Danîsha spoke at once, trying to cut him off before he made a fool of himself.

"Go to *Barazhân?!*" Perrely's exclamation packed in every ounce of what Barazhân stood for. Seven-foot giants. Icy mountains. Deadly weapons. Unrivalled power. The source of the pernicious teméyn trade. "No outsiders ever go to Barazhân! Never mind the problem of getting there — with *those* four." She gazed at him sadly, like a mother telling her child he can't play with the nice lion. Shivan felt a flash of annoyance.

"Just listen! If we go to Barazhân we can make sure Brakhól will be... will be properly looked after. Shakhere talks about taking him back to their 'parents' — maybe older relatives? — who'll care for him. We can improve Brakhól's chances by telling these people... we can tell them what we've learnt about his... gift. Things they may not know, from after... the Strongholder had him."

Shiván sent up a wordless prayer that he would remain coherent long enough to finish explaining the idea.

There was a moment's silence.

"That's a good point, Shiván," Frengor said with a warm smile.

"But what about the journey?" Perrely persisted. "Where would the scouts take us? Brakhól's too young. We can't sleep under bushes or in damp, chilly caves..."

"You're forgetting about Nist! She has a network here in Stillárre, and regularly gets supplies through Grûzhack-held territory to the mountain people, the, um... the Galeronden. She can guide us to one of their settlements. There we'll have proper food and shelter, and we can stay on for... a day or so."

"Oh!" Perrely was taken aback.

"That's a wonderful idea!" 'Neesh exclaimed. Lannie was nodding, her eyebrows raised in faint surprise. Their reactions were balm to Shiván's soul.

"How long would it take to get there?" Perrely asked.

"I believe Nist does the outward journey in three days," Frengor put in. "And I would guess you'd need about the same from there to Barazhân."

"One of the Galeronden could show us to the border," Shiván added. "Then it would be over to... Shakhere and his boys."

"Hmm," Bishop Harlon pondered. "But should we be risking Restorers' lives just to make sure Brakhól is well cared for?"

"Ah, but there's... more," Shiván said. "We've seen the effect Brakhól has on other Grûzhack when he's singing to the bellaril. It's incredible! Shakhere and his friends forgot their mission, their training... everything, and just came running to Brakhól. And 'Neesh, each time you play the bellaril with Brakhól, the scouts are all— are all, well... shook-up and tearful.

"Shakhere asked me last Anderil after the Hearth service where this happiness came from, and... and why it is so powerful. Once in Barazhân, mightn't the One use Brakhól—and you—in a similar way? Brakhól's talent was developed by... it was developed by, er... the Stronghholder as an instrument of destruction—a Child of... Despair."

Shiván himself felt despair growing as the grey mist seeped back into his mind; but he forced himself to stand up, placed his hands firmly on the table and looked around, catching every person's eye.

"Now let him be a Child of Hope! Let him broadcast... *joy* to his people."

A thoughtful silence followed. Shivan let out a pent-up breath and sat down again.

There was a slow nodding of heads. The Bishops and Frengor exchanged glances.

"Shiván," Frengor said, "you may have put your finger on the One's purpose in bringing Brakhól and Shakhere together here, with us." He paused. "But you said 'we'—and so did Perrely. To have any chance of returning alive, your group cannot include Dûrians— only foreigners, who won't instantly be tagged as the enemy. That rules you out, Perrely. Secondly, we dare not risk our *Aténnelor*, the Overguardian, on this mission. That rules you out, Shiván." The old priest's sharp eyes bored into Shiván's, and his heart sank.

"I fully agree, Frengor," the Bishop said.

Shiván looked at them doubtfully. Was he being sidelined again? But Frengor continued, "That leaves Alanya and Danîsha here at this table." He looked at 'Neesh. "*Mâra Atémbellar*, are you willing to go?"

"Yes, I am." 'Neesh was nodding solemnly, but there was fire in her eyes. Shiván knew how much she'd always longed to bring God's good news to those who'd never heard it.

Bishop Harlon was shaking his head. "Mâra, you have our greatest respect. And our prayers."

Frengor turned to Lannie. "What about you, younger sister?"

Lannie hesitated. It was obvious to everyone that nursemaiding Brakhól on a long and difficult journey was the last thing she wanted to do. The Bishop saved her embarrassment. "I think Alanya *Atémban* is needed here in Stillárre. She is widely known and respected in sorting out complex legal issues—of which there are more than enough at present."

"But Danîsha can't go all by herself... with a bunch of, um... Grûzhack warriors!" Shiván blurted out.

He wanted to say more but Frengor interposed quietly, "Then Gelmion will have to go."

Taken by surprise, Shiván sputtered into silence while the Council thought about Frengor's suggestion.

"That would not actually be a bad idea," Lannie said. "With his experience in the Bishop's Guard, Gil is a skilled longswordsman. He'd be a good protector, 'Neesh."

"It could mean a lot to him, too," Perrely added. "Gelmion's been a loner among us for so long. This would show that we accept him."

Frengor looked at the Bishop. "Are we agreed, then?"

"I think so. Let's pray about it."

They asked God to shed his Light on their plans, while Shiván struggled with a sense of let-down. With difficulty he put it aside. After his first positive contribution to the Council in weeks it was Gil who'd be benefitting, not himself; but maybe Gil needed it more than he did.

* * *

As the four Grûzhack scouts padded warily into the Fraternity Room, their eyes darting this way and that, they reminded Lannie of felines entering alien territory. Harlon gestured for them to sit, and they took chairs on the opposite side of the circular table from the Council members.

When Shakhere heard the proposal that Danîsha and Gelmion should accompany them, his response was immediate: "No."

He translated for his comrades, and they all tilted their heads to one side in the Grûzhack gesture of negation.

While the Council digested this, Lannie focused her attention on Shakhere and silently asked the One to give her insight.

"Why not?" Shivvie asked.

"Us not do dis."

"Gelmion and I can help you with Brakhól," 'Neesh urged.

"Brakhól my brudder."

"Yes, but look at what happened last night! If Brakhól gets upset while you're travelling, you may be caught by your own army. You don't want that, do you?"

Shakhere shrugged.

"*Why* is it so bad for Danîsha and Gelmion to go with you?" Perrely persisted. "They only want to help you, and they won't stay long in your country. As soon as Brakhól is settled, they'll leave. That will make it easier for Brakhól, too."

"No." Four tilted heads.

"Well, here's a challenge," Frengor murmured, an intrigued smile playing round his lips.

Harlon heaved a sharp sigh. "It looks like we have more praying to do."

Lannie had heard enough. "Shakhere."

He looked at her. She waited.

"You speak?"

"Yes, I speak. If you will not allow Danîsha and Gelmion to go with you, Brakhól will stay here."

"Lannie—" Shiván protested. She raised her hand—a signal they all understood: Alanya was following her gift.

"Brakhól my brudder," Shakhere repeated in a flat voice. "He come wid us."

"Not without Danîsha and Gelmion."

"No."

Lannie smiled. "Yes."

She sat, her eyes locked with his. The rest of the Council was silent.

Shakhere looked away first. He said something to his comrades, and there was a sharp exchange. He turned to Bishop Harlon, stretching out a hand in appeal. Lannie noticed he only had five fingers. The other Grûzhack had six.

"Woman not decide. What say Beeshop?"

Harlon answered coldly. "I say that in this Council, both women and men decide. Alanya speaks for us all."

Another hurried consultation. Shakhere told Lannie, "Grûzhack law say foreigner not come to Barazhân."

"And what does Grûzhack law say about scouts who leave the army without permission?"

Shakhere's translation was followed by a clash of fiery Grûzhack as all four spoke at once.

"If foreigners caught in Barazhân, all die."

Lannie's eyes narrowed. "All? Including you?"

"*All* die."

"Then you'll just have to make sure Danîsha and Gelmion are not caught."

After a fast and furious discussion with his comrades, Shakhere faced Lannie again. She saw the beginnings of a grudging respect.

"We take Daneesh and Gelmin. Dey go where we say and obey."

"In Barazhân they will do that. Before then, some of our people will escort you to the Galeronden country, and the Galeronden will put you on the path to Barazhân."

Shakhere stared at her, aghast.

Chapter 9: *Answering machine*

IT WAS MID-AFTERNOON in the Stillárre Domicile, and Gil was preparing to go out for a solitary walk. As he pulled his fur jacket on in the ornate entrance hall, Bishop Mâron came hurrying in.

"Hold on a moment, Gil, and I'll join you," he said in English.

"Okay. I thought you'd be otherwise occupied."

"No, no, I need to get out." He shot Gil a keen glance. "You look bushed. Bad night?"

Gil shrugged. "The usual."

"Another nightmare, I suppose. I'm sorry. You're carrying a heavy burden."

"Don't I know it."

Estaron suddenly appeared at Mâron's side. "Your Serenity, there are several urgent matters needing attention—"

"Not now, Estaron. You know I have a weekly arrangement with Gelmion, and I intend to keep it."

"I wouldn't intrude, Serenity, only…"

"This is my day off, Estaron," Mâron said with asperity. "Even if every refugee from Darthane were hammering at the door, I would still go for my walk! Whatever it is can wait."

Estaron bowed his head and steepled his hands in submission to the Bishop's authority. Then with an impassive face he left.

Mâron shook his head. "That man will be the death of me," he muttered. "I'll get my coat before he discovers a new national disaster to be dealt with."

A smile hovered round Gil's lips as he watched the harried Bishop taking the stairs two at a time. When he spoke English he became Father Martin again, the unassuming vicar of Leston whom Gil had met back in England. Also known as Dr. Martin Fellowes, a linguist respected in academic circles. But here in Dûrion he was the Kindler of Sûrilane—as well as Bishop Suffragan. An apparently miraculous situation in which he was transferred by God from one world to the other without losing any time in either. Gil the academic would have laughed at such a story, if it weren't for the fact that he had met the man in both places—and had himself been 'miraculously' transported three times between England and Dûrion.

But in either world, this was a man he could relate to. He was profoundly grateful that Martin was joining him.

They left the Domicile by a back door to avoid the crowd loitering around the main entrance. After slipping down a number of alleyways and side streets, they hunched their shoulders, pulled their hoods over their faces and slipped unrecognised through the south-western gate of the city.

Beyond was open countryside, bright in the spring sunshine. They left the southern highway as soon as possible and took a rural lane bordered by low hedges that ran through fields shimmering with new green. Throwing back his hood, Martin drew a deep breath. "Freedom at last!"

For a while they walked in silence, soaking in the sunshine and serenity. Gil glanced at his companion. His face was relaxed and his eyes had lost that intent look.

"How long is it since you were back in Leston?"

Martin sighed. "Too long. With all the recent upsets I suppose God wanted me here." He looked at Gil. "It doesn't happen to order, you know. I can ask to go back—and I have!—but I never know in advance which mornings I'll wake up in the vicarage, and which mornings I'll be here."

Gil shook his head. "I can hardly imagine what it must be like, living two parallel lives. Don't you struggle to make the switch-over sometimes?"

"Yes, I do. I think that's why God arranges it after a night's sleep. By the time I've had my morning coffee—or chass—I've reassembled the jigsaw and can more or less remember where I left off last time. I do forget things, though. Once, in Leston, I blamed it on a bad dream. Since then, whenever I'm forgetful, people say, 'Oh, the vicar's been dreaming again!'"

Gil smiled. "But when you're there, you remember what happened here, and vice versa—even though no time has been lost in either place?"

"Oh yes."

"Amazing."

They walked in silence up a low hill crowned with a small copse. From the top a panoramic view opened up across hamlets and fields to the River Mest, which gleamed silver in the westering sun. By unspoken agreement they settled on the grass beside the trees.

"What do you think of this 'travelling between worlds' thing?" Martin asked. "After all, you did it, too, when you first arrived here. I imagine my idea that it's an act of God, overriding the laws of his own universe, wouldn't fit in your world view. Do you have an explanation for it, or is it one of those mysteries that science has yet to unravel?"

Gil pondered a moment, chewing on a blade of grass. "'An act of God' sounds like a cop-out. I suppose right now I'd have to say it was a mystery."

"But you do believe in God—we discussed that last time."

"Yes, I've had to accept the existence of God. Neither atheism nor agnosticism provide a credible explanation for life. But accepting a supernatural power behind the normal laws of the universe is a big enough leap right now, without trying to account for the abnormal ones."

"Is that such a large extra step? If there's a God who created all life, surely his abilities can't be restricted to the laws that we are able to understand?"

"No, of course not. There's vastly more in the universe that we don't understand than the few things we do understand. The only rational explanation is that it's the work of a supreme Intelligence, which our human science is still discovering."

"An impersonal Intelligence?"

Gil shrugged. "Probably. I do have a problem with assuming, as you do, that such an advanced Intelligence would interfere in his own creation on behalf of individual human beings—like altering his own laws to bring us here, or to perform miraculous healings. But we've discussed this before, too."

"And I'll repeat what I've said before," Martin murmured. "In that case there's no hope for us. The kind of Intelligence you describe is impersonal, uncaring. He—or It—has created a huge, marvellously complex universe... and abandoned it to its fate."

Gil looked away. "I admit I find your concept of a 'good', caring God very attractive. And I have to concede that the Lightist—or Christian—faith is the most consistent and comprehensive world view I've come across. It accounts for the origin of the universe, the existence of good and evil, the complexity of human behaviour, the phenomenon of conscience... a whole host of things that would otherwise be 'accidental'."

"So what's stopping you from believing?"

"Lack of clear evidence. All these things are logically possible, but I have yet to be convinced that they're true. The existence of God—yes. The existence of the Lightist kind of God—no. And I can't go running after some emotional experience of 'enlightenment' which bypasses logic."

Martin shook his head. "Chasing an experience seldom leads to a deliberate, carefully considered choice, which is the only logical response if 'our kind of God' exists. But that's something that has to be accepted on the balance of probabilities; it can never be conclusively proved."

"I'm not convinced the balance of probabilities is in favour of your kind of God. So little is known about him—as you yourself have said. The only concrete evidence concerns the historical events surrounding Jesus Christ and Prince Orrénne, who both claimed to be the Son of God. And that evidence is circumstantial."

"Well, I believe there comes a point when the evidence runs out, and we simply have to trust the unknown. You can never know all there is to know about God—therefore you can never know absolutely, with zero margin of error, whether God is the caring and trustworthy Person we claim him to be."

"Exactly."

"Ah, but wait: Think of air travel on Earth. An ordinary passenger can never know absolutely whether the aircraft they are boarding is fully trustworthy. But at the same time, they have no compelling reason to doubt it. Therefore—without even thinking—they place their trust in the unknown, and board the aircraft. Only by doing so will they find out whether it is trustworthy or not."

Gil frowned. "I see the analogy, but God surely can't be reduced—"

"Analogies are never perfect. My point is that reason and logic have their limits. So many questions cannot be answered; so much about God remains unknown. But if he *is* the kind of God who intervened in human history—and did so on your behalf—then he cannot be ignored. Such an unprecedented action by an Intelligence many orders of magnitude greater than ours demands a response."

Father Martin's direct gaze was both sympathetic and challenging. In a quieter voice he said, "Logic and evidence can't help you here, Gil. Now you must ask yourself a different question. Not: *Do I have any compelling reason to believe in a caring, personal God?* — but: *Do I have any compelling reason* not *to?* If you haven't, then the time has come to step out of the box and trust the Unknown."

Gil stared into the sunset. The sky had turned into a blazing canvas of scarlet and vermilion, the river a sheet of molten gold. A casual display of breathtaking splendour — here now, gone in a moment. The Artist? Unknown.

"That's — something to think about."

Martin grinned. "Good. We'd better head back before it gets dark." They stood and dusted themselves off before heading back towards the city. "Oh, and by the way, I have a message for you."

"A message?"

"Well, a request, actually. From the Bishop's Council."

"Now you've got me intrigued."

Martin glanced at him and smiled. "They're wondering if you'd be willing to accompany Danîsha, Brakhól and the Grûzhack scouts on a trip to Barazhân."

* * *

That evening Gil sat on the bed in his tiny room in the Domicile. The only other furniture was a stool and a clothes chest; but he was grateful to have this small space to himself. His eyes were far away as he pondered the request Martin had brought from the Council.

An actual job to do. A difficult and essential job, for which no one else was available. He was amazed that they would trust him with it after what he'd done to them last year. Their vote of confidence opened a sliver of light at the end of a long, dark tunnel.

This trip would be dangerous. Neither he nor Danîsha might return. He'd asked for time to think it over... But there was no doubt what his decision would be. Martin had seen it in his eyes.

His thoughts went back to this afternoon's discussion. Eight months ago an exchange like that would have been unthinkable. In a matter of minutes he would scornfully have flattened the priest's card-house of assumptions.

But a lot had changed in those eight months. His self-confidence had been severely dented. He'd been mindbent. He'd seen more sheer evil than in all the rest of his life. He'd personally witnessed metaphysical events for which there was no rational explanation. He'd had no alternative but to concede the existence of 'supernatural powers' — including a supreme Intelligence behind the order and complexity of the universe.

He was no longer the sceptic who ridiculed anything he couldn't understand. He could no longer reject out of hand that 'Unknown' whom Martin had talked about. Perhaps the 'supreme Intelligence' he'd acknowledged *was* the Lightist God: a Person of absolute goodness, who intervened in human affairs to help those who turned to him.

He didn't know. As Martin said, he couldn't know. But he had no compelling reason not to believe it — only the balance of probabilities. Here he was, facing a hazardous undertaking that might cost him his life. What if God *was* a Person — one who could set aside his past actions, as the Council had done? If ever there was a time to try Martin's recipe of trusting the Unknown, it was now.

He had no idea how to 'pray'. Last year, under Shambor's control, he'd mimicked the Lightists' devout postures and pious clichés. He wasn't having any of that now. He wouldn't say or do a single thing that wasn't completely genuine.

Sitting exactly as he was, without closing his eyes, clasping his hands or raising his arms, he muttered under his breath, "God, if you do exist, I still think the balance of probability is against you being a person. But in case you are, and you're listening, I'm going to ask you to look after Danîsha and me on this trip. I'd... be grateful if we could come out of it alive. And I'd also like you to do something... well, something unusual. I don't know what, but something I'd never have expected. To help me find out whether you *are* the person they say you are. Um... That's all. Thanks."

It felt like leaving a message on an answering machine. Well, he'd find out in due course whether anyone was monitoring this particular machine.

Chapter 10: *Good governance?*

347 NF / Seventeen years ago

KONNAR STIFLED A YAWN. The distinguished visitor was late. He was tired of waiting, and he was tired of this depressing building.

He glanced around for the umpteenth time. The sanctuary in the training temple was ancient, and it showed. The stone in the pillars supporting the high, ridged roof was flaking in places. The same applied to the raised altar in front of the row of devotees. The narrow rectangular windows along each wall let in hardly any light, and the wooden benches were unforgiving after an hour of sitting.

Conversation among the assembled temple staff and local dignitaries had died a natural death about half an hour ago. Even earlier for Konnar. The other devotees tended to avoid speaking to him — and vice versa.

He heaved an involuntary gusty sigh. He'd been with the Mindbenders for five months now, and disillusionment had begun to set in. He might be the star student, but everyone had great plans for him and fought with each other about them. He was beginning to see that these Mindbenders — who were supposed to be ruling the country — only cared about their own personal power and wealth. Good governance was nowhere on the agenda.

Just the other day a local man had been caught trespassing in the temple grounds. He'd been mindbent and added to the gardening staff. Never mind his terrified pleas that his son was desperately ill and he'd taken a shortcut to find the herbalist.

Then there was the festering injustice of the water supply. Several years ago the temple had dammed the local river to safeguard its own supply, and to add freshwater fish to their diet. No one cared that in dry spells — like the present — the villages downstream, and even some outlying districts of Orselm itself, suffered water shortages. A delegation of prominent residents had come to the temple to complain. They had been sent packing.

He wished Bari were here. It would be so good to discuss situations like this with him.

Konnar swallowed another yawn. Bored noises rose from the front six rows of the sanctuary: smothered yawns, rustles of clothing, coughs, the creaking of benches as people tried to ease their aching backsides.

Well, at least his mind could range freely without the fear of being monitored by his superiors—a freedom his fellow devotees, and even the junior Mindbenders, resented. Many times in the past months the senior Mindbenders had tried to mindread or coerce him; but his mind had always brushed them aside. As they grew more desperate to control him he suspected that they'd attempted actual mindbending while he was asleep. But his mental barriers had still proved too strong for them. He was proud of that.

When he was ordered to do things he didn't feel were right, he simply ignored the orders. A number of Mindbenders in the temple had suffered when they tried to compel him.

So basically, they didn't know what to do with him. He was outside the normal hierarchy. He was too dangerous to expel, which would leave him free to wreak havoc beyond their walls; yet he was also too dangerous to antagonise within their walls. And they couldn't alert higher authority for fear of bringing wrath down upon themselves.

Therefore they had to negotiate in order to live with him. Konnar was quite happy with that. He didn't want to return to his miserable existence outside. At the same time he hoped that he might, in time, be able to bring some of Bari's good governance into mindbending.

Footsteps! There was a universal turning of heads and craning of necks, accompanied by a buzz of comment. Yes—finally!—His Superiority Mindbender Belyeru, of the Strongholder's personal staff, was entering the building with Training Master Nemisu. Konnar wasn't the only one to breathe a sigh of relief as they all stood.

Mindbender Nemisu—a tall, cadaverous man—conducted his Superiority to the altar, where they turned to face the standing audience. After declaring that Mindbender Belyeru needed no introduction to those assembled here, Nemisu proceeded to introduce him. Konnar filtered most of that out, playing instead his favourite game of mentally sussing out the new arrival.

Belyeru looked short beside Nemisu, though he was probably of average height. He had a smooth, shiny face, small eyes, and a permanent false smile. What Konnar saw in Belyeru's mind at first impressed him even less. It was a glutinous pit of arrogance and ambition. But a deeper look revealed that it contained a vast storehouse of knowledge about Selmion, the Strongholder, and current events, policies and strategies. He would have liked to explore further; but it was a little dangerous, and Nemisu was moving on to the next stage.

"Now, your Superiority, I would like you to meet our temple staff, students, and citizens of the local community." He nodded to a pair of stewards, who arranged the first row of presentees in a long line in front of the visitor. Konnar found himself standing next to one of the local citizens, who had been pointed out to him earlier as a prominent teméyn merchant. A solidly-built man in a costly purple robe trimmed with gold. He had a slight paunch and a fleshy, aggressive face. Konnar idly scanned the man's mind for his name—Galisiu Ankarida.

Then he stiffened mentally. Violent feelings were seething in this man's mind. He read them, and found that merchant Galisiu was intent on disrupting the meeting by demanding compensation from their distinguished visitor! For what? Looking a little further Konnar discovered that the man's daughter had been raped by one of the Mindbenders at this temple several years ago. The resulting child had now reached school-going age.

Merchant Galisiu was steeling himself to demand payment for the child's education from the visiting Mindbender, since his approaches to the temple itself had been brushed aside.

Before Konnar could do anything, Mindbender Belyeru reached the merchant, hand raised for the Selmian palm-press greeting. The Training Master announced Galisiu's name and occupation. But instead of pressing his palm against the Mindbender's, the merchant burst into angry speech.

"Your Superiority, I have been wronged! Six years ago my daughter was raped by a member of this temple. The child is now of school-going age, and I—"

"Konnaru! Falimu! Take this man out," Master Nemisu barked.

At that, something in Konnar snapped. When that poor trespasser had been mindbent, he'd done nothing. When the water-supply delegation had been ignored, he'd done nothing. He couldn't stand idly by any longer.

Devotee Falimu had already grasped the merchant's other arm and was pulling him towards the door. "I demand justice!" Galisiu was shouting. "Payment for schooling…!"

Konnar mind-shouted "*Stop!*" and Falimu froze. To the gaping visitor and appalled Training Master Konnar said quietly, "I think this man has a legitimate grievance that needs to be heard." He took pride in his fluency: if this place had done nothing else for him, it had cured his stutter.

For a long moment there was a frozen tableau as the Training Master, the visiting Mindbender and the merchant stared at Konnar. Konnar could see desperation building in Master Nemisu's mind. He knew only too well the impossibility of getting Konnar to obey orders. At the same time indignation was rapidly coming to the boil in Mindbender Belyeru. The visitor turned an outraged face to the Training Master. "You're going to allow this, Nemisu?"

The Training Master put on a convincing act. "How dare you, devotee? Take the man out at once!" Konnar felt sorry for him. He had no other choice.

Konnar turned to Galisiu. "Let's hear your story."

"Well, I— It's only right—" the merchant stammered, thrown out by the strange turn of events.

Infuriated, the visiting Mindbender sent a whiplash of pain on Konnar. Konnar bounced it back on him, and Belyeru screamed and clutched his head. Galisiu broke off in mid-sentence. In fury Belyeru attempted to seize control of Konnar's mind. Konnar struck back, and the Mindbender crumpled to the floor, his face ashen.

In the utter silence that followed, Konnar turned back to the merchant. "Please continue."

Galisiu gulped. Addressing himself now to Konnar he said, "It— ah—it was like this, sir. My—ah—daughter went berry-picking in the country with some of her peasant friends. A Mindbender was passing in his carriage, and he stopped and—ah—watched them for a while. Then he spoke to his attendants, and they… chased the girls."

His face grew red and his words more fluent as he continued. "They caught my Alenyi and dragged her to the carriage. The son-of-a-whore Mindbender raped her right there, in broad daylight! Then he threw her out on to the road like a— a chewed bone, and drove off."

He paused, watching with smouldering eyes while two devotees directed by Master Nemisu carried the collapsed Mindbender out of the sanctuary. "It's all right, sir," Konnar said to the Master. "I've purged his mind. He'll remember nothing of this incident." Murmuring broke out among the assembled temple staff. Memory erasure was something else devotees were supposedly unable to do.

"Well, so, her friends brought my Alenyi home," Galisiu continued, "and we were left to care for her. She fell pregnant, and her son is now ready to start school. The temple is responsible for this child! They have paid nothing for his upkeep these past six years. The least they can do now is to pay for his schooling!"

After a moment of silence Konnar turned to the Training Master. "Sir, an injustice has been been done here. What recompense are we going to make?"

Master Nemisu sighed. "Now is not the time, Konnar. We are here to welcome and entertain our guests. We can talk about this later."

No. Konnar was having none of that. His thoughts went back to the impromptu justice he and Bari had imposed on younger kids. Bari had always insisted that the time to deal with wrongdoing was now, not later. Leave it till later, and the guilty party always found a way to wriggle off the hook.

"No, sir," he said, his eyes hard. "Merchant Galisiu has waited too long already. We will give him justice before this meeting ends."

Protests broke out around the sanctuary. Master Nemisu stared at Konnar and shook his head. Then he raised his voice above the noise and said, "The public part of this meeting is now over. Will all guests, adherents, devotees and junior Mindbenders please leave. We will continue to address the issue Konnar has raised in private."

Konnar opened his mouth to countermand the Master's order, then thought better of it. It was really only the senior Mindbenders he needed. The subordinates would have been unable to speak spontaneously with the seniors monitoring their thoughts. And for the temple's good name—which in a strange way he still cared about—it would be better to exclude the other local dignitaries.

Once they had left, the senior Mindbenders rounded on Konnar and began voicing their objections. Merchant Galisiu watched, amazement etched on his features. There were loud voices declaring that if the Mindbenders' authority were challenged like this across the country, people would rise up in revolt. Others (a few) were more sympathetic, but demanded that the offending Mindbender should be identified as he was the one responsible, not the entire temple.

Konnar turned to Galisiu. "Do you know who the Mindbender was who raped your daughter?"

"He doesn't. We went through this when he was here before, Konnar," the Training Master said wearily.

The merchant shuffled his feet, looking unhappy. "It all happened so quickly. Alenyi was terrified... She's never been able to say exactly what he looked like." Konnar suspected that the Mindbender might have blurred her vision — or her memory.

Feeling he was losing control, Konnar walked among the eight senior Mindbenders checking their thoughts. He was shocked to discover that most of them had raped local women. Not that he himself was averse to the occasional amorous adventure, but always by mutual consent. It disgusted him to find that among the senior Mindbenders, grabbing and raping local girls while passing in their carriages was almost a popular sport.

But none of the Mindbenders seemed to remember raping this particular woman, and demands for the guilty Mindbender to own up met with solid silence. Not wanting to compound the injustice by choosing a victim at random, Konnar was nonplussed. He found himself wondering how Bari would have handled this.

Back up front with the Training Master and the merchant, Konnar surveyed the Mindbenders. He couldn't back down now. He'd declared his stand for immediate good governance; now he had to make it happen. But he couldn't ignore the argument that too generous a settlement would weaken the temple's position: they'd then have everyone and his second cousin clamouring for similar compensation.

After a longish pause during which he could feel the anger of the assembled Mindbenders buffeting his thoughts, a solution finally occurred to him, and he felt himself relaxing.

"Here's what we'll do," he announced. "This man's daughter was abused by one of us, but even the guilty person does not know for sure whether he was responsible. Therefore the temple as a whole has to take responsibility."

He silenced the resulting outcry and turned to the merchant. "Your grandson, sir, can attend the Mindbenders' school at no cost to yourself." He beamed at the man, delighted with this solution. It would save the temple actually paying out cash, and minimise the weakening of their authority in the community.

But the merchant didn't smile back. Shock and horror chased across his face. "No!" he declared. "I'm not giving the boy to you Mindbenders! I want payment for him to go to a normal school!"

Amid derisive laughter from the Mindbenders Konnar tried to persuade Galisiu that the Mindbenders' school was a good one, providing a high standard of education, and assured him that his grandson would not be forced to become a Mindbender. But the merchant was adamant.

As the argument trailed away into an obstinate stand-off, Konnar realised that he could hardly blame Galisiu: he himself knew only too well the fear he and his mother had once lived in that he, Konnar, might fall into the hands of the Mindbenders.

Konnar sighed. Fixing Galisiu with a hard stare he told him, "This offer of free education is a fair one, and it's the only one you'll get. Take it or leave it."

Galisiu turned on his heel and stumped out.

The assembled Mindbenders laughed. With a grim smile Master Nemisu said to Konnar, "Now perhaps you understand why we're not too concerned about abstract justice, Konnar."

Turning to the rest of the group he announced, "The midmeal is ready, and I'm told our honoured guest has recovered. Let us go and join him."

They walked out, chatting and laughing among themselves, several throwing Konnar a mocking glance as they left.

Konnar sank down on the hard bench feeling like X-marks-the-spot. He'd done his best to apply good governance, but had ended up making a fool of himself and pleasing no one.

Yet despite that, he'd done something. He hadn't stood idly by in the face of injustice. The fact that the merchant had refused to accept his settlement didn't alter the principle of the matter. In fact the incident only strengthened his belief that the Mindbenders *could* rule justly if they used their powers in the right way.

If only Bari were here! Together they could make it happen…

But Bari was long gone, so he would have to manage on his own. He wondered if the Strongholder would get to hear of the incident, but doubted it. Everyone would be too busy protecting their own hides. His Supremacy would not react kindly to the news that one of his training temples was unable to control its own devotee.

But supposing he did hear… Could Konnar stand up to *him?*

A shiver of fear passed down his spine.

———————————————

Chapter 11: *Hazardous journey*

357 NF / Seven years ago

ESTARON HAD FAILED. He sat on the bed in his apartment at Darthane University, unable to believe what had happened.

At his first 'boards' assessment this year — the twice-annual oral examination by senior scholars — he'd misunderstood a crucial question: it was only afterwards, as he'd puzzled over the board's sceptical response, that he realised what they'd really asked, and how inadequate his reply had been. And the second assessment... It was beyond belief — but he'd got the time wrong! When he turned up an hour late the assessors had all left. That had been the previous week, and there'd been no sympathy for unpunctuality: none at all. The very next day he'd been summarily 'cancelled', as the withdrawal of University privileges was called.

So here he sat, his career abruptly terminated at twenty-six and his hopes of high office dashed. A heavy weight of depression threatened to overwhelm him.

Nothing had gone right in the last two years. He'd done very well at the Academy of Law in Astenar, winning a place at the University to do postgraduate legal studies. These could have fitted him for high office... But from the moment he arrived in Darthane it had been one failure after another. He'd invested the endowment his parents had given him with a merchant whose business had gone from profit to bankruptcy in a few short months. Carrilay, the girl he'd loved, had run off with a Gadeshite the evening before their betrothal. He'd had three interviews with delegates from prominent Dûrian towns looking for a young, enterprising Civic Elder — all of which had come to nothing for completely random and irrelevant reasons.

And now the ultimate disgrace: 'cancelled'.

He'd have to pack his bags and return to Astenar. It was all he could do. He dreaded the look on his parents' faces when they heard what had happened. He'd find work as a legal assistant — the lowest of the low, but it was all he could hope for now.

For a long time he sat on the edge of the bed in his comfortable postgraduate apartment, his mind churning, searching desperately for some kind of loophole, anything other than a career-killing legal assistantship. But the black stain of cancellation blotted out all other options. No town would consider him now for Civic Elder. The road to public advocacy, and thence to the prestigious office of arbiter, was closed. Ironically that road would still have been open, though longer, if he had moved straight into professional life from the Academy instead of wasting time on these disastrous postgraduate studies...

The door-chime suddenly rang. Estaron's head shot up. Who could this be? No one paid social visits in the middle of the morning.

A messenger in the red tunic of the Cathedral stood outside the door. With a small bow he handed Estaron an envelope. Estaron frowned and thanked him before returning inside.

He stood in the small reclining room, holding the heavy white envelope with both hands and staring at it. His frown deepened. It was inscribed simply with his Dûrian name: *Estaron don Geldor*. Who at the Cathedral — the seat of government, both religious and secular — would be writing to him?

Taking a small fruit knife from the kitchen, he made himself comfortable on the recliner by the window. He carefully slit the envelope and removed a thick sheet of cream paper with a blue-and-silver embossed crest at the bottom. He started reading.

At first he couldn't take in what the letter was saying. Then it dawned on him: this was beyond his wildest dreams!

"Bishop Shambor dom Beldet offers you the post of private secretary, in view of your intelligence, excellent reputation, high moral character, (etc., etc.), being prepared to overlook your cancellation at the University as an unfortunate mishap counterbalanced by your outstanding record at the Astenar Academy of Law..."

Private secretary to the ruler of Dûrion himself! Estaron's hands sank into his lap holding the letter, his eyes staring unseeing over the red roofs of Darthane. Wide vistas opened before his stunned mind: Administrative experience... legislation... policy-making... diplomacy... If he'd had complete freedom to design his own career, he could not have come up with anything closer to his long-term ambitions, and those of his family!

Of course, it would mean working with Suffragan Bishop Shambor. Along with other Lightists in Dûrion, Estaron was not overly impressed with Shambor. He had done, and not done, a number of things that followers of the Prince found disturbing: like transferring local government from village elders to a much smaller group of Land Elders or barons, all beholden to him; and, especially, turning a blind eye to the proliferation of the Lightless cults, which now flourished as an open secret in many towns.

But at least the cults were still not legal: they could not own property or build temples. And regarding the Land Elders, it might be argued that centralising control of agriculture had increased productivity... though Estaron wasn't sure about that. But as Shambor's private secretary, if he handled himself well, he might over time develop some influence in matters like these. The prospect was very attractive — especially when compared to the dead end of a legal assistantship.

He wondered how Shambor had heard of him, and how he had known so quickly about the cancellation of his university privileges. Then he remembered being told that the Bishop Suffragan was frequently on the lookout for talent among the student legal fraternity, and would keep an eye on anyone who showed promise. He must have been one of those.

Possibly Shambor saw his cancellation as a positive, not a negative factor: by rescuing Estaron from an impossible situation Shambor would earn his complete loyalty; and in any case, Estaron would have nowhere else to go if he tired of the job.

He sat staring out of the window for a long time. If this didn't work out, he'd be trapped. Was he willing to take that risk?

On the other hand, what was the alternative?

He had to decide now. The Bishop wouldn't wait.

He asked the One for wisdom. After a while he felt tension draining away and peace taking its place. Whatever happened, God would watch over him.

Estaron went to the shey-nut desk, took a sheet of his best bond paper, and slowly began to write.

* * *

Present day

A stiff breeze was humming through the rigging of the ships at Stillárre's riverside wharf. Jomel stood with other members of the Bishop's party who had risen at this early hour to see Brakhól and his entourage off on their hazardous journey to Barazhân. The travellers had said their goodbyes, and were gathered at the gangplank

of the three-masted schooner that would be taking them to Bronnilar on the southern shore of the lake.

Nist was there, as large and overpowering as ever: her network of agents had in the past saved many—including themselves—from former Bishop Shambor's wrath by taking them to safety among the Galeronden in the Tallissôr Mountains; and she still worked as a link between the reclusive Galeronden and the rest of Dûrion. She stood now halfway up the gangplank delivering a final pep-talk, which Shakhere was translating for his fellow Grûzhack. Jomel's lips quirked. The scouts all wore stony expressions. To be commanded by a Dûrian *woman* was clearly the ultimate insult. They had almost rebelled at first, but Nist had rolled effortlessly over them.

The group at the gangplank included two of Nist's network— hard-bitten men in dark tunics wearing swords—along with Danîsha holding Brakhól's hand, and Gelmion.

Looking at the man whom she had betrayed into the Bishop's Guard, who had later abused and raped her, and who was now heading into mortal danger, Jomel acknowledged a tiny sliver of sympathy for him. His slightly haggard appearance testified to the nightmares that still tormented him. He avoided her, as he avoided everyone except Shiván, Danîsha and Mâron.

She felt a grim sense of rightness about this. Didn't the Book say, *Whatever a man sows, he will in due course reap?* Gelmion was reaping the reward for his own co-operation with the darkness that had ruled Dûrion—and for what he had put her through. Her sliver of sympathy was tiny and temporary.

Danîsha and Gelmion turned for a final wave before climbing the gangplank on to the schooner. Brakhól was staring up at the sails. She would miss the happy little tyke! Gelmion's eyes briefly met hers, then he turned and walked up the ribbed plank.

She watched the ship as it drifted free of the wharf, then picked up speed down the river. The figures waving from the stern gradually dwindled and became indistinguishable. She waved a final farewell, and turned to leave with the rest of the send-off party.

* * *

Perrely looked at Shiván as they walked together, the last to leave the dock. She smiled warmly, hoping to lighten his mood. "This was basically your idea, that Danîsha and Gelmion should go to Bara-zhân with Brakhól and the scouts. It's brilliant! And once Danîsha gets Brakhól singing with the bellaril, they could have a huge impact."

Shiván grinned. She could always rely on her smiles having that effect. "Yes, well... And it solves two problems at once, because... otherwise... ah..." He fell silent.

Perrely's heart plummeted. There it was again—losing his train of thought. He looked away, shamefaced. She'd agonised over his growing mental confusion, and had so hoped that the recent episode might be the first sign of recovery.

She'd spoken to Frengor, and he hadn't minimised the problem. But after declaring categorically that Shiván wasn't mindbent, and admitting that he couldn't identify the curse—if that's what it was—the only solution he'd come up with was prayer and fasting. He and all the priests had spent two days without solid food, praying for Shiván between other duties; and she, Danîsha, Jomel and Bishop Mâron had joined them. But it didn't seem to be working.

They walked on for a moment in silence. Then Shiván said diffidently, "I haven't spent any time under the Ambon... in the last couple of days."

"Under the ambon? What do you mean?"

"Um... you know... Sitting under it. In the Hearth."

Perrely turned and stared at him. "You've been sitting at the front of the Stillárre Hearth, under the Ambon of Sûrilane?"

He smiled hesitantly. "Yes. It helps. That's where I was when I got the idea about... you know... that idea."

"Really?"

"Yes."

They entered the city square, and walked in silence through the bustling crowds until they reached Bishop's Avenue on the other side. Perrely didn't know what to make of what Shiván was telling her. The *Ambon* was clarifying his mind? It didn't make sense. The Ambon's powers were to do with summoning: summoning the Restorers from another sky, summoning followers of the Light to oppose evil. Personally she suspected that 'that idea' was a fluke, and attributing it to the Ambon was clutching at straws; but on the other hand, she should support anything that boosted Shiván's confidence.

"Shiván, that's wonderful! If the Ambon is helping you that way, you must sit under it more often. Every day!"

Shiván grinned. "I will!" And his hand reached for hers.

Embarrassment swept over her, and she jerked her arm away. How could he do that in public? How often had she told him it was not acceptable?

Then she realised that this was just another manifestation of his present malaise. "I'm sorry," she murmured. "I know you didn't mean it."

He nodded, his face miserable.

They walked on in strained silence.

———————————————

Chapter 12: *Kidnapped!*

351 NF / Thirteen years ago

KONNAR GLANCED ROUND the Training Master's spacious office with satisfaction. How could he have imagined five years ago, when he was first brought as a trembling schoolboy to this temple, that he, Konnaru Galenida, would be its Master in just a few years' time?

It had taken a little manoeuvring, but in truth the senior Initiates at the temple had been relieved to see him finally in charge. The former Master, Mindbender Nemisu, had moved on to higher things; and though as the youngest Initiate Konnar was far from the obvious choice to succeed him, none of the others had relished the prospect of trying to keep Konnar in line. A little prodding had produced the desired result: let Konnar do things his way, and if he messed up it was someone else's responsibility.

It didn't hurt that former Master Nemisu had nurtured the impression in higher circles that Konnar was a rising star — though he hadn't done it for Konnar's sake, but for his own protection should rumours of Konnar's resistance to authority become damaging.

Konnar seated himself in a comfortable leather chair beside the window overlooking the grounds. So. Temple policy was in his hands now. He could at last begin to realise his — and dear departed Bari's — dream of implementing principles of good governance. Of course it would be within the context of mindbending, which Bari wouldn't have agreed to. But Konnar still believed it was possible; and to honour that lost friendship, if for no other reason, he was going to do all he could within the small domain of this temple to make it work.

He gazed out of the window at the pleasing vista of well-manicured lawns dotted with flowerbeds, stretching down to the river. Or rather, to the dam. A grim smile touched his lips. The dam would be the first thing to go. The river's water would be shared freely with all who lived along its length. Then there was that gardener... Was that him, watering a distant flowerbed? The one who had been mindbent merely for taking a shortcut through the temple grounds. He would be set free...

Konnar settled into a comfortable reverie as he totted up all the wrongs he could begin righting.

* * *

Present day

Estaron walked along the narrow alley deep in thought. He was taking his normal route to the Domicile from the lodgings where he'd moved recently. Despite the private office Brother Ongaret had found for him, the noise and constant interruptions at the Domicile had proved too distracting. A widow in a quiet part of the city had been glad to rent a room to the Suffragan's secretary. He was able to bring unfinished work back there in the evenings and burn his own lamp oil deep into the night.

At this early hour the sun had not yet reached the depths of the alley, but there was a brighter light up ahead where it joined a wider thoroughfare. Estaron briefly noticed an unusual vehicle standing there — an enclosed two-person racer. Pulled by teams of swift, dog-like sinélle, these small carriages achieved impressive speeds on the highways; but they were normally open to the elements. Dismissing it from his thoughts, Estaron began running over the arrangements he'd have to make to settle the next group of Darthane refugees. About a quarter were still in temporary lodgings, without work. Those with relatives in the area had been settled first, followed by people whose trade was in demand. The task became progressively more difficult as he worked his way through to casual labourers and —

A hand clamped over Estaron's mouth, and two others locked his arms in an iron grip. He was jerked off-balance and hustled along the alley. They came to the enclosed racer, where his head was forced down and he was thrust through an open door which slammed shut as soon as his feet were inside. A dim figure in the other seat seized his neck in an arm-lock, and a dagger pricked him in the ribs.

"*Yahaaya!*" a voice up front shouted — the Selmian *Get moving!* command. The racer leapt forward. It picked up speed, and Estaron heard the cries of pedestrians as they jumped out of the way. But he could see nothing. The windows were covered with heavy hangings.

* * *

100

"We have just received word from Berûvis and Mandilane that an enclosed racer passed through those two towns at speed," Garset told the Bishop's Council.

Shiván frowned. "Through Mandilane as well? Beyond that it's the Strongholder's territory. Could they be taking Estaron to Selmion?"

Perrely smiled at Shiván, pleased that he was able to make a sensible contribution to the discussion. For the past ten days he had been spending all his free time in the Hearth, sitting under the Ambon. He attributed his greater mental clarity to the Ambon itself, but she still found that farfetched. Personally she put it down to the quiet restfulness of the house of worship, where his strained mind could relax and restore itself.

Perrely's heart sank. "But if he falls into the hands of the Strongholder—"

"—we must assume the worst." Shiván completed her sentence, doing what so many had done for him recently. "He will be mindbent. Which will give the Strongholder a whole lot of very valuable information if he's planning an attack."

"We should send a rescue mission at once," Alanya declared.

Bishop Harlon shook his head sadly. "*Atémban*, I'm afraid sending a rescue mission would be... What was that phrase of Gelmion's you used the other day, Shiván?"

"'Beyond the sphere of practical politics,'" Shiván translated.

Harlon smiled briefly. "I like that. Sending a rescue mission is beyond the sphere of practical politics. Mandilane is controlled by the Strongholder, and his forces are advancing westward towards us in order to enclose Darthane and wrest it from the Grûzhack. I'm afraid Estaron is already beyond our reach. All we can do now is to pray for him."

"Just pray for him?" Alanya protested, her eyes fiery. "We can't let the Strongholder get hold of him! Shiván said it—he knows too much! Surely, even if he's in enemy territory now, we have to at least *try* and rescue him!"

Garset sighed. "*Atémban*, I have discussed this with my commanders. At most we could send two of my best troopers in a similar racer—any other means of transport would be too slow. Even so, it would be virtually impossible to catch up with them with so much distance already between the vehicles. And a racer coming in from the west would certainly be stopped—which would mean the end of the mission." He paused. "As my lord Bishop says, we are left with no option but to pray and trust the One for our own protection."

Alanya snorted. "Well then, we must increase our vigilance! What measures have we taken against a Selmian attack on Stillárre, Garset?"

"We already have scouts bivouacked at hidden locations along the road from Mandilane to Berûvis. That's the only route the Strongholder can use to attack us without running into the Grûzhack. But as Bishop Harlon said, we believe his goal is not Stillárre, but Darthane: to approach the city from the north and west as well as the east and south.

"Today I also started recruiting unemployed Darthane refugees to act as our eyes and ears here in Stillárre, in case he's planning something... more clandestine."

Alanya didn't look happy, but she nodded. "Right. I suppose that's the best we can do."

"Thank you, Garset," the Bishop added. "We will keep watch and pray."

Perrely nodded with the others. Garset had avoided mentioning her own deepest fear: that the Strongholder would use Estaron's knowledge to infiltrate Stillárre and kill or, worse, mindbend the Dûrian leadership: the Bishop, Mâron, Frengor, Alanya... and Shiván.

* * *

Estaron and his knife-wielding companion had been sitting silently on the racer's back seat for over three hours, swaying with the vehicle's rapid movement. They'd passed through three towns— Histen, Berûvis and Lômack, Estaron thought, though he'd seen nothing from inside the enclosed vehicle. They'd left the highway after the third, and Estaron reckoned they must now be on the local road through Mandilane to Selmian-held Astenar, his childhood home.

His guess was confirmed when the man beside him pulled the coverings from the windows. The knife he held glinted in the fresh light, still resolutely angled towards Estaron. There was a sardonic smile on his swarthy face as Estaron blinked at the bright countryside rushing by, immediately recognising the farmland west of Astenar. They swept past a troop of Selmian cavalry in their tan uniforms.

"Welcome home," the man said in Selmian. His gravelly voice defiled the tuneful language.

"Thanks for the ride. My parents' house is in Candlemakers' street. You can drop me there."

His captor's smile widened. "That *used* to be your parents' house. Now it's unoccupied, so there's no point dropping you there. I think we may as well continue to Orselm, don't you, Your Highness?" The knife point never wavered.

Estaron shrugged. His parents had committed suicide many weeks ago when the Strongholder captured Astenar. He'd heard it from a neighbour who'd escaped, and the pain was still fresh. His captor's arrogance infuriated him, and not for the first time he considered grabbing the knife hand and overpowering him. But what would that achieve? He was sure the other kidnappers were following not far behind on horseback. His only chance would be when the racer stopped to change sinélle teams—which must be soon: he was amazed the present animals had kept up this gruelling pace for so long.

That hope was disappointed when the racer started slowing down after leaving Astenar. Four horsemen appeared, riding alongside the vehicle. Distracted, Estaron didn't notice his companion's sudden movement. The next thing his neck was once more in an arm lock and the knife's point was pricking his ribs.

"Nice and easy now, Highness, while we change the sinélle."

The change was made and the long journey continued. The well-made Dûrian roads ended when they left Starmane and entered Selmion. As they rattled along the uneven stones of the highway to Orselm, Estaron stared out of the racer's windows, all his old distaste for the Strongholder's domain rising up again. The countryside was beautiful enough: lush green water meadows, stately *ileya* trees trailing their fronds in the river, the cries of waterfowl, and the flowing herds of horses for which Selmion was famous, wheeling and galloping with their young. But the villages they passed through were clusters of squalid wattle and daub huts with thatched roofs, huddled in the shadow of an Initiate's mansion.

The Initiates of Gadesh, both priests and Mindbenders, ruled this land with an absoluteness Shambor had never achieved in Dûrion.

A growing stench wafting in through the windows warned Estaron they were approaching a town. Dûrion had long ago pioneered urban drains and sewage systems, but Selmion had not bothered to follow suit.

The racer swooped across a wide bridge and was waved through a massive gatehouse in the walls of Andelmera. He knew that centuries ago Delmerane, as the Dûrians called it, had been a beautiful town, nestled between the arms of two rivers. Now it reeked of sewage and rotten garbage, and the grey stone houses had an uncared-for look. The only exceptions were a few ostentatious buildings in the market square, including the Temple of Gadesh, a couple of merchants' houses, and a large inn. Yet there were no slums; nor was there a gaol, guardhouse, or beggars on the streets. These were non-existent in a society where the poor and the unruly were either terminated or enslaved.

Night was falling when they finally reached the ancient port city of Orselm, oldest in the Dûrai lands. Caught in the dying rays of the sun, it crouched like a despotic grey spider beside the sea. The Strongholder's web reached out from here over the whole land, from the Thunderfall in the north-west, to the Sestiar Wilderness in the south, and to Andelara in the north-east—the birthplace of Prince Orrénne.

The racer wove its way through other traffic to enter the great west gate of the city. They rattled along the cobbled streets past tall buildings wearing the grime of ages. Finally they reached the central square, and Estaron caught a glimpse of the fabled royal palace on its green hill in the middle of the city. A soaring edifice of white stone and marble, it stood out in stark contrast to the drabness all around. It was many centuries since a king had dwelt there; it had been the Strongholder's residence since the last king of the elder line had become the Chief Initiate of Gadesh, combining the two offices in one person. From then on the titles of royalty had been dropped: though they occasionally resurfaced, as his companion with the knife had shown.

The gates of the royal park opened before them, and the racer swept up a well-paved drive to the marble portico and huge blackwood door of the Palace itself. The knife man's weapon vanished, and with a crooked grin he ushered Estaron out of the vehicle. Servants in white Selmian half robes trimmed with silver appeared, forming two lines from the racer to the Palace door, which now stood open. Bright light streamed out, against which a slight figure was silhouetted. Estaron had no choice but to walk between the ranks of servants to the figure at the door.

As he mounted a long flight of shallow stairs, the man at the top stepped forward. His half robe was plain white, his head uncovered, the blond shoulder-length hair edged with gold from the light behind. Beneath it Estaron could make out a youthful face.

"Your Highness!" a tenor voice exclaimed. It was oddly familiar. With a sweeping bow it continued, "Welcome to your palace!"

Estaron began mounting the flight of shallow steps to the doorway. His eyes were riveted on the face emerging from the shadows.

When he was one step from the top the figure froze. Estaron also stopped.

"Bari?" the man gasped, his eyes wide.

"Konnar!" Estaron exclaimed. Shock threatened to overwhelm him.

A moment later, in a rush of emotion that swept away decades of pain, they embraced.

_____

Chapter 13: *Together at last*

THE MAN IN WHITE STOOD BACK and held Estaron at arm's length. He searched his face, wide eyes devouring every feature.

"Is it possible?" he murmured. "I've *found* you again, after all these years?"

"You didn't have to kidnap me, Konnar. You could simply have invited me."

"But I didn't know... Wait! We have to talk." Konnar reached up to drape an arm around his slightly taller friend's shoulder. "Come inside! You've had a tiring journey. I think chass and sherili cakes are indicated, don't you?"

Estaron smiled at the reminder of their childhood snack. He allowed himself to be led through the blackwood door into the palace.

An imposing figure in white and silver strutted forward to meet them, flanked by lesser functionaries. His Importance opened his mouth to speak, but Konnar cut him short. "Tell the Strongholder I am giving our guest a preliminary debriefing. Bring chass and sherili cakes." He led Estaron past the man's gaping face without a second glance. They crossed the marble entrance hall with its priceless black statuary and silver ornaments. "These servants think they own the place," he muttered as he ushered Estaron into a small reception room. Soon they were lying on facing recliners, a crackling fire warming their feet, the refreshments served in silver dinnerware on a blackwood table between them.

"So, Bari—how long has it been?" Konnar said, his eyes still hungrily devouring Estaron as he nibbled a sherili cake. Estaron sensed strong emotion in his old friend: joy at the reunion warring with a deeper unease. His own delight was mingled with a sense of dream-like unreality. He'd yearned so long for this moment—but here? In the Strongholder's palace? He half-expected to wake up at any moment to that old, devastating loss.

"It's been twenty years," he said softly. "My parents searched everywhere for you when we came to Orselm in 345. We'd planned a special celebration for our fourteenth birthdays—just you and me. Where did you disappear to?"

Konnar sighed. There was a glint of moisture in his eyes, and his voice was unsteady. "It's a long story, Bari—a very long story. I was... taken up by a Mindbender."

"Oh..." Estaron exhaled noisily. "I'm sorry." His heart sank, but he had half-expected it, finding Konnar here in the Strongholder's palace. That worst-case scenario had occurred to him many times before: even as a small child, Konnar's mental abilities had been exceptional.

"You were the only one who appreciated my gift, Bari. My only real friend. The other kids thought I was a freak and avoided me. I lived for your yearly visits."

"Me, too," Estaron muttered. "When we moved to Astenar I could never speak about where I'd come from. I became a loner—those annual holidays were the only thing that kept me going." He drew a deep breath. "So— What happened? Why are you here?" He glanced around. "Is it safe to ask?"

Konnar nodded. "Quite safe, Bari. No one is eavesdropping—I'd know. And I'm now... autonomous. There's no Mindbender listening in."

"You're a Mindbender yourself now, aren't you?"

"I'm afraid so. You won't like that, I know."

Estaron felt a sadness in his friend's shiláy. He struggled with mixed reactions. "Well, I— The Mindbenders have always been our family's enemies. But you had no choice... No, that's not true. You *did* have a choice. You could have refused advancement. But you decided to go along with them and follow the way of Gadesh."

"My branch of the family have not been Lightists for three generations." He leant forward, his eyes pleading. "Try to understand, Bari. I only saw you once a year. My life was empty—I had no other friends. I was always fighting with the other kids, and after you left I couldn't help using my... powers. Mother and I had to keep moving because of trouble with the neighbours or at school. That was why you didn't find us in 345. Eventually a Mindbender spotted me mesmerising a gang of bullies, and took me in." He heaved a shuddering sigh. "He enrolled me in the training temple, and suddenly there was *hope* again, Bari. I was *somebody* in the Realm of the Mind. I was respected for exactly the things I'd been rejected for by the other kids."

"If only we hadn't gone to Dûrion," Estaron murmured, his eyes bleak.

"Yes. If you'd been around… Anyway, in the Cult of Gadesh I rose quite fast through the ranks, and here I am now."

"In what… capacity? I mean, what exactly is your rôle in the Strongholder's service? Why did you have me kidnapped? Surely the Strongholder isn't interested in fostering old friends' reunions."

There was a momentary flash of anger in his friend's eyes that struck Estaron like a slap in the face. Then it vanished in a smile. "Whoa! Too many questions at once. I brought you here on the Strongholder's behalf, Bari—I'm one of his advisors. But we didn't know it was *you*."

"What do you mean, you didn't—? Oh."

He'd been so immersed in the discovery of his old friend that he'd forgotten his original interpretation of why he'd been abducted. This confirmed it. He'd been kidnapped, not as 'Bari', childhood friend of the Strongholder's advisor; nor as Estaron, secretary to the Bishop Suffragan of Dûrion; but for an older, more sinister purpose. His heart sank.

Konnar was nodding, the sadness back in his eyes. "I didn't know it was you, Bari. What an amazing keeper of secrets you are! You never told me, and in all our years together I never guessed.

"I never once read your mind, Bari. I also promised you that I never would, and that still holds. Even though I'm now… a Mindbender. You are my friend, and I will *never* invade your mind."

"Thank you," Estaron murmured. Konnar's earnestness was reassuring. He hoped the promise would continue to hold, and that Konnar could protect him from others in this hotbed of mindbending.

"Anyway, now I know why your family moved. And I'm… really sorry about your father and mother."

At the reminder of his parents' recent suicide when the Strongholder captured Astenar, Estaron felt an unaccustomed surge of emotion which he quickly suppressed.

He shrugged. "Fortunes of war. But anyway… You've got me here. And you're telling me it's pure accident that we turn out to be old friends. So what now? What do you want of me?"

"To fulfil the purpose you were born for," Konnar said softly.

"That's impossible while the Strongholder still rules."

"Is it? What if the Strongholder were to offer you the recognition you deserve, with real authority under his general oversight?"

"*What?*" Estaron stared at Konnar, who was watching him through narrowed eyes. "He would never do that. It runs counter to everything he and his predecessors have worked for."

Konnar nodded. "Nevertheless… That is what he is offering."

Estaron leaned back on the recliner. This was the last thing he'd imagined. To be offered something so close to his highest dreams — just like that. One word, and it was his. The Strongholder must indeed be desperate. *Teméyn!* That was it. As his stocks of the drug dwindled due to the Grûzhack war, the Strongholder could foresee his coming demise and was trying to side-step it by setting up a figurehead acceptable to the people. *Himself?* This was unreal. In any case, it was no part of his dreams to become a figurehead.

Yet Konnar had spoken of having authority. "What kind of authority?" he queried.

"The real kind. Your own decisions, without reference to the Strongholder or anyone else. Within the bounds he sets — which would be very broad."

"Ah! So I couldn't, for instance… abolish mindbending?"

There was a faint smile on his friend's face. "No. Though if we lose the war, mindbending will disappear anyway."

"And what would these 'bounds' to my authority be?"

"All in good time, Bari. The details can be worked out once you've accepted the offer."

"*You* are empowered to make this offer? Wouldn't the Strongholder want to discuss such a critical matter himself?"

"The Strongholder shuns public appearances. He has appointed me his spokesman in most matters, including this one. So what do you say? Will you at least consider it?"

Estaron sighed. This was not how he'd envisaged their first conversation after being reunited. "And if I refuse? Would I then be allowed to return to Dûrion?"

Again Estaron saw a brief flash of anger in Konnar's eyes, which hit him like the flick of a whip. But the anger changed immediately to hurt. "You'd want to leave so soon? When we've just found each other again after so many years?"

Estaron felt he needed to tread carefully. "No, of course not. We'd spend some time together first. We have a lot of catching up to do! But eventually I'd want to go back. After all, Dûrion has been my home for many years now."

"It's also the home of my enemies," Konnar said softly. "Those so-called Restorers have done a lot of damage. They started the Grûzhack war..." He paused, then continued briskly, "But we can talk about returning to Dûrion later, if it arises. The question now is, will you consider the Strongholder's offer?"

Estaron stifled another sigh."I'll consider it, Konnar. You must realise, though, that to rule on behalf of someone else is not what I was born for — no matter how much real authority is included. But — the Strongholder's offer is generous, and I will consider it."

"It also ties in with our dreams of 'good governance'," Konnar murmured, his eyes narrowed. "Remember how we used to talk about that? You yourself often said what a good team we'd make, and how we would right wrongs and rule with justice and mercy. That is exactly what... the Strongholder is offering you."

"The Strongholder wants good governance?" Estaron couldn't keep the incredulity out of his voice.

He was amazed to see his friend's eyes moisten. "Yes, Bari. The Strongholder wants good governance. Believe it or not, but he has longed and striven for good governance for years. And he needs *you* to help make it a reality."

Estaron didn't know how to respond to such an extraordinary statement. He stared at Konnar. Did his old friend really believe that himself?

Seeing his scepticism Konnar appeared to change tack. "You haven't had the recognition you deserve for a long time, have you, Bari?" he said, regarding Estaron with hooded eyes. "What has your job been for the past five years? A secretary, nothing more. Yet by all accounts you've been running the government of Dûrion almost single-handed. Before then? A failed student. If Shambor hadn't scooped you in, what would you be now? Maybe a legal assistant in some Dûrian town — not even a qualified advocate."

Estaron felt the blood draining from his face. "How did you find all that out?" he demanded.

"We hear many things in the Strongholder's palace. I'm sorry, Bari." His face was concerned, the old Konnar who always read his friend's feelings—though never his thoughts. "I didn't realise it was *you*. If I had— Anyway, have you thought about all those failures? Before you went to Darthane University in 356, you were pretty successful. Top student at the Hearth School. Outstanding graduate from the Astenar Academy of Law... How could you have failed your board exams at the University?"

"I honestly don't know. It was a monstrous series of accidents."

"Yes, and for the last exam you arrived an hour late. The assessors had all left. That's not like you, is it?"

"No, it's not. It's never happened to me before or since. From the day I arrived in Darthane it seemed as if everything went wrong. Nothing I set my hand to succeeded."

"Exactly." Konnar heaved a sigh. "But it wasn't your fault, Bari. It was ours. You were the subject of a curse. Have you heard of the Curse of Futility?"

Estaron stared at his friend. "No, but it sounds appropriate." A curse! That would make sense of a lot of things.

"It's the most powerful curse there is. You were singled out, because— Well, you know why. It happened years ago, when things were different. I'll say it again—we didn't realise it was you! Our agents found you under your *real* name—the name you hid from everyone, both in Selmion and Dûrion. They linked *that* name to the Estaron don Geldor living in Astenar. The name Bari, which you were known by in Selmion as a child, never came into it!"

Estaron nodded slowly. His real name—and those of his parents—was their most closely guarded secret. They had used aliases for everyday life in both Selmion and Dûrion. What Konnar was saying made sense.

"But now the Strongholder will lift the curse. If you accept his offer." Konnar gazed at his friend with compassion.

Estaron shook his head. He spoke softly. "Is this a bribe, Konnar?" He steeled himself for the whiplash, which didn't come. Instead there was a rueful smile.

"No, Bari. If it weren't *you*, it would have been. But I know you can't be bribed. I'm just saying, if you could bring yourself to accept the offer, freedom from the curse would come with it."

Silence fell between them. Estaron could not avoid thinking of what it would mean to have the darkness in his mind lifted. To be free of the failures that had dogged him all these years! He thought of Carrilay, the girl he'd loved, who'd run off on the eve of their betrothal. Of his lost inheritance. Of the three failed opportunities to become a Civic Elder. Of his disastrous 'cancellation' by the university.

Yes, if it hadn't been for Shambor, he'd have ended up as a petty legal assistant, doing all the work while his superiors reaped the glory. He looked at Konnar.

"Did you arrange the job with Shambor?"

Konnar shook his head.

Well, that made sense. Shambor's offer had seemed like a return of good fortune, and in the beginning it had been. Until he'd discovered he was little more than a lowly scribe, an errand boy, a whipping post... and childminder to a deeply-disturbed megalomaniac. Meanwhile *he'd* been the one doing all the day-to-day running of the country. Bishop Mâron had been a huge change for the better; yet the basic situation remained unchanged: he, Estaron, was the one resettling refugees, dealing with the Stillárre Elders, coping with the thousand-and-one demands of government, while his superiors got on with the long-term strategic planning that was his birthright, and that he knew he would be good at.

A longing filled him, to be free of failure and to achieve his own goals instead of helping others achieve theirs. He found himself wanting to accept the Strongholder's offer, despite knowing it could never match his birthright.

Yet... Something was wrong. Certain anomalies had been nagging at his thoughts throughout their discussion. There was Konnar's simple attire, markedly different from a Mindbender's grey robes, or those of the ornate dignitary who'd met them in the entrance hall. There was the sadness in his shiláy. Those brief flashes of anger at being questioned or refused. The genuineness that accompanied his offer of 'real authority' — as if the authority were his to grant. And the unlikelihood of his claim that the Strongholder had entrusted such crucial negotiations to a subordinate.

He looked at his old friend and swallowed. Was it possible? Was he about to sign his own death warrant? But he had to ask.

"Konnar. This offer. Is it from the Strongholder? Or from you?"

His friend's face relaxed into a warm smile. "Dear old Bari," he murmured. "It always was hard to fool you. The offer is from me. I am the Strongholder."

Map 3:
Barazhân

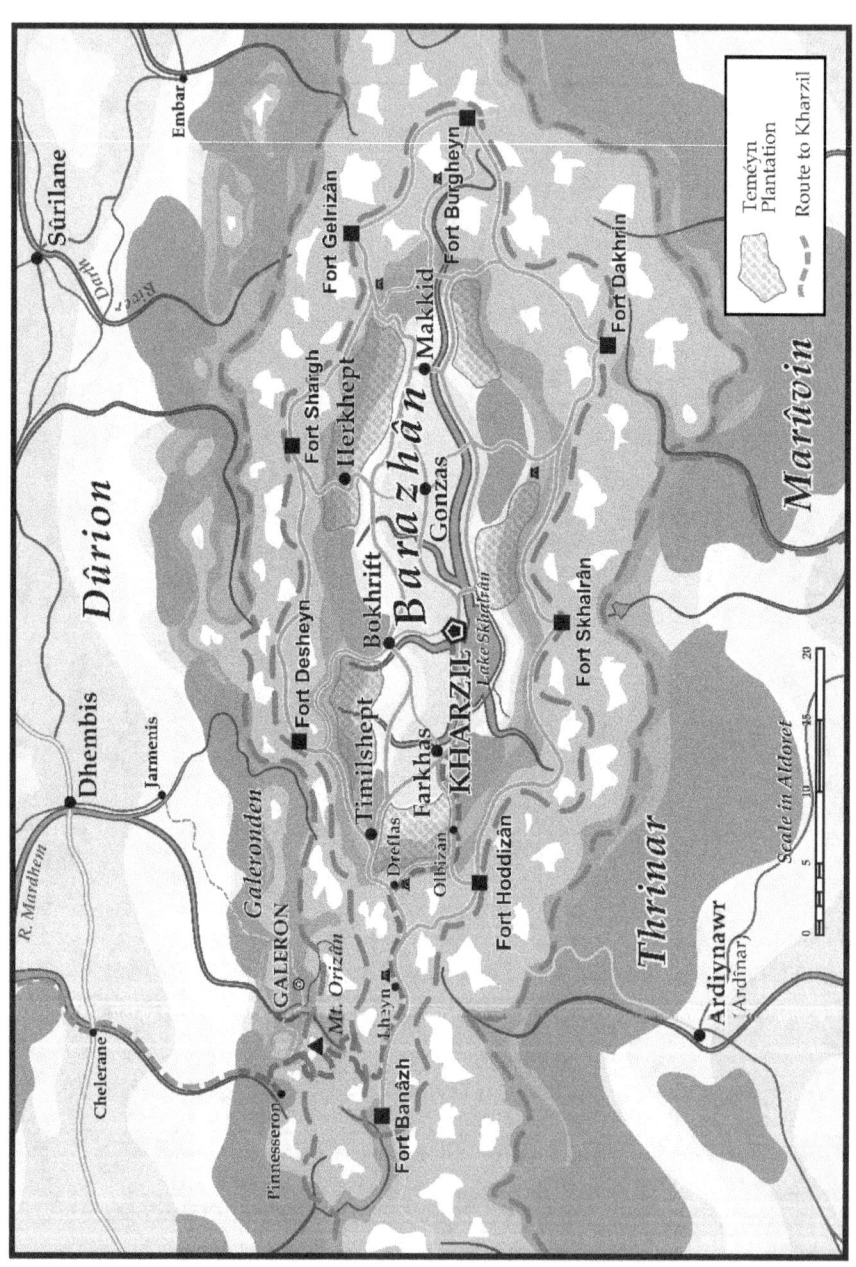

Chapter 14: *Mountain paths*

THE LAST ONE STILL LIVING *stared up at Gil with pleading eyes. All around in the darkness of the Manor basement the rest lay dead. This was a young girl – Teynel, Danîsha's favourite. About ten or eleven. A cascade of dark hair framed her narrow, winsome face. The command came, he raised his arm, and bewilderment filled the innocent eyes. In the deep recesses of Gil's mindbent brain his true self screamed as the blow fell...*

"Gelmin! Gelmin, wake!" A hand roughly shook his shoulder. A hoarse cry was still on his lips as he forced his eyes open. He almost cried out again at the sight of a white, heavily-ridged face only a few inches from his own. Nearby a child was screaming. *Teynel...?*

"Gelmin! You dream. You scare Brakhól. Wake!"

Slowly the present returned. This was Pinnesseron, a remote settlement of the mountain-dwelling Galeronden. Nist had smuggled them here through Grûzhack-held territory. The contorted features in front of him were Shakhere's; the screams were Brakhól's. The child's pain made him jerk in fresh agony, and his hammock swayed alarmingly. Behind Shakhere in the rustic wood-built lodge the other Grûzhack scouts were trying to calm the child.

A swelling murmur of voices outside and a banging at the door announced that the rest of the settlement had arrived. Flickering torchlight showed that it was the middle of the night. The scout Dellikh hurried over and opened up.

The first person to burst in was Danîsha with her bellaril. She thrust the instrument at Dellikh and seized Brakhól from the other scouts. The child clutched her, and gradually his screams subsided to a high keening. As soon as she could she sat Brakhól beside her on the rough settee and began playing a simple song on the bellaril. Slowly his distress eased and everyone began to breathe again.

Many of the blond, bearded Galeronden had crowded into the lodge with Danîsha. One of them addressed Gil in the ancient mountain dialect. "Tha had best seek the One's aid f' thy dreams, Gelmion, if tha thinkest t' reach Barazhân alive." There were nods and dour murmurs of agreement as they left.

115

Gil had eased himself out of his hammock and now sat shivering in a chair beside Danîsha and Brakhól, with a bearskin wrapped round his sweat-soaked clothing. Shakhere and Dellikh were rebuilding the fire in its stone hearth at the centre of the room. The other two scouts were preparing a pot to make the Galeronden herbal infusion *benoriss*. Brakhól turned a tear-stained face to Gil. He ruffled his hair. "It's okay now, Brakhól. I'm sorry I frightened you." The kid nodded doubtfully.

Gil sighed. "I've said it before, and I'll say it again. I don't know what we'd do without you, 'Neesh."

"Well, it's a good thing I don't sleep as soundly as those scouts. If I'd been nearby tonight, I'd have woken you before it got this far."

"As you did a couple of times on the way here."

"Yes." She gave him a troubled look. "You know, that Galeronden was right, Gil. From all we've heard, getting into Bara-zhân is going to be ten times more difficult than the journey here. If your nightmares continue, it'll only take one lapse on my part and we'll be done for. Can I pray with you that they'll stop?"

Gil's frazzled nerves couldn't take any more. "No!"

Danîsha's eyebrows shot up, and Brakhól whimpered. "Sorry, 'Neesh, but the last thing I need now is a religious quick-fix. I'll get over this. It means extra worry for you, I know, but... well, I'm sorry."

"I'll pray for you anyway," 'Neesh declared. Gil groaned silently. If there was one thing he couldn't stand, it was being prayed for.

* * *

Despite the broken night, they set off at first light the next morning. Many of the Galeronden were already up, and others came out of their lodges to see them off. Nist and her two henchmen were there; and so was Destor, the Galeronden leader, leaning on the arm of a younger man. He looked old and frail. Danîsha felt a pang of guilt, remembering that it was the Restorers' arrival among the Galeronden last year that had triggered the Grûzhack invasion and the loss of most of their settlements.

In the Galeronden manner the crowd was silent. The glances that came her way were not hostile; but there was no doubt they'd be glad to see the Grûzhack leave. Destor pronounced a brief blessing; then they set off, following the guide he had lent them.

As they climbed through the dense conifer forests surrounding Pinnesseron the scouts chattered away in their own language, happy to be going home. Shakhere was carrying Brakhól on his back; the boy's infectious laugh rang out from time to time. Danîsha glanced at Gil as they plodded along in the rear. Strapped upright to his back, the hilt protruding over his left shoulder, was the longsword he'd worn as a mindbent Bishop's Guard. The Council had insisted he bring it, to protect her and the child. But now his face was strained, the shadow of the nightmare still hanging over him. Had that wretched sword played a part in it? Well, whether he liked it or not, she would pray.

She shifted the bellaril case into a more comfortable position on her back. Gil had also brought the blaise, and she was glad of that. Before setting out this morning they had been in touch with Lannie using all three instruments. It was a comfort to have both sight and sound of their friends back home.

Conversation died as the way became steeper. After a long climb they suddenly emerged into cool, bright sunshine. Blinking, Danîsha looked back the way they'd come. "Oh, what a view!" she exclaimed, clutching Gil's arm.

"Pretty much the whole of western Dûrion," he murmured.

They both stood for a moment, staring at the fields and rivers and tiny towns of the country they'd come to think of as home. Danîsha wondered, not for the first time, whether she'd ever see her Earthly home again, her family, her dear grandchildren… She prayed for them every night, but oh, what a joy it would be to hold them once more in her arms. *Dear Lord, please. One day.*

She turned, and soaring heights confined her vision. Her eyes followed the steep slopes up and up, craning her neck till she saw a massive snow-capped peak gleaming against the azure sky.

"Mount Orizân," their guide told them. He pointed to the rough track they'd just joined, which followed a level course around the mountain. "This be your path."

The scouts were looking in every direction, trying to orient themselves. Shakhere uttered an exclamation. An outburst of Grû-zhack followed. "We know dis way. We lead now." He nodded dismissively at the Galeronden guide and set off at a brisk pace. Danîsha hurriedly thanked the man, who shrugged as if to say,

What can you expect? He turned and disappeared into the woods below.

Many weary hours later they stood on a rocky outcrop above a deep gorge. The shadows were drawing in, and from far below rose the hollow roar of a river swollen with meltwater. Above them towered the other side of Mount Orizân. They had spent the day walking around it, hardly climbing any higher. But the journey had not been easy, the path in some places shrinking to a two-foot-wide ledge along a sheer cliff face. The sure-footed scouts had barely restrained their impatience at the flatlanders' slow progess. Brakhól had started crying—which hadn't helped.

"Where's this cave, Shakhere? Brakhól needs food and rest."

The Grûzhack glanced at her. "Is here."

Turning away from the gorge, he and the other scouts pushed through some bushes, Brakhól cowering against Shakhere's back. Danîsha followed awkwardly, thrusting the springy branches aside, and Gil brought up the rear holding the bellaril. A tall, dark crack appeared ahead of them in the cliff face. Danîsha had to squeeze through sideways.

Inside there was the *snap!* of a firestick, and flame leapt up. The scouts began lighting small clay lamps, and Danîsha exclaimed in pleasure. It was a large cave with a dry sandy floor. Towards the back was a blackened area flanked by a stack of firewood. The albino scout Ganid moved a stone covering a recess in the rocky wall, and began pulling out earthenware jars and containers. Metal fire irons and pots appeared from elsewhere. Soon, to Danîsha's relief, they were enjoying a hot savoury porridge garnished with herbs and thin slices of dried meat that had softened in the cooking.

Shakhere grinned at her. "See? Grûzhack not bar-barian. Dis cave always ready for scouts. Have furs for lie on, too. You sleep well tonight."

They did.

* * *

They woke at dawn the next morning to the welcome aroma of a hot breakfast. "Eat much, long day is come," Shakhere told them. Gil yawned and stretched. He looked around. Danîsha gave him a cheery *"Ney li tarrend,"* echoed by Brakhól, who came running over to him. He gave the reply—*"Illen steylend"*—and tousled the boy's hair. To his surprise, Gil felt good this morning. No nightmare, he supposed. A welcome relief for once.

Gil was glad to tuck into another heaped plate of the savoury porridge. He, 'Neesh and Brakhól were still finishing off when Shakhere said, "You stay in cave, get ready. We go, find wood, water, for next time." The other scouts gave them a brief nod and filed out of the cave entrance after Shakhere. Each carried a sack and a medium-sized water jar. Gil nodded. It made sense that users of the cave would replenish stocks for the next arrivals.

When they'd finished eating they washed the dishes in the bowl the scouts had left ready, then repacked their few possessions into their shoulder pouches. There was not much else they could do to prepare for the coming journey. Shakhere had spoken of finding a Grûzhack road in the high mountains; they hadn't fully understood his broken Dûrian, but Gil gathered that this would be the dangerous bit, when they were most exposed. The road was the only way into Barazhân; but they dare not be caught on it.

The scouts still hadn't returned, so they sat down by the warm embers of the fire. "Today's Anderil—the One's day," Danîsha said. "Why don't we sing some songs and pray while we're waiting?" Gil's heart sank, but Brakhól responded enthusiastically. 'Neesh fetched the bellaril and began strumming. Brakhól recognised the tune, and soon they were both singing lustily—something about 'Father keep our feet today, as we walk your Way'. Gil endured the childish words and Brakhól's high-pitched singing, but as always his heart was warmed by the child's unfeigned delight.

When they'd finished 'Neesh looked at Brakhól and said, "Shall we ask the One to bring us safely into Barazhân?" The boy nodded eagerly. They both looked upward and raised their arms in the Dûrian prayer posture.

Danîsha prayed a simple prayer asking God to protect them from being discovered on the road into Barazhân. Brakhól's clear voice followed: "Daddy, Shakhere and me, we want to go home. Bad people want to stop us. But Daddy, *you* come too. You're big and strong! They'll see you and get scared and run away." He was quiet for a moment, then exclaimed, "It's okay! *Daddy's* coming!"

Brakhól was grinning up at them. Gil and Danîsha exchanged a glance over the child's head. His simple trust had moved them both. If *that* was prayer, Gil thought, he could believe in it.

A noise at the cave entrance brought their heads round. Shakhere and the scouts were standing there, staring at Brakhól in amazement.

The boy jumped up and ran to his brother. Seizing his hand he cried, "*Shakhere! Naghi giresh!* Baaba *daney ferktil.*"

The scout nodded. He took a deep breath, then turned to the Restorers. "We go now."

* * *

They huddled under a clump of wind-twisted bushes on a steep rocky slope. Danîsha was shivering convulsively, despite her three layers of furs. She couldn't remember ever being so cold or so tired before. Gil shivered next to her. Shakhere was holding Brakhól, a shapeless lump completely covered in an extra fur. The other three scouts were reconnoitring. At the top of this slope, apparently, was the Grûzhack road.

At last Dellikh appeared, holding a hand up with six fingers splayed. That had to be the all clear, because Shakhere jumped to his feet, turned to them, and pointed up the slope. Danîsha groaned as she levered herself off the ground, earning a glare from the scout leader. Not once but several times on the gruelling climb up here they had been warned that on the road they must be silent and imitate exactly what the scouts did.

Shakhere bounded up the steep slope like a mountain goat, still carrying Brakhól. Well, if he thought she was going to imitate *that*... Danîsha and Gil struggled up with flatlander awkwardness, sometimes on hands and knees. Danîsha's legs ached, but at least Gil was carrying the bellaril, and when he could he gave her a hand up the difficult bits.

They reached the crest and stopped, stunned. There, just below them, was the road. But *what* a road! Wide enough for two chariots abreast, it appeared to have been carved out of the solid rock. Their eyes followed it as it wound up into the mountains further west. Huge masonry pillars supported it where it flowed smoothly over ravines. The surface was coated with a gritty substance not unlike asphalt, grey-green in colour. A low masonry parapet ran along the outer edge, scant protection from the gulf of air beyond. In the distance more mountains stood in serried ranks, their snow-clad tips a delicate peach colour in the late afternoon light.

They became aware of movement below, and saw Shakhere waving his arms wildly at them. They hurried down, and with a searing glare the scout leader turned and began trotting eastward along the road. Danîsha groaned inwardly. All this, and now we have to go jogging? But she knew Shakhere wanted to get off the road as soon as possible, for fear of army patrols.

Somehow she got herself moving. At least it was downhill, though she didn't know how long she could keep it up. Gil trotted beside her and the albino scout Ganid brought up the rear.

An age passed. Danîsha knew only the road, her aching legs, her increasingly laboured breathing. Bends, bridges and clefts flowed by. They came to an upward incline, and she could take no more. With a gasp of agony she staggered to the cliff side of the road and subsided against the rock. Gil joined her, too winded to speak. Ganid gave a low whistle, and Shakhere came loping back with the other two scouts, Dellikh carrying Brakhól.

"Daneesh, we not stop!" he hissed. "Soldiers come soon from Fort Banâzh—bring letters. I know dis, I work dere before. Come! We go!" He took her arm and tried to pull her up. Danîsha yelped, and Brakhól uttered a sympathetic cry. Shakhere let go, and Brakhól struggled out of Dellikh's hands. "*Brakhól, ghân!*" his brother snapped.

Everything happened at once. Brakhól began crying in earnest, his distress enveloped them like a dark blanket, and a distant pounding of feet came from the west.

"*Dakhez shaktol! Berakht, berakht!*"

Shakhere grabbed Brakhól and the scouts sprinted off up the road. The child let out a yell of protest, and Shakhere stumbled and fell. The others ran on. With a cry Danîsha struggled to her feet. "Let's go!" Gil said, grabbing her hand. Gasping, Danîsha tried to run, but her legs refused. The thud of feet was drawing closer.

They reached Shakhere, who had staggered up and was rubbing his left knee, his face contorted. Brakhól seemed undamaged and ran to Danîsha. She thrust the bellaril at Gil and embraced the child. Taking his hand, she broke into a laboured trot following Gil, Shakhere hobbling behind.

The running feet were gaining on them. There was no way they'd make it.

Chapter 15: *Daddy came*

TAL GHA-DERID CLIMBED INTO HIS TOWN CAR. He settled himself on the plush suede seat and opened the curtains. He enjoyed seeing the city in the mellow glow of the afternoon sun. He raised his hand, and the car moved off.

Not smoothly, though. Tal frowned. He'd have to speak to his steward about the replacement puller, who had *not* been properly trained. The new man was second on the right, and he actually glanced backwards. Tal gave him a cold stare. Fear crossed the fellow's face as he quickly looked away.

The car glided into the traffic on its sprung wheels and picked up speed. The tubular towers of the Seminary for History and Culture dwindled behind them. The car's green and gold livery—and the lead puller's constant cries of *"Lhiftack! Gha-Derid Lhiftack Zhondickad!"*—had pedestrians scrambling out of the way, while all except the other gold-trimmed vehicles pulled aside.

The title *Lhiftack*—Docent—was useful in traffic; but Tal was glad to leave the rôle behind for another day. His elevation to second rank under the Savant, the head of the Seminary, had been welcome in terms of status and stipend; but he'd soon discovered it was the Docent who ran the place, and he missed personal contact with his students.

Tal let his eyes wander affectionately over the towers of Kharzil as they passed by. He loved this city, which was always finding new ways to express the power and grandeur of the Grûzhack people. It was a city of towers: there were square towers, circular towers, triangular, hexagonal and octagonal towers, all in different colours of stone. They sped under graceful arches and passed gardens bursting with spring blooms and fountains that created fantastic water sculptures.

In the centre of the city soared the lofty magnificence of the Magistry tower, its six sides symbolising the Endeavours that were the foundation of Grûzhack society: Knowledge (his family's Endeavour for generations past); Production; Trade; Construction; Beauty (art, music, sport); and, of course—he grimaced—War, which now had the ascendancy. The tower's conical roof stood for the Overmastery—which held the peace between the other six Grandmasters.

Tal sighed. If only the present Overmaster were stronger! But Farshan, like all the others, was under the spell of Rimmezh, the Warrior Grandmaster. It was thanks to Rimmezh that the wisdom of past generations had been abandoned, and the Grûzhack had poured out of their safe mountain valley on an ill-considered war of conquest. *All* was now at risk, Tal thought bitterly. Their prosperity, with the cessation of the teméyn trade; the Endeavours, with war taking priority over everything; and their future, with so many young lives being squandered. (He cut off any thoughts of the boy; that would come soon enough.)

Of course, there had been few periods in history when Barazhân had been completely at peace. That was why War was a permanent Endeavour. At least twice a century invaders tried to capture the source of 'green gold' — of teméyn. But hitherto the Grûzhack had only fought in self-defence. The ring of eight mountain forts, completed at great cost sixty years ago, had established a new peace, allowing the arts and sciences to flourish. During that time there had been no sabre-rattling on the Outside; their principal rival the Strongholder had been content to maintain a mutually-beneficial ceasefire. Now Rimmezh had to go and destroy all that by playing the invader...

The car slowed as the pullers panted their way up a low hill, approaching the suburb where Tal lived. Before they reached the top the gate was thrown open and they passed through. Ah, the buds on the *khift* trees that lined the Avenue had opened in today's sunshine! He savoured the delicate scent of the pale violet and yellow blossoms. Above the trees on either side loomed the slender towers of his neighbours' dwellings, echoing the towers of the city in miniature.

They turned a corner, and there was Tal's own dwelling with its ground floor commonrooms surmounted by private turrets, all in warm rose-stone. The groundkeeper swung the gate open, and they swept in without pausing. The car came to a stop at the front portico—smoothly, Tal was glad to see. He climbed out, ignoring the sweating pullers, and walked up the broad rose-stone steps. Behind him the lead puller barked an order and the car moved off at walking pace to its shelter at the back.

The steward opened the front door and stood aside as Mistil Na-ReyDerid came out to greet him. His wife was as lovely as that day twenty-five years ago when her glossy, blue-black hair, smiling eyes and upturned mouth first ensnared his heart. Childbirth had thickened her a little, but not much. They extended their arms, twelve fingers spread, and clasped hands in the marriage greeting. Then she led him inside to the living room. They sat side by side on the red leather sofa while maids brought in a tray and poured them each a steaming cup of sweetened *zakheyn*. They spoke of their small daily doings until the servants left.

Then Mistil looked at him, her eyebrows rising anxiously. His heart sank, though he'd known it was coming. He tilted his head— *no*. She turned away to hide her emotion.

When she'd mastered herself she said, "How can there *still* be no news? He sent a message to Barkt and Felhis every sixday, faithfully. It's now been almost five sixdays!"

Tal said nothing, gazing at her sadly. Her life centred around the boy. Once before she'd given him up for dead, and he'd miraculously returned. If he'd died in this ill-begotten war …

She seemed to read his thoughts. "No… *No!* They send news of deaths immediately. They *cannot* have left it this long!"

"He could be out on a mission, Mistil. In wartime, those can last many sixdays."

"Can't you use your influence to get a response from his Warriormaster?"

Tal wearily repeated what they had discussed many times. "I dare not do that, for Barkt and Felhis' sakes. But even if I could, you know how little influence the Knowledge Endeavour has now."

She buried her head in her hands. In all their years together he'd never seen such a display of emotion. In a muffled voice she said, "If Shakhere is dead too, I don't know how I'll carry on."

Tal stroked her shoulder helplessly.

* * *

On the Grûzhack mountain highway the running feet were steadily gaining on the intruders from Dûrion. Gil glanced back and saw that Shakhere had fallen behind, slowed by his injured knee. A large pier of rock hid their pursuers from view, but it sounded as though they would appear at any moment.

" 'Neesh, wait!" he gasped, taking the bellaril off his back and laying it on the road. As he hurried back to the grey-faced scout, he reached over his shoulder and drew his longsword. "Shakhere, sit. I'll—" The Grûzhack tilted his head in the negative gesture, and produced a dagger from under his tunic. He positioned himself beside Gil facing the way they'd come, his weight resting on his good leg. Glancing behind, Gil saw Danîsha pick up her instrument and subside against the cliff with Brakhól. The child was still crying, casting a dark pall of misery; and Gil's whole being shuddered at the feel of the longsword in his hand. This was the moment he'd hoped would never come. He steeled himself to use the weapon, reminding himself that this time he'd be protecting the innocent. He'd send a few Grûzhack soldiers to whatever hell they believed in before they could reach Danîsha and the child.

The thud of boots was louder now, apparently just round the corner. But Gil knew how deceptive sounds could be in the mountains. He found it difficult to estimate how many were approaching. More than three, definitely; probably less than ten. That left a range of odds between two to one, and over four to one—depending on Shakhere's support, which couldn't last long.

He avoided looking to his left where solid ground ended at the road's low parapet. Anyone forced over there would fall a long way before meeting the ground again. On the other side was the unscalable cliff from which the highway had been carved. There was nowhere to hide or gain an advantage. He'd have to rely on taking them by surprise.

The steady breathing of healthy runners reached Gil above the heavy footfalls. They would appear any second now. Then from behind him came a sound never before heard in these mountains: Danîsha playing the bellaril. At that instant a couple of Grûzhack soldiers in turquoise tunics burst around the bend. Gil yelled and charged with the longsword raised. Another warrior appeared. Confusion reigned as the three tried to stop and draw weapons, hampered by others rounding the corner and cannoning into them.

But by the time Gil had covered the distance, the first three soldiers were facing him with swords poised for action. They seemed unaffected by the bellaril. As he approached Gil swung the longsword in a vicious circular sweep, taking advantage of its greater reach. As the weapon bit home one man reeled back, dropping his sword. Another leapt aside in the wrong direction and went over the parapet. His scream vanished into the depths below. The third warrior collapsed.

Gil came to an unsteady stop, panting, the longsword raised for further action. But none was necessary. The Grûzhack weren't looking at him. Their eyes were focused behind him, and horror was spreading over their faces. Crying out in terror, they dropped their weapons and ran. Gil stared, bemused, as the turquoise tunics disappeared round the bend. Their shouts and thudding footsteps continued back the way they'd come.

He looked behind him. Nothing. Just Shakhere a few paces away; and Danîsha with Brakhól further up the road. Both adults looked stunned; but Brakhól was bouncing up and down with excitement.

"Did you see? Did you see?"

"See what, dear?"

"Daddy came!"

* * *

They found the other scouts a little further on, waiting in what Shakhere called a 'wayhouse'. To Danîsha it looked like an elongated bus shelter built into the side of the cliff. It had a bench for about twelve people, nothing else.

Shakhere hobbled up to his comrades, eyes blazing. "*Khaliskey gatiib! Deftas nakhilar, borkh anept? Anept dezh?* Anept?"

The scouts hung their heads while Shakhere raved at them. Danîsha climbed gratefully on to the high bench with Brakhól. Gil carefully wiped the blade of his longsword with a cloth from his pack, then sheathed it and laid it on the ground beside the bellaril before climbing up beside Danîsha.

Suddenly Brakhól leapt off the bench and yanked his brother's tunic. "*Shakhere, ghân! Kheftileyn ghâdessikt!* Baaba *daney ekheftil!*"

An exchange of pungent Grûzhack followed. The other scouts raised their heads to listen.

Shakhere turned a puzzled face to Gil and Danîsha. "Brakhól say we not have to fight. 'Faader' fight for us. So we not shamed. What he mean?"

Danîsha looked at the child, her heart swelling. *Out of the mouth of babes...* "Tell us what you saw, Brakhól."

"I saw Daddy! Didn't you? *Bi-i-i-g* —" Looking up, he stretched his arm as high as he could. "—and *strong*, and *bright*, and he had a huge shining sword, and he *charged* at the bad soldiers. They were scared! They ran away, and he ran after them!" The boy was grinning with delight.

"That's wonderful! And you asked Daddy to come with us this morning, didn't you?"

"Yes!" He turned to his brother. "See, Shakhere? Don't worry! *Baaba daney ferktil.*"

The scout leader was frowning. "Who be dis Faader? Faader, Mudder of Brakhól live in big city of Grûzhack, in Kharzil."

"He's the One Creator God, Shakhere. Brakhól is *his* son now, as well as the son of your parents in Kharzil."

"*Ayee!*" Shakhere made a warding sign, right hand raised obliquely above his forehead. There was a barrage of queries from the other scouts. Shakhere explained, to a fresh flurry of warding hands. All four stared at Danîsha, their eyes wide.

"Creator *God*, he drive away warriors? Brakhól *see* him?"

"Maybe it was his... warrior." She couldn't think of the Dûrian word for 'angel'. "Sometimes people see the One's warriors. Could that have been who it was, Brakhól?"

The boy looked doubtful, but nodded. She glanced at Gil. He seemed shaken, his eyebrows high. In English he murmured, "An angel? Really?"

"Yes! There are plenty of places in the Bible where angels appear to people. And it still happens today." She continued in Dûrian to Shakhere. "We asked the One to guard us this morning, and I believe he's sent his warrior with us. That's who Brakhól saw."

The scout stared at her for a long moment before translating for his comrades. There was a muttered conversation with wide eyes and vigorous gestures. Then Shakhere turned back to Danîsha.

"Grûzhack soldier *never* run away," he said huskily. "Today dey run away. Can only be *great* God make dat happen. God greater dan Grûzhack goddess Makhril." Again the warding hands. "If true, dis God save our life. Maybe we fear Great God more dan Makhril. But now we help you and Brakhól, because you his children." He bowed his head, and the others followed suit.

Danîsha cleared her throat, slightly taken aback by the turn of events. "Well really, um, we just can carry on as before. Take us to your parents in Kharzil. That's where the Creator God wants us to go."

The four looked up. Shakhere raised both hands with palms open. "We obey."

* * *

They slept that night in the small mining village of Lheyn, tucked into a fold of the mountains. Shakhere knew some of the workers, who smuggled them in as night was falling.

As he lay on the low pallet bed Gil's mind was in turmoil. What had happened with the Grûzhack warriors was impossible. Shakhere had spoken the simple truth: the Grûzhack did *not* run away. Their courage was legendary. So was their fear of being shamed, as the scouts had shown in the Stillárre Hearth. But dropping their weapons and *running*? From one man with a sword, whose injured companion had only a dagger? Unthinkable! Yet it had happened.

His thoughts went back to that evening in Stillárre when he'd prayed to the One Creator God. As if talking to an answering machine, he'd asked God to protect them on this journey; and to do something he would never have expected. Well, if anything qualified as an answer to that request, *this* did.

Today Brakhól had asked 'Daddy' to protect them; and with childlike trust the boy took it completely for granted that he had.

Was this truly who God was? A Father who listened to his children's requests, and answered? But that meant—

That meant everything Shivvie, Danîsha, Father Martin and the others had been saying was literally true. His mind boggled at the implications.

<hr>

Chapter 16: *Welcome to Barazhân*

"Sssst, Gelmin! Come!"

Gil jerked awake. Where was he? The bed was hard, the room bitterly cold and dark. A faint light outlined the doorway and the silhouette bending over him.

"Come! Time for eat!"

Memory flooded back. He was in a worker's hut in the small mining village of Lheyn, high in the Grûzhack mountains. They must be having breakfast at this unthinkable hour. He struggled up, pulled his bearskin cloak tighter around him, and stumbled after the scout through the pre-dawn glimmer towards a larger building. A warm glow shone invitingly from the windows. Now for a steaming cup of hot coffee... *If only!*

The others were there already, brought together from the various huts where they'd spent the night. They were sitting at a half-cleared trestle table, one of six. At the near end of the room was a crackling fire. He went and stood by it, soaking in the warmth. It was some comfort to see the scout Dellikh rubbing his eyes and Danîsha trying to smother a huge yawn. Brakhól was still asleep against 'Neesh's shoulder.

"Masters and workers, dey eat already," Shakhere said. "We eat quickly now before kitchen people finish. Masters mustn't see us."

Two of the kitchen staff were already carrying in a steaming pot and wooden bowls and spoons. Gil brought a pile of fur coats and arranged them on the bench as cushions for himself and 'Neesh. The table was the right height for a seven-foot Grûzhack, but not for them.

The kitchen workers—a man with stooped shoulders and a harried-looking woman—ladled savoury porridge into the bowls and stood watching while they ate. It was a silent meal. Gil didn't mind that. His thoughts were still busy with yesterday's events.

Once the bowls were empty, the woman hurried forward to collect them. At that point Danisha turned to Shakhere. "Before we go, let's ask the One Creator God to protect us again today."

Shakhere made the announcement. The woman with the bowls stopped where she was, heaving a theatrical sigh. The man watched impassively. Shakhere looked at 'Neesh, with his brother beside her.

"Daneesh and Brakhól, you pray for us. Today we go to Olbizân. Dat is place where Brakhól and me grow up." There was a smile and a sudden shaft of joy from the child. The two kitchen workers looked startled.

"I thought your parents lived in Kharzil?" 'Neesh asked.

"Yes. Is udder parent live in Olbizân. Dey dead now."

"You had *two* fathers and mothers?"

"Yes."

'Neesh let it go. She started praying, asking the One Creator God to send his angel with them once more, and to bring them safely to Shakhere and Brakhól's childhood home.

Gil couldn't bring himself to do the raised hands thing, but he echoed her silently. He was aware of a new reality. This was quite different from his last prayer — the one-way message he'd left on the celestial answering machine. After yesterday he had to accept that there *might* be Someone listening, though every rational instinct rebelled against it.

Danîsha had barely finished speaking when, with another sigh, the woman carrying the bowls resumed her collection round.

But then Brakhól started praying. In Grûzhack.

The bowls clattered to the floor. For a moment all eyes were on the kitchen workers. They were staring open-mouthed at Brakhól. The child continued praying. Gil heard him repeat the word *Baaba* over and again — "Daddy".

Brakhól stopped, and there was total silence. Then a babble of Grûzhack broke out, the kitchen workers still staring at the child and demanding explanations. A rapid conversation followed with the scouts. After a minute or so 'Neesh cut them short.

"Shakhere, we must go! Now. Before the Masters find us."

They collected their bags, and Gil strapped on his longsword. Shakhere led them out into the growing daylight, leaving two bewildered kitchen workers gazing after them.

* * *

They made it to the village of Dreflas without incident. On the crest of a small hill they sat down for a moment to take in the magnificent scenery that had opened up before them. From here the highway plunged steeply downwards, like a snake slithering over terrace after terrace of green growth into woodland far below. Beyond the woodland a velvety green carpet stretched out, surrounded on all sides by mountains. The carpet was criss-crossed by grey roads, and dotted with multi-coloured fields and small towns. In the middle distance a lake shimmered grey-blue. Beside it stood a city whose many pastel-hued towers they could just make out.

Shakhere pointed. "Kharzil. Lake Skhalran."

So this was Barazhân, the Hidden Magistry of the Grûzhack. The source of teméyn.

"It's beautiful," Danîsha murmured.

Shakhere led them off at right angles to the highway, on a side road that followed the contour of the mountain. Ahead of them the near-vertical slopes had been terraced as far down as they could see; and the terraces were were filled with rows of dark green plants.

"*Darkhel*. For making teméyn."

After a while their view was blocked by a tall hedge, beyond which they heard voices and the sounds of men working. Shakhere told them that this was the Olbizân teméyn plantation, where he and Brakhól had grown up.

It was about midday when they reached the main entrance. A wrought iron gate barred their way, and beyond was an open courtyard surrounded by utilitarian buildings of grey stone. As they stood there a crowd of underfed people in threadbare clothing gathered to gawk at them; and a large, authoritative-looking Grûzhack in a thick brown coat came striding up. His shoulders were hunched and his face was set in a truculent scowl. Gil's right hand hung free, ready to lunge for his longsword. He surprised himself by silently asking the One to make that unnecessary.

"*Barkt!*" Shakhere called out.

The big man stopped, the scowl changing to a puzzled frown.

"*Barkt! Eghéey, Shakhere!*"

"*Shakhere?*" Astonishment spread over the thick ridges of the man's face.

"*Aa! Deghift akhtigar shelmikhent lhaftick. Daney gôr tishept?*"

There was a swelling murmur from the crowd, and cries of "Sha-khere!" The man called Barkt came striding forward. "*Hah! Shakhere khaliskaleyn!*" With a broad grin he gripped the scout's forearm through the bars of the gate. Shakhere introduced the other scouts. Then he turned to Gil and Danîsha, standing at the back. 'Neesh was holding Brakhól's hand; the boy stared at the big man with wide eyes.

When he saw the two foreigners the smile faded from Barkt's face. He had a sharp exchange with Shakhere. Barkt's head tilted in the negative gesture, and Gil's heart sank.

Then Brakhól spoke. "*Daneesh khaliskey ghân?*" he asked in a small voice.

Barkt did a double take. His eyes widened. In an awed whisper he said, "*Brakhól?*"

"*Aa!*"

The boy's burst of joy hit the crowd. There were cries of delight and amazement. After a further rapid exchange between Barkt and Shakhere the gate swung open. Shakhere took Brakhól's hand as Barkt led the way to a door in one of the buildings. The crowd followed, all eyes on the two brothers, many pushing forward to grip their forearms. The few glances that came Gil's way were a blend of hostility and disgust.

Once inside they found themselves in a small, three-room apartment. A Grûzhack woman no taller than Danîsha accompanied them—she appeared to be Barkt's wife. She had sharp features and keen, close-set eyes that darted everywhere. They called her Felhis; Gil the linguist noted that the middle consonants of her name were hissed, like the double *l* in Welsh.

Beaming at Shakhere and Brakhól, Felhis ushered them to the two extra chairs at the central table. She and Barkt sat in the other chairs, and the scouts squeezed on to a bench against one wall. There was nowhere else to sit. Gil and Danîsha stood awkwardly by the door as the air filled with excited Grûzhack chatter. Then Felhis noticed them. Her face darkened, and she jabbed a finger towards the floor. "*Lakhtim!*"

Gil glanced at 'Neesh. She shrugged and leant her bellaril case against a dresser. Gil unbuckled the scabbard of his longsword, which he couldn't wear sitting. Shakhere saw what was happening and spoke sharply to Felhis. She responded in kind. Their voices rose, Barkt's bass joining in. Shakhere stood. His glance went from Danîsha to Gil, and he pointed at the chairs. "Please, you sit." He raised both hands, palms open.

There were horrified outcries from both Barkt and Felhis. Shakhere made a forceful reply, and again motioned towards the chairs. Danîsha sat down with Brakhól on her lap, facing their scowling hosts; but Gil pointed to Shakhere's injured knee. The scout nodded his thanks and raised both hands — provoking a further outburst from their hosts — before resuming his seat. Gil leant against the door, and for a while the argument raged on. Tears formed in Brakhól's eyes, and heaviness filled the air.

Then Shakhere's voice predominated. Gil guessed he was filling them in on what had happened. He was proved right when both Barkt and Felhis gasped and made the warding gesture. The story of God's warrior. Only it wasn't a story. It had happened. Brakhól broke into his brother's narrative with an excited comment, and Gil felt the warm glow of the child's enthusiasm. Barkt and Felhis felt it too, and their faces softened.

After that their hosts' attitude toward them mellowed. They were regarded, not exactly with friendship, but with wary respect.

When the midmeal was over they went out to the teméyn terraces with Barkt.

"Does he own the plantation?" Danîsha asked Shakhere in an undertone.

The scout laughed. "No, he overseer of men. Master Belkhiz, he owner. He away now."

A good thing for us, Gil thought. Had the One arranged that, as well?

Felhis had disappeared in the direction of the stone buildings round the courtyard. "She lead women," Shakhere said. "Over dere dey make teméyn powder from darkhel."

On the terraced mountainside the men were spread out along the rows of plants, weeding, mulching, removing dead fronds, clearing the irrigation channels, and sprinkling a milky liquid that Gil assumed was pesticide. Work stopped when he and Danîsha appeared, all eyes turning to the mysterious foreigners. A buzz of conversation briefly filled the air, cut off by a sharp command from Barkt. Surreptitious glances kept coming their way.

Gil bent down to examine one of the darkhel plants. The top had fern-like fronds, but the stems were thick and waxy. "So this is where teméyn comes from," he muttered. "Along with most of the problems in this world."

"I wish we could burn the whole mountainside. No, Brakhól — you can't do that!" 'Neesh hurried after the kid, who was trying to help one of the workers with his weeding. The man had a withered arm, but it didn't seem to hamper him.

"These plants look quite small, Shakhere."

"Yes, dey young ones. Soon grow big."

"When will they be ready for... making teméyn?"

"In summer. Den more small ones be planted — ready in autumn."

Gil stood up. Being this close to the source of all his heartaches in the past six months gave him a choked-up feeling of anger, outrage and pain. Just a simple plant, growing *only* in this mountain valley; yet what untold misery it caused all over the planet. He forced himself back to the conversation with Shakhere.

"If these plants are not yet ready, the women have nothing to make teméyn from. What are they doing now?"

The scout laughed. His three companions glanced at him, and Dellikh asked a question.

Shakhere replied briefly and turned back to Gil. "Women very busy! Dey grow new plants for autumn. Not easy. Must take root from old plant, put new branch in." He demonstrated, pushing his right forefinger into his bunched left fist. "Many not grow well, must start again."

Gil's eyebrows rose. "The plants don't grow from seed?"

"No! Plants is cut for teméyn before dey make seed. If dey make seed, dey not make good teméyn."

So. It all had to be done by grafting? "What happens if the teméyn crop fails — if all the plants die from frost, or disease?"

Shakhere shrugged. "Den no more teméyn. Barkt and Felhis make dat not happen."

After their tour of the terraces, Gil and Danîsha went back to the apartment with Brakhól, where Gil gave 'Neesh a break by translating some well-known English fairy tales for him. Then Danîsha played the bellaril softly — and they were glad Barkt and Felhis were out when the music was suddenly overlaid by a voice speaking out of nowhere. They all recognised the speaker: "Lannie!" Brakhól exclaimed.

Gil brought out the blaise, and holding both handles he focused the glass lens on the light wooden suface of the table. A slightly wavy image of Lannie and Shiván appeared, sitting in one of the rooms of the Stillárre Domicile. Lannie was holding the bess to her ear using both hands; and with the bellaril acting as a speaker, they could all see and hear her. Once Brakhól had said his enthusiastic greetings, they told Shiván and Lannie how the One had protected them and brought them safely to Brakhól's old home in Barazhân—to the relief and delight of the two in Stillárre.

The news from Dûrion, however, was not so good. In sombre tones Lannie told them the Grûzhack had just captured the major town of Janulane, halfway between Stillárre and Darthane. "They'll be arriving here any day now," she added.

They all prayed together, placing those in Stillárre under the protection of the One Creator God. For Gil this was suddenly real: Brakhól's 'Daddy' was a God who was there for those who trusted him.

* * *

In the evening Shakhere returned with Barkt and Felhis. The other scouts, he told them, would be sleeping with the workers. Brakhól was happy to see the overseer and his wife, and Felhis made a great fuss of the child, her eyes glistening. "She happy he alive," Shakhere explained. "Before, when parents away, she look after him."

"What work did your parents do?" Danîsha asked.

"Dey drive wagon, take teméyn to udder country."

"So they were the ones who died when the wagon crashed and Brakhól was captured?"

"Yes."

"What about your parents in Kharzil?" Gil said. "The ones we're going to stay with. What is their work?"

"Faader big teacher in learning place. Mudder—she stay home."

"A learning place... for children?"

"No. For grown people. He teach about... what happen before."

Ah. Gil's eyebrows rose. A history teacher—in what sounded like a university or adult college. Rather higher on the social scale than their 'other' parents.

Danîsha returned to a well-worn question. "But, Shakhere, you've never told us—how can you and Brakhól have *two* mothers and fathers?"

The scout shrugged. "Is happen here in Barazhân. Not in Dûrion."

Both Gil and Danîsha drew breath for another question, just as Felhis came bustling in from the small kitchen with a stack of wooden bowls and spoons and a volley of imperative Grûzhack. A steaming pot soon followed. Barkt and Shakhere had brought extra chairs, and they all squeezed in round the table.

As Felhis dished out the fragrant stew, Gil murmured to 'Neesh, "Two sets of parents, one pair with menial jobs, the other clearly middle class or higher. This seems to be a two-tier society — masters and servants. But Shakhere and Brakhól have it both ways."

Barkt spoke to Shakhere, who turned to them. "Barkt hear you say our names. He ask what you say."

Gil took a spoonful of stew before replying. It had a strong meaty taste mixed with other flavours he couldn't identify.

"I was wondering if your parents in Kharzil are Masters — like the Master of this plantation."

"*Ay!*" Shakhere stared at Gil, his eyes round. He relayed Gil's reply to Barkt, triggering a volley of exclamations and comments.

"Barkt say your God show you truth. Yes, parents in Kharzil be Grûzhack."

Danîsha frowned. "What do you mean, they're 'Grûzhack'? Aren't you *all* Grûzhack?"

Shakhere tilted his head in the negative gesture. "We not Grûzhack. We Grûzhileyn."

"Grûzhileyn?" Gil said. "What's the difference?"

"Grûzhack be true-born. Grûzhileyn be false-born."

Gil glanced at Danîsha. Her eyebrows were as high as his own. "What does *that* mean?" she demanded.

Shakhere passed on the question and there was another flurry of conversation. Felhis spoke decisively, and Shakhere translated.

"Felhis say true-born has no mistake, not even small one. False-born has mistake."

'Neesh turned to Gil, her face a puzzled question mark. But for him, light had dawned.

"You say *you* are Grûzhileyn, Shakhere... What is your 'mistake'?"

The scout leader held up two open hands. Gil frowned, then he got it. He nodded.

"What does he mean? I don't understand," 'Neesh said.

"Five fingers. Haven't you noticed? All the others have six. That's his blemish. What they're saying is that this is a caste system based on physical perfection. A true-born child has no imperfection or 'mistake'. Those are the Grûzhack. A false-born child has some kind of blemish — like Ganid, the albino scout, and Dellikh with that cast in his eye. Among the teméyn workers I saw a birthmark, a shrivelled arm, a bad limp. Those are the Grûzhileyn."

"So they're—separated out? Like an inferior race?" Danîsha demanded indignantly.

Gil turned back to Shakhere. "Are the Grûzhileyn all servants? Or are some Masters?"

The scout laughed without humour. He translated for Barkt and Felhis. Their dour responses said it all.

"That's terrible!" Danîsha exclaimed. "What is Brakhól's... 'mistake'?"

"If he happy, udder people happy. If he sad, udder people sad."

"His telepathy," Gil muttered.

"The very thing that makes him so special!" 'Neesh snapped. She was getting hot under the collar, and Brakhól felt it. "Mâra?" he said, looking at her anxiously. Danîsha put an arm around him and bit off what she was going to say.

For a while they ate in silence. Gil mulled over the Grûzhack social structure. A system in which the larger lower caste all had deformities of one kind or another. Which pointed to an unusually high rate of birth defects. Why would that be?

The spoon stopped halfway to his mouth as light dawned.

"Shakhere, you make teméyn here in Barazhân. Do you also take it yourselves?"

The young man nodded, and translated for Barkt and Fehlis.

"You take teméyn every day? Everyone, Grûzhack and Grû-zhileyn?"

"Yes. We put in food, also in drink. Just a little. It help us work better. But not for you!" he added hastily, seeing the dawning horror on Danîsha's face. "I tell Fehlis, she leave out from dis food here."

Gil smiled. "Thank you. I just wondered." To 'Neesh he added quietly in English, "Tell you later." Turning back to Shakhere he resumed the previous topic of conversation.

"So your Grûzhack mother in Kharzil... She is your *real* mother? She gave birth to you?"

"Yes."

"And your other 'parents' here... Did you come to them when you were very young?"

"Yes."

"So they were really foster-parents," Gil murmured in English.

"First me come here, den Brakhól," Shakhere told them. "True-Faader, he make sure we have same false-parents. Den he send money for look after us. Sometimes he bring true-mudder, she see us."

Shakhere translated what he'd said for Barkt and Felhis. They told Gil and Danîsha what a fine man the boys' true-father was. He had broken some of the strongest Customs to keep in touch with his children. He was the only Master they knew who would do such a thing.

"Udder Master not care," Shakhere said. "Children have mistake, trow dem away. Never see again. Just Grûzhileyn. Just... *slave*." He spat out the Dûrian word.

Barkt spoke, and Shakhere translated. "Barkt say udder Master very bad for you, too. Way to Kharzil dangerous tomorrow. Any Master see you — we all dead."

Then he smiled. "But one ting dey not know." He paused, eyebrows raised.

"What?" 'Neesh asked.

"Dey not know 'bout warrior of God!"

———————————

Chapter 17: *Brakhól comes home*

THE WAGON WAS ONE OF SEVERAL trundling along in the slow lane of the Kharzil highway. On either side were fields green with spring plantings. The wide grey-green ribbon of road stretched out ahead, following the southern bank of the River Farkh up to the bridge, then on to the pastel towers of the capital city. At regular intervals travelcars and Endeavour vehicles in a variety of colourful liveries swept past with a loud rumble of wheels and clatter of feet, their teams of speeders running with smooth, sinuous power.

Shakhere glanced across the wagon's crowded bench. The four of them could only just squeeze on, but that was nothing unusual. Most of the wagons coming into the capital were crowded with Grûzhileyn hitching a free ride. He and his comrades had exchanged their distinctive scout camouflage gear for the threadbare clothing worn on the plantations. Dellikh was holding the reins at the moment, sporting a floppy brown hat and an unbleached tunic. The four massive puller-beasts plodded on impassively.

"So, Shakhere." Migezh was next to him on the outside, one hand gripping the rail in front of them. "What's this secret weapon of yours to get us into your true-parents' suburb?"

Shakhere glanced at his fourth in the scout patrol and grinned. From inside his tattered grey jacket he produced a leather wallet. He unfolded it and carefully extracted a sheet of heavy cream paper. He held it up, and the others all craned to see the green writing on it. In the centre at the bottom was a complex pattern of flourishes in green and gold.

"Would you look at that!" Ganid breathed. "A Letter of Authority, no less."

"My true-father gave it to me when I joined the War Endeavour," Shakhere said. He tucked the paper lovingly back into the wallet.

Migezh narrowed his eyes as if in thought. "Hmmm. Yes. I think that might *just* get us in."

"Your true-parents must really care about you." There was envy in Ganid's voice.

"About you and Brakhól, yes," Dellikh said, "but not the foreigners. They won't give them shelter. No Master would break Custom *that* far."

"My true-father will! When I explain everything he'll invite Daneesh and Gelmin to stay in his house. You'll see."

Dellikh shrugged. "I hope you're right. If we went back to Olbizân with them still under the tarpaulin, Barkt would throw a fit."

A large travelcar pulled by six speeders swept past, its breeze lifting Dellikh's hat. Shakhere sat staring ahead, his eyes stony. Dellikh had touched on his own secret fear. Tal and Mistil had been unbelievably good to him and Brakhól. But would their generosity stretch *this* far? He had to believe that. He was now Daneesh and Brakhól's First Warrior, and it was his responsibility to look after them, along with Gelmin. If his true-parents wouldn't accept the foreigners, he'd have to make other arrangements. But what?

Migezh cleared his throat. "Then there's the little question of what we do if Brakhól makes a fuss again."

Shakhere had been thinking about that. A while ago, as they were turning on to the highway at Farkhas, there had been a shrill outcry from the back of the wagon that had drawn startled glances. No Masters had stopped their vehicles to enquire; but another time they might not be so lucky.

"I have an idea," he said. "Dellikh, you do a good imitation of a woman's voice."

"Oh, *stop* it, you flatterer!" The others cackled at the high pitched squeal.

"Okay, here's what we'll do." He outlined his plan.

A couple of hours later they were crossing the wide bridge over the River Bokh. The multicoloured towers of Kharzil loomed before them, glowing in the late afternoon sun. To the right the waters of Lake Skhalrân were dotted with pleasure craft from the many mansions along the water's edge. Shakhere was driving now, and once over the bridge he steered the puller-beasts left toward his true-parents' suburb, which covered a low hill overlooking the river.

Shakhere and his comrades were silent as the beasts plodded slowly up the hill. At the top a pair of wrought iron gates blocked the road, and a couple of guards stood silhouetted, watching their approach. He found himself repeating a few of the words Brakhól had used when asking for the Creator's protection — followed (to be on the safe side) by a ritual petition to the goddess Makhril.

Shakhere reined in the pullers as they reached the gates. The wagon lurched to a stop and the guards came forward.

"Your business?" The guard leader was a large, thickset Grû-zhileyn with a cold eye and a deformed nose. The other was shorter and younger. His spear was lowered not quite towards them.

"Delivery for Tal Gha-Derid."

"Delivery note."

"It was a rush request — no time for the normal paperwork. But I have this." He handed the leader his Letter of Authority.

The man's eyes widened as he took it in. The other guard peered over his shoulder.

"Well, well! Quite the pampered favourite, aren't we?"

The leader gave the paper back and stood in thought, his gaze wandering over the wagon while Shakhere's heart hammered.

"The letter authorises you to enter, no one else. Your friends can return with the wagon in the morning. They'll be let in if Gha-Derid says so."

"Nonsense! Gha-Derid ordered these supplies urgently, and he wants them *today*. What d'you think he'll say when he learns *you've* stopped them from reaching him?"

The reply was drowned by a high-pitched shout that burst from the wagon, along with a wave of anger and frustration. Both guards leapt as if whipped, the younger one dropping his spear. At the same moment Dellikh hurtled off his seat, shrieking in a high falsetto and clutching his leg. He hopped about on the road, keening, then let out a heavy groan and limped back to the wagon.

"My friend gets this terrible cramp in his injured leg," Shakhere told the gaping guards. "Now, please open the gate."

The leader scowled and walked over to Dellikh, who showed him his scar. "It cramps if I sit for too long."

"He needs rest," Shakhere said. "Gha-Derid will not be happy if you make my friend sit even longer."

Glowering at them, the guard leader motioned to his comrade, who opened the gates.

Shakhere shook the reins and shouted *"Kharréy!"* The beasts moved ponderously forward and the wagon rolled into the Grû-zhack suburb.

* * *

Tal Gha-Derid looked at his wife sadly. Reality was settling in. The boy was not coming back. She hadn't even asked tonight. Her eyes had lost their sparkle, and a strand of hair was hanging loose from its pins. She was still a beautiful woman, but... something had died. His own heart ached with that loss. He didn't want to think about the future.

They sat silently in the living room sipping their *zakheyn*. When they'd both finished a maid removed the tray, her face sombre. The whole house was in mourning. But the worst thing was that they couldn't express their grief. To do so would damage their standing in society and possibly cost Tal his job. After all, Shakhere was only a Grûzhileyn — not even officially their son.

A faint sound of voices drifted through from the front door.

"Oh, I can't face visitors!" Mistil rose from the sofa. "Tell them I'm unwell." She hurried out.

Tal sighed. Then frowned. The voices from the door were raised — but not in anger. A moment later his steward came in at an undignified trot.

"Sir! You must come!"

"Doykhid, calm yourself. What is it?"

"You must see for yourself, sir. I'll call the mistress."

"The mistress doesn't want to be disturbed."

"She'll want to be disturbed for this, sir!" The old man's face was shining.

Doykhid hurried off to their personal tower, and Tal almost ran to the front door. He could think of only one visitor who would cause the steward to forget himself like that.

He reached the portico — and there he was. Shakhere. Dressed not as an army scout, but in a disreputable old jacket and threadbare tunic. But no matter. His son was alive! In the background he was dimly aware of three other Grûzhileyn in similar clothing.

With a Herculean effort Tal subdued his emotions. "Shakhere!"

"Father." The boy's eyes were bright. He looked older and leaner. Tal's eyes devoured him. He held out a hand, but Shakhere stepped forward and embraced him. The feel of his son in his arms cracked Tal's restraint, and to his embarrassment tears sprang to his eyes.

Then Mistil arrived. Her mouth formed a silent O, but before she could speak the boy folded her in a tight embrace. Her cheeks were wet when he released her. "Shakhere," she whispered, her fingers tracing the outline of his face.

Tal cleared his throat. Others were watching, news might get about. "You've come back." The inane words restored normality. "Your tour of duty is over?"

Shakhere moved slightly away from Mistil. "Yes, Father." He gestured to the Grûzhileyn behind him. "These are my comrades." He introduced the rag-tag bunch—also scouts, apparently. Beyond them stood a plantation wagon, its contents covered with a tarpaulin. A tendril of doubt invaded Tal's happiness. This wasn't how warriors returned from active duty.

"Father! Mother!" Shakhere's face suddenly split into a broad grin. "I have something very special for you!" He turned and went to the wagon. Tal looked at Mistil. She smiled back, her face glowing.

* * *

Danîsha huddled uncomfortably in the near-darkness under the tarpaulin, fingering Teynel's comb in her pocket. Brakhól was next to her with his head resting on her shoulder. Gil sat beside them hugging his knees. They could hear the muffled voices outside. Their cramped hidey-hole in the back of the wagon was covered by a wooden board, and all around were crates, some empty, others containing a random selection of piping, rusty farm tools, and whatever Overseer Barkt could risk losing.

"I want to get *out!*" Brakhól whispered mutinously. Danîsha said, "We'll get out soon, Brakhól, and you'll see your Mummy and Daddy."

"Will they be nice?"

"Of course they will. They've been missing you. They'll be so happy to see you! You'll be happy, too." Her heart clenched. It was hard to think of handing this precious child over.

"Mâra and Gelmin will be there, too?"

"Yes, we'll be there." She desperately hoped so—at least till the child was settled.

Gil grunted.

There was the sound of footsteps approaching, and Danîsha put a gentle finger on Brakhól's lips. A few minutes later light flooded in as hands pulled off the tarp and removed the board covering them.

"Shakhere!" Brakhól exclaimed as his brother's head appeared in the opening. Looking from Gil to Danîsha, Shakhere clamped a hand over his own mouth in the Grûzhack signal to remain silent. Brakhól scrambled towards him and Shakhere lifted the boy out of the wagon.

* * *

Tal watched, puzzled, as Shakhere leant over the wagon, his back to them. Was that a *child's* voice? Shakhere reached in and lifted something out. He turned, and — yes — he was holding a child! He pointed towards them and murmured to the youngster.

The child said *"Ammi! Baaba!"* and a wave of excitement swept out from him.

Tal went rigid. It was impossible.

Brakhól!

Mistil screamed, hand to her mouth. Then she was running. Shakhere met her halfway and gave her the child. Tal's legs came to life, and in a moment he was with them. Mistil was clutching Brakhól, crooning over him, sobbing as she hadn't done since childhood. Tal felt the tears streaming down his own cheeks.

After a while Brakhól pulled back and stared solemnly at Mistil. "Ammi?"

"Yes, Brakhól." Her face was radiant through the tears. "I'm your mother. Do you remember me?"

He shook his head.

"But we remember you. We lost you, and now you're back!" She turned to Shakhere, who was grinning with delight. "How did it *happen*? Where did you *find* him?"

"It's a long story, Ammi. I'll tell you about it later."

She held Brakhól out to Tal. "This is your father."

"Baaba."

Tal took the child and looked him over, his heart full. Brakhól had grown a lot in the three years he'd been missing. The face looking back at him was that of a child who had suffered, yet was at peace. The grey eyes held the same depths of emotion they'd always had, along with that disturbing sense of power under restraint. The power that had led the physician six years ago to pronounce him a false-birth.

"I'm your father, Brakhól. Now you are home, I will always look after you."

A puzzled expression crossed the boy's face. "And Mâra? Gelmin?"

"Who?"

"Will 'Neesh and Gelmin look after me too?"

Tal turned to Shakhere. "I don't understand. What's he saying?"

The lad's smile had faded, replaced by a tense expression.

"Daneesh and Gelmin were looking after Brakhól when we found him, father—they and their people. They rescued him from the Mindbenders."

"Then we owe them a great gift of gratitude. Where are they? I'll see that they receive abundant recompense, even if it has to be sent through enemy lines."

Shakhere blinked, then swallowed. In a quiet voice he said, "They're here, father."

"*Here*? What do you mean?"

"In the wagon."

Before Tal could respond, Shakhere hurried over to the vehicle. He leant over the side, and the next moment two... creatures stood up amidst the crates.

Mistil gasped, and turned her face away. Tal stared in horrified fascination. They were squat, with broad, flat faces. Their eyes were large and virtually lidless. Their complexions were the dirty pink of infected skin. As they clambered awkwardly down to the ground, it became obvious how stunted they were.

Brakhól wriggled out of his grasp and ran to the apparitions crying, "Mâra, Gelmin!" followed by a string of gibberish. He grabbed the hand of the shorter of the two—a female—and started pulling her towards them.

That was too much for Mistil. She charged at the female shouting, "Let go of my child!" and snatched Brakhól away from it. Brakhól cried out in surprise and indignation, and everyone cringed. Tal gasped under the onslaught of his son's emotion, but anger welled up in him that Brakhól should have become attached to these monsters.

While Mistil held Brakhól and tried to comfort him, Tal rounded on Shakhere. "How dare you bring such creatures here! Don't you know that you *and* they could be executed?"

146

Shakhere's face was a mask of anxiety. "Yes, father, I know. But they saved Brakhól's life! You were just saying you wanted to reward them. *Please*, father—don't turn them away. We could never have got here without the woman, Daneesh. She cared for Brakhól, and calmed him down when he might have got us into trouble."

Tal glanced round. Half the household had come out to watch. "Inside, everyone! Back to your duties." To Shakhere he said, "Your comrades can stay the night. Ask Samilgezh to find them beds. He can also get that wagon out of the way. As for the aliens... Take them to the kitchen, they can wait there. I'll decide what to do." He laid a hand on the boy's arm. "Shakhere, I can never thank you enough for bringing Brakhól home. Remember this, whatever happens to the foreigners."

With a doubtful nod the boy turned to escort his entourage to the back of the house.

Tal put an arm around Mistil and Brakhól, the magic child they thought they'd lost forever.

Chapter 18: *Battle of Stillárre Docks*

LANNIE AND SHIVÁN entered the upper chamber of the gatehouse on the Stillárre city wall that rose above the tunnel leading into the city from the docks. From here they had the best view of the newly-arrived Grûzhack army. Shiván was wearing the Blade of Darthane and Lannie had her bow strapped on her back. They peered through the two narrow front windows. On the opposite shore of the wide Carreck River the Grûzhack were embedding their cannon. A field of brown tents had sprouted beyond the four metal mouths that gaped at them. Lannie shuddered. Were these the mouths that would finally devour them and end their mission in Dûrion? *Dear God, please protect us.*

"We should be okay," Shiván murmured. "The light's already fading. They won't start the bombardment until tomorrow."

Lannie shook her head. "How did they get here so quickly? It was only a couple of days ago we heard they'd captured Janulane. Then Palderen, then Rosten..."

"Yeah. But those towns only had small garrisons. Stillárre should hold them for a while."

"Oh, great. And then what?"

Shivvie gave her a crooked grin. "Dunno." She looked away, her heart sinking.

Below them the last sailing vessels — a three-master and a smaller two-master — were slipping downstream towards the lake, probably making for Jern on the western shore. From the dock itself the sound of breaking wood drifted up as workers destroyed the two ferries and the few remaining dinghies and rowing boats.

They went to the rear windows. The scene behind the wall was frantic. Soldiers were hurrying people along as they ran in and out of their houses gathering treasured possessions. The streets were crammed with horses and vehicles of all descriptions, from tiny handcarts to farm wagons, all struggling to leave the eastern suburbs of the city.

Lannie sighed. She felt so helpless. Where were the Restorers of last year — the ones who had defeated Shambor? Half of them were escorting a child home; the other two... Well, here they were. Waiting for the wall they were standing on to be demolished.

Above all, where was the Shiván of last year? The live-wire always fizzing with ideas that actually *worked*? He'd got himself more together recently, but as Overguardian he was a washout.

Should *she* be taking his place? No, that was out. She knew what the One's place for her was, and she was in it: discerning and rooting out the lingering evil of the Shambor years. Only last week she'd heard the deceit in a Stillárre merchant's voice, which had led to the breaking of a teméyn-smuggling ring. That was her job. Not thinking up war strategies.

Shiván had returned to the front windows. Suddenly he leapt away. "Lannie, *down!*" He grabbed her arm and she tumbled with him to the ground. "Cover your head!"

There was a loud explosion, then a crash of fractured masonry somewhere behind them. Screams filled the air.

They ran to the rear windows. The corner of a house had been demolished. People were trying to pull someone from the wreckage. Horses were bolting and a wagon had overturned.

There was another bang, and they dropped to the floor as a tremendous crash above them shook the whole tower. Dust filled the air and fragments of stone peppered them from the ceiling.

"Range-finding shots!" Shiván yelled. "Let's get out of here!"

They scrambled for the stairs.

* * *

Shiván didn't sleep that night; he was sure hardly anyone in Stillárre did. The whole city was dark, tense, waiting. The very air itself seemed thick with menace. Gloom pervaded his thoughts as he struggled to hold on to the One's protection.

Finally, at first light, the storm broke.

A thunder of explosions shook the city. *Cannon were demolishing the ancient wall!* His heart went out to the thousands of ordinary Dûrians who had fled for shelter within that impregnable barrier, never dreaming it could so easily be shattered.

The barrage continued all morning, and by midday the wall along the river had great gaps in it and many of the houses behind had been reduced to rubble. The Dorbians were guarding the northern bank of the Carreck as far as Carlis, and Garset had scouts out elsewhere. But in the city itself there was nothing they could do: they were at the mercy of the Grûzhack cannon.

Shiván sat praying under the great Ambon in the Stillárre Hearth, asking God for protection. At the council of war last night they had made what few decisions they could; now it was over to the One in whom they trusted, their Shelter and their Defender.

When the sounds of tramping feet and shouted commands drifted into the Hearth from the city square, Shiván donned a helmet and coat of banded armour, throwing his green infantry cape over his shoulders and fastening it at the neck. He strapped on the Blade of Darthane and picked up a small metal-plated Dûrian shield. Then he went out to join Garset and his troops. He had won the Council's reluctant permission to see once more whether the Blade's powers would work.

"The Grûzhack are preparing to cross the river," Garset told him. "If you still want to do this, now's the time."

Garset led two companies down to the dock area. The cannon fire had eased off, though there were still sporadic shots. "In case we get bored," Cârin said. Shiván knew the lieutenant was there as his minder, but he was glad of his cheerful presence. Shiván's own thoughts were gloomy.

When he'd parted from Perrely earlier on, she'd been tearful—which threw his emotions into turmoil. She cared for him, yet wouldn't consider anything closer than friendship. Then there was the constant fear lurking on the edge of consciousness, that this might be where it would all end—for him, maybe for all of them. What good were the Restorers now? Apart from his suggestion of trying the Blade—a long shot at best—he and Alanya had been barren of ideas in the Council last night. It was Garset who had proposed the only strategy with any hope of success.

His dark musings were cut short as they halted in the tunnel under the shattered gatehouse. Peering out, the first thing Shiván saw was an armada of boats on the other side of the river. They were of every shape and size—barges, ferries, fishing smacks, rowing boats, skiffs. There couldn't be many craft left in the harbours of Rosten, Palderen, and the other waterside villages the Grûzhack had overrun. Teal-coated warriors were clambering aboard. Several missed their step and fell into the muddy water, and some of the smaller boats capsized.

"Those landlubbers!" Cârin chortled. "We can stand here and watch 'em drown!"

But the first boats were already on their way across, and the way they were handled showed that not all the Grûzhack were landlubbers.

Intermittent cannon fire continued. A shot struck the gatehouse above them, and everyone leapt back as rubble rained down across the opening.

Garset sent his longbowmen scurrying behind what remained of the wall. Others went with them carrying steaming buckets and braziers with glowing coals.

Cârin frowned. "Those archers must have cold feet."

"Whatever, they're brave men," Shiván muttered, as a cannonball struck a section of the wall the archers had just passed.

But now the leading boats were more than halfway across, and the Grûzhack cannon fell silent.

"Overguardian," Garset said. This was Shiván's moment. He swallowed down a surge of panic and turned to the infantrymen behind him in the tunnel. Every eye was on him. He swept the Blade of Darthane from its sheath and shouted, "*For the One!*" The air quivered with the roared response of the Dûrians as they charged after him on to the docks. They fanned out from the gatehouse to line the whole length of the wharf, swords aloft.

Nothing happened. Far from turning their boats back in terror, the Grûzhack rowers seemed to pull even harder. With a heavy heart Shiván lowered the Blade. *Why, dear Prince?* Hours of prayer had made no difference. Whatever he tried came to nothing.

He resigned himself to fighting as an ordinary soldier.

A hand clasped his shoulder. "*Aténnelor*, the Lord Marshal says you should join him at the gatehouse to share oversight of the defence."

Shiván glanced at the man. "Give Garset my thanks, but tell him the Blade is a fine weapon, and it's needed right here."

The messenger hesitated, opened his mouth, then closed it and left.

Cârin — still at his side — raised a quizzical eyebrow. "Defying the Council, are we?"

"No. Just giving their instructions wider scope."

They turned back to the river. The Grûzhack flotilla was drawing closer in a line that stretched the length of the docks.

"They'll have a hard time getting up on to the wharf from those little boats," Câr said.

"Not if they mow us all down first with their muskets."

"Hah! You think those landlubbers can shoot their little fire tubes from a moving boat? They'll fall off!"

Shiván smiled grimly. "Or we'll rock their boats before they get a chance to shoot." He thought of the acrid-smelling buckets that had gone with the longbowmen.

The motley flotilla drew closer. Shiván could make out the ridged faces of the Grûzhack warriors, some perched uncomfortably in the smaller craft, others standing close-packed on the decks of the barges and fishing boats.

"*Kaskhidez!*" The guttural Grûzhack command rang out over the water. Up and down the flotilla teal-clad musketeers took the weapons from their backs and levelled them at the defenders on the wharf. On the decked vessels the front row of musketeers knelt, while those behind aimed over their heads. At either end of the deck archers nocked arrows into their short bows. Several of the smaller boats rocked dangerously, and one spilt its complement into the water. Cârin sniggered as the waterlogged warriors made futile attempts to climb back aboard.

Shiván waited anxiously for what he knew must come. Why were their own longbowmen taking so long? If the boats came much closer many Dûrians with him on the wharf would be killed. The Grûzhack archers would soon be within range; and if they got close enough for those massed muskets to fire, the carnage would be horrible.

But Garset knew what he was doing. His order suddenly rang out: "*Fire!*"

There was a whizz of arrows behind them. A stink of burning pitch wafted over the infantry on the wharf, and a blazing shower rained down on the Grûzhack flotilla, less than a hundred paces away.

Within moments the sails and woodwork of the two fishing vessels were alight, and there were shouts of terror as their occupants leapt overboard. The current swept them lakeward. On the other craft the Grûzhack dropped their weapons and raised metal shields. The arrows skipped off the shields, but many fell between the gaps and set the warriors' tunics alight. Others lodged in wood, which caught fire. Several more of the smaller boats capsized as their occupants thrashed violently to rid themselves of the burning pitch. Others were so busy dousing the flames that their boats drifted harmlessly downstream. A roar of jubilation rose from the Dûrian troops.

But a remnant of the flotilla reached the wharf. A wide barge came in where Shiván stood. A few arrows and scattered musket shots flew wildly at the Dûrians as it approached, but little damage was done. The Grûzhack reached out for the mooring rings, their heads just high enough to see over the top of the wharf. For many that was their last sight. Swords swept down, the Blade among them, and deep-throated yells of agony split the air. Before long the barge drifted off downriver, its cargo a tangle of teal-coated bodies. The same story was repeated all along the dock.

Except at one point, where the cries and clashes of battle still filled the air.

"To the ferry landing!" Garset bellowed, and the Dûrian troops ran to assist their comrades fighting in the water on the sloping ramp. A barge had disgorged its warriors into the gap in the wharf where the ferry entered. Here the taller, stronger Grûzhack were evenly matched against the Dûrians higher up on the entry-way.

Shiván reached the edge of the dock above the ramp, and the first thing he saw was a teal-coated Grûzhack raising his sword to finish off a young Dûrian recruit. Without thinking Shiván leapt down on the warrior, who crumpled under him, his yell ending in a strangled gurgle. The warrior thrashed about violently in the water, but Shiván clung on as if to an untamed stallion, gripping the head with both hands and holding it under. Cârin stood guard, fighting off a couple of the warrior's comrades. Finally Shiván's opponent went limp. Shiván staggered to his feet, panting and shivering from what he'd just done. Deliberately killing a man still felt like murder.

"Hey, Hero, no more fancy stuff!" Cãr exclaimed. "Stick to what I taught you. *Watch out!*"

Shiván dodged a vicious swipe from another Grûzhack wading up the ferry ramp. A Dûrian lieutenant stabbed the warrior from behind, and the Grûzhack turned to engage him. Shiván drew the Blade, and the warrior soon had more than he could handle.

Shiván flinched as the cannon thundered again, and there were cries further down the dock. At least they wouldn't target the ferry ramp. Thank the One these Grûzhack had all soaked their muskets jumping off the barge.

A Grûzhack officer in a soggy green tunic was forcing his way through the water towards Shiván, sword raised. Shiván waited until he was within reach, then parried his first blow and followed up with a swift lunge at the exposed neck. It was one of the manoeuvres Cârin had taught him, and it worked. The Grûzhack staggered back, his second blow went wide, and Shiván swept the Blade in a devastating arc. The officer disappeared into the red-tinged water as Shiván blocked another sword coming at him from the right. No time now to be queasy.

Shiván drove his new assailant back into deeper water. The warrior grabbed a mooring ring on the wall of the ramp, and a Dûrian soldier on the dockside slashed his hand. He uttered a cry of pain, lost his footing, and disappeared under the crush of Grûzhack still struggling up the ramp. Shiván wondered how many more of the enemy had drowned with only minor wounds.

He felt his mind beginning to cloud, and his heart sank. Already? His times of prayer under the Ambon usually gave him about two hours of normality—after which the fog set in again. Had it been that long already? Dear God, help me last out this battle!

A Grûzhack came swirling up to Shiván in a wake of disturbed water. Cârin was otherwise engaged. Shiván parried the initial blow, but could feel his reactions slowing. The screams and groans and the clang of striking metal distracted him. He was too late with the thrust to the neck, and barely deflected the warrior's second strike. Summoning all his strength he ducked under the third, surged inside the warrior's guard, and rammed the Blade home. The warrior's eyes widened, and he stood stock still as Shiván yanked the sword free.

Shiván looked past his enemy. Another boatload of warriors was approaching. With so many lost in the first engagement, they were still sending more? He watched as the barge drew nearer. Where were the Dûrian longbowmen?

Then his recent opponent toppled towards him, an arm wrapped itself round his shoulder, and Shiván collapsed backward into the water under the dead weight of a seven-foot armoured Grûzhack.

Chapter 19: *Barriers broken*

GIL SAT WITH DANÎSHA on a bench in the kitchen, their feet dangling off the ground. On the floor beside them were all their worldly goods —a couple of shoulder pouches and the bellaril. Gil's longsword had been confiscated.

"Now we know what it is to be treated like slaves," Gil muttered.

'Neesh shook her head. She looked exhausted. "Worse than slaves. Subhuman. That woman grabbed Brakhól away from me as though I was a dangerous animal."

The Grûzhileyn kitchen staff threw them disdainful glances as they cleaned vegetables, stoked ovens and prepared the evening meal. Gil sniffed. There was a faint, rather unpleasant tang in the air. His eyes went to a glass jar one of the servants was holding. It contained a grey powder. She took a small spoonful of it and sprinkled it on one of the dishes.

Teméyn. He decided not to mention it to 'Neesh.

A jolt of unhappiness surged through the house, and everyone froze. The servants looked at one another with raised eyebrows, then resumed their tasks in silence. Heaviness hung in the air, and there was a volley of deep sighs.

"Oh dear," 'Neesh muttered.

"'Oh dear' is right. They've upset Brakhól again."

A few moments later Shakhere came hurrying in. "Daneesh, Gelmin! True-faader, he say you not stay here. Brakhól get unhappy, say he want you. I say you make Brakhól happy again. Come! Bring bellaril!"

Danîsha slid down, grabbed the instrument, and they both set off after the scout.

They walked through a number of passages and circular rooms, each more opulent than the last. Some had curving staircases that Gil realised must lead to the towers he'd seen. The light of many small lamps showed up the satiny surfaces of the walls, which had delicate repeated flower or animal designs. The windows were draped with matching curtains that hung to the floor.

Finally they entered what had to be the living room, decorated in subtle variations of rose and red offset by creamy satin walls. The boys' parents were sitting on a leather sofa. Their father had a high, intelligent brow, piercing black eyes and strong features; Gil could see the likeness to Shakhere. The mother's carefully waved blue-black hair framed a face more rounded than most Grûzhack, and there were laughter lines around her dark grey eyes. But she was not laughing now.

They both stiffened when they saw Gil and Danîsha. The lady turned her head away again, and the man stared at them with distaste. But Brakhól leapt off his mother's lap and came running to them, his tear-stained face full of delight.

"Mâra! Gelmin!" He grabbed the bellaril case and began pulling it — and 'Neesh — towards his parents. "Play *Prince Loves Me!*"

They stopped in front of the sofa, facing the Grûzhack couple. The mother still couldn't look at them.

"Can I sit down to play?" Danîsha murmured to Shakhere.

In answer he stepped forward and said a few words to his parents, holding out an arm first to Gil, then to 'Neesh, and mentioning their names. Gil felt an absurd inclination to bow. The mother glanced at them briefly; the father made a snappish reply.

Indicating two chairs, Shakhere said, "Sit! Daneesh, you play. Brakhól, sing!"

They perched on the high chairs, provoking outrage from the parents. The father subjected Shakhere to a tongue-lashing, then stood and bellowed a summons.

"*Play!*" Shakhere urged Danîsha, his face contorted.

'Neesh struggled to extract the instrument from its case. She finally had it in her hands when three burly Grûzhileyn in dark maroon tunics appeared at the door.

Danîsha struck a chord. As the rich harmony filled the air everyone paused. The mother turned, astonishment raising her brows.

Then 'Neesh began playing Brakhól's favourite song. The child sat on the arm of her chair and began to sing — hesitantly at first, then letting go so that his strong, pure voice filled the living room with praise to the One Creator God.

Watching the parents was like seeing a slow-motion replay of a building being demolished. The stiffness in their posture softened. Their hard expressions dissolved, changing from anger to shock, from shock to amazement, from amazement to wonder. Tears began to flow as their long-lost child sang to an unknown God in an unknown tongue. The joy that poured from him seemed to reach down to the depths of their hearts.

When the song ended a profound stillness filled the house. Gil saw that the room was full of servants, staring at 'Neesh and Brakhól with tear-streaked faces and open mouths. He marvelled at the shattering effect Brakhól had on his own people. This went way beyond anything he'd seen among the Dûrians.

Shakhere broke the silence. In a small voice he asked his father a question.

Like a man waking from a dream the father slowly turned his eyes from Danîsha and Brakhól to his older son. He stared at Shakhere, then bowed his head and raised it again.

Brakhól leapt from the chair, his face ecstatic.

"Mâra! Gelmin! You can stay!" He was jumping up and down.

"For now," Shakhere added with a tense smile.

* * *

Danîsha slowly released a breath she hadn't realised she'd been holding. The tension of the past twelve hours had been weighing on her, along with her fear for Brakhól's welfare if she were abruptly sent away. The child was still standing beaming at her. She gave him a hug, then gently pushed him toward his parents.

"Go to your mother now," she whispered. He nodded solemnly and trotted over to the Grûzhack lady, who took him into her arms. She looked at Danîsha and her damp eyes said a wordless thank you.

No one made any move to leave. The father cleared his throat and asked Shakhere a question. The lad attempted a reply, with many hesitations. The father spoke again, pointing to Gil. Shakhere turned to him.

"Faader, he ask what dis song say."

Gil looked at Danîsha, but before she could answer Shakhere said urgently, "Not Daneesh! Faader ask *you*. With Grûzhack, man speak before woman. You tell me, I tell Faader."

For the first time since Danîsha had known him Gil looked flustered. His mouth half opened and he looked back at her.

Danîsha's heart was full. God was always one step ahead. "It's up to you, Gil. You know what the song says, and what it means. Tell them."

Gil swallowed. Then he turned to Shakhere, and his voice was strong when he spoke. "The song is about the One Creator God and his Son, Prince Orrénne."

Shakhere translated.

"It says that the Creator loved everyone under the sky so much, that he sent his own Son to live among them. Those who accept him find great joy and peace. When they are part of the Prince's family, they are... free." There was a quiver in Gil's voice.

Shakhere translated, and his father asked another question. Danîsha heard Brakhól's name. "*Aa*," Shakhere said. Yes.

A flurry of further questions came—from the mother, the steward, the cook, Ganid the scout. Shakhere answered smoothly, and Brakhól was grinning. The distinction between Grûzhack and Grûzhileyn, master and slave, was forgotten.

Shakhere turned to Danîsha and Gil between questions. "Dey ask if Brakhól and you part of Prince's family. I tell dem yes, dat is reason Brakhól so happy, why he make *us* happy." His eyes were bright.

But a frown had gathered on the father's face. He held up a hand, and the chatter ceased. He asked a question, his eyes on Gil.

Shakhere's face was solemn. "Faader ask if Creator God more powerful dan Grûzhack goddess Makhril."

Gil returned the Grûzhack's steady gaze. Danîsha sent up a silent prayer. "Yes, the Creator is more powerful," Gil said through Shakhere, "because he made everything there is. Any strength that others have, comes from him."

The father stared at Gil from under heavy brows. Shakhere relayed his reply. "You answer well. But Grûzhack say different. How can a person know which is true?"

Gil smiled at Shakhere. "You can tell him."

Shakhere stared. "The Warrior of God," Gil murmured. The lad's face cleared, and he turned to his father, launching into an animated flood of Grûzhack with wide, sweeping gestures. Brakhól and the scouts chipped in eagerly. The rest of the household hung on their words.

Danîsha breathed her thanks to the One.

* * *

The long evening was over, and the household had finally retired to bed. To Gil's relief, before they'd eaten Shakhere had slipped into the kitchen and told the staff to prepare a simple meal without teméyn for him and Danîsha. He took his responsibility for them seriously. Still looking dazed, and without their former disdain, the servants had hurried to obey.

Gil and the scouts had been squeezed into a hastily-converted stall in a sinélle stable. His bed was a pile of straw on the ground with a couple of blankets thrown over it. The three Grûzhileyn were chattering in hushed voices; and through the wooden partition on the right came an occasional whiffle or rhythmic scratching, along with a rich aroma of sinélle.

As he lay staring up at the sloping roof beams, Gil's thoughts went back over the amazing day. Their journey in the back of the wagon, unhindered despite Brakhól's outbursts; their acceptance in the household, against all the odds; and the way he—Gilbert Denbigh, the confirmed sceptic—had spoken with full conviction to the master of the house about the all-powerful Creator.

Gil discovered that he had meant every word. He knew there was a personal God, a Creator who cared for his creatures, who intervened on their behalf. It wasn't a matter of evidence or logical proof—but it was beyond question. It seemed the most natural thing in the world to speak to the One Creator God and thank him for keeping them safe.

* * *

Mistil sat on a plush red side chair in the living room, staring dreamily out at the well-manicured grounds. Tal had left for work, and she was reliving every moment of yesterday's reunion with her sons. She could still hardly believe they were *both* back. It had been the best day of her life. They had changed: Shakhere broader, stronger, his face weathered in more ways than one—no longer the young, eager recruit who had set off to war. And Brakhól... Still the same outgoing, bubbly personality, but—an innocent toddler no more. There was a depth to his young eyes that spoke of suffering beyond his age. She must find out more of what he'd been through in the three years he'd been away. But oh! It was so wonderful to have him back.

And that song he'd sung last night... It had reached into her very soul. The memory trembled within her, fragile but vivid. Who would have guessed that her little Brakhól could make such music? The whole household was walking around today with distant eyes, like people who had seen a vision and could not shake it off.

Of course that muscial instrument had set off Brakhól's voice beautifully. It was something like the six-stringed *lhendift* that virtuosos of the Beauty Endeavour played at public concerts — but bigger, and the sound was far richer. The female alien had played it well. After last night Mistil could almost begin to think of the alien as a person — if only it didn't look so revolting.

Doykhid interrupted her reverie with a discreet cough. "Visitors, madam."

"Who is it?" Mistil was puzzled. Social calls were rare before mid-morning.

"Two ladies from the neighbourhood, madam. Shall I admit them?" There was a significant look in the steward's eye.

Oh, goddess! She and Tal hadn't foreseen this. They'd assumed Brakhól's joy last night had been a private family matter, contained within the thick stone walls of the house. Obviously not! How could they have known his power had grown so strong?

Now these ladies had arrived to investigate.

She felt a surge of panic. What could she say to them? Only her closest friend Shandis knew about Shakhere; and even *she* didn't know they'd also kept in touch with Brakhól during the first three years of his life. Brakhól, to the neighbourhood, was merely a freak birth she'd suffered years ago. He'd quickly been disposed of, and that was that.

What would the ladies say if they found out that, not only were they illegally harbouring their false-born children, but also a couple of loathsome aliens? How long would it take for that information to reach the Magistry? Mistil twisted her hands together anxiously under Doykhid's sympathetic gaze. She wished Tal were there.

She couldn't turn the ladies away. That would be an admission of guilt. She'd have to feign ignorance.

She drew a deep breath. "Show them in, Doykhid."

"Yes, madam."

"Oh, and Doykhid? Give orders that Shakhere, Brakhól and the aliens are to be kept out of sight." She hesitated before adding, "The female can look after Brakhól." It had shown sensitivity last night in returning the child to her.

Doykhid raised both hands, palms open, and left the room. Mistil went to a tall wall mirror. She patted her hair and straightened her coral tunic and matching jacket, relieved that she'd taken time dressing this morning. She sat herself carefully in a corner of the sofa, ready to rise gracefully and greet her guests.

They turned out to be her friend Shandis and another near neighbour, Dilmey. They weren't dressed for visiting—in fact they seemed to have come just as they were. Both stared at her intently as they grasped her right hand and locked fingers in the friendship greeting. Her heart sank.

Shandis came straight to the point. "What happened last night?"

Mistil affected a surprised titter. "Shandis! How abrupt. You make it sound as though we were up to something... *evil!*"

"Not evil. Wonderful!" Dilmey's eyes were red-rimmed. "Such... happiness! It sort of poured across to us from your house. I haven't been able to sleep thinking of it!"

Shandis nodded. "The same with us. I would have come over there and then if Haftarg hadn't stopped me."

Mistil tried to swallow unobtrusively. "Well, I don't know what to say. I'm flattered that you find us so... attractive!"

Shandis' eyes hardened. "Mistil, please stop pretending you don't know what we're talking about. Something... very strange happened here last night. What was it?"

Doykhid reappeared, saving Mistil. But not for long.

"Three more ladies, madam."

Mistil tried to smile. It must have looked ghastly. "Show them in, Doykhid."

Hilgin, Karlis and Shistilg entered. They were slightly more distant neighbours, and looked as if they hadn't slept either.

"Mistil, what *was* that last night?" Karlis blurted.

"Nothing at all," Shandis said. "Mistil is just surprised we find her house so attractive."

Doykhid appeared again, wearing a resigned look. "More visitors, madam."

"Show them in," Mistil said faintly. The situation was getting beyond her.

During the next twelve hundred heartbeats a steady stream of women arrived. When the last stragglers had entered, the living room was filled to capacity. Mistil stared around, dazed. There were over eight sixes of them, squeezed on to the sofa, the side chairs, the kitchen chairs, and even a wooden bench the servants had found. She herself was left standing, facing a hundred anxious eyes.

Shandis appointed herself spokeswoman. "You know why we're here, Mistil. If our men were not at work, they would be here too. Tell us what happened last night." There were murmurs of agreement all round.

Mistil heaved a shuddering sigh. Tal would be horrified, but there was no escape.

"Ladies." Her voice quivered. She was crossing a boundary; there would be no return. "I'm going to show you something that will shock you at first. Have patience! Then you'll experience again what you felt last night."

There was a collective sigh of anticipation.

Mistil murmured to Doykhid. The steward's eyes widened, then he nodded and hurried out. A tense silence filled the living room.

Two servants brought a small bench, which they squeezed in next to Mistil. Then Brakhól came running in. He stopped suddenly, gaping at all the visitors. There were murmurs of surprise and a couple of half-spoken questions were cut off by Mistil's raised hand. Finally the alien woman entered, holding her *lhendift*-instrument.

Uproar broke out, many of the women screaming and hiding their faces. Some leapt to their feet and tried to leave, but the crowd was too dense.

"*Wait!*" Mistil called out desperately.

On prior instructions the alien sat at once on the bench and started to play. Brakhól huddled next to her, staring at the turmoil with wide eyes. The alien spoke to him. His face relaxed, and he began to sing. It was a different song this time.

Mistil hardly saw the effect on the audience. Once again her eyes were riveted on her younger son as joy and peace poured out from him. The music plucked cords in her own heart that had lain dormant for decades. Now they rang in harmony with Brakhól's song, and she was consumed with an unbearable yearning to be in the place where he was, to know the peace that he knew.

The song ended, and she wished it would go on forever.

The utter silence was punctuated by an occasional whimper.

Finally Shandis whispered, "Who *is* he?"

Mistil told them the whole story. Not only the ladies heard, but also the crowd of Grûzhileyn servants from all over the suburb who were gathered at the open windows. More Grûzhack ladies arrived, and even a few men, and in deference they were allowed into the house. The passage to the living room quickly filled.

Questions followed, and Shakhere came in with the alien man to answer them. They spoke of the One Creator God, greater even than Makhril; and of his Son, who had lived under Malane, the sky of this world, as a Prince of the flatlanders. It was he who had brought this joy, they said.

Soon the questions coalesced into a single repeated plea: *Sing again!*
Brakhól sang, and the crowd grew.

Chapter 20: *From Prince to King?*

ESTARON WOKE SLOWLY from a ridiculous dream in which he'd been kidnapped and carried off to Selmion. There he'd discovered that the Strongholder was none other than his childhood friend, Konnar!

Bright light was shining in from an eastern window. That was odd. His attic room faced north.

He sat up suddenly and gaped at his surroundings. He was in a luxurious canopied bed with a soft mattress that bounced under him. A silk robe moved smoothly against his skin. The large bedroom was decorated in white and silver, the Selmian royal colours. A maid in royal livery had just pulled aside the window hangings, and he could see a blue-green horizon of sea below a sun-filled sky.

"Can I bring you the dawnmeal, your Highness?" the maid asked in lilting Selmian.

Memory came rushing back. He was in the Strongholder's palace in Orselm. And the Strongholder was indeed his long-lost friend Konnar. And last night, as his final action before parting, Konnar had lifted from him the Curse of Futility, which had blighted his life for the past eight years.

This morning—it was gone. A great weight had lifted from his shoulders. His thoughts were clear, his whole mind and body were bursting with energy. He felt ten years younger. The dark, confining boundaries of tunnel vision, which was the only way he'd survived the curse—limiting his attention to one important objective at a time in a constant struggle to avoid failure—had fallen away. He could hardly believe it.

"The dawnmeal... Yes, please," he said, smiling at the pretty girl. She blushed, steepled her hands, and bowed herself out.

While she was gone he prowled round his new domain. He found an adjoining bathing suite with a sunken marble bath already filled to the brim, and luxuriated in the steaming, aromatic water. When he came out to dress, though, he was annoyed to find that the clothes he'd taken off last night had disappeared. There was only a neat stack of white silk garments in the dressing room beside the bath: raiment for a prince. Muttering under his breath he pulled them on. Konnar was losing no opportunity to nudge him in the direction he wanted.

Catching sight of himself in a tall mirror, he paused. The royal attire, topped off with a white half robe edged in silver, did look good on him. He sighed. This was his birthright. But not as a gift from the Strongholder. He had a lot of thinking to do.

The maid reappeared, accompanied by a couple of footmen carrying trays of steaming food and a tall porcelain jug of chass. All the dinnerware was of antique design and gleamed gold in the sunlight. They must have dug it out of the royal treasury! He shook his head. Konnar over the top again. Yet despite knowing what his friend was up to, he could still hardly believe this was happening to Estaron, the barely-noticed flunky standing in the shadow of the Dûrian Bishop.

The servants laid out the sumptuous dawnmeal on a low table facing the window. There were hot rolls and butter, roasted gamebird and *cayet* slices, two red half-spheres of *miléss* fruit, spiced chass and honey cakes. Estaron thanked them, earning startled glances. The maid gave him a shy smile as she turned to leave.

Before sitting down to the feast he stood at the tall windows. Below the palace hill the grey buildings of Orselm stretched down to the docks, where the masts of many ships could be seen. Beyond them the sea moved gently in the calm of the day. White *galidiyana* hovered and swooped over the harbour, their haunting cries drifting faintly through the window above the background hum of the city.

This was what Konnar had offered him. To rule this city and all of Selmion under Konnar's oversight as Strongholder. When they'd talked later yesterday evening, Konnar had again pleaded earnestly that he would take up the offer. "Just think what we could achieve *together*, Bari! We understand one another so well. You could... tone me down if I go too far; I could give you all the resources you need to be a truly great ruler. And the monarchy would be restored! Just what your branch of the family has worked for for centuries. You would become what you were born to be: King of Selmion!"

It had been hard to stand against Konnar's overwhelming enthusiasm without seeming ungrateful. Somehow he'd managed it, though his friend's disappointment had resulted in another painful flick of the whip. "Konnar, this is... an enormous change for me. I need a few days at least."

Estaron returned to the table and began thoughtfully buttering a roll. *King of Selmion*. That was the problem. It was his rightful title: since his father's death when the Strongholder captured Astenar earlier in the year, the mantle of Heir of Selmion's Renegade Royalty had fallen on him. It was the title Prince Orrénne himself had borne: he was of the same family as the Prince, the younger royal line, which stretched back to the distant past when the elder house had abolished the monarchy and turned to the Cult of Gadesh. Their last king had become the first Strongholder, and the younger house had fled into exile. Centuries later Prince Orrénne had been born; and the younger royal house had barely survived the Strongholder's fury at Orrénne's challenge to his authority. Since then the surviving Renegade Royalty had lived in secret, hiding their titles behind everyday names and occupations.

Yet they had not forgotten who they were. Their Privy Council – the three or four senior princes – met secretly and did what they could to undermine the Strongholder's rule. Which had been little enough until now. Estaron's father – the Heir – had taken his family to Dûrion when the then Strongholder seemed close to discovering their identity. They had made the annual trip to Orselm for his father to meet with the Privy Council.

Then Konnar had disappeared. Sidelined as a loner among his age-mates in Dûrion, Estaron had thrown himself into his Selmian heritage. On the next few annual visits he learnt all he could about Selmian history, traditions and politics, attended meetings of the Privy Council, and spoke to many of the younger generation of Renegade princes.

But the annual visits became too dangerous, and his only outlet had been his studies. With no return to Selmion possible in the foreseeable future, he'd been forced to develop Dûrian ambitions. Those had burned bright until the long string of disappointments he'd suffered under the curse – which had been enough to destroy all his hopes.

But now Konnar had reawakened them. To be king... to set his own agenda and have others carry it out... to restore Selmion to the gracious kingdom it had once been... All his newly-released energies craved that freedom – though he could never accept it on Konnar's terms. That would be a travesty and a betrayal of the Renegade Royalty whose Heir he was.

Estaron took up a golden knife and forked spoon and started on the tender gamebird and sliced *cayet*. They were served in a spicy sauce, and tasted good. He found he was hungry; he hadn't eaten much last night.

Yet Konnar had not forgotten their boyhood dream of exercising good governance together. The earnestness with which he had reaffirmed that ideal last night had impressed Estaron. The adult Konnar was a complex and confusing character. Despite all the evil he was clearly involved in as Strongholder, it seemed that those early longings had not all died. And he was inviting Estaron to play a part in bringing them to fruition. Maybe there was a rôle for him to play here. Not as King, obviously. But as… Governor, perhaps? That was something he needed to give more thought to.

But there was also the matter of mindbending, the scourge of the age. As Strongholder, Konnar was at the very pinnacle of that vicious system. Yet his joy at finding Estaron, and at the renewal of their friendship, revealed an underlying desire for good that could perhaps be built upon. Konnar had admitted last night that stocks of teméyn were dwindling fast due to the Grûzhack war; there were only about two months' supply left throughout the Dûrai region. *And when the teméyn went, mindbending would go too.*

What would become of Konnar then? If Estaron were ruler of Selmion, perhaps their rôles would be reversed, and he could offer Konnar a position where his experience would come in useful. Maybe the shock of such a total loss of power would turn his heart to the one true God. Last night's conversation had encouraged Estaron to believe that despite the dark stereotype of 'Strongholder' that he embodied, his old friend was not beyond redemption.

But that remained to be seen. In the meantime, as Governor (or whatever), Estaron could make Selmion a better place by curbing the Mindbenders' powers and replacing tyranny with justice. And maybe—just maybe—realising their boyhood dreams together might open Konnar's eyes to the fundamental wickedness of the system that had brought him to power.

Of course all of this would mean abandoning his Dûrian friends in their time of need. Going over to the enemy, from their perspective. That did not sit well with him. But did he really have a choice? What would Konnar do if he flatly refused his offer? His friend had brushed that question aside last night. But the kidnapping indicated that he'd had a darker goal before discovering that Estaron was his long-lost friend: a goal which no doubt included mindbending and the destruction of the Renegade Royalty. A shiver ran down his spine.

However he was inclined to believe, for the moment, that Konnar would keep his promise and not mindbend him if he refused the offer. The delight of finding each other was too fresh. But to allow him simply to return to his old life in Dûrion? Never. Both for political and personal reasons, Konnar would keep him at his side. Perhaps find him some sinecure in the palace and dress him up like that carnival king at the door last night. Estaron's toes curled.

He heaved a sigh. He was here for the duration. Might as well do what good he could in the position Konnar was offering him. In any case it would only be until the teméyn ran out: two months. Then everything would be different. Maybe the Renegade Royalty would come into its own, restoring order in the inevitable chaos; and Selmion would at last have its true king.

Estaron smiled at his own wishful thinking. But if he accepted Konnar's offer he would insist on informing the Dûrian leadership that he was safe. He owed them that much, at least.

And he must think about getting a message to the Renegade Privy Council—without Konnar's knowledge, if he could manage it.

* * *

"So, Bari, what's it to be?"

Another day of luxurious living had passed. Estaron and Konnar were sitting on a marble bench in one of the outside colonnades overlooking the palace grounds. Well-kept lawns dotted with flowerbeds swept downhill to tall trees that hid the surrounding city. Only a distant rumble betrayed its presence.

Estaron looked at his friend, whose face was gravely attentive. "I've decided to accept your offer."

Konnar broke into a broad grin. "I knew you would!"

"I'm glad our old ideals of good governance are still important to you; I want to work with you to make them a reality."

"This will be a dream come true, Bari! Let's start by—"

"But—"

Konnar's grin faded.

"—not with the title 'King'."

Konnar's eyes hardened. "Why not? That's what you are."

"Yes, I know, but... please try to understand. My family has always had a high view of the Selmian monarchy. I could not call myself 'King of Selmion' if my actions were subject to your oversight. And I don't think it would be good for *you* to have a 'King' under you in Selmion, whose title implied he could do anything he liked. It might cast doubt on your own authority."

"You would be king of Selmion only. I rule *all* the Dûrai nations."

Including Dûrion? Estaron felt a stirring of unease. He pushed it aside. "Exactly. So you could overrule me if I made a decision you disagreed with. But don't you see, that's inconsistent with calling me 'King'? Call me 'Governor', 'Lieutenant', anything you like... Just not 'King'."

Konnar gazed at him for a long moment through slitted eyes. Then his face relaxed, and the boyish grin was back. "Dear old humble Bari! You never let on that you were a prince, and now you won't accept the title 'King'! Oh well, 'Governor' you shall be, then."

Estaron let out a breath he hadn't realised he'd been holding.

"Now," Konnar continued, "are there any other conditions you want to impose before we make the formal announcement?"

Estaron shifted uncomfortably on the hard marble bench. "Only... two. First, I need to send a message to my friends in Dûrion. Just to let them know I'm safe. No other details are necessary."

Konnar nodded. "And the other?"

"It's been many years since I visited Selmion, and I'd really like to reacquaint myself with the country before an announcement is made." He continued hurriedly as he saw the thunder clouds re-gathering on his friend's brow. "It needn't take long—no more than a month. You yourself could show me any current projects I'd have to take over, and you could assign people to bring me up-to-date on recent events, explain government procedures, and so on. Right now I know so little I could easily make unwise decisions and embarrass us both."

There was a tense pause as Konnar's cold eyes bored into Estaron's.

Finally he heaved an exaggerated sigh. "You really must get over this secretarial mentality, Bari. You'll have others to worry about methods and procedures. But, alright, to keep you happy... three weeks. Not a day longer. Now—chass and sherili cakes!"

Estaron matched Konnar's sudden grin, but his smile faded as he followed him back into the palace. Had he made the right decision? Only time would tell. One thing was certain: Working with the new Konnar would not be easy.

* * *

Konnar smiled back at Estaron as he left the small reclining room where they'd enjoyed their chass and sherili cakes. He relaxed on the recliner and closed his eyes. How differently this had all turned out from what he'd expected!

His original plan had been simple: to kidnap this unknown 'Estaron'—the Dûrian alias of Prince Nomariu Tarenida, the Renegade Heir; bring him to Orselm; then, after extracting the necessary information from him—either by mindbending or mindreading (neither of which could be done at a distance), to kill him along with the rest of the Renegades.

True, the Renegade Royalty had only been a minor thorn in the flesh until now. Their peculiar structure, with small independent groups that knew virtually nothing about each other, had prevented him and his predecessors from apprehending the ringleaders. But the threat they posed was so small that no one had tried very hard. And as long as 'Estaron' was working for Shambor, Konnar had been happy to leave him be. The Curse of Futility was keeping him in check.

But with those upstart Restorers killing Shambor and precipitating the Grûzhack war, the Renegades in Selmion had stepped up their subversive activities, burning teméyn stocks and attacking caravans. They might well be planning to bring their Heir back to foment a rebellion while Konnar's forces were otherwise occupied; and he'd thought to forestall that.

Then Nomariu, alias 'Estaron' in Dûrion, had turned out to be Bari—his former everyday name in Selmion! The shock was huge, and at a single stroke all Konnar's plans had collapsed. There was no way he could mindbend, much less kill, *Bari*: the only true friend he'd ever had, whom he'd thought of and longed to find again all this time! Never. Konnar had not invaded Bari's mind as a child, and he would not do so now—not even for a harmless, superficial mind-reading.

The Renegades would have to wait. He'd found real companionship again; and after years of loneliness he was not about to throw that precious gift away.

It had been some rapid on-the-spot thinking that had given him the idea of sharing authority with Bari. Not his wider power as Strongholder, of course: but ruling Selmion, which had always been their childhood dream. He'd delighted in his ability to offer his best friend the title that was his due, and to lift the curse he had unknowingly inflicted on him eight years ago.

It hurt him a little that Bari had been unwilling to accept his true title. Time had changed him — changed them both. After many years of secretarial servitude apparently all Bari wanted was to be a lowly 'Governor'. Well, maybe he would start aspiring to higher things as time went by.

The big question, though, was whether he would make the break with his Renegade and Lightist connections. Konnar could only hope he would remain loyal to their friendship.

If not… a world of pain lay ahead for them both.

Chapter 21: *Triumph in Carlis*

SHIVÁN FLAILED HELPLESSLY under the dead weight of the warrior he'd just killed. He was pinned underwater against the sloping floor of the ferry ramp. The seven-foot Grûzhack was covered in tempered steel armour, and felt like a ton of bricks. Shiván heaved on the shaped shoulder pieces with all his might, lifting the torso an inch or two. Then he lost his grip and the body fell back on his rib cage, forcing precious air from his mouth.

Shiván's lungs screamed for breath, his eyeballs felt ready to pop, and his mind was darkening. *God... help!* He heaved again, but his strength was failing. On the point of passing out, he felt a foot ram into his side, then sudden turbulence as someone stumbled over the two of them. The weight on his chest shifted, and with a convulsive movement Shiván jerked himself free. A moment later he had staggered to his feet and was sucking air into his mouth with great gasps between coughing spasms.

"Keldon hallár! Aténnelor!" A Dûrian officer steadied him with his hands. "Overguardian, are you all right?" Shiván saw that the remaining Grûzhack had been driven further down the ramp. All around them Dûrian soldiers were wading towards the last of the fighting.

Cârin suddenly appeared, pushing himself between the officer and Shiván. "I'll see to the Overguardian."

"What happened?" he hissed when the officer had left. "I mind my own business for a few heartbeats, and you vanish!"

"He fell on me— I went under..."

"This battle is over for you," Câr declared firmly. With a hand in the small of Shiván's back he propelled him up the ramp. Shiván didn't try to resist. The Ambon's influence had faded; to carry on now would be suicidal.

Once out of the water Shiván stopped and looked around. The Grûzhack cannon had fallen silent. There was no sign of any barges— the two at the ferry landing must have been sunk. The last few warriors were fighting to their deaths in the bloodied water between the walls of the ramp.

"We stopped them!" Cârin said, a smouldering light in his eyes.

"No thanks to me," Shiván muttered. He turned and walked toward the ruins of eastern Stillárre.

* * *

Early next morning the Grûzhack bombardment started again. The range of the cannon had been increased, raining destruction on previously undamaged areas of the city. Shiván ignored the general pandemonium and made his way to the old, grey Hearth building on the city square, which was mercifully out of reach of the Grû-zhack cannon. Walking to the front he knelt at the altar beneath the gleaming gold and silver Ambon.

"Dear Prince, you know how grateful I am that your Ambon has been clearing my mind. But you see how weak I am when I'm away from it. You sent me to Dûrion to be your Overguardian. To lead and encourage your people. But if that officer hadn't tripped over me yesterday, I would have drowned. Not because I'm a bad swordsman — Cârin has taught me well — but because I lost concentration. Because I was away from the Ambon.

"I feel so weak and useless. Do I have to carry on like this?"

For a long time he was silent, staring up at the Ambon, quieting his mind to hear the Prince's voice. The continuous roar and crash of the cannonade and the urgent cries of people outside faded into the background. In the silence of the Hearth he seemed to hear a softly-spoken response: *Be glad you're weak.*

Shiván blinked. "What?"

Because my power is made perfect in weakness.

"Oh!"

That's what Jesus had said to Paul when the apostle had pleaded to have his mysterious 'thorn in the flesh' removed.

The quiet voice of the Prince of Peace continued. *Don't rely on the Ambon of Sûrilane. Don't rely on the Blade of Darthane. Rely on me. I have used those instruments to help you carry a heavy burden. But I am the One who is strengthening you. And I will continue to strengthen you, even when every instrument fails.*

Slowly the truth sank in and relief flooded Shiván's heart. The more he thought and prayed, the more he realised that God *had* been strengthening him — ever since that night outside Starmane when the grey mist had descended on his mind. He'd learnt to concentrate really hard before making decisions. He'd re-learnt the technique of

173

thinking on the bright side and trusting God that had brought him through the severe depression of his teenage years. He'd pulled himself back many times from the slippery slope that led to despair. With no sense of pride he knew that he'd succeeded in living an almost normal life in circumstances where many others would have gone under.

But recently he'd been relying too heavily on the Ambon and the Blade. In a solemn moment he pledged himself to trust the Prince without them. The Blade, to him, would be an ordinary sword. The Ambon might still be a channel of God's comfort and clarity when he was in its presence; but when he left he would no longer count off the hours until the effect faded. He would trust the Prince to let it last as long as it was needed.

The hour of the midmeal passed. Chaos continued outside. Several people rushed into the Hearth and out again, but Shiván remained where he was. Perrely brought him some food. He tried to explain what the Prince was showing him; and though she obviously didn't understand, her sympathy was comforting.

As he thought and prayed through the afternoon a clearer picture gradually emerged. He would still lose focus away from the Ambon, but the intervals before that happened would steadily increase. He had to work and fight normally as Overguardian. The Prince would give him the clarity needed on a task-by-task basis. His part was to keep on trusting. A conviction grew in him that God was preparing him for an even greater challenge that lay ahead. He shuddered to think what could be greater than this; but, as his old King James Bible put it, *sufficient unto the day is the evil thereof*. If God could take care of today, he could also take care of tomorrow.

That evening a message came from Gwargif, whose warriors were still patrolling the northern bank of the Carreck. The Grûzhack had assembled another flotilla of boats at Rosten, further upstream. All the signs were that they would cross the river tomorrow. Shiván insisted on joining the force that went to assist his old friend, who had gathered the Dorbian Legion together at Carlis on the opposite shore.

* * *

The Dûrians reached the village in the grey light of early dawn. A heavy mist hung over the river and shrouded all but the nearest houses; it would disperse later. But from the number of stone buildings and thatched cottages that showed dimly through the haze as they moved down the main street, Shiván could see that Carlis was quite a large place. There was a sizeable inn, a weaver's house, a smithy. All the inhabitants had fled, however; a heavy silence hung over the empty buildings. It felt like a ghost town as they walked down the paved road, many cobbled alleyways vanishing into the gloom on either side. They crossed the central square, dominated by a substantial Hearth building, their footsteps making a dull echo that was quickly absorbed by the mist.

At the waterfront a single pier stretched out into the river, empty of any moored craft. The rest of the waterline consisted of a paved embankment and a pebble beach. The beach was packed with the shaggy, grey-white forms of the Dorbian Legion, making a surreal scene. Shiván, Garset and Cârin pushed their way through to the pier, where Gwargif was standing.

"Father of Warriors, you have come!" The great wolf-like creature had a broad smile on his intelligent face. He raised a six-fingered paw and clasped Shiván's outstretched hand. "Is today we fight together again!"

"Just don't let him into the water, High Commander," Câr said.

Gwargif's brow creased in a puzzled frown. "Warrior Father want to swim?"

Shiván laughed. "No—that's Cârin's little joke. I nearly drowned in the battle on Stillárre docks."

"Which is why you shouldn't be fighting in the ranks, Overguardian," Garset said heavily. He turned to Gwargif. "High Commander, you are in charge here. On behalf of the Bishop's Council I'm requesting that the Overguardian be restricted to a command rôle."

Gwargif regarded him thoughtfully for a moment. Then he looked at Shiván. "Shining One tell you bring sword and fight?"

"Yes."

The Dorbian leader turned back to Garset. "*Hrarborgh* say he fight. He Father of all Warriors for Shining One. Gwargif obey."

A look of resignation settled on the long lines of Garset's face. He bowed his head and left.

"Thanks, old friend," Shiván said.

There was a smile in Gwargif's eyes. "Is people of Doorin is love you, is not want you dead. But for Dorbi, best-loved leader is fight in front, not behind. Today is great day for Dorbi—Father of Warriors is lead Legion! Is every warrior is fight better today. Warrior who die, others tell family he die for *Hrarborgh*. Then family is glad, and dead warrior have great praise."

Shiván felt tears prick his eyelids.

"And if *Hrarborgh* die leading Dorbi, then is every warrior fight till all enemy dead, or all Dorbi dead. When story come home to Dorbai, is told to children's children's children." Gwargif's gaze was fixed earnestly on Shiván. He lowered his voice. "Shining One send you. *Lead* today. *Be* Warrior Father."

"I will," Shiván managed.

Gwargif left to speak to his officers. Shiván stood staring over the mist-shrouded river, overwhelmed by the Dorbians' vote of confidence. They knew he'd not been himself for a long time, but it made no difference. He was their 'Father of Warriors', and they would die for him. He squared his shoulders. *Prince, make me worthy of their loyalty.*

Cârin was watching him with a quizzical expression. "So, what now, Warrior Papa?"

"I've been given the rôle, so I'd better fill it."

"Uh-oh."

He stood on the pier with Câr, thinking. *If I were the Grûzhack commander, how would I plan this attack?* The Grûzhack had failed at the Stillárre docks. Why? Mainly because of the rain of fire from the Dûrian longbows, which reached their boats before either their own archers or their musketmen were in range. The result was that several boats capsized and many warriors landed in the river; and they inflicted very little damage on the Dûrians before reaching the wharf. Which in most places stood high out of the water, giving the unharmed defenders an unbeatable advantage.

So if he were the Grûzhack commander, how would he correct those errors now? Well, there was no high wharf at Carlis, so that problem fell away. What about the Dûrian longbows? The Grûzhack obviously didn't have any, or they would have used them. How would they avoid a repeat of the rain of fire? Garset had brought longbowmen, buckets of pitch and burning coals for exactly that purpose. The Grûzhack might try a roof of overlapping shields on each boat; but then they couldn't use their bows or muskets before landing. Could they try and come in very fast? No, hardly practical with such a miscellaneous collection of boats. The element of surprise...?

The mist!

Shiván froze. They'd taken it for granted that the Grûzhack would wait for the mist to rise. But what if they didn't...? His mind whirled. Then he charged off the pier, almost knocking Cârin into the water.

"*Gwargif!*" The Dorbian commander was sitting on his haunches nearby, speaking with his lieutenants. The great, wolf-like head whipped round. "Take your warriors out of the village and surround it. *Now!*"

After a startled pause Gwargif barked orders, and the grey-white sea began pouring off the beach. On the raised embankment Garset was overseeing the archers' preparations. He turned, frowning. With Gwargif loping beside him Shiván ran up to the Dûrian Marshal. "Garset, the Grûzhack flotilla will be arriving any minute. Forget the fire-arrows. Your longbowmen must be ready to shoot a normal volley the instant they appear — then run for their lives and join the Dorbians outside the village."

"But the mist —"

"The Grûzhack will use it to hide their approach! Tell your infantry cohort to come with me. I have a plan for them."

"Overguardian, they'll be needed —"

A low growl rumbled in Gwargif's throat. "*Hrarborgh* speaks."

"Lord Marshal, *now*. There's no time to discuss it."

Garset's lips tightened, but he gave the order. A hundred troopers filed after Shiván as he hurried with Cârin into the misty streets of Carlis. Gwargif loped off to organise the Legion. Shiván gathered the men in the central square and outlined his plan. The idea was new, but they were all familiar with the village, and they took to it enthusiastically. They dispersed in patrols of ten into the surrounding alleyways.

Cârin nodded appreciatively. "Good thinking, Overguardian."

"Pray that it lasts."

"Oh, I will, don't you worry. Otherwise I'll be the one pulling you out of trouble again."

They trotted back down the main street to a point where they could see the bowmen lining the embankment and the river beyond. Was the mist thinning a little? Shiván prayed it would linger just another fifteen or twenty minutes.

The minutes went by. The mist remained, but no shapes appeared in it. No soft splashing of oars. *Dear Prince, have I got it wrong?* The assurance came at once. *Wait.*

They waited. The line of archers stirred restlessly. Low murmurs were stilled by *Hssts* from the officers. Several glanced back into the village. Shiván saw Garset shaking his head. His heart sank.

Then a watery rustling sound made itself heard from the river. All along the line the archers straightened. At a murmured command they raised their bows, arrows already nocked. Muscular arms drew the strings back. The bows bent and tension filled the air as everyone waited.

Dim shapes appeared in the mist, drifting almost noiselessly towards them. Boats' prows and the blunt ends of barges and rafts became clear. A teal-coated lookout materialised on the nearest prow, eyes widening as he took in the long line of poised bows. His mouth opened, but before he could shout, Garset yelled *"Fire!"*

The twang of released bowstrings and whiz of arrows filled the air. At such close range the archers could hardly miss. A cacophony of deep-throated yells broke out, and many of the boats began rocking. One overturned as it emerged from the mist, fouling those alongside. But two rafts and a barge were stable, though fallen bodies lay among those standing on the decks. At a shouted command muskets leapt to teal-coated shoulders.

The Dûrian archers had not hung about, but were scrambling to safety among the houses as fast as they could. Shiván and Cârin were running up the main street as the guns roared. Cries from behind showed that not all the archers had made it.

While Garset and the archers' captain herded their men out of the village, Shiván and Cârin darted down an alley near the central square, where they joined the infantry lieutenant and the first of the ten-man patrols. In the lane opposite a hand was raised in salute. The second patrol was ready. Both patrols faded back into the misty depths between the houses.

Not long afterwards came the slap of sandals on the main street. As Shiván had anticipated, the Grûzhack hadn't sent any scouts ahead. Street warfare was unknown to them. They probably still thought the mist was in their favour.

The slapping of feet grew louder. The Dûrian lieutenant's eyes were on Shiván. All the men had drawn their swords. Shiván held the Blade loosely in his left hand. The first rank of Grûzhack warriors went trotting past their alley. As the second appeared, Shiván leapt forward yelling, "_For the Prince!_"

The cry was echoed behind him, across the street, and in eight other places. The Grûzhack column broke up in chaos as the warriors turned different ways, hindering each other as they tried to bring their weapons to bear. Shiván sent the Blade scything into a warrior who had dropped his musket and was trying to draw his sword. With a gurgling cry he collapsed.

Shiván yanked his weapon free and pushed forward, making way for the Dûrians behind him. At the same time the infantry from the second patrol were attacking the Grûzhack from the opposite side. Those in the middle didn't know which way to turn. But their officers were shouting frantic orders, and they were starting to find their weapons. "_Withdraw!_" Shiván yelled.

The Dûrians darted back into the shadows of the alleys. When the Grûzhack followed, Shiván, Cârin and a couple of others led them on, shouting fake commands and making plenty of noise, while the rest of the patrol slipped into side lanes and made hit-and-run attacks as the Grûzhack passed by. Soon the enemy were hopelessly split up and confused, small groups blundering through the dark alleyways. They ended up attacking each other as often as the Dûrians.

After eluding their pursuers, Shiván and his companions stopped to catch their breath in a narrow lane. He looked upward. The mist was lifting — time to leave. He stood up and yelled, "_Out! Out! Out!_" Câr and the troopers joined in, and across the village others took up the pre-arranged cry. Then they slipped silently through the alleys, avoiding the Grûzhack, until they reached open fields. There the rest of cohort quickly joined them. Of the original hundred, well over eighty had survived.

They all took a moment to clean their swords on the grass at the edge of the field, which was planted with _farn_ grain. The graceful, half-grown plants reached knee-height. About four hundred paces away through the thinning mist they could see a line of grey-white shapes.

"To the Legion!" Shiván shouted. He and his companions charged across the field leaving a flattened path in their wake. Clusters of disorganised Grûzhack began emerging from the village behind them.

An ominous, rumbling growl spread along the Dorbian line. *Oh no,* Shiván thought. *Don't let them mistake us for Grûzhack!* "This is Shiván!" he shouted, but his voice seemed to fall dead on the still air. A quick glance behind showed the longer-legged Grûzhack gaining on them. "*Faster!*" he yelled to his companions.

Now the mist was rapidly lifting. "*Hrarborgh!*" a wolf-warrior cried, and a swelling shout of recognition rose from the Dorbian ranks. Shiván and his troopers reached the front line and turned to face the Grûzhack—who had come to a sudden stop. A command rang out, and arrows rained down on the enemy from the Dûrian archers ranged behind the Legion. Many teal tunics fell into the young grain.

Before the Grûzhack could recover and raise their muskets Shiván swept the Blade of Darthane aloft.

"*Cha-a-arge!*" he bellowed at the top of his voice.

With a deafening roar the Dorbians leapt forward, Shiván in the forefront with the Blade raised high. He didn't know where the strength came from… —or rather, he did. *Thank you!*

As they crashed in among the enemy, Shiván found himself applying the techniques he'd learnt in martial arts: thinking of himself as 'water', flowing with the enemy's battle style, sliding away from their blows with skilled footwork, throwing them off with sudden changes in body posture. One teal-coated warrior after another fell under the Blade, until with a shock Shiván realised there were none left. The fields around Carlis were littered with teal and green-coated bodies. They had destroyed every last one of the invaders.

A great cry of triumph erupted from the throats of both Dorbians and Dûrians. Gwargif and Garset came over to Shiván, and the Lord Marshal clasped his hand and raised it high. "Overguardian, forgive me. You have more than proved yourself today." Shiván could only nod.

Gwargif's eyes were bright. "You are *Hrarborgh*! You fight better than *hrar*, than warriors; better even than *Hrarkhez*, the High Commander! Dorbi never forget this day, when Father of Warriors show children how to fight!"

He turned to the Dorbians gathered all around. "*Hrarborgh dakhran!*"

"*Hrarborgh dakhran!*" The ground quivered.

Gwargif led Shiván to a huge Dorbian and spoke a few words. A smile split the warrior's face, and he lowered himself to the ground. Gwargif gestured at the broad back. "You ride Hmengiz to city."

"What! No, Gwargif, I—"

"Is special honour for him. He save life of Gwargif today. You say no, he have no praise."

Shiván stared at the Dorbian leader.

"Nothing for it, Hero," Cârin murmured at his side. "That's your reward, so you'd better enjoy it. Just don't fall off." There was a broad grin on his face.

Chapter 22: *Changing rôles*

THE VOICE FROM BARAZHÂN WAS FAINT, but Lannie would be able to hear what 'Neesh was saying if the others would stop shuffling and murmuring. It was evening, and they were all crowded together on a recliner in one of the small reading rooms in the Stillárre Domicile. Lannie was clutching the turquoise bess two-handed to her right ear and feeling irritable.

She rounded on them for the third time. "*Quiet,* for crying out loud!"

"Yes, Ma'am!" Shiván threw a mock salute. He'd been insufferable since riding into town on a Dorbian's back earlier today.

"… hundreds of them, all round the house," 'Neesh's distant voice was saying. Lannie asked her to start again.

Finally she had enough to tell the others. "Danîsha's been playing the bellaril and Brakhól's been singing. Hundreds of the neighbours have been coming to hear him, and the authorities aren't too happy about it."

"Are they going to be arrested?" Jomel asked anxiously.

"We don't know yet, do we?" Lannie retorted.

"But the parents have accepted Danîsha and Gelmion now," Perrely said. "They'll look after them, won't they?"

"Do you want to sit here guessing, or do you want more news?"

Shivvie held out his hand. "Let me have a word." She gave him the bess gladly.

"'Neesh, it's me, Shiván. We'll ask the One to protect you folks. Yes … Yes … Well, we won an important battle today… *Im-por-tant — bat-tle…*"

Lannie switched off. She looked round the small, book-lined reading room and heaved a sharp sigh. She felt depressed — and that was triggering her irritability. The other Restorers were all doing something useful — even Gil! Shivvie seemed to have got over his muddled thinking and had done wonders on the battlefield today. 'Neesh was playing a crucial rôle accompanying Brakhól up in Bara-zhân. Gil, according to 'Neesh, had been a tower of strength, and was now actually answering questions from the Grûzhack about the Lightist faith!

And Lannie? In the chaos that was now Stillárre there was no place for subtle legal judgments. But she was a career girl, and this was the alternative career she'd carved out for herself in Dûrion. Now it had vanished overnight: no one called at the Domicile any longer asking deferentially if Alanya *Atémban* could come and resolve a dispute or break a deadlock between opposing parties. She was simply no longer required.

There was only one other thing she could do in this world, so she'd offered Garset the hard-won archery skills she'd developed with the shortbow over the winter. In the politest possible way he'd told her there was no place for her among his trained and experienced longbowmen. Shiván and his Blade was apparently welcome to help fight off the Grûzhack, despite his recent unreliability; but not Alanya and her short bow.

So instead she was helping with relief work and tending the wounded — along with hundreds of other non-combatants. If one day she didn't turn up at the makeshift care centres, no one would miss her.

Oh, to be back in Birmingham in the twenty-first century, entertaining Matt in my own little flat far away from all this madness!

She felt more like a fifth wheel on the wagon than at any time since arriving in Dûrion.

* * *

Estaron walked slowly through the palace grounds towards the marble bench and table where he and Konnar usually had their afternoon chass together.

Four days had passed since he'd accepted his friend's offer to become Governor of Selmion, and he was trying to make the best of the three-week handover period Konnar had grudgingly allowed. During the past four days he'd had free run of the palace, and had talked to several of the senior dignitaries: large, ornately-dressed Gedoriu, the palace major-domo, who had been in the foyer when he arrived; Otaru, Konnar's secretary — a slimy little man with an ingratiating smile that Estaron immediately mistrusted; and three senior Mindbenders on Konnar's personal staff.

Talking to the Mindbenders had grated on his nerves like an ungreased wagon wheel. Their kind had been his family's enemies for centuries past; treating them like colleagues and asking their advice went against every grain in his body — despite his years of rubbing shoulders with their counterparts as Shambor's secretary in Dûrion.

But Konnar's Mindbenders, like everyone else, had treated him with elaborate respect while saying nothing about the practicalities of running the country. Estaron had begun to realise that there was little or no structure in place: government was at the whim of the ruler, from Konnar at the top down to the lowliest district Mindbender. To say there was a lot of work to be done was an epic understatement.

He'd met at least once a day with Konnar—usually in the afternoons for chass & sherili cakes; but Konnar had avoided talking about government policy or practice, focusing instead on specific, small-scale wrongs that could be righted. That seemed to be the idea of 'good governance' that he'd gained from their boyhood days. Estaron had tried to broaden his thinking, without much success. Maybe today would be different...

That hope was dashed when Konnar came trotting towards him across the lawn, dressed in a sky-blue tunic and breeches and a broad grin. "Race you to the table," he cried, breaking into a sprint. Estaron found himself smiling in response, and set off half-heartedly after him.

They sat, panting a little, at the marble table where chass and sherili cakes had been laid out. "Remember how we used to race each other to our hideout?" Konnar said. "I always got there first."

"So you did. You haven't lost that ability. But you have lost your stammer."

"Yes. That was one good thing mindbending did for me—as you would say."

"You lost the stammer when you were first mindbent?"

"No, no. I was never mindbent."

"What? I thought all members of the Cult of Gadesh were mindbent before they became Mindbenders?"

"Normally, yes. They couldn't mindbend me, though."

"Really?"

"Nah. I was too strong for them." Konnar grinned as he bit into a sherili cake.

Estaron stared at his friend, eyebrows raised. So Konnar was a real prodigy. Well, he'd always known it, but he hadn't realised his powers were *that* strong. No wonder he'd risen so fast in the Cult of Gadesh.

Konnar laughed. "Anyway. We must go to the hideout again one day! It will look a lot smaller now, I expect. I wonder if our things are still there? The table—the lamp—your leather wallet—those story books... They will have fallen apart now. Remember the time we raced to the cave, and you had chass and sherili cakes in your bag, and when we opened it there was just this horrible pink mush at the bottom?"

Estaron chuckled.

They reminisced a little longer, then Estaron brought the conversation back to the present. "I wanted to ask about that letter I wrote to the Dûrian leadership telling them I'm alive and well: do you know if it's been delivered?"

"Oh yes, I had a report yesterday. It was carried in a racer to Dûrion and slipped under the front door of the Travelling Order's Domicile in Stillárre."

"Thank you." It was good of Konnar to have gone to that trouble.

Mention of the Domicile brought back bitter-sweet memories, and Estaron was silent for a moment. Konnar would of course have read his letter; but he'd taken that into account and kept it brief, saying only that he was alive and well, but could not return. He hoped they would read coercion between the lines, and not betrayal. But in either case they would be deeply worried. They would work out that he'd been taken to Selmion, and fear that he'd been mindbent and revealed all their secrets to the Strongholder. He asked the One to give them peace.

"On another matter," he said to Konnar, who was watching him with grave friendliness. "I've been speaking to various members of your staff here in the palace—about government procedures, and so on—"

"I know," Konnar interrupted with a grin. "I've heard all about your barrage of questions."

"I hope I'm not hindering their work."

"No, no. Most of them can do with being made to think."

Estaron returned his friend's smile. "But I would also like to visit various places in Orselm and elsewhere—one or two of the trading houses; the customs facilities at the port; a horse farm; the depots for road repair; and so on—to familiarise myself with conditions in the country. Would you have any problem with that?"

"Of course not!" Konnar declared expansively. "I'll give you an escort whenever needed, and you'll have immediate access to whatever places or individuals you want to see."

Estaron's reply was forestalled by a sudden rapt look on Konnar's face as his eyes lost their focus. He'd long been familiar with the signs of mindspeech, and waited patiently until the eyes sharpened again. "Sorry!" Konnar exclaimed. "I have to go now. Remember: dinner in the small dining room tonight. I'll see you then." He hurried off with a final grin and a wave.

Estaron sat for a while, pondering Konnar's response about leaving the palace. The mention of an escort was significant. As Governor-Designate of Selmion, of course, an escort would be his right according to protocol. But what would happen if he waived that right?

All the palace staff knew who he was — including the gate guards, he was sure. He decided to pay them a visit.

He strolled down the winding, well-paved carriageway through the trees to the main entrance of the palace. Beyond the high bars of the double gate he could see a bustling street, with hawkers shouting their wares, carriages rattling over the cobbles, runners trotting past carrying messages from one business house to another. A strong desire possessed him to join that throng of humanity; to be out of this luxurious prison.

Two soldiers in the white and silver uniform of the Royal Guard were on duty, standing on either side of the gate, which was locked and barred. Both came to attention as he approached. He walked up to the one on the left, who looked slightly older. The man gave a smart hand-on-heart salute, staring straight ahead.

"You know who I am?"

"Yes, your Highness."

"Will you open the gate, please? I wish to go out."

There was a long pause. The guard's eyes moved unwillingly to meet Estaron's. He cleared his throat. "Ah... Apologies, your Highness. Standing orders. All outside trips must have prior approval from the Strongholder."

Estaron nodded. "I see. Very well, carry on."

"Highness." Again the salute, eyes once more at the regulation angle, straight ahead.

Estaron turned and strolled back up the carriageway. Yes. He would need Konnar's escort. Ostensibly to guard him; but in reality, to watch what he did and make sure he came back.

And with an escort looking over his shoulder, how could he achieve his other immediate goal, to get a message to the Renegade leaders? He was their Heir: rumours would already be circulating about a prince in the palace; what would his Renegade uncles and cousins be thinking? And especially, what would they think when their Heir was announced as the Strongholder's governor of Selmion? Betrayal was the least of it.

Konnar seemed to be underestimating how strong his allegiance to the Renegades still was; maybe he thought it had been destroyed by the curse. In any case, Estaron had no intention of enlightening him. That was one area where their aims would always differ.

He had to get a message to his great-uncle, the Prince Regent. He knew where to send it: he had long ago had to memorise the everyday names and addresses behind which the Privy Council hid their true identities. But if he couldn't leave the palace without an escort, he would have to find some other way of getting it delivered — without Konnar's knowledge.

That would take some doing.

* * *

Konnar listened to the Guard captain's report and closed the mind-link. Then he leaned back on the recliner in his well-appointed study and considered this latest development.

While the joy of being with Bari again was still fresh, the whole basis of the relationship had changed. Whereas in their boyhood Bari had been the leader and Konnar the dependent (and how very dependent he'd been!), now it was the opposite way round — and the adjustment was hard for them both.

Like Bari assuming he could simply walk out of the palace gates whenever he liked. Even Konnar's closest associates could not do that! Perhaps in time Konnar would have enough confidence in Bari's loyalty to allow him that freedom; but the years apart had robbed them of the unquestioning trust they'd once had in each other. He, Konnar, had become Strongholder; and Bari had become a Dûrian Lightist — besides being the Renegade Heir. They could hardly be further apart on the political and religious divide.

He still didn't know whether Bari valued their friendship more than his former political and religious allegiances; whether, if allowed the freedom to leave, he'd stick with his best friend or return to his best friend's enemies. That doubt gnawed at him constantly. He wanted to trust Bari, but he couldn't; not yet.

Bari would have to earn that trust.

* * *

The next day Estaron met Mindbender Belyeru in one of the palace corridors, Konnar's head of personal staff, whom he hadn't spent time with yet: a slightly portly man with a smooth face and small pig-like eyes. They pressed their right palms together in the Selmian greeting; and Estaron steeled himself for a chat. They settled themselves in a small reclining room nearby.

Belyeru looked Estaron over, a smile hovering around his lips. "You are looking very well, your Highness."

Estaron felt his eyebrows rise as he murmured, "Thank you."

Belyeru hastened to explain. "I am aware of the curse your Highness was under before your arrival at the palace. I was with his Supremacy the Strongholder when it was cast several years ago."

"Eight years ago," Estaron murmured. "I am grateful to him for lifting it."

"Indeed yes. It must be a great relief to you."

"It is," Estaron admitted, wondering when he could turn the conversation to more relevant matters.

"Forgive me for saying so, your Highness, but I don't know if you are aware of how mild your sufferings were under that particular curse. Comparatively!" he repeated, raising a finger as Estaron's brows drew together in a frown. "I know you had many setbacks which must have been devastating at the time. But we are talking here about the Curse of Futility: the most powerful sanction that has ever been developed in the Realm of the Mind.

"The Curse was cast on you from Orselm, a great distance from where you were in Dûrion; and not on your person (which was then unknown to us), only on your office as Renegade Heir. That it had any effect at all under those circumstances is surprising. That it had as much effect as it did, is truly amazing—and a tribute to his Supremacy's mental powers." Belyeru paused, his sharp little eyes intent.

Estaron rose to the bait. "What would the effect have been if I had been known to you, and living in Orselm?"

The Mindbender shook his head. "Oh, your Highness. You can scarcely begin to imagine. From past occasions when it has been used, we know that it afflicts the individual with an inability to complete or retain a thought; the breakdown of all organised activity; failure to keep a job; collapse of family life and other relationships... In short, to a rapid descent into total incapacity, leading within a very short time to destitution and death. A few mentally strong individuals have survived; but they are the rare exception."

Estaron stared at the man, appalled. That was what *could* have happened to him? Then he had indeed got off lightly.

The conversation turned to more immediate matters; but the horror of what had been intended for him left a darkness in Estaron's thoughts for the rest of the day.

———————————————————

Chapter 23: *Slum singer*

"TAL, THEY'VE ONLY JUST COME BACK!" Mistil cried despairingly. "We *can't* send them away."

It was evening, and they were sitting in the living room on the second day of the madness that had gripped their law-abiding suburb. The window shutters were closed, and Steward Doykhid was with the groundkeeper at the gate, still turning visitors away.

Tal sighed. This was all way beyond him—beyond them both. "We have no choice, Mistil. If we don't send them away, the Magistry will. Savant Darzhan was summoned from the seminary today to appear before the Knowledge Grandmaster—to answer questions about this Docent of his who's causing so much trouble. He told the Grandmaster that I was dealing with the matter, and the disturbances would cease immediately. If that doesn't happen…"

Mistil was staring at him, appalled. He tilted his head sadly. His next words would be like knife wounds, but they had to be said. "Would you *want* us arraigned on charges of illegal harbouring? How could we ever help our sons after that—or even *see* them again?" Mistil's eyes filled with tears. "And what about *them*? Would you want Shakhere dishonourably discharged from the army? Brakhól handed over to the priestesses of Makhril for exorcism—or worse?"

"*Oh…!*" Mistil buried her face in her hands. Tal waited.

She flung her head up, a wild look in her eyes. "We must stop his performances! Turn everyone away! Say it was all a mistake…"

"Mistil, you know that won't work. The damage is done. People have been flocking here from all over Kharzil demanding to hear Brakhól. The interest is so high, I don't think we physically *can* turn them away. Our only hope is to send him elsewhere, secretly. Shakhere could look after him."

"But who would *have* them?" Mistil demanded, her voice unsteady. "Barkt and Felhis didn't want them back on the Olbizân plantation. And we don't *know* any other Grûzhileyn who would take that risk!"

"I do."

Both their heads turned to see Shakhere standing in the doorway.

He walked in. "I wasn't listening—I only heard what Ammi said now."

Tal dipped his head in acknowledgment. "Continue."

"Dellikh—my fourth—has been staying with relatives in Gorhiz." Tal nodded at the mention of the large Grûzhileyn slum on the other side of the city. "He said his uncle and aunt have invited me to visit—with Brakhól. I'm sure we could stay with them."

Tal looked at Mistil. Her face brightened. "They wouldn't be afraid, like Barkt and Felhis?"

"Gorhiz is a big place. No one cares what people do there."

Tal nodded. "And none of the true-born would soil their feet by visiting a slum. This sounds good, son."

"But a place like that …" Mistil was looking anxious.

Shakhere laughed. "Don't worry, *Ammi*! Brakhól and I have stayed in much worse places. We'll be fine."

"And what about the foreigners? They can't stay *here*!" she exclaimed in alarm.

"No, no. The woman will have to go with Brakhól, to keep him calm. But Dellikh said his uncle and aunt are so keen to hear Brakhól they'll put up with anything, even two aliens in the house. And once they hear Daneesh playing and Brakhól singing…"

Mistil nodded.

"Good, that's settled, then," Tal said before his beloved wife could find any further objections.

* * *

Danîsha suppressed a sharp sigh. Brakhól's face was set in an obstinate mould and his reddened eyes were angry. The small shack in Gorhiz quivered with tension. If this blew up into another tantrum, Dellikh's aunt and uncle would throw them out—and then what?

She broke eye-contact with the boy and glanced around the cramped living space. Squalid wasn't the word. She couldn't blame Brakhól for resenting the move from his true-parents' home. A steady drip-drip in the corner by the broken bench announced a leaky roof. Some unpalatable gunge was simmering over the fire in another corner, filling the confined space with its stink and a haze of smoke. Aunt Dekhtil loomed over the pot, stirring and radiating disapproval—not least because Shakhere had said she couldn't add teméyn. Uncle Rezhack sat on the floor beside Shakhere and Gil, keeping up his running commentary on child-raising. A gnarled finger stabbed out repeatedly at *her*. Shakhere, mercifully, had stopped translating yesterday.

The former scout gazed at her now with anxious eyes. Danîsha knew how seriously he took his responsibility for them. Brakhól's refusal to sing was putting him in an impossible position. She turned back to the child, her left hand rubbing Teynel's comb as she struggled to find the right words.

"Brakhól, I know this isn't as nice as your parents' home. But Dellikh's uncle and auntie specially asked us to come so they could hear you sing. If you make them happy, you'll be happy, too. You like it when people enjoy your singing, don't you?"

"*No!* I want to go back to Ammi and Baaba."

"We'll see them again soon. But first, won't you sing just one little song? What about *Prince Loves Me*?" She reached for the bellaril.

"*No!*"

There was a loud snort from the aunt, and Uncle Rezhack's commentary became more voluble. Danîsha's lips compressed as she let go of the instrument.

"Maybe we should ask the One for a little help here." Gil's face was grave, and there was no hint of mockery in his voice. Danîsha felt a stab of gratitude for his support, tinged with amazement at how much he'd changed.

"You're right. Listen, Brakhól —"

"No. Wait." Gil stood. "Shakhere, ask Rezhack and Dekhtil if they can give us a moment of silence while we talk to the Creator God." He gestured, and Shakhere and Danîsha rose to their feet as well. Brakhól stayed stubbornly on the bench.

Shakhere said a few words in Grûzhack. Another snort resounded from the cooking corner; but Rezhack stopped his commentary, staring up at them with a curious half-grin.

A blessed silence fell. Gil and Shakhere raised their arms in the Dûrian manner, and she did likewise. After a few moments Gil started speaking to God.

His quiet words soothed Danîsha's tension like a cool cloth on a fevered brow. There were no clichés, just a simple request for help to someone who could be relied on. When he'd finished Shakhere translated for the uncle and aunt.

They sat down, and Danîsha looked at Brakhól. The obstinacy had faded from his face, leaving the ordinary distress of a young child in a threatening situation. He began to cry, and she sat down and put her arm around him.

After a while she said, "Shall I play something now? You don't have to sing." He nodded, his down-turned eyes making him look like a woebegone St. Bernard puppy.

Danîsha took up the bellaril. She ran her fingers over the strings, producing a rising arpeggio that easily overrode the bubbling pot, the rain on the roof and Uncle Rezhack. Her heart gladdened at the sound.

She started on another of the Brakhól's favourites, *Let the Light shine in*, plucking the melody together with the normal chords. On the second verse, Danîsha started singing. Gil and Shakhere joined in. She glanced at Brakhól. Her heart leapt when she saw him mouthing the words. She smiled encouragingly. At the third verse he joined in. Glancing at one another, she and the two men faded their voices out, leaving the stage to Brakhól.

Yet somehow… it fell flat. Rezhack laughed, and Danîsha groaned inwardly. The magic was missing. This wasn't the normal Brakhól, singing his heart out to the Prince he loved. It was a little lost child, wanting to please those he depended on. Danîsha stopped at the end of the verse.

"Brakhól…" she said softly, leaning towards him. "The Prince *loves* you. Remember? And you love him. Don't sing for us — sing for the Prince. Can you do that?"

Something in the child's face relaxed. He nodded, and the old light began to dawn in his eyes. Danîsha started the fourth verse.

And now Brakhól sang. Uncle Rezhack's mouth fell open. Aunt Dekhtil sat oblivious as the pot boiled over. When the song ended they begged for more. Soon the little house was surrounded by a dense crowd hanging on every note.

Brakhól had arrived in Gorhiz.

* * *

Mistil sat with her friends in the soft rose décor of her living room sipping *zakheyn*. She sighed for the third time, fighting the pain their questions caused.

"I can't tell you, Shandis, I really can't. We sent him away because questions were being asked in high places. Do you think we *wanted* to?" She heard the emotion in her voice and took a grip on herself.

"Brakhól was causing disorder. People were coming here from all over Kharzil."

"That wasn't *our* fault," Hilgin remarked tartly.

"No, but..." Desperation overcame Mistil's diffidence. She leant forward and looked her friends in the eye one by one. "If I told you where Brakhól is, what would you do?"

"We'd go and —" Karlis began.

"Exactly. You'd go and listen to him. Others would find out, and soon there'd be disorder there as well — which would be traced back to us."

"This isn't like you, Mistil," Shandis said reproachfully.

"No, because I have a child to protect. It's bad enough losing Brakhól so soon — and not knowing what's happening to him."

"But Mistil!" Was there a glint of moisture in Shistilg's eye? "How can you not understand? Brakhól made us... he showed us... we were... —"

Hilgin came to the rescue. "Your false-born showed us that a different kind of life is possible. We were just starting to learn about this Creator God when you snatched him away from us."

"*Of course I understand!*" The ladies reared back at her sudden vehemence. "Do you think *I* don't feel the same? I'd give anything to be with him, to hear him again, to... to find that peace he has — But not if it means he'll be arrested, or tortured ... or *exorcised*. He's my son, and I'll do nothing to harm him!"

Steward Doykhid intruded respectfully into the heavy silence that followed.

"Lady Dilmey is at the door, madam."

"Show her in," Mistil said wearily.

Large, flamboyant Dilmey came bustling into the living room, giving voice before she'd even said hello.

"You won't *believe* what I've just found out! Hastid — he's the husband of a cousin of my dear friend Bellis — well, he was passing through Gorhiz last night — on business, you know — and he heard the most amazing singing! He and his driver just had to divert to find out what it was. And it turned out to be..." She paused theatrically. " — A Grûzhileyn child in a slum house, with an alien playing the *lhendift*!"

Mistil buried her head in her hands.

Chapter 24: *Children of Despair*

ESTARON CAREFULLY SPRINKLED fine sanding powder over the wet ink, waited a few moments for it to dry, then lifted the smooth, creamy sheet of paper from the writing table. It felt oddly reassuring to be acting as a secretary again.

He took the letter to the tall windows of his palace apartment and re-read it. A faint smile touched his lips. Yes, it would do. It introduced himself as the Governor-Designate of Selmion to Merchant Alenyu Destida, and suggested that it might be useful for them to meet. He requested that the merchant disregard any apparent *karinuto* that might have come to his notice; and assured him that he, Governor-Designate Barilu Dantorida, was fully committed to uphold standard business practice in Selmion.

Alenyu Destida was of course the everyday name of Prince Regent Sindetu Lenorida, head of the Privy Council of the Renegade Royalty. *Karinuto* were failures. The word had two related meanings: failure to pay financial debts; and failure to fulfil expectations. If the letter were opened and shown to the Strongholder, Konnar would assume that Estaron was promising payment to a merchant to whom the palace owed money (of which there were many). Such promises were seldom taken seriously, Estaron had learned: a palace official—in this case, himself—would meet with the merchant, and after a friendly chat in which various favours were mentioned, the merchant would depart, satisfied but unpaid.

But if it reached the addressee (whose real identity Konnar could not know, or Estaron would have heard by now of his capture or execution)—he had no doubt the wily old Prince Regent would read an entirely different message. To avoid any possibility of misunderstanding Estaron had included several code words which he and his parents had agreed years ago with the Privy Council, that identified him and indicated his need for a face-to-face meeting. He hoped the latter would be possible, though the Council might deem it too risky.

Taking a second sheet of paper, Estaron wrote *Alenyu Destida* in the middle of it, with the address—*Way of the Tall Houses, Orselm West*—nicely centred underneath. He placed the address page on

195

top, aligned the two sheets, and made the necessary folds. Finally he closed the letter with the palace's black sealing wax, pressing into it the Dûrian Bishop Suffragan's seal that he'd had with him when he was kidnapped. Konnar could hardly complain: there hadn't been time to have a new Selmian Governor's seal made. And for the recipient it would be an extra validation of his identity.

Of course he had no way of knowing whether his great-uncle Prince Sindetu still lived at that address; nor whether news of Estaron's arrival might have driven him into hiding, fearing that the Strongholder had mindbent him. But he had to try and make contact.

Leaving his apartment Estaron took the letter, together with similar missives to several other merchants, down corridors and staircases to the back foyer of the palace, which opened out on a large courtyard and stables. To one side of the foyer was a table with a black box for the regular 'outside post' operated by Gedoriu, the major-domo. In it was an untidy stack of papers of different sizes. He tucked his letters somewhere in the middle with the faint hope that they might escape censorship; but whether opened or not, he prayed the one to 'Alenyu' would reach its recipient.

* * *

Estaron rode a white gelding through the bustling streets of Orselm with his escort — four officers of the Royal Guard on their distinctive silver mounts, two flanking him on either side. Riding behind him was Dilenyu, a junior Mindbender whom Konnar had insisted should accompany him when travelling outside Orselm, to maintain mindspeech with the palace. Their constant presence was a little oppressive, but it was worth it to be free of the palace.

This was his third day of outside visits. The day before yesterday he had inspected the customs facilities at the port, and despite the fact that the customs officials were mindbent slaves, he was impressed by how well it had been run. In conversation with the Mindbender in charge he had learnt how the reorganisation of the customs service as a mindbent operation several decades ago had reduced theft, bribery and other abuses, while significantly increasing revenue to the state. In purely economic terms he could not argue with that.

Yesterday he had met the head of one of the more prestigious trading houses in Orselm. They were managing well enough without mindbending; but from the false warmth of their smiles and their suggestive comments about 'mutual advantage' he had a pretty clear idea of how a large proportion of their wealth was obtained. They would discover to their disappointment that the new Governor of Selmion did not play those games.

Today he was going to a horse farm some distance off the highway west of Orselm. It was a longish journey—about an hour and a half on horseback each way; but he was looking forward to the ride. This farm, like many others, mainly supplied the Selmian cavalry. He hoped to find out, among other things, how free they were to set their own prices.

The cobbles of the city streets gave way to the intermittent paving of the western highway as they rode out of the city. Green fields and forested hills lay ahead; Estaron felt his spirits lift. Not long afterwards they turned off the highway on to a rutted country road that wandered over hill and down dale. He breathed in the clean air and let out a sigh of pure pleasure.

Then, without warning, darkness struck. Estaron cried out as an overwhelming despair settled on his soul. He yanked his gelding to a halt and sat trembling in the saddle. People were speaking around him with rising voices, but Estaron sat in the middle of the road, frozen in place by an inner desolation beyond anything he had ever known.

Time passed meaninglessly. Hands plucked at his sleeve, but he hardly noticed them. His life was a mockery: his past a wasteland, his present an empty shell, his future a void. To go on was pointless. He might as well die now. He slumped forward in the saddle—

And the darkness lifted. He just stopped himself from falling off the horse.

"Your Highness, your Highness, are you all right?" bleated a high tenor voice beside him. The Mindbender. Dilenyu. "Sir?" queried the gruff baritone of the commander of the Royal Guard detachment.

Estaron took a shuddering breath. "No, I am not all right." He looked around. The sun was shining. The road and the fields were empty.

"Your Highness—" Dilenyu began, but Estaron rounded on him. *"What was that?* Do you know?"

"Y-yes, Highness. The Strongholder apologises—"

"Did you mindspeak him?"

"Yes, your Highness. It was an exercise involving the *Gorelenye* — the Children of Despair — which has now been halted."

"The *Gorelenye* are kept near here?"

"Yes, Highness."

A cold fury was rising in Estaron. "Then take me to them."

"Ah, Highness, the Strongholder — "

"Mindspeak him. Then *take me to the Gorelenye!*"

"Y-yes, your Highness."

A few moments passed during which Dilenyu wore the rapt expression of mindspeech. His eyes kept darting to Estaron, then away again as he met his icy glare.

Finally he let out a sigh and said, "The Strongholder approves the visit, your Highness."

Estaron muttered, "He'd better."

* * *

By the time they reached the *Gorelenye* barracks — a compound of gloomy buildings surrounded by a high fence, deep in the countryside — Estaron had his anger under control, though it continued to simmer.

A Mindbender with cold eyes and a skull-like face let them in at the gate. His greeting, "Welcome, your Highness," held no welcome at all.

Estaron ignored him. His gaze took in the three double-story stone buildings set around a paved courtyard, and the wide field beyond. Figures were moving about the field, picking up bodies. On the far side was another building where men in uniform could be seen coming and going.

"This way if you please, your Highness." Skull-face was moving towards one of the nearby buildings.

"What is happening on the field?" Estaron asked.

"In due course, your Highness. First — "

"Not in due course — now." Estaron snapped. "Answer my question."

Skull-face turned. "Your Highness, the Strongholder — "

" — has authorised me to investigate this facility. I am the Governor-Designate of Selmion, and you will answer my questions when I ask them, not at your own convenience. What is happening on the field?"

For a long moment their eyes locked and he thought the Mindbender would challenge his authority. The answer that finally came was brevity itself. "Staff are clearing up."

"After the... 'exercise' that affected us on the road?"

"Yes."

"Those look like bodies they're removing. Whose bodies?"

"Criminals who died."

"You staged a battle here?"

"That was the intention. It ended prematurely."

"Were the criminals killed by the *Gorelenye*?"

"By our own troops, with their help."

"Just in those few moments?"

Skull-face nodded.

"We experienced the childrens' 'help'. How is it produced?"

"By torture of various kinds. We can provide demonstrations, if you wish."

"I think not. How did their... attack reach us at such a distance? We have ridden at least six *alidoruto* to get here."

Skull-face became almost voluble. "These *Gorelenye* were chosen for the power of their mindspeech; and because they speak their feelings in the same way mindspeakers speak words. Their feelings are broadcast even further by our Mindbenders."

Estaron couldn't restrain a wince. "I see why you are located in such an isolated area. Take me now to the *Gorelenye*."

Without a word Skull-face turned and walked towards the nearest barrack building.

Inside some thirty boys and girls were seated on the floor of a large room. They appeared to be between the ages of about five and twelve. Four other Mindbenders in their grey robes were standing along the walls and at the back.

"Greet the Governor of Selmion!" Skull-face boomed as Estaron and his escort entered.

"Greetings, Governor Barilu," the children intoned in a well-rehearsed chorus. Estaron stared at the empty faces looking up at him, and tears pricked his eyes in a sudden surge of grief. They were faces that had lost hope. The blank eyes of the older ones were like windows in an unoccupied house. They had retreated to some hidden place where pain could no longer reach them.

And the younger ones… Little faces that still held faint vestiges of hope: has this strong man in his white and silver uniform come to set me free? Or fear: tension in every line of their bodies, poised to leap away if he raised a hand.

They were dressed in rags, and a sour, unwashed smell rose from them. All had bruises, burns and scars on their bodies, and some had fresh bandages. There were missing fingers and ears.

"Some of these *Gorelenye* have caused more than fifty deaths," Skull-face declared. "Tomaru over there—" he pointed at a nine or ten-year-old boy with a livid scar down one cheek "—has been known to kill at more than eight *alidoruto* just on his own." There was no reaction from Tomaru. "Sixteen of these *Gorelenye* were used in the Dûrian war, enabling the cavalry to break out at—"

Estaron interrupted the flow. "I think I've seen enough, thank you. We will leave now." He turned to those heart-breaking faces and fought down an overwhelming impulse to take them with him and raze this den of unimaginable abuse to the ground. But he was still only Governor-Designate.

"Goodbye, children," he said softly.

At a gesture from Skull-face the dull chorus replied, "Goodbye, Governor Barilu."

As they rode out of the gate Estaron announced that they would return at once to Orselm.

Konnar had some questions to answer about good governance and child torture.

* * *

After prowling the palace corridors for several hours, Estaron finally cornered Konnar in his private study.

"Bari! You're back. I'm sorry you were affected—"

"Good governance?"

"Yes, yes, I know, Bari. But you must understand that these *Gorelenye* have been essential to our military strategy—"

"*Children!*" Estaron exploded. "They're children, Konnar! As young as *five*. Not weapons. Not objects of wood or metal. *Children!*"

"Without those children we would not have broken the Dûrian siege of Starmane, Bari. Or continued to block the Grûzhack advance. They—"

" —are helpless kids whom you are abusing and turning into *things*. Have you visited that *Gorelenye* barracks? Have you looked into those empty eyes? Do you remember how *you* felt when you were nine or ten? When Dilaru's gang treated you like a weird *thing* and chanted 'Freak!' at you? *You* were able to fight back: you had your powers; I even had to restrain you. But these children are completely at your mercy, and you have tormented them way beyond anything that was ever done to you!"

Konnar was silent, pain in his eyes.

"If I am to be Governor of Selmion I want the *Gorelenye* project stopped, Konnar. I will not tolerate abuse of innocent children."

There was a long pause. Then a sad smile touched Konnar's face. "You're right, Bari. That's not good governance — and it will stop."

"Immediately?"

"As soon as possible."

Estaron frowned. "No. At once."

"Be reasonable, Bari. It will take a little time. There's the military to be placated, Mindbenders to be reassigned — and homes to be found for the children. You wouldn't want them left to fend for themselves, surely?"

"What about their families?"

"Most are orphans. Others were thrown out because there was no money to feed them, or their 'gift' was unappreciated. Only a few have relatives who might still want them back. They will be sent home."

Estaron took a deep breath. "Alright. But that place must not still be operating when I am inaugurated as Governor in a couple of weeks' time."

"It won't be. That I solemnly promise you."

Estaron nodded. "Thank you."

They went on to talk of other things until a mind-call interrupted Konnar and he gave his customary goodbye wave.

Estaron walked thoughtfully back to his apartment. Konnar had seemed shaken by the parallel with his own childhood; and his promise to close down the project had sounded genuine. But his initial attempts to justify this barbaric exploitation of children showed that for a long time now he'd had no concern for their suffering at all. Perhaps he now realised that he *should* be concerned; but Estaron feared that while he'd given way in this instance, he was still far from regarding individuals as people with a right to respect and fair treatment.

How many more issues like this would come up to highlight the differences between them? Could Konnar's vague desire to realise their boyhood ideal of 'good governance' compete with harsh realities like the need to win a war?

So much remained to be seen.

* * *

Konnar sat staring out of his study window, considering his old friend.

Being with Bari again was reawakening some of the old thoughts and ideals they'd had as children: reminding him of concerns they'd once shared — which he only now realised arose out of Bari's Lightist Renegade background. Like his concern for the *Gorelenye* as people, not military assets. He could now see how those principles had also animated Bari as a boy; how he had always been concerned for the underdog and for those suffering undeservedly. Such cases were at the core of his ideal of 'good governance'.

But surely the longer-term view should also be considered? Which was more important, the short-term welfare of a group of orphan children (who might in any case have been left to die by their dirt-poor relatives); or the long-term welfare of the state as a whole?

Yet he himself once, years ago at the training temple, had espoused the short-term welfare of a local man whose daughter had been raped by a member of the staff. He had placed that man's claim above the long-term welfare of the temple as a whole, which would suffer serious financial loss if all such claims were allowed. Nowadays, like Training Master Nemisu, he would reject such a claim out of hand.

Which was right? His earlier concern for the individual, or his present concern for the wider issues?

He buried his head in his hands for a moment. It was wonderful having Bari back, but he could do without these agonising differences of perspective.

Then he lifted his head. Right now, only one issue mattered: the survival of mindbending. That meant not only winning the Grû-zhack war, but also winning control of teméyn production. He could work with Bari to promote good governance in small, local matters; but not in anything that would jeopardise that overriding goal.

Which meant that he could not share the project closest to his heart with his old friend. He sighed. He'd been looking forward to discussing it with Bari, revealing its *magnificence* to him, getting his comments on its pros and cons, and especially on dealing with the outcome. But after Bari's extreme reaction to the *Gorelenye* today, that was out. Better that Bari knew nothing about the larger project until it was done.

And this was one thing that *had* to be done, without any scruples about individual suffering. His own position, his plans for joint rule with Bari, and the whole future of the present world order depended on it.

He would keep his promise to Bari about ending the *Gorelenye* project: but only after the greatest deed of the present age had been accomplished.

Chapter 25: *Mission accomplished*

"AGENT GEDORIU, your Highness."

Prince Sindetu Lenorida looked up from the table where he sat in the small, sparsely-furnished reclining room of the safe house. A couple of open packing crates stood on the floor beside a threadbare recliner, on which books and ledgers lay scattered. The table was several layers deep in correspondence, cargo manifests and shipping schedules.

Sindetu himself was a grey-haired man with a strong face, showing deep vertical lines of experience and suffering. He was wearing a house robe of fine blue silk. His thick eyebrows shot up at the steward's announcement.

"Gedoriu? At last! Show him in."

The steward bowed and withdrew. A few moments later the palace major-domo entered. "Highness," he murmured, going down on one knee, his head bent.

"Gedoriu, please, don't worry about protocol here. It doesn't fit." He surveyed the large man as he rose to his feet and gently shook his head. A man of few words and iron principles. He would continue to observe protocol wherever he was.

"Yes, your Highness. I apologise that I have not been able to come personally until now. But I believe I bring good news."

"Anything that will get me out of this rat hole will be good news."

"Yes, sir." Gedoriu reached into his white, silver-trimmed jacket and pulled out a letter. "This was addressed to you. It is from the Governor-Designate."

Sindetu's face settled into grimmer lines. "Oh. Our errant Heir. Let me see." He took the letter from the major-domo and examined it. "Hmm. Seal of the Dûrian Bishop Suffragan. Opened and reattached. You showed it to the Strongholder?"

"Yes, your Highness, as he instructed."

"And?"

"He joked about his new governor's conscientiousness."

"Really? That's hopeful. Let's see what amused him."

Sindetu opened the letter and read it aloud to Gedoriu. When he'd finished a slow smile crossed his face. "Clever. Nomariu — or

Bari, as we called him—has not lost his edge. The palace does owe me for a couple of shipments, as I'm sure he found out."

Gedoriu cleared his throat. "I think this confirms, Highness, that Prince Nomariu has not been mindbent."

"Yes, indeed. It's what we assumed, though we could not take any chances—which is why I'm holed up here. And what about yourself, Gedoriu? Are you sure *you* still haven't been mindbent or mindread?"

"Reasonably, sir. The Strongholder ignores me because he thinks I lack the intelligence to do anything beyond managing a household. I foster that idea by keeping my mind focused on my work, so if he does skim my mind that's all he sees. Besides, he is now quite anxious to identify and capture the Renegade leadership because of the damage our agents have recently caused with their attacks. If he had any idea I was a Renegade agent, I would not be standing here now— nor, I venture to say, would you be here either."

Sindetu smiled. "Fair enough, Gedoriu. But tell me, have there been any reports of the Royal Guard being sent to my residence?"

"No, sir. I came via the residence. There was no sign of a break-in."

A weight seemed to roll off Sindetu as he relaxed in his seat. "That's a relief, Gedoriu. Perhaps I can risk going home now. If the Strongholder had mindbent the Heir, he would not have sent a letter to contact me. He would have found my address in Bari's mind, ransacked my house, and then turned Orselm inside out to find me. I would have had to escape to... a long way away. And we don't know how much Bari remembers about the other princes. They would also have been in danger. It would have caused tremendous disruption; perhaps even the end of the network we have built up over so many years."

"We have had a fortunate escape, sir."

"Yes, we have. Though *why* is still a mystery. Kidnapping our Heir was a masterstroke. If the Strongholder had mindbent him immediately before we had news of his arrival, he could have wiped us out in a couple of days. Why didn't he? What does he hope to gain by setting the Heir up as a puppet Governor?"

Sindetu eyed Gedoriu keenly. He was their most important asset, their eyes and ears in the palace itself.

The major-domo stood silent for a moment, his eyes staring at the tall windows behind Sindetu. Then he said slowly, "Prince Nomariu and the Strongholder get on well together, sir. Certain things I've noticed suggest that they already knew each other before the prince's arrival."

Sindetu's eyebrows shot up. "Such as?"

"Well, sir, it was night time when the Heir first arrived. He could not be seen clearly as he came out of the vehicle at the palace entrance. The Strongholder was waiting for him with a mock-formal retinue and started taunting him as he approached the steps. Then as he walked up into the light they seemed to recognise one another. The Strongholder fell silent and stared at him. Then they each exclaimed the other's name — 'Bari!' and 'Konnar!' — and embraced with obvious emotion..."

He stopped as Sindetu stared at him, thunderstruck. "*Konnar!*" he breathed. "No, it can't be. But it fits... They embraced, you say? Can it conceivably be... that the Strongholder is *Konnaru Galenida*?"

With a puzzled frown Gedoriu said, "The original name of the Strongholder is never made public, as you know sir, ..."

The Prince Regent explained. "Konnaru was a childhood friend of the Heir's. They were very close. It was rumoured that Konnaru had certain... powers, even as a child. We advised the Heir's parents to terminate the friendship; but the boys so enjoyed each other's company that they hadn't the heart to. If the Strongholder is Konnaru Galenida... it would explain why Prince Nomariu has not been mindbent. The Strongholder still values the old friendship, and wants to keep the Heir beside him with this phony governorship..."

He paused. "But that works both ways. Prince Nomariu has accepted the governorship."

In the following silence Gedoriu murmured, "Can we trust him, sir?"

Sindetu heaved a heavy sigh. "The answer is, we don't know. He may have felt he had no other choice. But his statement about commitment in this letter does not entirely reassure me. He was devoted to the Renegade cause as a youth; but we haven't heard from him now for over a year, and only sporadically before then. In fact we have hardly had news of him since he started his ill-fated studies at Darthane University. Now he suddenly arrives here and accepts a subordinate position in government under his former best friend. No, I don't like it.

"Watch him, Gedoriu. Thank you for what you have told me today. Let me know if there are any other significant developments."

Gedoriu bowed his head. "Highness." Raising his eyes again to Sindetu he said, "You will not accept his request for a meeting?"

"Not yet. I want to see how his relationship with the Strongholder develops."

"Highness. And will there be a reply to the letter?"

"Not for you to deliver; you've taken enough risks already. I'll send a polite response by the normal channels. That will be all for now, Gedoriu."

"Highness." With ponderous dignity the Renegade agent and palace major-domo went down on one knee again before leaving.

* * *

In Barazhân, seven days had passed.

Tal stood on his toes and gazed around. There was standing room only in the disused warehouse he had hired for Brakhól's nightly sessions. The close-packed crowd consisted mainly of Grûzhileyn workers, but well-dressed groups of the true-born were scattered among them. The air was heavy with the smell of teméyn-laden breath and honest sweat.

There was a stir at the front of the crowd, and Shakhere mounted the steps to the makeshift platform of boards laid over upright barrels. Behind him came the short figure of Brakhól, followed by Daneesh and Gelmin. A roar of welcome arose from twelve hundred throats, spreading rapidly to the thousands outside. Mingled with it were cries of disgust from newcomers who hadn't seen the aliens before. Tal shook his head. It was hard to remember that he'd felt that way not long ago. Now the two foreigners were friends he held in high regard.

Daneesh sat on a specially-lowered chair and unpacked her *lhendift* instrument. A tense hush fell on the crowd. Brakhól took his place beside Daneesh. Tal felt a surge of pride. It was his son who had drawn all these people here. The 'false-born', whom his own people had disowned. But he and Mistil had never disowned him. And now here he was with a message that broke through every barrier of prejudice and custom: a message that *all* Grûzhack, true and false-born, desperately wanted to hear. He didn't know what the outcome of all this would be, but he knew one thing: there was a God greater than Makhril who was reaching out to the people of Barazhân through his son.

Daneesh struck a chord on the lhendift, and the silence deepened. She and Brakhól shared a glance. She nodded—and the child began to sing.

Tal had heard Brakhól's singing many times now; yet every time it was as if he'd never heard it before. He glanced at Mistil beside him. Her face was rapt, her eyes moist. There was a dampness on his own cheek—a source of shame in times past. No longer. These tears were bringing him to a place he wanted to be: the place where Brakhól was.

The music rose and fell, the rich chords of Daneesh's instrument perfectly complementing his son's pure young voice. All around were faces full of yearning. *People*, Grûzhack or Grûzhileyn, longing for the peace Brakhól was showing them.

It slowly came to Tal that there was a disturbance at the back of the room. He craned his neck, and was shocked to see the blue tunics of the Kharzil garrison pushing their way in. Had the Magistry sent them to break up the meeting? But the young Grûzhileyn recruits— too inexperienced to be sent to the war—soon came to a standstill, gaping open-mouthed at the platform. Tal smiled. Whatever the Grandmasters had intended, they'd reckoned without Brakhól.

The song ended, and a deep silence followed: the silence of unfulfilled longing, of seeking to hold on to a fading vision. Shakhere, the master of ceremonies, had learnt to give people the time they needed. Just as the audience began stirring he stepped forward.

"If anyone has questions for Brakhól or for the foreigners who taught him about the Creator God, ask now."

A workman called out from the back, his voice still husky with emotion: "Why does your religion make you so happy?"

Brakhól's clear voice answered without hesitation, "Because Daddy loves me!"

"Who is your Daddy, Brakhól?" Shakhere prompted.

"The Creator God!"

There was a short pause while the crowd digested Brakhól's response.

"But how can a god *love* us?" a cultured voice asked. "The gods and goddesses rule our lives. They demand obedience and offerings. Why should *they* give us anything?"

Brakhól looked at Gelmin. Shakhere translated the question. The foreigner answered at once in his strange, fluid language. Tal had come to appreciate Gelmin's sharp mind and his clear explanations. Shakhere relayed the reply.

"The Creator God *made* us. He made the whole world. He gave us everything we have. That's why he cares for us in a way no other god can. He wants his world to be perfect, and every creature in it to be happy. So when we are unhappy... he is, too."

After that the questions flowed thick and fast. Before long Gelmin was describing the part Tal found most difficult: that the Creator God had a son, and that he had sent this son to live under Malane three centuries ago as a prince of the flatlanders. That they had rejected his rule, and actually burnt the son of God to death! As if that wasn't enough, according to Gelmin God's son had *overcome* death and given unending life to his followers.

He would have dismissed that outright—if it weren't for Brakhól. The transparent reality of Brakhól's relationship with this reborn God confounded every argument.

Shakhere, he knew, had entered that relationship. It showed in the lad's eyes and the spring in his step. Mistil, too, along with several of her friends, had found Brakhól's place of peace. He was the only one of their family still looking in from the outside.

He must have a long talk with Gelmin.

* * *

Gil sank down on the edge of his bed in the small office he'd been allocated at the back of the warehouse. He was glad to sit at last.

It had been a long session. The most amazing part had been the meeting afterwards with the two hundred and forty warriors of the Kharzil garrison who had been sent to break up the gathering. They were totally overcome by their encounter with Brakhól and the Creator God. What worried them most was their military oath, which pledged allegiance to the Grûzhack goddess, Makhril.

Gil had had to tread a fine line there. Without naming Makhril, he'd explained that allegiance to the Creator superseded all other allegiances. He and 'Neesh had discussed that issue some time ago. They'd concluded that it wasn't necessary to make inflammatory statements against Makhril. Anyone who had experienced one of Brakhól's broadcasts would have the stark comparison staring them in the face.

The young soldiers had left looking thoughtful. If they'd been ordered to make arrests, they hadn't done so. Gil wondered what their reception would be back at garrison HQ. He breathed a quick request that the One would protect them and lead them to the truth.

And Tal. He'd just come from a long chat with him, via Shakhere. There was a man very like himself. He'd tried to pass on to him some of the things he'd so recently learned...

His eyes stared unfocused at the shabby wall opposite. It was completely natural, now, for him to share his inner thoughts with the Creator. God was real in his personal experience: he could say that quite calmly and factually. In fact, every criterion he'd set had been satisfied. He hadn't been whipped into an emotional frenzy. Somewhere on the way to Barazhân he'd started actively trusting the Unknown—as Father Martin had urged back in Stillárre. And the Unknown had responded, and become a Person he wanted to know. Prayers he'd uttered, without even knowing *how* to pray, had been answered. His simple request before starting out on this journey— that God would do something he could never have imagined—had actually happened. What more could he ask?

He spoke a silent word of thanks to the Unknown he was now learning to know.

* * *

Next day it was all over the city: the garrison had defected to the new movement!

In fact, all six hundred of them were now camped in the warehouse awaiting instructions.

Danîsha's heart was heavy as she sat discussing the situation with Gil, Shakhere and Tal. Where would this end? The regular army was in Dûrion, and the Magistry had no other means of law enforcement. Using the blaise, Gil had already observed sporadic outbreaks of lawlessness.

They sent the garrison troops out to perform their normal duties.

That afternoon many of them returned wounded. Fighting was breaking out all over Kharzil. The true-born were organising local militia groups composed of retired officers and servicemen. In the city centre normal business had ground to a halt, and there were running battles between Grûzhack and Grûzhileyn.

That night thousands of Grûzhileyn turned out as usual to hear Brakhól—but only a handful of Grûzhack. Through Shakhere, Gil pleaded for restraint. Hotheads shouted that the false-born had been oppressed long enough. Brakhól had shown them that everyone was equal before the Creator God. Now it was *their* turn to rule!

In the end Brakhól began to cry and the meeting broke up in disorder.

Tal, Mistil and their true-born friends had little option but to stay in the warehouse. Danîsha muttered a prayer of gratitude that they were surrounded by loyal Grûzhileyn who had entered the Light—and by the city garrison with their muskets. But would this really be the final outcome of Brakhól's singing, her playing, and Gil's explanations about the One Creator God? A *civil war*? She was tired and confused, and a sudden longing filled her to be sitting down with a hot cup of tea in her homely Birmingham cottage, chatting on the phone with Tim, Rose or Maureen…

The following day the news had spread to the countryside, and Grûzhileyn from other areas started pouring into Kharzil. The fighting began to swing against the Grûzhack. But the true-born had the courage of desperation; and they, too, received outside reinforcements.

A Grûzhileyn with contacts at the Magistry came rushing in to report that the Grandmasters had sent their fastest runners to recall the army. He added as an afterthought that they had posted a large reward for the capture or execution of 'the alien trouble-makers'. Gil used the blaise to inform Lannie in Stillárre about the army's recall: it was good news for them, at least.

That evening Tal, Mistil and Shakhere came to the two Restorers, accompanied by the garrison commander.

"You should leave now," Tal said, "while you can. Your lives are in danger. And before long the whole of Barazhân will be in chaos. Garrisonmaster Sargid here has an enclosed racer. He's willing to lend you eight men as pullers, to take you to the border." As Shakhere finished translating his eyes were moist.

Danîsha's heart lurched. "But Brakhól…"

"…will miss you desperately—at first. And you will miss him." Tal's tone softened. There was a new peace in his eyes. "We can never thank you enough for all you have done, and for all you have taught us. But the trouble brewing here now is *our* fight. You have shown us the Way. We must follow it alone."

As she stood, torn, Gil murmured, "He's right, 'Neesh. We've done what we came to do. I doubt if there'll be any more meetings after this."

After an early breakfast the next morning Shakhere ushered them out of the rear of the building, where they found a two-person racer waiting, complete with eight husky troopers in menial pullers' tunics. Garrisonmaster Sargid lifted the passenger seat of the conveyance to reveal a compartment stacked with muskets. They would have protection, if needed.

Tal and Mistil came out of the warehouse. They'd left Brakhól with Mistil's friend Shandis. Danîsha had said goodnight to him the previous evening, without telling him she was leaving and might never see him again. It was the hardest thing she'd done on this trip to keep her emotions in check so he didn't pick up on her distress. Even now she felt herself choking up at the thought of never hugging him again. Never sending his glorious voice soaring again in song with the bellaril. What would become of this precious child in the ugly civil war now brewing?

She felt the tears trickling down her cheeks as she embraced Mistil, whose eyes were also full as she murmured *Khalis dar*—Thank you. Shakhere moved hesitantly toward her, and Danîsha embraced him, too.

Tal held out a hand with splayed fingers to Gil, who grasped it in the friendship greeting.

Danîsha hurriedly climbed into the racer, cramming her bellaril into a space behind the backrest. Gil joined her. She called out, "Wait!" and rummaged in the bag at her feet. She pulled out a well-worn object, and thrust it at Shakhere.

He took her copy of the Book with a heartfelt "Thank you," his eyes shining.

Someone drew the racer's curtains, and with a jerk they were off.

They took a devious route, avoiding the spreading gunfire. That night they slept in an abandoned barracks. Next morning they reached the high path that led down to Pinnesseron. Gil had contacted Lannie with the blaise, and she'd arranged for Nist to escort them from there to Stillárre.

They climbed out of the racer for the last time, shivering in the icy mountain air. Danîsha could hardly believe they were leaving Barazhân. Her thoughts were still with Brakhól, Shakhere, Tal, Mistil, and the other new children of the Light whom they'd left so suddenly in the midst of the growing civil unrest.

They thanked their escorts, praying they would survive the return journey. Then they consulted the rough map Shakhere had given them, and set off on the steep path down to Pinnesseron.

Chapter 26: *Worst fears realised*

THE TEMPLE OF GADESH IN ORSELM was full to overflowing this morning. Estaron sat with other dignitaries in the front row of seats facing the raised altar. All around him a subdued murmur rose from the huge congregation as they waited for the rituals to begin.

Estaron glanced around the centuries-old building. It had the massive simplicity of an earlier age. The plain grey walls were punctuated by tall, rectangular windows. Unlike the domes found in more modern temples, the pitched roof was supported by a heavy ridge beam. Rafters ran up from the walls, with a dark blue ceiling between. The building widened around the altar, which was located in the centre. A cleverly-constructed metal flue extended down from the roof with a flared opening to catch the smoke of the altar fire.

Estaron had been told that priests and temple staff would normally sit on one side of the altar, worshipers on the other; and the recesses to the left and right would be used for ceremonial implements and sacrificial victims (human or animal). Today, however, every available space was filled with visitors. Estaron had been introduced to Mindbenders, Mindbenders' subordinates and Initiates of Gadesh from all over the country. To say that he felt out of place would be an understatement.

But there had been no option about attending. Konnar had simply announced that he and the Governor-Designate of Selmion would be joining a special gathering in the Temple of Gadesh today. Estaron's breakfast had been brought in early, and soon afterwards Mindbender Belyeru had arrived to escort him and several other high-rankers from the palace.

His mind was full of foreboding. Konnar had been strangely withdrawn this past week. They'd hardly met, and when they did the Strongholder was constantly interrupted with mind-calls. People were coming and going the whole time, Mindbenders wearing the rapt expression of mindspeech, palace staff talking in huddles, then falling silent when he approached. It was obvious Konnar was planning something he didn't want to share with his best friend.

And here, in the temple, were the *Gorelenye*. His eyes went again to the leftward recess beside the altar, which was filled with the thirty traumatised children manacled to the benches. The older ones stared grimly ahead with their empty eyes; the little ones craned their necks to see this strange place, fear etched in their faces. Behind them stood their grey-robed Keepers, whose pockets held who-knew-what instruments of torture.

And here *he* was on Anderil, the One's day, filled with a growing fear that an evil beyond imagining was about to be unleashed.

Finally the preliminaries were over. Estaron watched with dread as the vast congregation of Mindbenders and Gadeshites focused their combined energies outward, their arms raised towards the west, the south and the north. Konnar was standing beside the high altar wearing his black and silver robes of office. He was visibly carried up into it all, responding to the growing evil energy of the gathering, chanting words in Old Selmian.

Estaron could not follow all of the ancient language, but he understood enough to realise that an action was being taken today to guarantee victory over every enemy; and that similar gatherings were taking place at this moment in every Dûrai nation, including conquered eastern Dûrion.

He had a horrible premonition of what was about to happen.

The congregation joined in the Strongholder's chant. Their voices slowly grew in power. A cold wind moaned through the temple, slicing through Estaron's cloak and making his teeth chatter. Dark, writhing shapes appeared in the air. The *Gorelenye* started screaming, the stark terror in their childish voices flooding Estaron's mind with despair. He staggered, clutching his head in agony.

An acolyte lit the altar fire. The angry red glow emphasised the growing darkness.

The terrible crescendo continued to build. Raw pain now filled the children's screams. Estaron's knees buckled and he sat down suddenly. He clutched the edge of his seat, panting, struggling to retain his grip on sanity.

Screams and voices merged into a rising shriek of pure evil. Estaron saw a great figure of darkness rising from the altar and towering over the congregation: Worldruler Gadesh. An offering of a small, screaming body was thrust into the flames. Estaron closed his eyes.

After an eternity of agony the chant ceased. The pitiful whimperings of the surviving *Gorelenye* were silenced. Estaron opened his eyes. Blackened remains lay among the glowing coals on the altar. Konnar stood beside them, staring out over the congregation with bloodshot eyes. His right hand was raised in a clenched fist.

The Strongholder began to speak, his tenor voice unnaturally deep. His words fell into a power-charged silence. As the congregation echoed each pronouncement, Estaron felt a shock run through him: a shock that said, It is done. It cannot be undone.

"In the name of the Worldruler, of Almighty Gadesh,
   whose word is law, whose will is absolute:
Every enemy; every ruler opposed to the Realm of the Mind…
Every slave, servant, soldier and citizen of those rulers…
We curse your crops to blight –
   your livestock to barrenness –
   your products to uselessness.
We curse your hopes to despair –
   your power to impotence –
   your plans to failure –
   your thoughts to confusion."

Konnar paused. Staring upward he raised both hands with clenched fists and shouted,

"We curse you to futility!"

The congregation's roar shook the rafters.

Estaron's worst fears were realised.

Chapter 27: *Chaos falls*

GIL STOOD AT THE LECTERN in the Stillárre Hearth under the great Ambon of Sûrilane, looking out over a packed congregation. Not only the Hearth members were there, but a large contingent of travelling priests led by Frengor, whose deeply-wrinkled features beamed at him from the third row. Many of the Travelling Order's rather earthy followers had come along as well, adding a cheerful buzz to the normally staid gathering.

Gil's heart was full. What a change from the last time he was here! Then he was a useless appendage, a 'Restorer' who knew neither the One Creator God nor his own destiny. He had found them both in Barazhân.

He and 'Neesh had come back yesterday to a city in disorder, fires still burning near the river. But the citizens were in festive mood, because the Grûzhack had suddenly packed up their cannon and left. The two of them became heroes when people heard it was *their* exploits that had forced the enemy to retreat. A special thanksgiving hearthtime had been declared today; and he'd been invited to tell the story.

He cleared his throat. "My brothers and sisters in the Creator's family." Not a cliché: that's what they *were* to him now. People began slapping their thighs in a spontaneous round of applause. When they'd finished he continued, "The man speaking to you today is not the man who left Stillárre four weeks ago. Then, I did not believe in the One Creator God. Now, I can't help believing. I have seen him doing things I would never have thought possible. I have spoken to him, and he has answered. He has claimed me and made me his own."

There was another thunderous volley of clapping, mingled with cries of encouragement. Gil felt a tightness in his throat.

"As you know, Danîsha and I set out to take young Brakhól back to his home in Barazhân. But it was only through Brakhól's confidence in the Creator that we made it. That was my first lesson that God is real—through a child."

He went on to tell the story of the Warrior of God. How before they entered Barazhân, Brakhól had asked 'Daddy' to look after them. How their group had been trapped on the mountain highway with no way of escape, while the thudding feet of a Grû-zhack military patrol drew closer.

The congregation hung on his words.

"Then the warriors came round the corner, and I charged them with my longsword. But they were staring at something behind me. They looked terrified. Next thing they started dropping their weapons, and—"

Reality shifted.

A cold wind ruffled the window hangings. Colours seemed to fade to shades of grey.

The words froze on Gil's lips.

A moment ago all eyes had been on him. Now people were looking around, puzzled, as if wondering where they were. A swelling murmur arose, like a disturbed hive of bees.

Bishop Harlon stood up in the front row, half-facing the congregation. "Something has happened!" He turned to Gil. "I don't know what you've done, but..." He looked back at the people, who were also getting up, gazing around in confusion, gathering into knots of agitated conversation, hurrying out as if for a forgotten appointment. Children were crying and mothers were calling their names. People who had just hurried out wandered back in looking lost.

"Estaron!" the Bishop exclaimed. "Where is Estaron? He'll know what to do..."

Gil stood frozen in shock.

Harlon couldn't have meant that. He knew perfectly well— Gil came down from the lectern to speak to him. He opened his mouth to remind the Bishop that Estaron had... He felt a sudden surge of panic. *What* had Estaron done?

Shiván was standing at the other end of the row, gazing around with raised eyebrows. He would know! Gil hurried over, then faltered as he approached the young man.

What was he going to ask?

* * *

Shiván was seriously confused. Gil had been going great guns up there, then suddenly—wham! Everyone getting up and wandering about... the Bishop spouting nonsense... Perrely disappearing with some comment about finding Jomel—who was right behind them! Was he going crazy again?

He saw Gil and grabbed his arm. "What happened? Did I miss something? Did you see anything from the front?"

A look of consternation crossed Gil's face. "Miss something!" He felt feverishly in the right-hand pocket of his robe. "It's gone! My blaise. Someone's stolen it! Or, no—maybe I left it at the... where we live. I must find it!" He hurried off.

"Gil!" Shiván called after him. "It's in your *other* pocket!" Gil turned and waved vaguely without stopping.

Cârin came hurrying up to him. "Have you seen Shîr? Can't find him anywhere!"

Shiván stared at him, shocked. "Câr, Shîr's—" But the surviving twin had already dashed off.

A girl of about five grabbed Shiván's hand. "Daddy! I want to go home!" Tears streamed down her cheeks.

"I'm not your Da—" There was no point. He picked her up. She began sobbing, head on his shoulder, arms tight around his neck. He patted her back. "There, there. Don't worry, I'll take you to your home."

If he could find out where that was.

He wandered around for a while, carrying the girl and calling through the din for any parent who'd lost a child to come and claim her. No one did. Frengor said sadly that he wished he'd been invited.

A cold stone settled in Shiván's heart.

What in God's name was happening?

* * *

Lannie awoke the next morning feeling vaguely uneasy. She yawned, sat up, and looked around. She was in the small priest's cell that was her bedroom in the Domicile. Bedside table. Leather-bound copy of the Book. Slop bucket. Curtained hanging space where she kept her clothes. All present and correct. No problem.

So why was she feeling uneasy?

She glanced down, and blinked in surprise. Well, for a start, she was still wearing yesterday's clothes! How did that happen?

A dim memory came back to her of being lost in the streets of Stillárre. Had she really wandered around the *whole day*, looking for the Domicile? Yes, that's right—it was already getting dark when Shiván had found her. He'd brought her home, shown her to her room.

No, that couldn't be right! *Shivvie* was the one who got lost when he wasn't quite with it. She'd just had a bad dream. But, unlike a dream, the memory began to clarify. She remembered wandering down Bishop's Avenue in a daze, looking at the handsome store fronts and town houses and feeling annoyed that none of them were the Domicile.

Her unease turned to fear. Dear God, what was wrong with her? She knew where the Domicile was! It was on…

Her mind was blank.

How was that possible? She always knew where places were! The street where the Domicile was, where the bed was located on which she was now sitting, was of course called—

She leapt up in horror. She had to talk to 'Neesh about this. She hurried out of her room into the wide passage and knocked on the next door to the left.

Perrely answered, her face drawn and eyes red.

* * *

An hour later Shiván ushered eight very worried people into the Fraternity Room for an emergency Council meeting.

He himself was worn out. He'd been busy all day yesterday, and well into the evening, finding the lost sheep of the government of Dûrion. He'd guided them back to the Domicile; organised the few remaining priests to prepare a meal; prevented everyone from wandering off again; and finally escorted them to their rooms and made sure they got into bed. At least he'd been too busy to give way to his own depression.

The present situation was a nightmare. Had the whole of Stillárre suddenly gone down with Alzheimer's? The city was like a mediaeval vision of hell. People wandering about not knowing who they were or where they lived; meaningless arguments breaking out, sometimes ending in bloodshed; animals running amuck; children crying and screaming. He'd brought the little girl who'd 'adopted' him to the Domicile; he'd dubbed her Anna. One of the priests (he hoped) was giving her breakfast.

A large bunch of keys clanked on his belt. Last night he'd been round and locked every outside door — including the secret ones. He couldn't have his charges wandering off again.

He glanced at the faces in the Fraternity Room. This was the government of Dûrion, and he needed to find out if they were still capable of governing. Well, they'd all taken their seats at the circular table. That was a start.

Bishop Harlon cleared his throat. He looked haggard. Yesterday he'd been trying to find his way to Estaron's lodgings. Shiván wondered whether a search for Estaron would be the first item on his agenda.

But no. Harlon opened the proceedings quite reasonably. "Thank you, Shiván, for bringing us here. Something has happened, and we urgently need to take steps to deal with it."

He paused, looking at the others. There was a heavy silence.

Then Frengor spoke. His eyes were shadowed and his smile vague. "In a situation like this, we should first look to the Book to find God's way forward." He rummaged in his pockets for a few moments, then looked round puzzled. "I seem to have left my copy behind..."

"You can use mine," Perrely always kept her compact copy of the Book with her. But not today. Soon she and Frengor were both searching their pockets and looking under their seats.

"I could go and get mine," Danîsha offered, getting up. Then she paused, and her eyes filled. "Oh no! I remember. Shakhere took it. He took my Book. Now I can't read God's words any more..." She slumped back on her seat, tears trickling down her cheeks, her fingers busy with Teynel's little wooden comb that she always carried with her.

"Alright, alright!" Shiván exclaimed. "Let's not worry about having an actual copy of the Book. Most of us know large sections of God's Word by heart. What were you going to say, Frengor?"

"Say...?"

Shiván's heart sank. "You were making a comment about how to deal with this crisis."

"Ah yes. The One says that all those who *look* for his truth, will find it." He glanced round earnestly. "Brothers and sisters, we must *look* for it. We must not sit idly, waiting for the answer to drop into our laps. We must actively search for *his* way, *his* answer, *his* word for this time and place."

"How?"

The question came from Garset. He looked more rumpled than most. He'd insisted on wearing his mail shirt under his tunic last night.

Silence fell.

"Well, the first thing to do, obviously, is ..." Bishop Mâron broke off, looking puzzled. "I forget what I was going to say."

Shiván felt himself teetering on the brink of despair. This group couldn't run Dûrion. They had ideas, opened their mouths, then forgot them! He could see why in times past the Council had been quick to shut *him* up when —

Good Lord! Why hadn't it struck him sooner?

He leapt to his feet. "Your Radiance, please excuse me. I'll be back soon!"

"Well, Shiván, this is..."

He didn't wait for formal permission. Outside the room he hesitated, then locked the door behind him. He hurried downstairs to the entrance hall, brushing aside anxious priests. He unlocked the main outer door, slipped through, and re-locked it.

Terror-stricken people besieged him. It cut his heart to force his way through, ignoring their confused pleas. He made his way along side streets and alleyways until he reached the market square, where a large crowd milled about aimlessly. He ran through them to the Hearth before anyone could recognise him.

The Hearth was full. Many seemed to have slept there. He ran down an aisle, jumping over people, till he reached the altar — and beyond it, the Ambon of Sûrilane.

He reached up and carefully lifted the great emblem of Dûrion from its wall brackets. As he did so, he felt comfort and clarity flowing into him.

But the Ambon's power was diminished. He hurried back down the aisle, and people stirred as he reached them, new hope dawning on their faces. But by the time he'd moved on they'd slumped back or wandered off on new pointless errands. It hurt him to leave them like that; but the Bishop's Council had first priority.

He re-entered the Domicile by a back entrance and hurried upstairs to the Fraternity Room. Muffled voices raised in anger came through the door. He wasn't a moment too soon.

He came in with the Ambon raised. Garset and Gil stood frozen in the midst of an argument, their faces red. Perrely came running to him. Her distress gave way to wonder as she felt the Ambon's influence.

Shiván leant the golden rod with its silver circle against the wall behind Bishop Harlon. Relief spread over the Bishop's features. Shiván beckoned to the others. "Come close."

The two Bishops turned their chairs round, while the others pulled theirs up or sat on the floor at the foot of the Ambon. Once they felt its healing power they couldn't get close enough, like a crowd of frozen travellers huddling round a fire.

"Shiván... God bless you," 'Neesh murmured.

Gil passed a hand over his forehead. "What was I thinking? Garset, forgive me..."

"I'm as much to blame as you," Garset muttered.

Frengor heaved a deep sigh. "Praise the One for the Ambon. If I was talking nonsense earlier on... please overlook it."

"None of us have been ourselves," Mâron said, and Harlon nodded.

Lannie was looking at Shiván with a puzzled frown. "What made you think of the Ambon? And how come *you've* been okay?"

"I know why," Perrely said. "Shiván has spent a lot of time sitting under the Ambon." She turned to him. "You told me the Ambon cleared your mind. But I didn't believe you. Now I do." There was a catch in her voice. Shiván longed to hug her.

Lannie stared incredulously. "You mean... Whatever hit us yesterday is the same as the problem *you've* had all this time?"

"I think so. The penny dropped when Mâron lost the thread of his thoughts earlier. But this has been a lot worse than what I had."

"Only because it's affected more people!" Perrely exclaimed. "Don't undervalue yourself, Shiván. You've coped with what we've just experienced far better than we have, for months on end!"

"With no help from us," Lannie muttered. "The opposite from me, in fact. Shiván... I'm sorry. You deserve a medal."

"At the very least," Harlon added. "Right now you deserve the heartfelt thanks of every man, woman and child in Stillárre."

"Okay, okay!" Shiván exclaimed, feeling heat in his face. "I just— did what I had to."

"You showed your quality as the One's Overguardian," Frengor said softly. "Let none of us doubt you again."

"And now we should resume our Council meeting," the Bishop said, glancing around the close-packed circle. "This time in our right minds."

Mâron cleared his throat. "Before we deal with the problems in the city, I think we need to know exactly *what* we're suffering from. Could it be an illness of some kind?"

Danîsha shook her head. "An illness would hardly have struck everyone at exactly the same moment. There would have been a period of some hours, at least, during which people started feeling the effects."

"So if not an illness, what else *could* it be? Mass hysteria?" Gil muttered the last two words in English.

"No way," Lannie retorted. "Then people would have got carried away with the excitement of what you were saying. Instead there was a sudden switch from happiness to misery. That's not mass hysteria."

Shiván did his best to translate for the Dûrians. There was a buzz of comment.

Frengor had been staring into the middle distance. Now his voice cut through the babble.

"I know what this is."

One look at his grim face silenced the meeting.

"We travelling priests wandered through all the Dûrai lands in times past. We learnt many things about the Cult of Gadesh. One of those was the potency of its curses."

"A curse!" Danîsha exclaimed. "That's what you thought, wasn't it Perrely, when Shiván first came back from Starmane?"

Perrely nodded, her eyes wide.

"Curses cast in the name of Gadesh himself, the Worldruler, have great power," Frengor continued, " —even against those in the Light. And the most powerful curse of all, the one that strikes terror into all who know it, is the *Curse of Futility*."

In the silence that followed Shiván saw everyone, himself included, measuring that name against what they had experienced. It fitted.

"I believe we have just had the Curse of Futility cast upon us. How it could have been done with such strength as to affect the whole of Stillárre, I don't know. Curses are normally cast in the presence of the victim, or from very nearby. There has been some phenomenal power at work here."

Bishop Mâron frowned. "But the Cult of Gadesh no longer exists in Stillárre — or anywhere else in Dûrion."

"No, it doesn't — except perhaps a few small groups meeting in secret. They would hardly have the power to cast a curse on this scale. Which reveals the magnitude of what we have just witnessed. It must have been done over a great distance... maybe from eastern Dûrion."

"So the whole country could be affected!" Harlon exclaimed.

"That's quite possible."

After a shocked pause Lannie said, "But tell us more about the curse itself. How does it affect people?"

Frengor sighed. "All I know is that the Curse of Futility confuses the sufferer's mind and undermines their will and self-confidence. Which ties in completely with what we've been experiencing so far."

Shiván found himself nodding. Perrely and Alanya glanced at him with wide eyes.

"But that's only the beginning. Over time, everything they attempt comes to nothing. They lose the will to live. People I've heard of, afflicted by this curse, have ended up taking their own lives, or dying neglected by the roadside."

His words fell into an appalled hush.

"*Unless* — "

Hope dawned.

"Unless they follow the example of Shiván here, and walk with God as they've never walked before."

───────────────

Chapter 28: *Benevolent mindbending?*

THE REST OF THE COUNCIL left the Fraternity Room in fear and awe as they set out to follow Shiván's example of constant reliance on the One. But Lannie stayed under the Ambon. She needed a period of clear thinking before she tackled those rough waters.

She sat on the floor at the foot of the sacred emblem, closed her eyes, and allowed its healing influence to flow through her. "Thank you, God," she murmured.

After a while she straightened and opened her eyes. *What am I doing here?* she wondered. *I thought I'd made a success of embracing the new career God gave me discerning the truth; yet when it came to Shiván's strange behaviour, I just fell right back into my old way of jumping to conclusions and making snap judgments. For months he was there in front of me all the time, struggling, losing his train of thought, making silly suggestions, and I just dismissed it as... what? I don't know what I thought about it, because I never thought! It was "just Shiván", so I paid no attention. God, have mercy on me!* She buried her face in her hands.

Now I'm in the same place as Shiván, and I can only thank you, dear Prince, from the bottom of my heart, that Shiván isn't treating me the way I treated him. He brought me home last night; this morning he's been looking after us, in full control of his faculties; he brought us the Ambon – and he was the one who discovered its power against the Curse.

I can forget about a 'career', now: just to stay in my right mind I have to trust you as Shiván does, moment by moment. Teach me how to do that!

Her face went down into her hands again and remained there for some time. Her thoughts turned to her lost fiancé Matt, and her snap judgment that had dismissed him as a bully who persisted in browbeating others till he got what he wanted. *Was that true?* Probably not. She'd tried so hard to get hold of him in the few days between their break-up and when she'd ended up here. Maybe it was just as well that she hadn't. She'd have continued insisting that he'd bullied her, when really... *Of course! It was for* my *sake he was doing that! He knew I wouldn't do what I needed to without pressure, so he was supplying it.* Idiot! *How could I* not *have seen that?*

She sat up, took a deep breath, and leaned back against the wall beside the Ambon.

And the situation with Gil? Same thing the other way round. She'd got him up on a pedestal, and rationalised away everything that would have tumbled him off it.

Well, Lord, one thing is for sure. Now I have to trust you moment by moment. Will you keep me from making any more snap judgments?

She felt, rather than heard, the glad affirmation. Her brow cleared and peace settled on her heart. She stood — just as Perrely stumbled back into the room and made a beeline for the Ambon.

"It's all yours," Lannie murmured as she headed for the door. Now to walk with God as she'd never walked before.

* * *

Estaron stood on the balcony of his palace apartment, gazing out over Orselm. He was shaken to the core by what had happened yesterday in the Temple of Gadesh. Every single Lightist in the Dûrai lands was now afflicted with the same Curse that had blighted his own life — only in its worst possible form. It was unimaginable.

His thoughts kept going to Dûrion. What was happening there now? Mindbender Belyeru had given him a graphic description of the effects of the Curse of Futility when properly cast; and there was no shadow of a doubt that *this* curse had been properly cast. It had been cast on every ruler and every citizen opposed to the Cult of Gadesh — and that included Dûrion and the Grûzhack Magistry. The governments there would have collapsed... merchants would be incapable of running their businesses... food supplies would run out... His mind couldn't grasp the breadth of this disaster.

The only hope now lay with the Restorers. Would they have been immune, with their foreign minds? If not... It didn't bear thinking about.

He himself felt no different: Konnar must have exempted him. He ought to be grateful, but right now gratitude did not come easily.

Where did this leave him with Konnar? If his friend could take an action like this without consulting him, what basis did they have for co-operation? Would there even *be* any unmindbent people left in Selmion for him to govern? The Curse had targeted those 'opposed to the Realm of the Mind', i.e. to the Cult of Gadesh; and that probably covered most of the unmindbent Selmian population. The government here wouldn't collapse, but what about food production? Trade? Crafts? Would all of those now become mindbent operations, like the customs service? In which case there would be even less need for a Governor of Selmion.

Gone, now, was the reassuring prospect of mindbending ending in two months' time when the teméyn stocks ran out. They would not run out, because in a single stroke Konnar had won the Grûzhack war. His forces could now march into Barazhân virtually unopposed and take control of teméyn production at its source. That is, if the Grûzhack were as susceptible to the curse as the Dûrai peoples. But after seeing the effect the Grûzhack child Brakhól had on his own people—with his Selmian 'training'—Estaron had to assume the Curse would be equally effective.

And what of the Renegades? His wider family? They were finished now. Under the Curse their network would fall apart, and many would give their secrets away as the iron discipline of decades failed. Would Konnar execute them, or simply ignore them? It hardly mattered. Either way, he, Estaron, was totally on his own now.

He walked back into the apartment and sank down into a chair at the table.

So. Konnar had succeeded in establishing mindbending in perpetuity. He had a long reign of despotism to look forward to, with Estaron as his loyal sidekick. Doing what? Establishing good governance? That was a joke.

Estaron buried his head in his hands.

* * *

In the afternoon, at the time he and Konnar normally had chass together, Estaron was wandering through the scented flowerbeds of the palace garden. His feet took him to the marble table and bench, and at the last minute he realised that Konnar was there.

"Bari," his old friend murmured. His eyes were sad, concern etched in the lines of his face.

Estaron stared at him for a long moment. Then he sat down and drew a deep, slightly shaky breath. *"Why,* Konnar?"

Konnar's sad expression deepened. "I knew you wouldn't approve, Bari, but it had to be done."

"Did it? Thousands of people sentenced to death—maybe tens of thousands—to preserve your position as Strongholder and the future of mindbending?"

"No, Bari. To preserve *our* future and the transformation of mindbending." He leaned forward, his eyes intent. "I know Mindbenders have always been the enemies of your family. But try to look beyond that for a moment. You saw how efficiently the customs service works at the docks: a mindbent operation. The same can be true in many other areas. Criminals and people who would otherwise be a danger to society can be used to serve society instead. Life for everyone can become better.

"I know Mindbenders have abused their powers in the past, but that will change. And I need *you* to help bring about that change. To transform, first Selmion, then other nations, into well-run countries where mindbending works as a service to law-abiding citizens, not a parasite draining their resources. Can't you see the tremendous value of that, Bari?"

During this earnest appeal Estaron's heart had sunk even further, if that were possible. "You're turning everything on its head, Konnar. Mindbending involves power over others, and people with power will always use it for their own advantage. Are you seriously asking me to believe that your Mindbenders will suddenly start acting for the good of society?"

A touch of steel entered Konnar's voice. "You forget that they are *my* Mindbenders. If I tell them to act for the good of society, they will do so."

"So this will be imposed by force?"

"Initially, yes. But take Mindbender Menaru and his customs service. He takes pride in how well it works. To make sure it continues to do so, he also takes good care of his mindbent subordinates. Over the years, if you and I put our hearts into it, we can make that the norm for all Mindbenders. Just as in Dûrion some choose public careers like law, both to serve society with high ideals of justice and, secondly, to benefit themselves; so also in future I can see people entering the Realm of the Mind for similar reasons. It can happen if the right conditions are created. For that I need you, as someone brought up in the tradition of good governance."

"Good governance…" Estaron shook his head. "How can you even speak of that, Konnar, when you have just treated tens of thousands of people as mere obstacles in your way?"

Konnar sighed. "The entire vision was under threat, Bari. I truly regret the short-term suffering — especially for your friends and family—but it *will* be short-term. Once we have established control in the surrounding nations, the Curse will be lifted; and when Stillárre is captured, your friends will be unharmed. That I promise."

"You promised the *Gorelenye* project would be ended. And there those children were in the temple yesterday, being tortured. One was even sacrificed—burnt to death!"

"I had to use the *Gorelenye* this one last time, Bari. I'm sorry it was painful for you. But now the order has been given: in a couple of months that barracks you saw will no longer exist, and homes will have been found for all the children. I'm happy to give you oversight of that once you're sworn in as Governor."

Estaron stared at his friend. He had an answer for everything. Yet he couldn't seem to grasp the barbaric nature of his so-called solutions. Or was this all an elaborate game he was playing? Trying to string Estaron along with a cock-and-bull story about 'benevolent mindbending' in order to win back his co-operation?

No, looking into his friend's concerned eyes Estaron could not believe he was that cynical. To some extent Konnar genuinely believed what he was saying. Yes, he wanted power. He was not willing to meekly allow mindbending to end. But, ridiculous as it seemed, he truly wanted to turn it to good as far as that was possible.

Konnar broke in on his thoughts. "I don't have to be a Mindbender to see that you're doubting me, Bari."

"Not doubting you. Just trying to understand how you can think something good could be made out of mindbending. Can't you see, Konnar, that mindbending itself is wrong? You are invading someone's mind without their permission and imposing your will on them. Treating them like a thing, not a person. Nothing can justify that—no matter what wider good may come of it."

Konnar regarded him soberly for a moment. "Is that so very different from denying a person their freedom? Locking them up in a prison cell, as you Lightists do in Dûrion? Or in a so-called 'Care House', if their minds are unsound?"

"Yes, Konnar, I believe it is different. When you take control of a person's mind you overrule everything that makes them what they are. That's far more serious than simply keeping them locked up."

"And what if 'what they are' is a threat to society? I have had people released from mindbending, Bari, and they have been better people for it. Former criminals have started living law-abiding lives. I review the slaves of all my Mindbenders from time to time and insist they release any who seem capable of being useful members of society."

Estaron's eyebrows rose. That was certainly a step in the right direction.

"Yes. Despite your poor view of mindbending, I *have* been concerned about good governance, Bari. Since becoming Strongholder I have stamped out wanton rape and abuse of the local population by Mindbenders and temple staff; I have abolished the special privileges some temples and Mindbenders had given themselves—like exclusive access to water supplies, first choice of local produce and imported goods, and so on. I have opened temple schools to the public with subsidised fees, and we've made some progress in persuading people to send their children there.

"I so much want you to be part of this, Bari. Time and again I've longed to discuss issues like these with you, and now you're here! Please. Let's do this together."

Estaron was at a loss in the face of Konnar's intense gaze and apparent sincerity. He turned and stared out over the gardens. Did he really mean it? How could he reconcile such total opposites as mindbending and good governance? Yet he seemed to have it all rationalised in his own mind. How could he partake in such a manifest evil as casting the Curse of Futility on all the surrounding nations—yet still be concerned about Mindbenders abusing the local population? There was no point raising that question; Konnar would have an answer ready that satisfied him, but made little sense to Estaron.

He turned instead to the present situation. "What is left for us to do together, Konnar? I can no longer be your Governor of Selmion. As the Curse takes hold I imagine there won't be many unmindbent people still functioning for me to govern; and you won't want me interfering with your Mindbenders. I couldn't—"

Konnar interrupted. "Oh, but you're wrong, Bari. There will be plenty of unmindbent people for you to govern. The purpose of the ceremony yesterday was mainly to broadcast the Curse outside our borders. My enemies here in Selmion—like your Renegades—will be affected, but not as severely as those outside. And you might have noticed that you yourself have been completely shielded."

"I did. Thank you." Relief mingled with a faint sense of shame flooded him. His wider family had not been destroyed. But Dûrion would be a disaster area... How could he work with Konnar after this?

"I'll need some time to think, Konnar. Yesterday has... shaken my confidence."

Konnar nodded, that sadness in his eyes again. "I understand. Your inauguration is planned for the day after tomorrow; so that gives you until tomorrow to decide. But whichever way you choose, you'll be welcome to stay, Bari."

"Thanks." He managed a brief smile, then stood and walked slowly back to the palace.

* * *

Watching his friend walking off with bowed head, Konnar sighed. It had been a shock to discover that, like most other Lightists he'd come across, Bari was too sensitive to make a good ruler. For years he'd had Bari up on a pedestal in his mind: the political expert, the one who knew how to run a country properly. But recent events had shown that he would not be able to handle the hard, pragmatic decisions a ruler had to make. He would take the soft way... and suffer the consequences.

Well, as Governor of Selmion Konnar would be able to protect him from those consequences—but he hoped Bari would learn from them.

He shook his head. It took some getting used to, this reversal of rôles in their friendship.

If Bari accepted the governorship—as he still sincerely hoped he would—there were some stormy waters ahead.

* * *

Estaron lay on a recliner in his darkening apartment, thinking. But no matter how much he thought, he kept reaching the same conclusion: unpalatable though it was, he had no option but to accept the governorship and continue working with Konnar.

The alternative was to sit idly by and watch all the Dûrai lands fall under Konnar's despotism. Konnar had declared him welcome to stay: but not to leave. As a mere guest in the palace he would have far fewer opportunities to go outside its walls and possibly engineer a meeting with the Renegades — if they remained active.

And despite everything, it seemed that Konnar still valued his advice. Perhaps he could lighten the despotism in small ways. Though the prospect of doing that for the rest of his life filled him with despair...

The door opened and a maid came in with a firestick and fireclay. She lit the already-laid fire before noticing Estaron on the recliner. She screamed and almost dropped the burning firestick. "Highness! I didn't see you — "

"My apologies, I was deep in thought. Do carry on."

She bowed her head and hurried round lighting the lamps before leaving.

For a long while Estaron stared at the growing flames in the hearth. He felt at one with with the wood as it was slowly and inevitably consumed.

Finally he made the only decision possible. With a heavy heart he murmured, "Creator God, help me to be your instrument in this dark situation."

Chapter 29: *Spreading nightmare*

"NEXT!"

Lannie watched as the woman at the front of the line shuffled forward holding a small sack. Her wide eyes were darting round the reception room of the merchant's town house. Hangings with subtly co-ordinated colours decorated the walls, spring green dominating. There were two recliners with matching upholstery. Bookcases full of leather-bound volumes stood against the side walls; and at the end, facing the street door, was the highly-polished counter behind which Lannie and Shiván stood. Next to them were two large sacks of *farn* grain, jarring with the gracious décor. A door behind them led to the storeroom where the grain was kept.

Lannie sighed. The merchant who owned the house was sitting upstairs, counting and re-counting the coins in a large chest. He hardly seemed to care that they were dishing out his merchandise to the needy of Stillárre. *Dear Prince, please keep me focused.* It never got easier.

The woman with the sack was coming forward, when her gaze settled on a small lampstand with delicate filigree work standing on a side table. She veered towards it, stepping off the strip of coarse cloth they'd laid down to protect the dark green floor-cover. Immediately a watchful Dorbian trotted over and blocked her way. He gave a small growl. The woman screamed and dropped her sack. With a sigh Lannie hurried over and took her arm. The Dorbian picked up the sack, and Lannie gave it back to her.

"Don't worry, he's just reminding you to walk on the cloth. Come to the counter, and I'll give you your grain."

It was the fifth time something like that had happened this morning. They could never have managed without the twelve Dorbian warriors guarding the door and shepherding people in. Outside was the clamour of a large crowd.

She ushered the woman to the counter, went behind it, and picked up a small scoop. It held enough grain to feed an adult for a day. She asked the woman how many children she had.

"Three."

Ask a man that question nowadays, and he'd most likely stare at you blankly. Under the curse women retained their social and caring instincts better. That—and to avoid accidentally feeding a family twice—was the reason the Dorbians had strict instructions to admit women only.

"How old are your children?"

"My son's fourteen— No, fift-… Anyway, he's big; then there's Carrilay, she's eleven; and little Shinda is five. She's always crying, because—"

"Yes. Is your husband with you?" Lannie hated cutting them off, but otherwise the job would never get done.

"No, he got lost when— when all this…"

Lannie felt her focus fading. *Please, Lord!* With difficulty she pulled her thoughts together. Something told her she needed her full concentration for this woman.

"Oh, I'm sorry. Any other adults that you're feeding?"

"No… except for Uncle Tarlion. He's with us until Aunt Bessel gets back from…" She tailed off under Lannie's stern gaze.

"I don't think so," Lannie said softly. The woman's eyes dropped.

"I'll give you three scoops for you and your children." Lannie poured the grain into her sack, adding a little extra for the five-year-old.

As the woman left, Lannie silently thanked the One for her gift of hearing the truth. If Shiván was in doubt, he referred people to her. That is, as long as she kept trusting the One Creator God every moment. She'd had a few lapses, when Shiván had jumped in and taken over for a while. Then she'd retired to another room to pray. God had never failed to restore her focus. But oh, how she longed for the evenings when they'd all gather under the Ambon and bask in its healing power!

It was time for a break. She signalled the Dorbian officer at the door not to allow anyone else in, and sat on the half-empty sack as she waited for Shiván and Anna to finish with their latest customer. Shivvie had brought the child with him each day, hoping that some woman would recognise her; so far no one had. When Anna wasn't too tired or confused he allowed her to pour the grain into people's containers.

Shiván's client left with her grain, and he sat down on his sack facing Lannie. Anna scrambled on to his lap and snuggled against him.

Lannie smiled. "Quite the family man."

"I wish."

After a moment's silence Lannie asked, "How is Perrely coping?"

"Not very well. She's too confused to pray when the Ambon's not there, so she starts feeling guilty, unworthy, useless… all that."

Lannie nodded. "None of the Dûrians are doing well without the Ambon. Even with it they're not much good unless they're right up close. We foreigners seem better equipped—though 'Neesh and Gil are struggling." The other two Restorers had the Ambon with them as they worked with Cârin and Jomel elsewhere in the city, persuading householders to take in the homeless folk who could not remember where they lived.

"True, but everyone has improved over the past couple of days," Shiván said. "I think Perrely, Garset, Mâron and the other Dûrians will soon be able to do some relief work, if they take the Ambon. You yourself have come a long way since Sunday. Then, you'd forgotten where the Domicile was. Now here you are, as sharp as a needle, and no Ambon in sight. How have you managed that?"

Lannie smiled ruefully. "Constant vigilance. I can't say how much I admire the way you've coped all these months, Shiván. I thought, if Shiván can do it, so can I."

"Wow. And there I was thinking you had me pegged as a clown."

"Not any more."

"So what's your system?"

"Well, I pray! That above all. But I've also found it helps to concentrate on my gift of discernment. I've had some practice focusing my mind—like when I was mindbent last year; and a few years earlier, when I was paralysed. Ever since then, when I've heard people moaning in despair and saying they can't do this or that, I've listened and discerned what's true. Usually it's much less than the person thinks. So now I've started doing the same with my own thoughts. I discount my despair and ignore my lapses of memory. I act *as if* I have hope, though I don't feel any. That way I avoid making lots of mistakes, which encourages me—so then I make fewer mistakes, get more encouraged, and so on."

"And that breaks the cycle of futility. Wow. I'm impressed."

"You showed me the way, Shiván. You know that it's not easy. I can never relax, or I start slipping back. I expect you have the same."

Shivvie nodded. "Yeah. As you say, constant vigilance. It's a relief to get back to the Ambon."

There was a brief bark from the Dorbian officer at the door. Lannie sighed. "The customers are restless. Back to work."

* * *

The day ended, and the next one began. Looting and rioting had broken out in parts of the city. Dorbian patrols were loping from one trouble spot to another.

The Council was meeting under the Ambon in the Domicile's Fraternity Room—the only place of sanity in the spreading nightmare.

Gil held the blaise by both handles, focusing its image on the wall beside the Ambon. Behind all his thoughts was a continuous cry for help to the Creator. He had thought the situation in Barazhân had tested his new-found confidence in God. It paled into insignificance now.

The rest of the Council was clustered around him, looking at what the blaise revealed. It was a picture of Darthane, and the streets were full of grey and tan-cloaked Selmians.

"There was no resistance," Garset muttered. "The Grûzhack just abandoned the city."

"Their army has fallen apart," Gil told him. He slowly panned the blaise westward. There were exclamations of shock as the Council watched. A column of Selmian cavalry was advancing unopposed towards Sûrilane. In the town itself people were milling about, some grabbing possessions from their houses, others running to and fro aimlessly. The market square was covered with a pall of smoke. Through it they glimpsed burnt and ransacked buildings. There was a groan from Mâron.

On towards Dhembis they saw clusters of Grûzhack warriors streaming south in an unco-ordinated rabble. Many were wandering through the fields, disoriented. Abandoned weapons and equipment lay scattered on the roads.

"They've been affected as badly as us," Perrely murmured, her face drawn.

Wherever they looked, towns and villages were in disorder; it was every man or woman for themselves.

Gil put the blaise away.

Tears were streaming down Bishop Harlon's cheeks. "My people... my people."

Other eyes were red-rimmed; everyone looked shaken.

"Dûrion no longer exists," Mâron said unsteadily. "The nation is now this city."

For a while they mourned.

Finally Shiván said, "We can't let Stillárre go the same way as the rest of the country."

Frengor nodded. "We must do all we can to hold things together here. We must make Stillárre a place of refuge from the chaos outside."

Garset spoke. There were dark rings under his eyes. "The army can't give much help. We're little better than the Grûzhack. There are hundreds of desertions every day."

"The Dorbians seem to be unaffected by the curse," Shiván said. "They're already doing a good job of breaking up riots and stuff. But they're handicapped by working with your troops, who often don't show up. Maybe we should hand over the defence of the city to them...?"

A shadow crossed Garset's face. Gil could dimly imagine how painful that suggestion must be.

Garset sat for a long moment, his lips compressed. When he spoke, it was with difficulty. "I think— You may be right, Overguardian. But what will happen when the Selmians get here? The Dorbians are too few. They won't hold the city for long."

"I think the Selmians will head for Barazhân first," Gil said. "They have to get the teméyn flowing again, or mindbending stops." He made a cutting motion with his hand.

"Right!" Shiván exclaimed. "That gives us some time. And we've all been learning how to cope, haven't we?" He looked around. "Alanya can function almost normally without the Ambon. You too now, Gil?" Gil nodded. "Garset, you went out yesterday and made it back again."

"Only just."

"But you did it. We're gradually learning how to trust God and remain in control, despite the curse. The improvement may be slow, but it will happen. And there must be others in the city— devoted Lightists, strong-minded people—who are also learning to cope. We must find them. Enlist their help in restoring order, getting food supplies coming in again, putting others to work."

"I agree with you, Shiván," the Bishop said. "We *will* cope, because we must. As the proverb says, *He who can control his mind can control a city.*"

Garset nodded. "What's left of the army is being held together by people like that, both officers and men. We could keep them, and let the rest go."

"Good idea," Shiván murmured. Gil saw the sympathy in his eye.

"But they would become civilians, not soldiers. We would in fact be disbanding the Dûrian army." He heaved a deep sigh. "Your Radiance?"

"It seems the best course, Garset."

He bowed his head.

"We'll speak to Gwargif tomorrow," Shiván said gently.

Danîsha shook her head. Perrely was weeping silently.

They turned their attention to the details of disaster management.

* * *

"Is Dorbi is guard all of Stillárre?" Gwargif sounded dubious.

Another morning of relief work had passed. Shiván, Garset and the Dorbian High Commander were sitting in the mess hall of a barracks the Dorbians had appropriated. The benches, rather than the tables, were used to eat from. The two men had moved a couple of food bowls before sitting down. Gwargif squatted on his haunches in front of them. Dorbians trotted past the open door from time to time.

"That's what we're asking," Garset said heavily. "I can no longer rely on my troops, Gwargif. I can't trust them to stay at their posts or do what they're ordered. We... don't have an army any more."

"Your warriors are already doing a great job keeping order in the city," Shiván told him. "You're also patrolling the outlying areas to guard against the Selmians; and you're bringing in stray animals for food. We're asking you to carry on as you are. Only, there won't be any Dûrian troops to help."

Gwargif blew a heavy sigh through his nose. "We do this, because Father of Warriors ask. If Selmin come, we fight. We keep Stillárre safe—from outside, from inside. But find food... is hard. People of city, they not like Dorbi. If not listen, how we make them help? Is Dorbi is not do all by self."

"I'll send my best men with your patrols tomorrow, Gwargif," Garset said. "They'll explain to people that your officers are now in charge, and must be obeyed."

The Dorbian gave a slow dip of the head and a snort of agreement.

There was a two-way volley of barks from outside, rising in volume. It sounded like an argument, which quickly turned into snarls and snaps. With a yelp Gwargif jumped up and trotted out of the mess. "*Diftakh!*" he roared. The fight subsided to low growls, which faded away.

Gwargif walked slowly back inside. Shiván thought how his friend had aged since they'd first met him, a frisky young wolf-warrior. His face had more lines now, and there was a tired wisdom in his eyes.

He squatted down and looked at the two of them sadly. "Dorbi go same way as Doorin, only slower. Is darkness in mind, is make light more faint. Now warriors of *hrarkhoneyl* fight selves, not enemy!" Shiván's heart sank a few notches. So the Dorbians were not immune to the curse. "But we are pack, we run together. Gwargif lead. If Gwargif not follow darkness, pack not follow darkness. We keep city safe."

Gratitude welled up for the Dorbian's loyalty. "Thank you, old friend."

Garset added, "We praise the One for you and your warriors."

They gave Gwargif the raised Dûrian handshake, then left.

* * *

The daymeal was served, as always these days, in the Fraternity Room. When it was over the Restorers and Council members rose to leave. Danîsha caught Gil's arm and at the same time called out, "Lannie!" They both turned.

"Please! Can we try and contact Shakhere in Barazhân? With all three of our instruments, so we can see and hear? What you showed us yesterday... those Grûzhack warriors wandering about... I'm so worried about Brakhól and his family and all our friends."

"Of course," Gil said. "We should have done it sooner."

They took their usual places around the Ambon. The Council and several others including Cârin and Jomel stayed to watch. Danîsha laid the bellaril on the floor in the centre of the circle, and asked the One to allow the instruments to work. Gil and Lannie began searching for Shakhere with the blaise and bess.

Gil focused the blaise on the wall. The picture soared over the mountains into Barazhân, giving Danîsha a nostalgic reminder of air travel and making the Dûrians gasp. Then Gil brought them down over the lush fields and valleys of the mountain state. Columns of smoke were rising in many places. As in Dûrion, towns and villages were in chaos. People were wandering about on the roads—some with possessions, some simply looking lost. Danîsha groaned; it was just as she had feared. The countryside was dotted with the ruins of rural mansions; the aftermath of civil war. Bodies and weapons littered the ground where there had been fighting—but there was no fighting now.

They reached Kharzil, and there the devastation was even greater; buildings burnt to the ground or ransacked, crowds looting shops and storehouses. Many Grûzhack and Grûzhileyn were sitting or lying by the roadsides with agonised faces, some in convulsions. "Teméyn withdrawal," Gil muttered. Danîsha nodded—before they left they'd seen symptoms like that among the Lightist Grûzhileyn who had come off the drug.

"Find the meeting hall," she urged Gil. The blaise passed over a ruined area of Gorhiz, the Grûzhileyn slum; and there it was, the building where they'd so recently held their nightly meetings. It was a burnt-out shell.

Danîsha cried out, her hands flying to her mouth.

But before she could speak, Lannie found Shakhere and the bellaril came alive with muffled 'woody' voices.

"Shakhere?" —Lannie.

"*Makhril!*"

"Shakhere, is that you?"

A shaky voice. "Who dis speaking? Where you are?" A babble of Grûzhack in the background.

"It's Alanya. I'm in Dûrion. Here is Danîsha." 'Neesh eagerly took the bess from her.

"Shakhere! Are you all right?"

"Mâra?"

"Yes, it's me. Are you safe? How is Brakhól?"

"Yes, I safe. Brakhól too. We not hurt." Danîsha sagged with relief. "But how you speak like dis?"

"I— We— It's too hard to explain." The picture still hovered over the ruins of the hall. "Tell me where you are, Shakhere."

"You not know? I outside Magistry tower."

The picture swept over ransacked buildings and bullet-chipped towers to the centre of Kharzil, where a large crowd was surging round the great octagonal Magistry tower. Gil's brows were knitted in concentration as he focused his thoughts on Shakhere. The picture zoomed in towards a ring of Grûzhileyn facing outwards around the base of the tower. Some held muskets and wore tattered city garrison uniforms. Then they found Shakhere, looking grimy but fit, gazing up into the sky with a bewildered expression. Many of the Grûzhileyn stared curiously at him.

"Are your parents all right?"

"Dey okay." His eyes kept moving, trying to see them.

"What happened after we left, Shakhere? We've been so worried about you."

Shakhere explained that civil war had spread all over the country. It was worst in Kharzil, and on the fourth day their meeting hall was torched by a Grûzhack militia group. Danîsha gasped and Gil shook his head as Shakhere described how he, Brakhól and his parents had only just escaped with their lives. They had taken refuge in the Gorhiz slum, where his parents were known.

Then on the fifth day... "everyone get mixed up. Not know place, even name! Fighting stop. We tink because no one have teméyn any more." He went on to explain that many teméyn stores, warehouses, and processing rooms on the plantations had been destroyed by the Grûzhileyn. Thousands in Barazhân were now suffering without the drug.

"Shakhere, people didn't get mixed up because they had no teméyn. It happened to us, too."

A hiss of surprise echoed from the bellaril, and the upturned face in the wall image registered shock. The Grûzhileyn around him laughed and began jostling him in fun. Shakhere said a few pungent words in Grûzhack, then added to his Dûrian listeners, "I go inside."

Gil followed him with the blaise through a splintered wooden door that must once have been magnificent. Inside was an empty octagonal foyer, the floor and walls inlaid with black and pink marble. It was littered with debris and pockmarked with musket holes. Several shattered doors yawned open in the marble walls. The noise of the aimless crowd outside faded.

In the centre of the foyer was a spiral staircase. Shakhere sat on the lower step. He looked puzzled. "What is make Doorin and Grûzhack mixed up, all at same time?"

"It's a curse, Shakhere, cast on us by the Selmians." The young man's eyes widened. "But you're not mixed up, so you must be trusting the Creator. Is that right?"

He nodded. "Yes. Faader, he pray very much." Gil gave a grunt of approval. "At first we all mixed up, like rest. Den we pray. Brakhól, he talk all time to Daddy." Danîsha's heart swelled with joy. "We help friends keep open to Light."

Shakhere went on to tell them with obvious pride that his father, Tal, had gathered together a number of people who were resisting the curse — both Grûzhack and Grûzhileyn — and they were upstairs in the Magistry council chamber now, setting up a new government. He and the Grûzhileyn around him were guarding the building; they would be the nucleus of a restored city garrison.

Danîsha's heart fell as Shakhere enthusiastically described Tal's plans for a new Grûzhack state based on equality. She glanced round, and saw the others in the Council circle looking grim. "They don't know about the Selmians!" Perrely exclaimed.

Gil said, "Let me speak to him. He must warn his father."

Danîsha handed over the bess, and Gil passed the blaise to Shiván, squatting on the floor beside him. The picture disappeared briefly, then wavered wildly until Shiván had refocused it.

"Shakhere," Gil said, "this is Gelmin. There's something very important you must tell your father."

Shakhere's face brightened, then grew longer as Gil told him about the approaching Selmians. They should not try to fight them, Gil said, or they might be killed or mindbent. The first thing the new Grûzhack government had to do was to find a place where they could go into hiding when the Selmians arrived.

"Grûzhack not hide!" Shakhere protested.

"Tell your father to pray about this," Gil said. "I think the Creator will show him that you'll achieve more by resisting the Selmians from a secret place, than by allowing yourselves to be killed or captured. Meanwhile here in Dûrion we will be doing all we can to find a way of ending the curse."

After more argument Shakhere reluctantly started up the spiral stairway to interrupt his father's meeting. Gil put down the bess with a sigh.

"Ending the curse?" Lannie said with raised brows.

Chapter 30: *Impossible solutions*

AS THE OTHERS LEFT the Fraternity Room, Gelmion touched Jomel's shoulder. "Would you mind staying for a moment?"

She looked at him, her eyebrows raised.

"There's something I need to say to you... privately." His earnest gaze bored into her.

Gelmion had changed while he'd been in Barazhân with Danîsha. That was very clear. Though his account of their trip had been interrupted that terrible day in the Stillárre Hearth, Danîsha had since told her that he was a changed man. He had declared the One's truth to the Grûzhack, and had responded to their questions about the Lightist faith. He had prayed, and his prayers had been genuine. Furthermore, they had been answered.

Still... she found it hard to trust him. Once before he claimed to have met the One, and it had all been an elaborate lie. After that, while he was pretending to be a devoted Lightist, he had repeatedly forced himself on her, holding her family hostage for her compliance with Shambor's help. Yes, he'd been mindbent, but he'd obviously co-operated with the tyrant for his own advantage. And the emotional scars of his abuse were still very tender.

But, alright. If he wanted to talk, she'd listen. His apparent change of heart deserved that much, at least. She nodded.

They walked back to the circular table. Perrely was still sitting under the Ambon, but she hurried out with a brief smile as they approached. They resumed their former seats; there were a couple of spaces between them. Gelmion stared at her for a long moment with an unreadable expression, his arms resting on the table, hands clasped together. There was a sadness in his shiláy. Then he bowed his head as the foreigners did when praying. Feeling a little uncomfortable, Jomel looked away.

"Jomel." She met his intense gaze. "Last year I did some terrible things." He swallowed. "Some of the worst were the things I did to you. I— What can I say?" His eyes moistened. "I am so, so sorry." He looked down again at the table.

Jomel was stunned. This was Gelmion? *Apologising* to her? Did she want his apology? Could she accept his apology? She needed to process this.

He lifted his red-rimmed eyes to her. "I know I pretended to be a Lightist last year. But in Barazhân, thanks to Brakhól and Danîsha, I discovered who the One really is. And since then, whenever I've thought about what I did to you, my heart has been broken."

For a long moment he looked at her, his eyes tortured, pain radiating from his shiláy. Jomel could not doubt his sincerity.

"So please— I'm not asking you to forgive me; but please believe that I mean every word of what I'm saying now. I can't think, 'The One has wiped away my wrongdoing, so everything's fine now'. It isn't fine. I have abused you and hurt you deeply, and my being sorry doesn't take that hurt away. But I just want you to know that now your pain hurts me, too. Last year I didn't care; now the One has made me realise what an appalling thing I did. Can you accept that?"

Jomel stared at the man she'd once been attracted to. He wasn't asking her to forgive him, which she wasn't sure she could do yet. Just to accept that his sorrow about what happened was genuine— which it certainly appeared to be. That, taken with what Danîsha had said, was enough—maybe.

"Yes, I think I can accept that," she murmured.

Relief washed over his face. "Thank you."

* * *

Danîsha lay awake in her priest's cell in the Domicile, unable to sleep. The images they'd seen through the blaise, both in Dûrion and in Bara-zhân, kept replaying themselves in her mind. Two entire populations reduced to futility, and the conquering army of an oppressor worse than any Hitler sweeping in! Dear God. What would become of Sha-khere, Brakhól, Tal, Mistil, and the others she'd left in Barazhân? What would become of herself and her friends here in Stillárre? *Lord, help us.*

Gil had spoken of finding a way to end the curse. How could they do that? She, at least, could still barely function away from the... what's-its-name. There. Her thoughts were already getting confused.

She got up and pulled a robe over her night clothes. She'd go back to the Fraternity Room and pour herself some leftover chass.

After several wrong turns she arrived at the meeting room. She opened the door, and stopped. Someone had beaten her to it. A robed figure was silhouetted against the glowing embers at the far end. She spoke the evening greeting. "*Ney li silmend.*"

"*Illi ristend*. You're up late, 'Neesh." It was Shiván.

"I couldn't sleep." She walked over to join him.

"Me neither. Would you like some hot, overbrewed chass? It tastes horrible."

"Hot is fine."

He poured the dark, steaming liquid into a two-handled mug from a kettle hanging over the coals. Danîsha sipped, grimaced, and sipped again.

"Let's sit by the Ambon," Shiván suggested. She followed him gratefully to the other end of the room. As they sat on the Bishops' chairs facing the great emblem, Danîsha felt the heavy burden of trying to think straight slipping away. She sighed with relief.

"What brings you here so late, Shiván? Also thinking about this dreadful curse?"

"Actually, no." He was silent for a moment; then sighed.

"I was thinking about Perrely."

"Oh, Shiván. I'm sorry. Shall I leave?"

"No, please stay. I could use the company."

She couldn't see his face, but he was slumped despondently in the chair.

"I love her, 'Neesh. But the curse has affected her badly — you've seen how she spends every moment under the Ambon. I long so much to comfort and protect her that it hurts; but there's always that line I can't cross. It's become like this big... barrier between us. We can't even talk normally any more."

He turned towards her. She could see the agony etched on his face in the dim glow from the distant embers.

"It must be awful for you, Shiván. I only wish there was something I could do. I've spoken to Perrely, but she keeps insisting the One has called her to singleness. It's almost as if she's clinging to that, as if her self-respect demands it. I sometimes wonder whether it's a genuine calling, or whether she's... denying her true self in an effort to please God."

Shiván nodded vigorously, and relief swept briefly across his face. "Yes! You're right — that's exactly it! Thank you, 'Neesh. God told me the same thing when he sent me to Earth last year. I was blaming myself for jumping to the wrong conclusion about what the One wanted for us, but then he showed me it was actually Perrely who'd got it wrong. He *does* intend us to be together, I know it. But Perrely still can't see that." His voiced tailed off, and the old sadness returned.

"Have you discussed it with her, Shiván?"

He shook his head. "The One told me not to say anything. He will show her when the time is right. Once or twice I've tried to say something like, 'Are you sure?' — but she refuses to talk about it."

Danîsha's heart went out to the young man, so earnest, so sincere. Somehow, Perrely *had* to be made to see reason! But now wasn't the time, while she was still so strongly affected by the curse.

"All I know, 'Neesh, is that I can't stop loving her." He spoke with a quiet finality. "I'll wait for her — I'll never marry anyone else. I'll always be there for her, even if we're only friends. When we've finished our job as Restorers — *if* we finish it — maybe the rest of you will go back to Earth. But not me. If God gives me the choice, I'll stay on here in Dûrion. Because I can't bear to be away from her."

Danîsha laid a hand on his knee. "You know I'm praying for you both, Shiván. I do believe that some day, somehow, he'll give you the desires of your hearts."

He responded with a wan smile. "Thanks, 'Neesh. I'll hold on to that."

They sat together in silent companionship, their overbrewed chass growing cold.

*   *   *

Alanya hurried up the stairs to the Fraternity Room. Gil had seen in the blaise that Sûrilane and Dhembis had fallen to the Selmians without a fight. Everywhere Dûrian society was collapsing, and the Bishop had called another emergency Council meeting.

Harlon looked haggard as they all took their places under the Ambon. He glanced at each of them from under his white brows before speaking slowly and deliberately, pain etched in his face.

"Friends, what we are seeing around us is unprecedented. The sheer scale of the universal collapse of law and order and of any armed resistance to the Selmians has led Frengor and me to the belief that what we are seeing is an event that has long been foretold in our Book." He glanced at the head of the Travelling Order.

"Yes," Frengor said, his face grave. "Harlon and I have prayed and studied together these past few days, and we have come to the conclusion that this has to be the Great Darkness spoken of in the *Book of Visions*."

"The Great Darkness! Oh no," Perrely murmured, her eyes wide.

Harlon opened the heavy book on his lap. "*Visions* section seventeen, clause five, says: *A great darkness will cover all the lands, when every man's endeavours will come to nothing.* Does that sound familiar?"

There were sombre nods around the circle. Light trees stood on either side. Their soft glow was reflected in the gold and silver of the Ambon leaning against the wall.

Frengor added, "Later clauses speak of all that will be lost in the Great Darkness: lost goods; lost crops; lost people; lost families; lost homes and towns; lost thoughts and memories... lost lives. The prophecy speaks of *all the lands*. That goes beyond Dûrion and Bara-zhân. It includes all the Dûrai nations, maybe others as well. I believe the Curse of Futility must have been cast by the Strongholder himself in Orselm, probably with the support of every single Mindbender under his control."

"Dear Lord," 'Neesh muttered, aghast.

Lannie closed her eyes at the image of untold thousands waiting helplessly to be conquered. "He'll rule the world!"

"Unless he's stopped," Frengor said softly.

Harlon opened the Book to a different place. "You all know the Ambon prophecy." He glanced round the circle.

"*They will lift high the Rod of Truth to summon the faithful,*" Perrely quoted.

Harlon nodded. "*Return of the Prince*, section 36, clause 3. We saw that fulfilled last year, didn't we?"

There was a general murmur of assent as they remembered how the Ambon—the Rod of Truth—had drawn thousands to the Restorers' cause.

"But do you remember the rest of the Ambon prophecy?"

"Yes," Perrely said, puzzled. "It goes on to say, *They will raise it over the altar of darkness, and release my captive people.*"

"What 'altar of darkness' does that refer to?"

"The darkness of mindbending."

Harlon and Frengor exchanged a sad smile. "That's how we all interpreted it," Frengor said, " —until now. We took the 'altar of darkness' as a poetic reference to the Cult of Gadesh, the religion of the Mindbenders, exalting itself over the true Way."

"But what if it was meant literally?" Harlon suggested.

There was a pause.

"Then it would refer to the altar of Gadesh," Garset said.

"Exactly."

"But surely that comes to the same thing?" Perrely protested.

"No." Mâron looked grim. "I see what his Radiance and Frengor are getting at. You—and most of us—are thinking of the altars of Gadesh that existed in this country until recently. But that prophecy was written in Selmion, several centuries ago. At that time, there was only one altar of Gadesh."

"The altar in… Orselm." Perrely's voice fell to a whisper, horror dawning in her face.

"That is the only place where a curse of such power could have been cast," Harlon said softly. "And we believe the prophecy is telling us it's the only place where it can be lifted."

There was a moment of shock, then an outburst around the circle. Everyone spoke at once. Lannie's voice rose above the rest. "You're saying we have to take the Ambon to *Orselm*? To the *capital* of the Strongholder's own country? Then calmly stroll into the Temple of Gadesh and hold it up over the *altar*?"

"We believe that is the only way this Great Darkness can be ended."

Lannie stared at the Bishop in disbelief. "We might as well try and walk into the White House and put a bomb in the Oval Office," she muttered in English.

"How could the Restorers possibly reach Orselm?" Garset demanded. "It would take an army four times the size of the one we *used* to have!"

"And even if we went on our own and somehow got past their soldiers, what about all the Mindbenders in Selmion?" 'Neesh exclaimed. "They'd spot us at once!"

"Their *shilâyet* would give them away!" Perrely added, her eyes straying anxiously to Shiván.

Frengor raised a hand. "Nevertheless," he said, his voice quiet but compelling. "That is our only hope. Otherwise the Strongholder will win a victory so total that these lands may never know freedom again."

An appalled silence settled over the Bishop's Council.

Finally Shiván cleared his throat. "We'd have the Ambon…"

"Oh yes, we'd be in our right minds," Lannie shot back, " —until we got caught."

"Nothing is too difficult for the Creator God," Gil said quietly. "If he says we'll raise the Ambon over the altar of Gadesh in Orselm, then that's exactly what will happen."

Lannie stared at Gil. Surprise warred with frustration within her. He was now the believer, she the sceptic.

Frengor sighed. "You're right, Gelmion. But nothing is said in the prophecy about what will happen here, while you are gone. We will also pay a price."

"It's impossible!" 'Neesh burst out. "If we take the Ambon away, you'll all be left… in the dark! Stillárre could end up like those other towns we saw in the blaise. There'll be no government, no law, no *hope* for anyone in Dûrion!"

"Ah, but there *will* be hope. The hope that one day, against all the odds, you'll succeed. That's what will keep us going."

"Prince have mercy on us," Garset muttered.

Chapter 31: *Into the darkness*

GIL AND LANNIE MANOEUVRED a large wooden box through the front
door of the Domicile. Behind them twelve Dorbians held a
clamouring crowd at bay. The box was full to the brim with non-
perishable foodstuffs which they would need on their journey:
biscuits made from *farn* grain, dried fruit, chunks of hardened sweet-
tree syrup, nuts, dried fish, small bags of *histay*, which looked like
rice; and even a packet of preserved meat which they'd bought from a
Thrinari merchant.

"Whew!" Lannie observed as the doors banged shut and they put
the box down on the marble floor. The reception hall was littered
with boxes, bags, cooking pots and other equipment assembled for
their hurried departure. "Remind me never to go camping under a
curse again!"

Gil smiled. He appreciated Lannie's lively spirit, though there was
nothing between them any more. "There are still those sheets of
waterproof fabric to get for our lean-tos."

"No, oh no… I *have* to have a break before going out among that
lot again."

Her wish was granted. Shivvie came bounding down the stairs
and skidded to a stop when he saw them. "You're back! Frengor has
something he wants to show us all."

They trooped up to the Fraternity Room.

The rest of the travelling party was gathered round the Ambon:
'Neesh, Garset, Perrely, Cârin and Jomel. The Council had decided
the four Restorers should be accompanied by an equal number of
Dûrians, to dilute their foreign shiláyet. Jomel was included
because her father was Selmian, and she spoke the language
fluently.

Frengor was standing with the others, holding a leather tube
about two feet long. "Ah, here are our missing travellers. Gelmion,
I particularly wanted you to see this."

They all clustered round Frengor at the end of the oval table
nearest to the Ambon. He worked a circular cap off the end of the
leather tube, then carefully pulled out a roll of thick, creamy paper.
"You hold this end," he said to 'Neesh, who pressed her palms on

the left edge of the sheet. Frengor rolled the paper out across the table, and Perrely gripped the other end.

At first the swirling black marks meant nothing; then the penny dropped. "A map!" Gil exclaimed in English.

Frengor glanced at him. "I knew we had a *darlis* of Selmion somewhere in our archives, and last night I found it. You can take this with you. It was made during the brief period when our Dûrian Founders restored the monarchy in Selmion; it's about three hundred years old, but well preserved."

"Oh!" There was disappointment in Danîsha's voice. "So it won't be very accurate."

Frengor laughed. "It'll be accurate enough for you. Nothing much changes in Selmion. Now, look, here's the way you should go ..."

He traced a route through the northern part of the country to the coast, then south to Orselm, avoiding the major centres. Gil's heart sank. Even so... How could they cross the entire country undetected?

Frengor turned the map over. On the back was a city plan of Orselm, the River Selm winding along its southern edge. Most of the symbols were obvious: thick black lines marked the streets, and enclosed shapes were the buildings, many of them labelled in Selmian. Frengor showed them the Royal Palace—now the Strongholder's palace—the city square, the harbour, the law courts... and an unmarked shaded rectangle. "That," he said grimly, "is the Temple of Gadesh. In the Founders' day it was destroyed. But it has long since been rebuilt."

They stared in a dark, foreboding silence at their impossible goal.

As if reading their thoughts Frengor said, "It may not be as impossible to get to as it seems. I will give you details of someone to contact if... when you reach Orselm. For that you will need Jomel here. I understand you speak Selmian well?"

She nodded with wide eyes. "My father is Selmian, and I lived there as a child."

"That may be crucial on this mission. Anyway, the person you contact will put you in touch with the Renegade Royalty—who do all they can to oppose the Strongholder. I'll tell you more about them later. But the Renegade Royalty can give you access to *these.*" He put his finger on one of a network of dotted lines that criss-crossed the map.

"What are they?" Perrely said.

Frengor grinned. "I'm glad you asked. These, my friends, are the ancient tunnels under Orselm."

"Tunnels!" Danîsha exclaimed. "What are they for?" They all leant forward to peer at the dotted lines on the map.

"They are underground roads that connect important homes and buildings with one another. Here is the palace, and this —" his finger traced a dotted line from the palace to a long rectangular building near the west gate of the city "—leads to the cavalry barracks." His finger moved to another dotted line. "This connects the palace to the City Provost's house."

"And this," Shiván said, putting his finger on a dotted line running to the shaded rectangle, "leads to the Temple of Gadesh. Wow!"

"Well, that's all very nice," Lannie said, "but aren't these tunnels guarded? Surely we can't just walk in?"

"If you make contact with the Renegade Royalty and show them the Ambon, I'm sure you'll do exactly that. You see, the tunnels were built during the troubles before our Founders liberated Orselm; but after that they were blocked off because some of them became flooded. As far as the Strongholder knows, that is still the case. But in more recent times the Renegade Royalty have reopened the tunnels, and they found many that are still dry. They recruited a number of masons to repair and maintain them, and they use them now to move about the city unseen. Only the Renegade leaders and their most trusted agents know about the tunnels."

Gil nodded, and smiled at Frengor appreciatively. "So if we make it to Orselm we have a good chance of reaching the Temple of Gadesh unhindered. Thank you, Frengor. That makes the whole enterprise seem more hopeful."

"*If* we make it to Orselm," Lannie muttered.

* * *

Perrely shivered as the procession began its slow progress from Stillárre's market square to the Berûvis Gate. Shiván was in front, holding the Ambon, and she was at his side because she needed its sustaining influence. Behind them were the other three Restorers, followed by Garset, Jomel and Cârin. They were each leading a camel-horse with a large pack strapped behind its rear hump. The four men wore their swords. Danîsha carried the bellaril on her back. Overhead was a dark sky.

The street to the gate was lined with everyone in Stillárre who had any degree of mental control. They watched the group pass by silently, their faces grim. Tears streaked many cheeks. One despairing statement was heard over and over: *The Restorers are leaving.*

Perrely's heart ached for the people of Stillárre. They were entering a long tunnel of darkness with only a thin sliver of light at the end: the forlorn hope that these eight travellers would succeed in their all-but impossible task.

Just inside the gate the two Bishops and Frengor were waiting. The travellers stopped, holding their horses, and the onlookers closed in behind them. Harlon climbed the first couple of steps that led to the wall, so that all could see him. Overnight he seemed to have aged ten years. Yet when he raised his right arm and spoke the priestly blessing, his voice was strong:

"*The One bless you and keep you.*

The One make his Light shine upon you, and be gracious to you.

The One smile upon you, and give you peace.

"My children, you go with the prayers and longings of all who follow the Light. May the Prince strengthen and uphold you every step of your journey!"

Shiván handed the reins of his horse to Perrely. He thanked the Bishop and climbed the steps to stand beside him, holding the Ambon. He turned to face the silent crowd.

"Friends, don't lose hope! Remember the Prince in his darkest hour. His enemies had him at their mercy. He had lost everything. They mocked him, cut him, tortured him, then threw him on the flames like rubbish to be burned. *But God did the impossible!* He was re-made in the fire and lived again! He defeated his enemies so completely that they no longer have *any* power over those who live in his Light. That's *us*. The curse may hold us back for now, but it cannot hold us forever!"

He paused. Perrely's heart was full. All eyes were riveted on Shiván; and maybe, just maybe, there was a lessening of the stark despair. At that moment the clouds parted and a ray of sunshine lit up Shiván and the Bishop on the stairway. Harlon's robe glowed bright crimson, Shiván's cloak a deep, rich blue; and the Ambon sparkled gold and silver.

Shiván laughed and raised the Ambon high. Light flashed from it and a clear, piercingly sweet trumpet call rang out. All crowded closer, their eyes wide. Shiván cried, "This present darkness *will* be lifted, my friends! The One has said so. It will happen. Look to him every moment in the days that follow, and *keep on hoping.*"

There was a roar of assent.

Shiván took a deep breath. "We'll be back! Until then, the One be with you all."

"The One be with you!" Garset echoed, and Perrely and the others joined in. There was a chorus of response. Then someone began singing, *God above all kings and powers, blessed be your name.* Others joined in, and the sound swelled to an anthem of praise, defying the darkness.

The brief sunlight faded, and they turned and led their horses into the gate tunnel. As they passed Frengor and the Bishops, each received the Dûrian high handshake. Frengor murmured an encouraging word, and Bishop Harlon blessed them again, his eyes filmed with tears. When they reached Mâron, his wife Shindorel stood beside him holding Shiván's adoptee—the little girl he'd named Anna.

"She'll be all right with us," Mâron said, his kindly face showing the strain of the times.

"Thank you so much."

Shiván took the girl in his arms. "Be good now, with Uncle Mâron and Aunt Shindorel." She nodded solemnly. He gave her a kiss and passed her back.

On the outer side of the gate the Dorbians were ranged in a triple line along the city wall, far enough from the gate to avoid startling the horses. Shiván and Garset walked over to say farewell to Gwargif. The Dorbian commander reared up and placed his paws on Shiván's shoulders.

"Go, *Hrarborgh*. All Dorbi is bless you. We watch Stillárre, you kill darkness." A wet tongue touched Shiván's forehead.

Shiván placed a hand on the Dorbian's shoulder. "The Shining One be with you, my friend." Garset nodded his agreement. "Dûrion owes you a debt we can never repay."

They returned to the highway, where the whole group mounted their horses and set off at a brisk trot.

Behind them the Dorbians raised a long, drawn-out howl filled with sorrow and longing.

———————————————

Chapter 32: *Teméyn in jeopardy*

JOMEL RODE BESIDE PERRELY AND SHIVÁN as they approached Berûvis. This was where Perrely had grown up, and tears ran down her cheeks as she surveyed the neglected fields, the fire-ravaged homes, and the corpses lying abandoned at the roadside. Behind them the sun was setting in a riot of red and gold, casting a lurid glow over the curse's handiwork. Jomel's heart went out to her cousin. She reached across the gap between their horses and clasped Perrely's hand, winning a brief smile of gratitude.

They had been travelling for nine hours since leaving Stillárre. Everywhere the sights were heartbreaking. A well-ordered society had fallen apart in two short weeks. There was little traffic on the roads, but the many crashed or abandoned vehicles slowed their journey. Some, full of merchandise, had been plundered by the ragged scavengers who now roamed the countryside.

"We turn here," Perrely told Shiván, pointing to a gateway on the left. It would have been imposing, if one of the wrought iron gates hadn't been hanging askew.

They threaded their way between the gates and set off along a tree-lined drive that wound its way up a hill. Jomel shook her head. She doubted the wisdom of coming to Perrely's old home; but her cousin had argued that it would be safer than the town, and the others had agreed.

They came out of the trees, and there was the house. Jomel's voice chimed with Perrely's in an involuntary cry of shock. The large, single-storey building hadn't been burned; but that was the best you could say. The front door was missing. The windows had been smashed and the hangings removed. Broken furniture and utensils — the debris of looters — were scattered about the forecourt. They dismounted and tied their horses to the hitching rail at the far side, then took their shoulder pouches into the house.

Perrely stood in what remained of the elegant reception room, clearly struggling to control her tears. Jomel slipped an arm around her. The dark burgundy floor-covering was stained and ripped by the heavy objects that had been dragged across it. Not a single intact piece of furniture remained. Shards of smashed flower bowls and wall mirrors littered the floor.

As they walked through the manor house they found that every room had been looted; but there was a guest bedroom on the far side of the central courtyard that still had a heavy bedstead and mattress. They leaned the Ambon on the wall next to it. Perrely sat on the mattress, staring around the empty room in disbelief. Danîsha and Jomel joined her while the others went exploring.

Danîsha took out the bellaril and started playing. The sweet music lifted their spirits, though it brought back memories of happier times.

After a while Alanya came in to tell them that the bathing rooms still had running water. "Oh!" Jomel exclaimed in delight. The thought of a bath, even a cold one, was delightful. Perrely and Danîsha followed her as she hurried after Lannie.

Later, refreshed, they brought their packs to the rear of the house. By unspoken agreement the large bedroom became their communal dining chamber and sleeping quarters. Jomel could see that, like her, none of the women wanted to sleep separately from the men; that was a luxury they could not afford on this journey.

They found wood and kindling in the kitchen, and cooked up a supper of *histay* grain and dried fish from their supplies. Cârin brought in a light tree that was only slightly damaged.

Afterwards people began preparing to sleep — the women sharing the bed, the men on the floor. Shiván went outside, taking the first watch guarding the horses. Then a thought seemed to strike Gelmion, and he turned to Danîsha. "Shall we find out what's happening in Barazhân?"

Mâra looked pleased. "Lannie?"

With a sigh Alanya rose from the bed, where she'd been lying with her eyes closed. She took the bess out of a pocket in her robe. The three of them sat on the floor facing the empty wall. Jomel and the others clustered behind them as Gelmion and Alanya began searching for Shakhere with the blaise and bess.

"I hope Tal managed to get his people out of Kharzil before the Selmians arrived," Danîsha muttered while the other two Restorers concentrated.

"I thought it was the Grûzhack army they were worried about?" Jomel whispered.

"No, last time Shakhere said only a few of their soldiers had returned. They were running towards Kharzil from the Selmians, who had driven them out of Fort Desheyn. By now the Selmians must have reached the city. The Grûzhack army won't stand a chance. Oh, I do hope Tal and his family are safe…"

"Shakhere!" Alanya exclaimed.

"Mâra?" came a woody voice from the bellaril. At the same time a flickery picture appeared on the wall — Gelmion had found him with the blaise. It took Jomel some moments to realise that it was a fire inside a cave. Shakhere's head was in the foreground, silhouetted against the flames. Other shadowy figures appeared and faded behind him as the firelight shifted.

"Here's Mâra," Alanya said, handing the bess to Danîsha.

"Shakhere! Praise the One! You've found a hiding place?"

"Yes. We in caves in mountains. Selmin not find us here."

"Are your parents and Brakhól all right?"

"Dey fine."

"Is your government there, too?"

"Yes. Also many strong people, Grûzhack and Grûzhileyn. And shoot-sticks. We attack Selmin." The young man's pride was obvious, even in the muffled tones of the bellaril.

A voice spoke from behind him, and the silhouette turned away to listen. After a short exchange it turned back. "Faader say to tell you, is no more Grûzhack army. Selmin now rule in Kharzil. But we give dem big trouble. Mindbenders take many warriors for going just a few aldoret. We kill two already! We also break teméyn plantations."

"Ah!" Gelmion exclaimed, then said a few words to Danîsha which Jomel couldn't follow. They must have been in Inglish.

Mâra put the bess back to her ear. "Gelmion says that's good, Shakhere. Stop the Selmians getting teméyn, and mindbending will end."

"We know. Faader say dat too."

"We ourselves are on the way to Selmion, Shakhere, with the great Ambon. We are obeying a prophecy in the Book. Where is that written, Perrely?"

Perrely sighed and thought for a moment. "*Return of the Prince*, section 36, clause 3."

Danîsha repeated the reference to Shakhere. "Find that in my copy of the Book. We're trusting the One Creator God to enable us to raise the Ambon over the altar of darkness in Orselm. We believe that will end the Curse. Tell your father this. And pray for us."

"That is good! I read, and we pray."

A child's voice clamoured behind Shakhere. "*Mâra!*"

"Brakhól!"

The others in the bedroom got up, smiling, as Danîsha and the child chatted happily together. Even Perrely's wan face softened. Jomel gave her a hug before tumbling on to the bed. She pulled her robe over her, then tucked her travel pack under her head. Gelmion was sitting by the window. He had an attractive profile in the dim light from outside...

What was she thinking? That meant nothing any more.

* * *

In the great dining hall of the royal palace in Orselm the Strongholder was giving a banquet. Konnar was resplendent in his ceremonial black and silver finery. Estaron sat on his right, as befitted the Governor of Selmion, wearing the simple dark blue Governor's robe he had chosen for himself. All around the table, which formed a hollow square, Mindbenders' grey robes mingled with the tan uniforms of military officers. Wealthy merchants and other prominent citizens unaffected by the Curse added a touch of colour. In the centre of the square a fountain sparkled under the many light trees that hung from the ceiling. At the far end of the hall a band played soft music.

Estaron admired the décor, but he was not in sympathy with the purpose of this banquet. He had completed his first week as Governor of Selmion without too many hitches; he did not need a reminder that he might be spending the rest of his life in this job.

"Your Highness, let me congratulate you on your recent appointment." The merchant on Estaron's right was beaming at him. A large, florid man with multiple chins. "We are all delighted that you are relieving his Supremacy of local concerns." Estaron bristled at the patronising tone. "I'm Kaleniu Narida—I trade in exotic spices." He held up his hand, and they exchanged the Selmian palm-press greeting. "So, tell me, what have you achieved in your first week?"

"Well, let me see..." Estaron narrowed his eyes and stared at a point above the other's head before continuing. "I have made a start on reviving the old Royal Post, to allow rapid communication between different parts of the country."

"Ah, yes. Without mindspeech that would be important for you."

Estaron eyed him. "I have closed down the *Gorelenye* project, relocating the children to foster homes."

Kaleniu's eyebrows shot up and his smile faded. "Really? The Strongholder..."

"...has accepted my initiative in this. I have also—just today—cancelled the trading privileges that gave unfair advantage to a number of merchant houses. I believe business enterprises should succeed by their own merit, not through patronage. Don't you agree, Merchant Kaleniu?"

The smile was now definitely gone. "I— Yes, of course. Of course, Highness. But—ah—good business relations do play a part, don't you think? I mean, it's important that there should be—ah—cordiality between..." The merchant on his right spoke, and he muttered "Please excuse me—" before turning abruptly away.

Estaron hid a smile. The message would spread through the merchant community that the new Governor had teeth. There was no need—yet—to completely antagonise them by announcing his planned tax increases.

A trumpet sounded, and Konnar stood up to speak. The band fell silent. Gedoriu, the major-domo, depressed a lever on the wall and the fountain subsided into its flower-bedecked pool. A deep hush descended over the banqueting table.

"My dear friends, tonight we celebrate a major milestone: our troops' resounding victory in Barazhân." There was a thunder of hands slapping the table, in which Estaron did not participate. "We now control all teméyn production under Malane; the Realm of the Mind has been permanently secured." Applause broke out again.

"Soon the teméyn caravans will again be travelling our roads, and we'll have the supplies we need to start repairing the damage done by the Curse of Futility. Damage that was deplorable, but unavoidable. When law and order is restored, the Governor and I intend to turn these lands, together with Selmion, into realms of good governance. The curse will be lifted, and freedom and justice will prevail."

His voice dropped and he continued in a steely tone: "There will be no exploitation of citizens in these lands. There will be no profiteering from our victory. We will be rebuilding, not feathering our own nests. I hope everyone in this room understands that."

There was total silence in the hall. A few heads nodded; others stared at the Strongholder like birds mesmerised by a snake.

"Now — we are here to celebrate! Enjoy the feast!"

A babble of relieved chatter broke out. Servers fanned out around the table bringing in the first course: grûn-tail soup with chunks of meat and doughy *hîrin* floating in it. In deference to his Lightist vegetarian principles Estaron received a clear *argis* soup dotted with chopped young sprouts of the vegetable. It was delicious.

Give Konnar his due, he had not gone on at length about their 'resounding victory' in Barazhân. Mopping up the Curse-struck remnants of the formerly fearsome Grûzhack army was hardly an epic achievement. And he'd made a public declaration — for the first time, it appeared from the reactions — of the good governance policy they'd discussed together. That gave some grounds for hope.

Nevertheless… Teméyn supplies would now be replenished and the status quo maintained. Estaron did not share Konnar's enthusiasm for 'benevolent mindbending'.

He could only wait and see how things worked out in the weeks to come.

* * *

Shakhere attacked the large teméyn press with a will. His axe crashed down on the frame, splintering it. Two more blows, and the perforated metal pan through which the juice flowed clattered to the floor. Barkt, the Overseer of the Olbizân plantation, brought a sledge-hammer down on it, and it shattered into a dozen pieces.

"Now the filters and precipitation trays," Barkt gasped, panting with the unaccustomed effort. All around them the Grûzhileyn workers leapt eagerly to obey. As usual, Shakhere hadn't found it hard to persuade them. Freedom had been within their grasp, then the Selmians had arrived to impose a far more terrible servitude. They would do anything to prevent that. When their present vandalism was done, a chosen few would escape with him to swell his father's army in exile. The others would disperse to stay with relatives and friends. The plantation, like many others, would be ruined and abandoned.

A while later later someone shouted, "Now the drying ovens!"

"No, wait!" Shakhere called out. "First burn all the seedlings!" There were cries of agreement as Barkt's wife Felhis led the women at a trot to the greenhouses where next season's plants were laid out in long rows. They came running back, each carrying a tray. It took several trips, but soon every potential source of new teméyn was burning as the men stoked the ovens.

Shakhere felt a fierce joy. Few outsiders knew that teméyn was not produced directly from the wild *darkhel* plants found in Barazhân. It was a refined, high-yield strain selectively bred over many centuries. It could not survive in the wild on its own. His father had said that the knowledge of how it had been developed was now lost. Destroy the seedlings in every plantation, and generations would pass before any teméyn fit for the Mindbenders' use could be produced.

Let the teméyn workers destroy the equipment. It satisfied their rage. But what they were doing now — destroying next season's seedlings — was all that really mattered.

* * *

"*What!*" Konnar barked.

Estaron jumped. They were in the middle of their weekly meeting with Chief Mindbender Belyeru, discussing a new law Estaron was proposing that would ban the mindbending of ordinary citizens without due cause. Someone had just mindspoken the Strongholder — with bad news, it seemed.

Konnar was on his feet, staring fixedly at the bookcases on the wall of his study. It was a wide, plush room with a spacious desk and several recliners, reminiscent of Shambor's reception chamber in Darthane Cathedral.

"What do you mean, 'there's no teméyn'?" Konnar exclaimed. The conversation continued in silence, only the slight twitching of his face marking the exchanges. Estaron and Belyeru shared a glance with raised eyebrows. After that Estaron kept his face neutral, hiding the sudden hope that had sprung up in his heart.

Finally Konnar sat down again. His nostrils were pinched and his eyes hard. "*Now* they tell me! Too afraid to, earlier. There's no teméyn in Barazhân. Can you believe it? Many of the storehouses were destroyed in the revolution, and the Grûzhileyn are busy right now, burning the rest. *In spite of the Curse!*" He fumed silently for a moment. "My new Mindruler has all his troops out suppressing these slaves. They're also searching the plantations for any teméyn that may have survived."

He paused, boring a hole through the bookcases with his eyes. "But, by Gadesh, they _will_ find teméyn, or produce more." He addressed his subordinate in Barazhân again, speaking aloud in his agitation. "Randenyu! Listen to me. Teméyn supplies must start flowing again — _soon!_ Old stocks or newly-produced, it doesn't matter. Do you understand? No troops are to leave Barazhân until that happens — including those you were going to send to Stillárre. The conquest of Dûrion is on hold for now."

He sat muttering angrily to himself. "No teméyn for Gadesh-knows-how-long! The whole programme on hold!" Estaron and Belyeru maintained a discreet silence.

Then Konnar burst out, "Those rebels in Stillárre somehow held out against the Grûzhack, and now they'll have time to rebuild and re-equip! This is intolerable!"

Estaron couldn't let that pass. "You promised to keep my friends in Stillárre safe, Konnar. Isn't this contributing towards that?"

"_I'll do that in my own way and my own time!_" he snapped back, glaring at Estaron. Estaron's eyebrows rose and he stared back at his friend.

Then in one of his mercurial changes, Konnar's frown suddenly cleared and was replaced by a rueful smile. "You're right, Bari! This just means your friends in Stillárre will be undisturbed a little longer."

"They'll also be under the Curse a little longer."

"Believe me, this delay will be as short as we can make it. And as I said to you before, when we do take the city our troops will ensure that the Restorers and all members of the Dûrian government remain unharmed. Provided they do not actively resist." He glanced briefly at Belyeru, whose eyes blinked. A touch of mindspeech there, Estaron thought.

"If they're still under the Curse they'll hardly be able to resist."

"Well, the Grûzhileyn in Barazhân are doing so... Anyway, that's something for a future discussion. Right now we were considering the conditions under which the mindbending of ordinary Selmian citizens might be acceptable. Only persistent criminals or the feeble-minded, you were saying."

They returned to the discussion of Estaron's new law; but within himself he revelled in a fierce hope: dear Prince, let those Grû-zhileyn succeed!

* * *

The meeting broke up and Estaron and Belyeru went their separate ways. Shortly afterwards Konnar made mind-contact with Belyeru.

"What news of the Restorers?"

"My sources report that they are spending the night in Berûvis, your Supremacy."

"This foolish expedition of theirs will never succeed."

"Should our troops in eastern Dûrion apprehend them?"

"No! Didn't you hear what I said to Prince Barilu? For his sake they are not to be touched."

There was a short pause.

"But if they actually enter Selmion...?"

"Then they are Barilu's responsibility."

If Belyeru could have seen his master at that moment, he would have been surprised. Belying the grimness of his mind-tone, the Strongholder's face was etched with anxiety.

Aloud he muttered, "What will you do with them, Bari? Which friendship will be more important—ours, or theirs?"

———————————————

Map 4:
Selmion

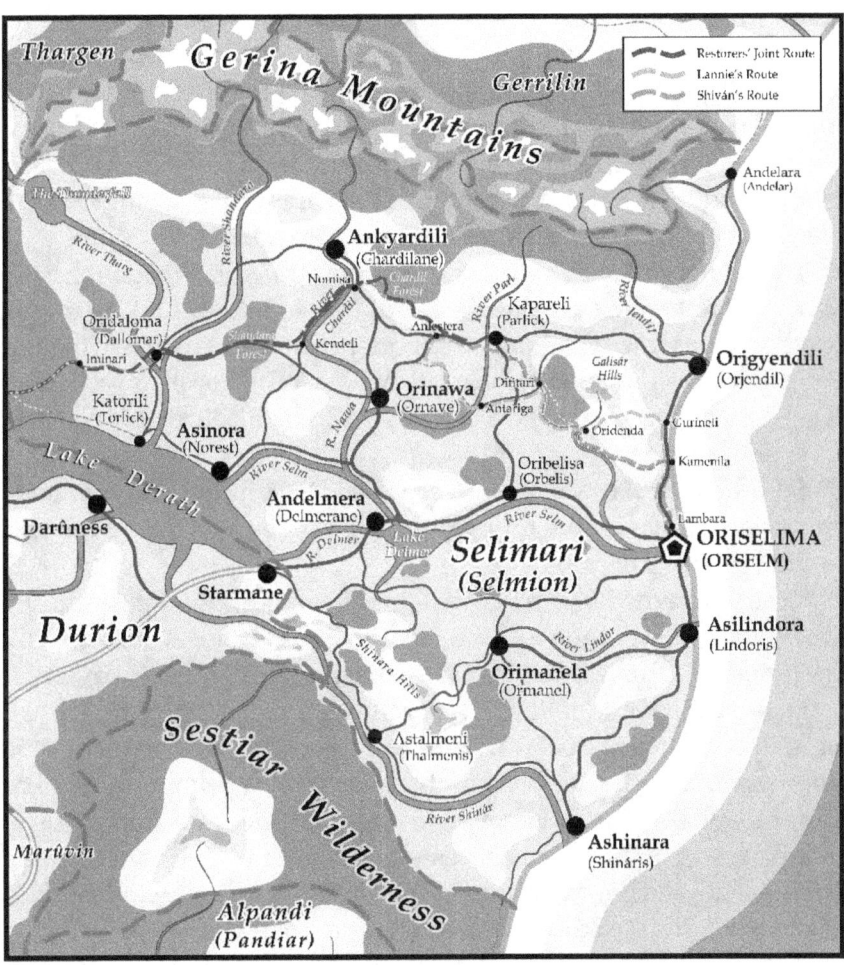

Chapter 33: *Entering Selmion*

KONNAR SAT DRUMMING HIS FINGERS on the shey-nut desk in his study. Today he'd dispensed with the services of four top-level Mindbenders, along with their 1,445 slaves—who included 212 Royal Guards. He'd never remotely dreamed such a thing could happen— but it had. With no teméyn coming in from Barazhân and local supplies dwindling rapidly, what else could he do?

The Mindbenders had to be imprisoned: they knew too much to be allowed their freedom once released from his control. Of course they would be in mindlock for one or two months, which made it easier. When more teméyn arrived they could be re-mindbent. The lowest level of slaves knew nothing of importance and could be returned to their families to be cared for during mindlock. But for the two middle levels, there was no option but to have them killed: he couldn't imprison or care for them all.

So much for Bari's good governance! Well, at least he wouldn't find out. The slaves due for execution would be sent to join the war and disposed of en route.

What concerned him most was the threat to his own position. He was now losing four of the sixteen Mindbenders he directly controlled; and unless teméyn started arriving soon from Barazhân, more would have to follow. The army was already stretched to the limit in both Barazhân and Dûrion; and six of his Mindbenders were with them. That meant he now had only six in Selmion itself. The Royal Guard in the palace was reduced to the bare minimum to guard prisoners and man the gates; and a number of areas in the countryside and in other towns had lost their local Mindbenders. There would be breakdowns of law and order.

That was intolerable. They *had* to have a breakthrough in Barazhân!

* * *

Lannie was plodding along the forest track, so absorbed in her own thoughts that her horse almost ran into Gil's when he suddenly stopped. He had his hand raised, and beyond him the trees ended.

Everyone urged their horses forward to join him, their animals blowing and stamping on either side of the track. Dark mountains loomed to the north. In the middle distance stood a small village amid a wide field of farn grain. The huts—they could hardly be called houses—were made of wattle and daub, the roofs of thatch. A river glinted silver near the horizon under a lowering sky.

Selmion.

The dread name re-echoed, dark with menace, in Lannie's mind. There were small intakes of breath around her. This was the land of the Strongholder, the black, pulsing heart from which mindbending spread its evil tentacles into all the surrounding nations. This was where the fate of the present age rested: and it rested squarely on their shoulders.

Cârin, however, was not impressed. "So that's the Strongholder's country," he murmured. "Doesn't look much to me. If the houses are anything to go by, it'll be a walkover. Orselm, here we come."

"Don't you believe it," Garset muttered. But Lannie and several others managed a smile. Cârin was always trying to keep their spirits up.

Shiván spoke softly to Gil. Ever since entering the Forest of Astenar three days ago, they'd been keeping their voices down. "What's the name of this village again?"

"Iminari." Gil was staring into the blaise. He had been appointed navigator and keeper of the map Frengor had given them. "No one's there," he said. "They're out in the fields." He pointed to several clusters of dots moving among the half-grown grain. Beyond them, on a small hill, stood a forbidding grey building, part-castle, part-country house. With a shock Lannie realised it was not unlike Carreck Manor, where she and the other Restorers had found refuge when they first arrived in Dûrion.

"That'll be the Mindbender's mansion," Jomel murmured beside her. Lannie nodded. They'd be making a wide detour around *that*, as well as the village.

"It's getting late," 'Neesh said. "Why don't we go back to that stream we crossed a while ago, and stay there for the night?"

"Good idea." Perrely wheeled her horse around and led the way back into the forest. Lannie was relieved the girl had recovered from that night in her family home. She was her old, perky self again. Except when the 'curse-haze' crept up on them...

That was something they'd learnt the hard way. At first they hadn't recognised it. On the second day they'd skirted Berûvis, taking byroads to the north of the town. When they reached the village of Shilmis everyone was feeling numbed and slightly dazed by the pathetic sights of disoriented people, shattered lives and plundered houses. An hour later Gil woke up to the fact that they were on the wrong road. They had to backtrack and cut across country. Since then they'd made a habit of stopping every three or four hours and resting, with the Ambon out of its leather case and propped up vertically.

During their three-day journey through the Forest of Astenar those rests had been a life-saver. They had taken to the forest after skirting the Selmian-held town of Mandilane. Frengor had advised them to follow the little-used forest route to Selmion, adding that it would bring them to the least-populated and least-guarded area of the country. He had given Gil a rough, hand-drawn map of the paths to follow; but finding the turnoffs — or even the overgrown paths themselves — had needed constant vigilance.

Now they went back to the stream they'd crossed earlier and found a small glade nearby where they prepared for the night. They set the Ambon upright against a tree and all heaved sighs of relief as the curse-haze, which had been growing in them, dissipated.

Lannie took the first watch. The others covered themselves with extra clothing and wriggled into the most comfortable hollows in the ground they could find; while she sat down beside the Ambon and laid her shortbow and quiver beside her. Not that anyone had bothered them in the forest: it seemed one of the most forsaken, desolate areas of Dûrion. But the bow made Lannie feel that here, if not in Stillárre, her hard-earned skills over the winter had some value. She thanked the One for that.

And this job as archer on the team wasn't *her* plan — a new line of work that the career girl had wangled for herself. It was something God had brought about in his own way and time, completely unforeseen. She found a new kind of comfort in that. *He* was in control; and he knew what he was doing. This moment-by-moment trust they'd learned in order to combat the Curse actually had a lot going for it.

And they needed it, badly.

Tomorrow they would enter enemy territory, and the real test would begin.

* * *

After a final night in the forest they were trotting eastward on a rutted track through Selmion. No one spoke; they were all on edge. There were no trees, hedges, or any kind of cover: just a wide green expanse of waist-high grain. To the left, a couple of aldoret away, was the Mindbender's mansion. Gil found his eyes continually drawn to it, and knew the others were looking that way as well. They were painfully exposed — the only travellers on an otherwise empty road.

Were eyes in that mansion following them right now? Would the Selmian equivalent of the Bishop's Guard be waiting round the next corner? *Creator God, protect us.*

They'd wanted to make a wider detour, but this was the best they'd found. Frengor's map only showed the main routes. Another track headed north-east from Iminari, but it was equally exposed, and passed closer to the mansion on the other side. They had discussed travelling at night, but decided there was too great a risk of losing their way.

He raised a hand. "Blaise check." Jomel spurred her horse to catch up with Cârin, who was scouting ahead. Garset was performing the same function behind. They dismounted and stood beside their horses, holding the reins. Gil handed his to Shiván and took the two-handled glass from his pocket, causing his longsword to bump against his leg. Shiván, Cârin and Garset also wore their swords under their cloaks; and Lannie's bow was easily available behind her saddle.

Gil looked into the blaise and thought of the mansion. It zoomed towards him. He slowed up, watching for any sign of movement. Well-kept grounds filled the slopes of the hill. He passed over the tree tops and circled the building. A servant in green and brown livery came out of a side door. Gil veered away. If you zoomed in too close, people became aware of being watched. That was why he wasn't going to risk looking inside and disturbing the Mindbender. He moved up to roof-level and peered over. As he'd expected, there was an inner courtyard. A woman was scrubbing clothes in a trough at the centre.

After scanning some outbuildings on the other side of the hill — stables, a large barn, servants' quarters — he let out a slow sigh of relief. "No unusual activity," he reported to the others. There were several gusts of released breath. "I'll just check the surroundings."

A few moments later he gave the okay. There were the usual groups of labourers working in the fields around the mansion, but no one else. They remounted and set off again.

After another hour of cautious riding they found a small stand of trees and took an Ambon break to clear their minds. The Mindbender's mansion was well behind them, and they were breathing more freely. Despite that first hurdle, Gil had begun to appreciate Frengor's choice of route. This part of Selmion was sparsely populated; they had met no one else on the road.

They continued on into the afternoon, travelling slowly while he kept checking their surroundings. They took a wide detour to the north of the village of Oridaloma (or Dallomar, as the Dûrians called it), fording two rivers and slipping across a larger road. As evening drew in a man in a tattered half robe gave them a fright when he stumbled across their path, babbling in Selmian. Jomel spoke to him briefly; then he was on his way, running across a field, weeping.

"He says he's lost his family," Jomel told them.

They watched silently as the man disappeared into a copse.

"So Selmians are affected by the curse, too," Perrely murmured.

Gil nodded. "They can't *all* be mindbent. I daresay the Strongholder has plenty of enemies in his own country. Maybe this one was a secret Lightist."

A few aldoret further on they found an abandoned barn. They took refuge there for the night, barricading the door with a small cart. There was plenty of hay, and a full water trough. The horses were happy.

Garset volunteered to stand the first watch.

* * *

The next day they continued eastward until they reached a fork in the road. There were still no other travellers, though they had to make several detours to avoid small clusters of wattle and daub houses. The fields of farn grain had given way to empty swathes of grass on which bovines and horses grazed. A line of woodland loomed up ahead.

"Shandara Forest," Gil murmured. "We take the left-hand track through there towards Kendeli village."

Shiván heaved a sigh of relief twenty minutes later as they rode in under the trees. Cârin uttered a muted whoop, startling his horse. Everyone was grinning.

"It's so good not to feel *watched*," 'Neesh exclaimed.

"That does not mean we can let our guard down!" Garset exclaimed testily.

"Give us a break, Lord Marshal," Câr protested. "We're all as taut as bowstrings at full stretch. Keep this up, and we'll start snapping. Allow us at least to ride together and chat a little here in the forest. Hey, Shiván?"

Câr had voiced Shiván's own thoughts. "I think we need to unwind a little, Garset."

"We should at least keep watch ahead and behind."

"Yes, of course. Cârin and I will ride in front. Will you continue as rearguard?"

"Very well."

"What about an Ambon break?" Jomel asked.

"We've only been travelling a couple of hours," Gil said.

"Oh." She made a little moue of disappointment.

"*Felleneynor!*" Shiván said, waving his arm forward. "Let's continue!"

Time went by as they rode along the forest track, chatting together. It felt good not to be constantly looking over their shoulders. Perrely came up to join Shiván and Cârin, then Câr dropped back to talk to Gil. Large drips began to spatter down at irregular intervals, and Perrely laughed.

"It's raining outside! The Prince gave us this forest at the right moment."

Shiván grinned at her, and she pulled a face at him before adding, "It will be good to reach those tunnels Frengor talked about in Orselm. I'll feel a lot safer underground."

"Me too. Let's hope—"

Without warning the trees ended and they rode out into the rain. Marching towards them on the road was a six-man Selmian infantry patrol.

Perrely screamed. A voice cried "*Kedasa!*" Both groups came to a sudden stop a few paces apart. They stared at one another, stunned.

Thoughts whirled through Shiván's head. *We haven't been keeping watch! The curse-haze has crept up on us. What now? No choice...* He drew the Blade and thrust it upward. "Attack!" he shouted—a fraction after the Selmian sergeant yelled, "*Eri tikasa!*"

What followed was pure confusion. The Selmians advanced with lowered spears. Shiván spurred his trained warhorse at them. Perrely tried to get out of the way, obstructing Cârin and Gil, who were trying to come forward, hampered by a rocky outcrop to the north. Garset was shouting something from the rear.

As two of the Selmians lunged at him, Shiván's warhorse reared and let fly with its hooves. Shiván was almost unseated. He recovered to see one of the Selmians collapsed on the ground, the other coming at him with a sword. He slashed down with the Blade. Out of the corner of his eye he saw a Selmian poised to loose a spear at Perrely. His heart lurched, then the man fell with an arrow through his neck. *Thank the Prince for Lannie!*

Cârin appeared at his side, sword whirling. With a cry of *Hoy! Hoy!* Shiván wheeled his horse towards the Selmian sergeant. The man ducked nimbly away from the flying hooves, and there was a jarring clash as their swords met. In the background Shiván was dimly aware of the bellaril playing, but it was having no effect. Then it suddenly stopped. There was a yell from Cârin. Had he fallen? Was 'Neesh all right?

Prince, help us! Using his height advantage he brought the Blade scything down on the sergeant's shoulder. With a howl of pain the man crumpled to the ground. Shiván's horse brought its hooves crashing down on him. Shiván grunted with disgust and pulled the animal away. He reared back just in time to avoid a jabbing spear. Gil was beside him, making wide sweeps with his longsword. Shiván engaged his fourth man, then a Selmian command rang out behind him: *"Dilinasa! Sinye lo dilinasa!"* His antagonist leapt aside, and with amazing agility dodged past Gil, left the road, and disappeared behind the rocky outcrop, heading for the forest.

"Stop them!" Garset shouted from the rear. Shiván and Gil swung their horses around and spurred them after Garset towards the forest. Fleeting impressions lodged in his mind through the shifting curtain of rain: Lannie standing on the outcrop, bending her bow; Cârin cursing fluently and limping after his horse; the Ambon propped against a boulder; Danîsha lying at the side of the road with Perrely and Jomel bending over her.

Garset disappeared into the forest following one (or more?) of the Selmians. A little way to the north Shiván glimpsed his former antagonist ducking among the trees. They couldn't let them escape!

He'd followed Garset's thinking. These troops were not mindbent—otherwise they would have been affected by the bellaril. Therefore every one of them had to be killed to prevent word reaching the Strongholder.

He spurred his horse off the road. The well-trained animal took the rough terrain in its stride. They crashed in among the trees where the Selmian had entered. There was no sign of him. Shiván's eyes darted around. A broken twig. He urged his mount in that direction. A flash of tan fabric ahead to the left! The horse needed no encouragement, leaping a bush and galloping after their quarry.

The man had gone to ground in a patch of undergrowth, but he wasn't quick enough—the outer branches were still quivering. Shiván quickly dismounted.

What followed was messy, and Shiván hated it. Charging into the bushes he found the man scrabbling to get away, and stabbed him in the leg. The soldier broke free, tried to run, and couldn't. Shiván had to kill him in cold blood, filled with regret and a half-coherent prayer for his family.

Shivering with shock and a sudden onset of the curse-haze, he remounted and rode slowly back to the others. *Dear God, we've attacked the Strongholder in his own country! What will happen to us now?*

Garset and Gil had returned with grim faces and bloodied blades. "Are they all dead?" Perrely asked, her voice unsteady. Shiván nodded.

They dismounted and clustered around the Ambon. Shiván sighed with relief as he felt its healing influence. 'Neesh was lying on a blanket, her eyes shut and face pale. She was breathing shallowly. Her bellaril lay nearby, apparently undamaged.

"What happened?" Shiván asked.

"Spear wound in the side," Lannie said. "Perrely and Jomel have bandaged her up."

Cârin was sitting on a rock, wrapping a cloth around his right thigh. In answer to Shiván's look he shrugged. "What can I say? I fell off my horse. Selmian jabbed me before I could ram the spear through his guts."

"Can Danîsha ride?" Garset asked urgently.

Her eyelids fluttered open. "I'll manage. I have to," she croaked.

"Then we must leave at once, Overguardian. If anyone finds us like this, they will also have to be killed."

Shiván winced. "Okay. Everyone who can, get those bodies out of sight!"

They dragged the other three Selmians off the road and hid them as best they could under bushes and behind rocks. Then they took Lannie's pack off her horse and added it to Danîsha's. They strapped Danîsha's saddle behind the second hump of Lannie's camel-horse in the 'rear-mount' position. Lannie was one of the better riders, having spent long hours on horseback during the winter. It took her a few moments to adjust to the different position, then slowly, with great care, they eased 'Neesh into the front saddle. She groaned, clutching the pommel like a lifeline. Perrely lengthened the reins and passed them to Lannie so that they ran on either side of Danîsha.

Gil put the bellaril back in its case and slung it over his shoulder. Cârin remounted with difficulty. "It's your job to *keep* me here," he muttered to his horse.

They set off, slowly increasing speed as Danîsha proved able to stay in the saddle. Shiván and Gil were in front.

"We'll have to make a wide detour round Kendeli," Gil said, "and take the road to Nomisa. We can spend the night in the Chardil Forest. It means leaving the route we planned with Frengor, but we need to get away from here—fast. I'm worried about Danîsha, though. She's not looking good."

Shiván glanced back, and his heart sank. 'Neesh's face was grey, her eyes closed.

Prince, please watch over her.

Chapter 34: *Flying in God's arms*

EVERY MOVEMENT OF THE HORSE sent shafts of pain searing through Danîsha's body. She clung to the pommel, focusing all her energy on the simple task of staying upright. She saw nothing beyond the horse's grey-brown neck and lighter grey mane. Time had stopped. Every now and then as if from a great distance she heard Lannie muttering, "Hang on, 'Neesh." Every time she thought, I can't hang on any longer. Yet she did.

The horse suddenly swerved and Lannie grabbed her shoulder with one hand as she almost fell off. She felt something give within her, followed by a warm wetness around the wound that seemed to keep spreading. Agony battered her mind. She cried out, then clamped her lips shut, breathing rapidly through her nose to stop herself from panting. She couldn't slow the others down. They had to keep going.

Lannie's distant voice sounded anxious. "Are you all right?"

Danîsha nodded. *Dear Prince, help me!* A cold clamminess was seeping into her bones, and she began to shiver.

The hoof beats and the pain continued. After an age of agony there was a shout from the rear.

"Hold on, 'Neesh," Lannie said. "There are riders behind. We'll have to speed up…"

The horse's movement changed and Danîsha felt the breeze grow stronger on her face. The saddle shifted under her and she thought she would fall—but strong arms were holding her steady. She looked down; there were no hands to be seen. Words came to her from long ago: *Don't be afraid, for I am with you… I will strengthen you and help you. I will hold you up.*

Relief flooded her mind. Thank you, Lord.

Then a strange thing happened: The horse, the breeze, Lannie's voice, faded to the very edge of perception. She was flying in God's arms.

Do you like it?

Yes!

You know my arms have always been around you, don't you?

Yes, Lord. I'm sorry I've so often forgotten.

I haven't. I can never forget you.

A tear trickled down Danîsha's cheeks.

I remember you when you were born. So small, but such a loud voice! I remember you at school, going your own way, ignoring me, giving your parents grief. Then, one day, my servant spoke to you about me. And you listened! Do you remember?

I remember, Denise whispered. That had been her name then.

I was so thrilled! You came to me out of your darkness, and I brought you into the Light. And the whole of heaven overflowed with joy! Someone who'd been lost, was found. Someone who'd turned her back on me, became my daughter. I loved you so much.

Denise felt as though her heart would break.

Then came the long years you served me in England. You thought they didn't count. You wanted some 'special' kind of service, didn't you?

Denise found herself nodding, the tears flowing freely. In the far distance she could still hear the horse's hooves and feel the breeze on her face; but they seemed unreal.

But what you did, caring for your husband, telling your children about me, showing my love to the youngsters you taught – those things meant more to me than any sacrifice you could have made overseas.

Would… would you rather I had stayed home? Denise whispered.

No, my child. I knew what you wanted, and that's why I brought you here to share my love with the people of this world. There was a pause, and Denise almost thought she heard a chuckle. *Remember how surprised you were when you first arrived?*

Denise smiled inwardly.

It took you a while to realise that this was what you'd actually asked for! But then I gave you the bellaril, and you began singing my song. So many have heard the truth through your music! It became a channel for my Light. To some, it brought joy and strength; to others, it brought pain and weakness; but to all it brought Truth. Have you enjoyed playing my music?

Yes, Lord. Very much.

You've played it well. You helped overthrow Shambor; and many have come to the Light through you. You and Brakhól were a partnership I planned long ago, to reach my people in Barazhân.

Will they be alright? Brakhól and Shakhere and Tal and Mistil…

Yes, they will. And so will the others you have cared for: Little Teynel, at Carreck Manor; she's with me now. She loves it here in the Light – it's the most beautiful place you can imagine. She can't wait to show it to you. Oh, and she wants you to give her hair comb to Gil.

Her comb? Oh, but Lord… that's been such a comfort to me.

I know. But now you don't need it any longer, and Gil does. Can you give it up, for him?

Yes of course, Lord.

The gentle voice continued. *Margay and Frem are here too, along with Denny, Damion, and your other friends who died. As for those still in the shadows – Gwargif, who you took in when the Dûrians would have driven him out; Perrely and Jomel, who you've been like a mother to; Shiván, Lannie and Gil… They have so needed your wisdom and your caring heart.*

After a long pause Denise whispered, And my family, back home? Tim, Rose and Maureen? Ben and Ellie? Penny, Anthony and Christopher…?

My arms are around them, too.

Even Rose and Bill? They haven't found you yet…

My dear daughter, you've prayed and wept for them so often. Your tears have not been wasted.

Denise rode on in the arms of her Father. At last as the day was drawing in they entered the shelter of a forest. When the horse finally came to a stop, the voice spoke softly again:

There's something else I want you to do for me.

* * *

The group made their way through the trees of the Chardil Forest until they found a place to camp in a glade beside a stream. As soon as they'd dismounted and leant the Ambon against a tree, Shiván started issuing crisp orders.

"We must look after Danîsha before the light goes. Perrely, stay with her. Lannie and Jomel, cut some bracken for her to lie on. Gelmion and Cârin, can you get a fire going and heat some water? Garset, you and I can cut poles for a lean-to."

Perrely hurried over to Alanya's horse. Danîsha was still sitting in the saddle, her face a deathly white but strangely peaceful. Perrely laid a hand on hers.

"We'll get you down as soon as Alanya and Jomel have made a bed."

Danîsha nodded, smiling faintly. Perrely marvelled at her calm.

After a few moments the two women came back with armfuls of springy foliage. They found a level spot nearby and laid it thickly on the ground. Jomel ran back to get more while Alanya fetched a long cloth. Within minutes they had prepared a soft bed for Danîsha.

Then Gelmion and Cârin left their fire to help her down from the horse. She groaned and sweat broke out on her brow as they laid her, clutching her robe closed, on the bed.

"We'll get ropes and a waterproof sheet for the lean-to," Alanya said. She and Jomel hurried off to unload the travel packs. Gelmion and Cârin went back to the fire, which had died out.

Perrely squatted down beside Danîsha. She reached a hand out. "Let's open your robe so I can get you ready to bathe the wound."

But Danîsha clasped the edges of the robe tighter. "First I need — to talk — to you," she gasped.

Perrely shook her head. "Treatment first, talking later. Frengor gave us some wonderful herbs that will ease the pain and prevent infection." She undid the cloth belt at Danîsha's waist and took a firm hold of the nearest edge of the robe.

"Promise me — you won't — call the others. Yet." Danîsha's eyes held an urgency Perrely didn't understand. Reluctantly she agreed. Danîsha let go of the robe and she peeled it open.

She had to clasp a hand to her mouth to stop herself crying out. The bandages had worked loose and Danîsha's once-cream tunic was drenched in blood. More was still oozing out of the gaping wound in her side.

Perrely leapt up, her mouth open to shout for help. Danîsha clasped a hand round her left ankle, gripping it with surprising strength. "You promised," she gasped.

"Danîsha! That wound is terrible! We must do something at once — "

"Perhaps nothing — will mend it. The One may be taking me into his Light."

"No... No... *Mâra* — " Perrely felt her face crumple.

"Sit, my dear. We need to — talk."

Perrely glanced around desperately. Lannie and Jomel were struggling to get the travel pack off Garset's horse. Gelmion was feeding the fire with some larger branches Cârin had just brought. All of them were doing what needed to be done. She looked back at Danîsha. Her gaze was peaceful and steady. With tears running down her cheeks Perrely sat down again. She clasped Danîsha's right hand with both of hers, unwilling to let her go.

"First, there's something — you must give — to Gelmion." With her left hand Mâra fumbled in the pocket of her robe and brought out a small wooden hair comb. "Tell him— it belonged to Teynel. The One said— she wants him— to have it." Perrely nodded silently and took the comb, her eyes glued to Danîsha's face.

"And I want you— to have the bellaril."

"Mâra, no..."

"I also want to talk— about Shiván. I believe— you have a deep desire— to be with him. I think you have been— denying it. Am I right?"

Perrely's defences were in tatters. "Yes," she said in a shaky voice. "But I thought it was wrong. The One called me to singleness..."

"Maybe he did. For a time. To test your— obedience. There's a story in our Book... Ask one of the others. About Abraham and his son. But now... you have obeyed. Loved God— more than yourself. So he is— giving you Shiván."

Perrely sat staring at Danîsha, gently massaging her cold hand, her heart in turmoil.

"Shiván— spoke to me. In Stillárre." Danîsha's voice was getting fainter. Perrely leant closer, torn between the urgency to fetch help and a desperate need to hear what Mâra was saying. "Shiván told me— he'll never marry anyone else. He won't— let go of you. He will always— be there for you. Even if it costs— his own happiness. He will stay in Dûrion. Because he can't bear— to be away from you."

Danîsha's words were becoming slurred. She sank back and closed her eyes.

"Mâra!" Perrely half started up to call the others.

Danîsha's eyes opened, and her face was transformed by a smile. "You and Shiván— belong together."

Her eyes closed again, and her face settled into peaceful repose. The smile still lifted the corners of her lips.

"*Mâra! No...*" Perrely's cry of anguish echoed through the glade.

Chapter 35: *Devastating loss*

THEY ALL CAME RUNNING. Shiván knelt beside Danîsha, horrified by the sight of her blood-soaked tunic and fearing the worst. He felt for a pulse—and relief flooded through him. "She's alive! She just passed out."

"Oh!" Perrely cried, and started sobbing.

The next few minutes were chaotic. Lannie and Jomel cleaned the wound with warm water, and Garset used his battlefield experience to stitch it with washed threads from his tunic. Gil and Cârin put the last touches to the lean-to, and they gently placed Danîsha on a makeshift stretcher and carried her to the shelter while others remade the soft bed for her to lie on.

When she was settled Shiván looked for Perrely, and saw her sitting on a rock, still weeping. He walked over and stood in front of her. "Perrely, what is it?"

She looked up at him, and to his amazement her face was radiant. She stood, and the next moment his amazement shot off the charts as she put her arms round him and buried her face against his chest. He hesitantly returned her embrace, then more confidently, his heart overflowing.

They stood together for a long time. At last she gently disengaged and looked up at him; and there was something in her eyes that he hadn't seen for a long time.

"Thank you," she whispered.

* * *

They prepared a warm evening meal round the fire, during which they agreed that they needed to stay here until Danîsha was well enough to ride again—to Perrely's relief.

As they ate her thoughts were swirling. What she had thought were Danîsha's last words had overturned all her self-punishing arguments about Shiván; and she needed to readjust her thinking. Their earlier embrace had been completely spontaneous; but oh, it had felt so good. He was sitting beside her now, and she kept glancing at him. When he caught her eye he would give her a quizzical smile, his eyebrows raised.

Should she speak to him? What would she say? Could they allow themselves that kind of physical contact? It went totally against all her Lightist upbringing. Yet they were in a desperate situation; they might not live long enough to marry…

Suddenly, like a breath of fresh air, Danîsha's words came back to her: "You and Shiván belong together." Yes. It was the simple truth. She'd known it all along, but suppressed it. She wouldn't worry about the conventions any more. She was Shiván's, and he was hers. She took his hand, and the delight in his face as he looked at her was all the confirmation she needed.

* * *

After the meal Gelmion began walking towards the lean-to, and Perrely remembered the other task Danîsha had given her. She hurried after him.

"Gelmion."

He turned towards her.

"Gelmion, Danîsha gave me something. For you." She handed him the small wooden comb.

"What's this?"

"It belonged to Teynel. The One told Danîsha that she wanted you to have it."

"*Teynel* wanted me to have it?"

She nodded.

For a long moment he stared at the comb. Then before Perrely's eyes his face dissolved. He sank down to the ground. Gelmion, who nobody had ever seen weeping, was racked with great sobs that shook his entire body. He cradled the comb in his hands as if it were made of gold.

The others came crowding round. "Gil—what's wrong?" "What happened?"

"Danîsha gave him Teynel's comb."

* * *

Gil knew that the Creator God had forgiven him for his part in the brutal murder of his friends at Carreck Manor—including poor, innocent Teynel. But he'd never imagined *they* could forgive him.

He saw again the child's bewildered eyes as he raised his longsword to kill her — eyes that said *Why?*

But now… she'd given him a gift. She'd *forgiven* him. Something deep within him broke, and the waters of pain, dammed up for so long, came pouring out. He wept as he hadn't wept since early childhood.

Minutes — or hours — later the tears eased. His thoughts went back to the Manor massacre and he realised that now, for the first time, he could think of those dead faces without feeling overwhelming grief for the atrocities his hands had committed. Behind the pain-laden faces he now saw someone else in agony: the picture switched between Prince Orrénne, dismembered but still alive on the altar fire; and Jesus Christ on the cross. The Son of God had taken the grief and guilt on himself — and had suffered the full penalty. Teynel and the other friends he'd killed now saw him as the One saw him: *Forgiven*. At last he understood the full, incredible breadth of that word.

Gratitude beyond speech rose from his heart to God.

* * *

Three days had passed in the forest, and Danîsha was on the mend. The fever had spiked on the second day, but quickly came down as the Dûrians dosed her with Frengor's herbs and the juice of the *elaney* plant, which was plentiful in the forest. Margay had used it at the Manor: it was a natural antibiotic. Danîsha spent much of that time reading Shiván's Bible; the peace in her face spoke of a different kind of healing.

Lannie had found herself sitting with 'Neesh, fetching herbal chass for her, helping to clean and re-dress her wound with a poultice of elaney leaves; and generally, well, *cherishing* her, as everyone else was doing. Perrely, Shiván, Jomel and Gil, especially, had spent time with her when she wasn't resting; and Lannie was doing the same.

She was surprised at her own strong reaction to nearly losing Danîsha. She hadn't realised how fond she'd become of this wise and loving older lady. She'd long ceased to be "Mrs. Thompson", the knitter and flower-arranger in their Birmingham church: she was the Lady of Song who had saved them so often with the bellaril; the fearless prophetess who had confronted Shambor with the truth; the missionary to the Grûzhack, who with Brakhól and Gil had turned a nation upside down. Above all, she was *Mâra*, her friend and kindly mentor. Life without her was unthinkable.

Yesterday Danîsha had walked to and fro very carefully, and declared she could ride. So today they were leaving. The sun was just rising, and Lannie helped Shiván, Garset and Jomel fold the waterproof sheet they'd used for the lean-to.

At last all was packed, and they assisted Danîsha up on to her horse. She winced several times, and gave a little gasp as she settled in the saddle. Then she turned to them. "What are you all staring at? Let's go!" Laughing, they set off at a gentle pace.

When they reached the edge of the forest, Gil made a careful survey with the blaise. There was no one in sight. They came out under a grey sky and followed a footpath running south-east beside the trees. To their right, empty swathes of yellow-green grass rose towards them, punctuated by rocky outcrops. To their left, beyond the forest, stood a range of mountains. From Frengor's map Gil was able to tell them that these were the Gerina Mountains, forming the northern border of Selmion. Lannie breathed a prayer of gratitude for that map. They were way off course; but without it they'd have been totally lost.

A couple of hours later they made a wide detour around a squalid wattle-and-daub village labelled Anlestera on the map, which straddled what counted as a highway here in Selmion. Danîsha was obviously tiring, and once safely past the village they took a break, helping her down on to a comfortable seat made from their packs.

After half an hour they set off again, rejoining the dirt road. In the distance ahead was a glint of water, and beyond it a smudge of grey.

"That must be the town you mentioned," Shiván said to Gil. The two men and Lannie were riding together; Cârin was scouting ahead as usual, and Garset bringing up the rear. Behind them Perrely, Danîsha and Jomel were talking quietly in Dûrian.

"Yes, that'll be Kapáreli — or Parlick, as Garset calls it. The River Parl is between us and the town."

"Is there a way round?"

"I'm looking for a footpath so we can cross the river somewhere to the south."

"We'd better pray, then," Lannie said. There were few footpaths in this bleak countryside.

A shout came from behind. They wheeled round. Garset was riding rapidly towards them. Beyond him, galloping out of the village of Anlestera, was a compact group of horsemen. Tan-coloured capes fluttered from their shoulders. "Oh dear God," Lannie breathed.

Selmian cavalry.

Shivvie took a rapid look around. Lannie could read his thoughts: No shelter. No side paths. Uneven terrain, dangerous for riding. One invalid.

"How many?" he demanded as Gil took out the blaise. Garset and Cârin reached them. Danîsha, Perrely and Jomel sat white-faced in the centre.

"Ten."

"Those of you not fighting, get at least a hundred paces off the road behind us. Raise the Ambon." Jomel and Perrely nodded. 'Neesh's face was pale but determined. "Lannie, position yourself on the right flank. Nock an arrow, but keep the bow down until I bring out the Blade. The rest of you, wait for my command. When we're at close quarters, Lannie, guard our back." Lannie saw Garset give a quick nod.

They hurried to obey his orders. As Lannie slung the quiver over her shoulder and fitted an arrow to the bow, a fierce joy filled her that she could at last do something useful with her shortbow. But at the same time she wondered if this would be the end of their mission to Orselm. If they had to escape, would Danîsha survive a gallop? *Dear God, please help us.*

The cavalry drew rapidly closer. A quick glance behind showed the three other women sitting side by side on their horses a short way off the road. Jomel was holding the Ambon upright. Perrely's arms were raised in prayer. 'Neesh's head was bowed. She wasn't trying to play the bellaril. As they'd learnt last time, ordinary Selmian troops were not mindbent.

Lannie held the bow at her side pointing downward, poised to be raised in an instant. Beside her the knuckles of Shiván's left hand were white on the hilt of the Blade.

The thunder of the horses' hooves grew louder, and the ten riders with their raised swords filled the road. The stories Lannie had heard about the dreaded Selmian cavalry flashed through her mind: the finest fighting machine in the whole Dûrai region, crafted by a nation of skilled horsemen; only once defeated in the last hundred years…

As if in answer Shiván spoke. "Remember who we are! Restorers of the Way. The Lord Marshal of Dûrion. Soldier of the Lightist Rebellion. We have a bow, a longsword and the Blade of Darthane, none of which they're expecting. Garset and Cârin between them have survived hundreds of engagements. We will defeat them — *in the name of the Prince!*"

He swung the Blade aloft. A moment later a clear, sweet trumpet call sounded and a brief flash brightened the dull sky. Lannie swung round to see Jomel holding the Ambon high.

The Selmians cried out. The patrol faltered, some reining in, others swerving. Lannie swept up her bow and fired off several arrows in quick succession. One of the cavalrymen went down, another plucked an arrow from his shoulder. But it was only a few moments before their training kicked in. The ensign in command rapped out an order. They pulled together and resumed their charge.

Lannie managed a final shot at point-blank range, and another rider went down. Then she peeled off and took up a position in the rear.

The two groups crashed together. Shiván, Gil, Garset and Cârin fought as if possessed by the Light, not allowing the Selmians through. Gil was causing havoc with his longsword. Shiván ducked and wheeled, the Blade scything in again and again. Garset and Cârin parried and thrust, giving better than they received.

When any of the Selmians tried to break round the side of the mêlée to encircle them, they were Lannie's game. One fell to her bow and another was injured before they dropped that tactic.

Shiván swayed to one side as a trooper lunged at him, and with his free hand he yanked the outstretched sword arm. The rider shot out of the saddle under his own momentum. Lannie looked away as Shiván's warhorse trampled him.

Just then the cavalry ensign called the retreat — "*Gyelasa!*" The remaining cavalrymen — only four; the road was littered with tan-coated bodies — wheeled round and tried to disengage. Shiván and his comrades were on to them immediately. One horse went down, and Garset chased the rider as he tried to flee on foot. Lannie moved forward to try and get a shot at the fleeing rider.

At the same moment the ensign broke free of the mêlée and made straight for Perrely, Jomel and 'Neesh, his sword raised. Lannie cried out, but Shiván and Gil now blocked her way, fiercely involved with the other two cavalrymen. Cârin spurred his mount after the officer. Jomel screamed and the three desperately tried to turn their horses, but ran foul of each other. Jomel was clutching the Ambon. As the cavalry officer bore down on them Cár angled in to cut him off. The ensign saw him — his sword described a flashing arc — and with a cry Cârin crashed to the ground. A moment later the Selmian reached Jomel, ripped the Ambon out of her hand, and galloped off westward with it.

The Ambon! With a yell Lannie leapt her horse past Shiván and Gil and set off after the fleeing cavalry officer.

Chapter 36: *Death and pursuit*

THE STRONGHOLDER REGARDED HIS MAJOR-DOMO with distaste. He was fussing about the study straightening papers and cushions.

"Gedoriu, hurry up and leave. I want to be alone."

It irked him to use normal speech, but the man wasn't mindbent. As chief of the palace staff he had a myriad of duties, and he functioned better this way.

"I've told you a thousand times, Gedoriu. Others can look after my private quarters."

The functionary threw him a harried look. He was sweating in his ornate white and silver uniform. "But, your Supremacy, it wouldn't be fitting for the lower servants to have access to these rooms…" He dropped a cushion, picked it up, bent down to retrieve a book Konnar had left on the floor, and lost hold of the cushion again.

Konnar smiled. "It's not so much fun being a Lightist these days, is it Gedoriu?"

The man jerked upright and dropped the book.

"Oh yes, I know about those Lightist scriptures of yours, cleverly hidden behind a loose stone in your bedroom wall."

"Sir —" His face was a mask of shock.

"But Gedoriu, you know what?" He clapped the man on the shoulder. "I rather enjoy watching you battling the Curse. It's good entertainment. You've done well so far; if you carry on this way I may even release you from it." His voice changed. "Now pick up those things and get out!"

The man obeyed as quickly as his stateliness allowed. After replacing the cushion on the recliner and laying the book on the polished shey-nut desk he walked to the door.

"But Gedoriu?"

The major-domo froze.

"If you let me down…"

There was a pregnant silence. Then the man turned, bowed briefly, and left.

On his own at last, Konnar allowed himself a chuckle as he settled on to the recliner. It was fun making old stuffed-shirt Gedoriu squirm. *Gesh*, he actually thought he'd kept his Lightism a secret! Konnar had known it from the moment he'd met him in a wealthy merchant's home. But Gedoriu was so impressive that Konnar had relieved the merchant of his services and appointed him palace major-domo. No danger that he would pass information to outside parties: he was a prisoner in the palace, and no one, but *no one*, entered or left without Konnar's permission.

Now to the matter in hand. His temporary good spirits faded. The cavalry must have caught up with those Dûrian intruders by now. He focused his mind on Lingetu, leader of the spies who had been shadowing them.

"Report."

"There has been a battle, your Supremacy."

"And?"

"Ensign Keloru captured the ambon."

Relief washed over Konnar.

"And the Dûrians? There better not have been any casualties."

"Only one, Supremacy."

"What? Keloru will answer for this!"

"It wasn't one of the foreigners, Sir. The young Dûrian soldier tried to prevent Keloru from gaining the ambon. Keloru had no option but to cut him down."

"Let me see."

Lingetu was silent while Konnar scanned his recent memory.

"What's this? One, two, three–four, five, six… Almost the entire patrol lying dead on the road!"

There was the mental equivalent of an embarrassed cough. *"They did kill the entire patrol, your Supremacy. Keloru was the only survivor."*

"Geshu!"

Konnar leant back, aghast. Those 'Restorers' and their hangers-on had just killed all but one of an elite cavalry unit! The carnage the other day near Kendeli could be excused: that foot patrol had been up against armed men on horseback. Even so they'd seriously injured the foreign bellaril-player. He was glad she'd recovered in the forest, saving him from breaking his promise to Bari. These intruders must be left intact for the new Governor to deal with.

But this…! He'd instructed the cavalry not to inflict casualties, but he'd never expected they would pay such a high price. The foreigners' achievement in getting this far despite the Curse and *still* decimating his best troops was disconcerting, to say the least.

It could only have been some Lightist magic in their ambon that made it possible. While travelling they stopped at regular intervals and clustered around it. He knew of its power of summoning, of course; the Dûrian Founders, who made it, had used it that way; and so had these so-called Restorers last year in their war against that fool Shambor. But this... 'reviving' power was new. Anyway, he'd relieved them of it now. Maybe they'd start falling apart as they should have done days ago...

He turned his mind back to Lingetu.

"Show me what's happening now."

He watched through Lingetu's eyes as the spy slowly raised his head above the crest of a low hill. In the distance three women were sitting next to a body sprawled on the grass beside the road. The men were digging a grave for their fallen comrade.

"Lingetu, I see only six people around the dead man. There should be seven."

"The seventh rode off after Ensign Keloru, Sir."

"By the dark flame, Lingetu, do I have to squeeze information out of you one drip at a time? So one of them is chasing Keloru? Which one?"

"I crave your pardon, Supremacy. The younger foreign woman. She's a better archer than we thought. She accounted for three of our dead."

"Is she a good rider?"

"Yes, Sir. She handled her horse well while shooting from the saddle."

"Gadeshu strike her! Which way did Keloru go?"

"Back through Anlestera, Supremacy, taking the quickest route to Orinawa."

"Very well. Continue following these six, Lingetu. I'll deal with the other one."

A quick conversation with the garrison commander in Orinawa, and he'd done all he could. Heads would roll if they failed to secure the ambon.

Geshu! These intruders had him on edge the whole time. It ran against every instinct to allow them to continue. He itched to send an entire cavalry squadron after them, drag them to Orselm, and make them suffer for their insolence.

But Selmion was Bari's domain now. Konnar needed Bari to learn of the Restorers' presence in the natural course of events, so that the full responsibility would rest on him. Bari had been building up his own lines of communication, reviving the old Royal Post under a different name and appointing representatives and post riders in all the major centres—including Orinawa. He would soon be hearing about the intruders. If not, Konnar would make sure he did.

And then… Then he would learn the true extent of Bari's loyalty.

Would Bari eliminate this threat to their joint rule?

Or would he side with his former friends against Konnar?

The Strongholder chewed a nail as he stared unseeing at the rich floor-cover and shey-nut furnishings of his study.

* * *

Cârin was galloping like the wind to cut off the cavalry officer and had almost reached him, when the rider's sword flashed in the sun and the razor-sharp weapon bit deep into the one gap in his banded armour, on the lower right side. He screamed as pain beyond imagining exploded within. For a moment his eyes darkened, and he felt his own sword fly from his hand as he tumbled from his horse.

He landed hard and felt something—maybe several things—break. He rolled a couple of times, ending up on his back. He tried to sit up, only to yell again in agony. He dimly heard the clashes and cries of the others still fighting, and a scream from Jomel. A horse leapt over him, and there was the cavalry officer galloping westward, and— was that the Ambon he was holding? A cry from Alanya, and she was off in pursuit.

There was nothing he could do. He'd failed. The Ambon was on its way to the Strongholder. He lay there, his breath coming in laboured gasps, staring at the sky and feeling a warm wetness gathering under his right elbow.

Jomel was the first to reach him. "Cârin! Oh no, dear Prince, Câr!" Her face swam into view, filled with shock. Perrely joined her, her eyes wide and tear-filled. They tried to lift him, but the pain made him almost pass out. Then he dimly heard Danîsha's voice telling them to pack his tunic into the wound to stop the bleeding. He felt their clumsy efforts and the pain soared, but his mind was receding from his body. It wouldn't be long now, he knew.

More faces over him. Garset. Gelmion. Shiván, his face contorted with shock and grief. Somehow Cârin managed to clasp Shiván's arm where it stood beside his chest as he leant over him. "Thank you," he wheezed, amazed at how faint his voice sounded. "For being… my brother."

"Stay with us, Câr! We're going to fix you. We'll go back to the forest—" As he spoke, Cârin watched with mild surprise as tears trickled slowly down Shiván's cheeks.

Then Shiván's face morphed into Shîrin's. The twin he'd lost last year. He was smiling. "Come on, you slacker," he quipped. "I won't wait here forever!"

Shiván was still speaking, but Câr cut him off. "No," he said softly, which was all he could manage. Shiván fell silent. "Gotta go now. Shîr's... waiting. Can't let... him... have all the fun."

Shiván's face faded, and there was Shîr, grinning, his hand outstretched, a golden white beyond. Someone else stood beside him, and all the joy in the universe radiated from him. Pain fell away, and Cârin gladly let his brother pull him up to join them.

* * *

Shiván saw the light fade from Câr's eyes and dropped his head, weeping. Garset felt the wrist for a pulse. "He's gone," he murmured.

For a long moment they stood or sat where they were, unable to take it in. Cârin's body lay unnaturally twisted on the ground, his tunic soaked in blood. He'd been brought down by a hundred-to-one chance when his enemy's sword found the only gap in his armour.

Using the two small shovels they'd brought from Dûrion, they managed to dig a shallow grave beside the road. They laid their friend's body in it, and Perrely shakily read a few words from the Book. In the silence that followed Garset said, "He was once a rebel and my enemy, but he became a good friend. He was a fine soldier, and a swordsman without equal."

Danîsha added, "He cared for those he was with and always did his best for them."

Gil nodded. "He was the first to volunteer for difficult jobs. He was there whenever help was needed."

Between sobs Jomel said, "He made us laugh!"

Perrely's voice quavered as she added, "He died trying to protect us."

Shiván's heart felt numb. "Since Shîr died he's been my brother. He always had my back in battle. He saved my life many times when I first suffered from the Curse. He was always cheerful. Travelling with him was— it was—" He fell silent, too choked up to continue. Perrely squeezed his hand.

They stood in silence for a while, then by unspoken agreement they filled in the grave. Shiván stared at the forlorn mound of earth. *Thank you, dear Prince, that this is only his physical body. The real Cârin is with you now, and with Shîr, and I know his joy is overflowing.*

With difficulty they turned to other matters needing immediate attention. They dragged the fallen cavalrymen off the road. There was no place to hide them. The horses had already trotted off towards Anlestera.

Then they sat down beside the grave to wait for Alanya. All around them the yellow grass lay silent and empty, reflecting the desolation they felt.

Gil cleared his throat. "Well, this confirms one thing. The Strongholder knows we're here."

"Does he?" Perrely asked, her hand tightening in Shiván's. "Couldn't these soldiers have found us… by mistake, like the other ones when we came out of that wood?"

"Hardly," Garset said. "They were already charging when we saw them."

"And their officer deliberately took the, er… the Ambon," Gil added.

"It makes no sense at all," Garset muttered. "Why only ten men? Why not a whole… a hundred men?"

"Perhaps they…" Jomel stopped. "I've forgotten what I was going to say."

Alarm bells rang in Shiván's mind. "Listen, everyone." He waited till he had their attention. "We've lost the Ambon. My mind is going fuzzy, and I think you're feeling the same—even more so than before. We've got to keep trusting God moment by moment—as we learnt to do in Stillárre in the early days after the Curse was cast. That's the only way we can keep thinking straight."

They slowly nodded and murmured assent. Shiván sent up an urgent prayer for clarity himself. It was definitely harder now.

He looked round the group. "Let's pray together, shall we?"

They raised their hands. After thanking the One again for Cârin's life and committing him into the Father's care, Shiván asked for guidance and clear thinking in the situation they now faced—and that he would restore Alanya and the Ambon to them soon. 'Neesh asked for peace of heart for them all. A long pause followed. Perrely managed a few words, then fell silent. Finally Shiván committed them all to the One's protection.

"So what are we going to do?" Gil said, looking at Shiván. In fact all their eyes were on him, and he realised how desperately he, in particular, needed the One's enabling. "Without the Ambon our mission is over," Gil continued. "Should we ride after Alanya? Or should we wait here for her? But the Strongholder knows where we are, so if we wait we may be caught…" His voice tailed off.

Jomel muttered "Dear Prince," and buried her face in her hands.

Shiván nodded. "You've summed up the problem, Gil. I don't think it's any use riding after Alanya. She's on a fast horse and she has a long start. How about we wait here for her a little longer? Not too long—we can't stay out in the open like this, and we have to find shelter for the night."

"But if we move, how will Alanya find us?" Garset asked, frowning. "That is, if she does recapture the Ambon and escape."

"Oh, it all sounds so hopeless," Perrely groaned. Shiván could feel her shivering as she leant against him. He tightened his arm around her.

"It's never hopeless while the One's in charge," Shiván said quietly. "Alanya knows the route we're following, and we'll just have to trust that she can ride faster on her own and catch us up."

"I hope she does know the route," Gil muttered. "She was never much interested in looking at the map."

"Gil, why don't you try contacting her with the blaise?" Danîsha said.

"Great idea, 'Neesh!" Shiván exclaimed. "We should have thought of that sooner!"

Gil felt in the pockets of his robe and brought out the square glass lens. Holding both handles and focussing on a bare patch of ground, he let it soar over the surrounding countryside. He found the small village of Anlestera to which the officer and Lannie had been heading, and cast around from there checking the roads and paths out of the village. But ten minutes of diligent searching failed to find more than a few pedestrians, a couple of carts, and a farmer herding a flock of sheep.

"Nothing," Jomel sighed.

"Then all we can do is to continue to follow our planned route and trust that the One will enable her to catch up," Shiván said, infusing as much hope and confidence as he could into the words. "The sooner we reach the safety of those tunnels in Orselm, the better. Actually, all

Alanya needs to do is to travel east to the coast and then follow the coast road south to Orselm. We'll wait as long as we can near each village on the way."

There were mutters of agreement. Danîsha added, "And let's pray that *she* manages to contact *us* with the bess. She'll need the encouragement! I hate to think what it'll be like for her—alone in a foreign country with her foreign shiláy, not knowing the language, without a map, and maybe carrying the Ambon as well. She'll stick out like… like a Grûzhack in the Stillárre Hearth!"

They prayed again that the One would keep Lannie safe and bring her back to them with the Ambon. "Oh, I hope she comes soon," Jomel groaned as they finished. "I'm feeling so… strange and mixed up."

"I know, Jomel, we all are," Danîsha said. "We must keep trusting the One."

Shiván nodded. "We absolutely have to. But while we're waiting, Perrely and Jomel, can you check Danîsha's wound?" Cleaning and re-dressing the wound would take their minds off their own problems for a while.

They waited half an hour longer, but there was no sign of Lannie. Conversation faded as the curse-haze settled over them more heavily.

Finally Shiván roused his silent flock, and herded them south-eastward off the road to cross the River Parl and head towards the next village on their route, Difitari. The horses struggled across rough country until they hit a path heading towards the river, glinting in the distance under a grey sky.

Far to the south lay their final destination: Orselm—and the safety of those tunnels Frengor had told them about. Shiván prayed with every step that they would live to see them.

* * *

Lannie bent low in the saddle, urging her horse on after the dust cloud ahead. The cavalry officer had given her a good run through Anlestera—scattering chickens, dogs and villagers—and had swung left on to a southerly road that she guessed led to a larger town. Now his heavier cavalry mount was tiring, and she was slowly gaining on him. She reckoned she'd draw level in about a quarter of an hour.

But what then? She was useless with a sword. Her only hope was an arrow from behind. But at this speed? It would be the shot of the century.

She carefully reached over her shoulder to feel the arrows in her quiver. In a moment of heart-stopping panic her fingers found nothing. She scrabbled about in the mouth of the quiver, and finally found feathers. *One.*

Bent over like this, the others must have fallen out.

She pulled the base of the quiver downward to avoid losing her last arrow. *Lord, help me!*

The countryside on either side of the road was turning greener as she pounded on. The dust cloud ahead was drawing nearer. *God, let me get this right. I'll only have one shot!*

As the distance between them shortened she made out the horse and rider at the centre. There was something odd about the way the officer was carrying himself. Lannie realised he was clasping the Ambon tightly under his left arm like a mediaeval lance, while supporting it with his hand to keep the other end away from his mount. The long rod kept wavering to and fro with the speed at which he was riding, threatening to bump the horse. She realised the difficulty he was under, and admired his skill. But that gave her an advantage…

Something caught her eye further along the road, beyond the rider. Another dust cloud coming towards them, at its centre a cluster of dark dots. Travellers? No, it was moving too fast. More cavalry! Dear God.

The officer must have seen them, because he shouted and picked up speed.

Lannie was about to lose her one and only chance. With a yell she struck the horse on the rear hump. It responded to the challenge, finding a new lease of energy.

The approaching horsemen disappeared behind a hill. Lannie was drawing closer to her quarry. With one hand she undid the fastening on the bow in front of her. Nearer still.

Now less than a hundred yards separated her from the officer — well within bowshot. She slowed her mount, took out her last arrow, swept up the bow, and fitted it.

He was pulling away from her. *Dear Prince, help me!* She drew the bowstring back with all her strength and sighted down the arrow shaft. The horse was moving smoothly. The bow was steady. She compensated for speed and distance, and with a final gasped prayer —

— she let the arrow fly.

Chapter 37: *Recapture, escape and contact*

FRENGOR SIGHED as he and Mâron made their way through the streets of Stillárre. On all sides were the crumbling brick walls of derelict houses, many gutted by fire. Thin figures in rags scuttled down alleys as their Dorbian escort approached. The centre of the city had become a wasteland.

They crossed the market square. The Hearth building, the great merchants' houses, all were ruined shells. The sun came out from behind a cloud, throwing the desolation into stark relief.

"It'll take years to rebuild all this," Frengor commented.

"If we ever get the chance," Mâron replied. Optimism had been hard to come by since the Restorers left.

They continued through the ravaged city until they reached the north-western suburbs, where a semblance of normality remained. People opened the rough barricades they'd thrown up and clustered round the two men. The Dorbians gave them room, but remained wary, their eyes darting everywhere.

Questions flooded in from people with drawn faces and threadbare clothes. When would the next food convoy be arriving from the western farmlands? Had more building materials been located? Had the promised cloth come in from Histen and Nerick? And repeatedly there were murmured queries about the Dorbians, with anxious glances towards their escort. Was it true that there were *dark* Dorbians on the rampage in the countryside? Were *all* the Dorbians turning away from the Light? Was the city still secure?

With a heavy heart Frengor said what little he could to allay their fears, and Mâron did likewise. They were on their way right now to find out if there was any truth in the rumours of dark Dorbians attacking food convoys and outlying farms. Supplies had been promised, and they would make sure they got through. The city was still safe, and there was no sign of the Selmians...

Eventually they resumed their journey. The Dorbians led them to the army barracks Gwargif was using as his headquarters.

The grey-white Dorbian commander greeted them with muted enthusiasm. "Fathers of city, welcome. Is good you come." He conducted them to the sparsely-furnished cell that was his lair.

Frengor and Mâron sat on the edge of a low table that was the only furniture. Gwargif squatted down facing them. "Is Dorbi is make trouble in country. This you want to ask, yes?"

"Yes."

The Dorbian commander heaved a deep sigh. His eyes were troubled. "Is curse is work on Dorbi too."

Frengor exhaled. His worst fear, confirmed. "So they *are* yours."

"I thought they must be," Mâron said. "There haven't been dark Dorbians this deep inside Dûrion for centuries."

Gwargif bobbed his head sadly. "Is many problems with Dorbi here in barracks. Many fights. Some warriors get vicious. Only think of self, not of pack. Get punished, and fight officer! That *never* happen in *hrarkhoneyl* — in Dorbian Legion." His voice sank and his eyes were moist. "They become like... animal. Then, last few days, they run away. *Is* now dark Dorbi at Stillárre."

There was a moment of silence. Then Frengor extended a hand and Gwargif lifted one of his. Frengor gripped the fingered paw-hand. "Gwargif, my friend, I'm sorry. This must be difficult for you."

The grey-white helmet of hair above the intelligent face bobbed again. "Is Dorbi must fight Dorbi. Yesterday, today, Gwargif send trusted warriors, find darkened ones. Bring back, or... kill." The pain in his brown eyes spoke for itself.

The two men were silent as they left the barracks. After a while Mâron sighed. "Dear Prince. So now we have civil war among the last defenders of our city."

"We *cannot* lose hope," Frengor declared. "We must hold on to what Shiván said when he left: This darkness *will* be lifted. This curse *will* be overcome."

They walked on through the desolation that was Stillárre.

* * *

Lannie's arrow curved through the air towards the fleeing cavalry officer. It began to fall, and she held her breath. Then it struck. Not in the middle of the back, but the left shoulder. The officer flinched — and the Ambon under his left arm swung with his movement. It must have struck the horse's muzzle, because the animal suddenly veered right, and the rider lost his balance. He teetered for a moment, yawing out to the left at a bizarre angle, then with a cry he crashed to the ground. The Ambon glinted as it shot from his hand.

Lannie let out a whoop and galloped up to the fallen man. He lay still—whether stunned or dead, she had no time to find out. The rumble of hooves was growing louder further down the road. She leapt to the ground. She needed two things: the Ambon, and her only arrow. The arrow lay nearby, but the Ambon was nowhere to be seen.

Frantically she cast around looking for it. The road was empty. The officer's horse had trotted on towards its approaching comrades. Where could the Ambon have got to? It couldn't have travelled far; the man had already been been falling when it left his hand...

The coming hoofbeats were just around the corner when she finally found the Ambon stuck half-hidden in a bush. She seized it, sprinted for her horse and leapt into the saddle, narrowly avoiding her enemy's mistake of striking the animal with the emblem. She clasped it horizontally under her arm like a lance, as he had done, then urged her mount off the road eastward towards a hill that she hoped would hide her from sight. As she rounded the slope of the hill she heard shouts and the confused thudding of horses being reined in as the newcomers discovered the fallen officer.

She rode as fast as she dared. It was a strain to keep the Ambon steady. If only she had its leather case! But that was strapped to their pack animal, along with her travel bag. She concentrated on putting distance between herself and her pursuers. She could already hear shouted commands and the sound of horses picking up speed in her direction.

A few minutes later to her relief she found a well-trodden country track running eastward, and urged her horse to a gallop. For a while she thought she was shaking off the men behind her; but then she heard hoofbeats and a distant cry of triumph. They'd spotted her. She didn't risk looking back.

She could only hope that these cavalry did not include mounted archers. She smacked her horse's rear hump, and it found a new burst of speed.

Up ahead the track disappeared into a winding line of trees. The glint of water could be seen under the lower branches. An idea came to her. *Dear God, don't let the horse refuse!*

Lannie plunged under the trees at full speed, then pulled her mount up sharply as it splashed into a shallow stream. The path continued eastward on the other side. She wheeled right, clutching the Ambon tightly, and urged the horse down the stream bed. For a heart-stopping instant it hesitated, rearing up; then it started picking its way downstream. As rapid hoofbeats approached, Lannie turned the animal into the shadow of a large clump of bushes by the bank. She held it stock still as about twenty cavalrymen galloped across the stream in an eruption of water and spray.

Then she turned her mount and continued downstream, ducking from time to time to avoid low branches. She switched the Ambon to her other arm. After quite a few twists and bends she paused as she heard the distant splash of horsemen re-crossing the stream from the other side. She felt a glow of satisfaction. They hadn't tumbled to her trick. But they might still do so. Before then she had to gain more distance.

Half an hour later she came out of the stream and rested her horse in a cluster of trees on the eastern bank. Faint shouts came to her from a long way off. For now she was safe.

She left the copse and rode beside the stream. A pale sun had come out, and from the shadows she guessed she was travelling roughly south-east. Her mount was tiring now, so she kept to a gentle trot, her ears pricked for any sound of pursuit. But there was none. Her hand savoured the feel of the Ambon's shaft. The mission hadn't failed. Yet.

Lannie rode on through lightly wooded country until the sky began to darken. Then she found a copse large enough to hide herself and her mount. She tethered the horse and settled down as best she could for the night, shivering a little in the early evening chill.

She took the bess from the pocket of her robe. Holding it against her ear with both hands she murmured softly, "Shiván?"

* * *

Shiván and his weary band were having a long and difficult journey. As the curse-haze settled more heavily on them they travelled more slowly and had to stop more often.

They rested under a small knoll for the midmeal — taken from their dwindling supply of dried food. Everyone was conscious of the two great gaps in their midst. Nobody said a word, but Shiván knew their thoughts were along the same lines. Cârin would never again enliven their breaks with his wisecracks. And Lannie... Would they see her again, or would she die somewhere unseen, her body rolled carelessly into a ditch? Had they lost the Ambon, their mission, their future?

No! He would not fall prey to defeatist thinking. That way lay the rapid slide down into depression. He above all must remain strong. *Dear Prince, please help me.*

Jomel began weeping, setting off Perrely. Gil sat down beside her murmuring, "It'll be alright". She glanced at him and struggled to stifle her tears. Shiván put an arm around Perrely, and she gave him a tearful smile before snuggling up against him. He marvelled at her new warmth. Was this a positive effect of the curse-haze? Danîsha sat on Perrely's other side and gave Shiván a knowing look, her lips quirking upward. Had Perrely said something to 'Neesh? But now was not the right moment to ask.

After a while Shiván tried to focus their minds on God and his presence with them in every situation—even without the Ambon, and without their two friends. 'Neesh supported him with wise comments, and the tears eventually eased. Shiván hoped Perrely and Jomel had begun to understand the way of moment-by-moment dependence on God, which was the only thing that kept him and Danîsha going. Lannie, and to a lesser extent Gil and Garset, had developed their own ways of coping; but the two younger women had depended heavily on the Ambon; and the curse-haze they were suffering now was definitely worse than they'd coped with before.

Over an hour passed before they'd dressed Danîsha's wound and resumed their journey.

They had to stop four more times en route to their goal, the River Parl. Twice they turned aside to avoid others using the path. Twice they just needed to rest. Unfortunately, this was open country. *Grûnet* cattle could sometimes be seen grazing in the distance, with two or three herdsmen sitting nearby. There were few copses to hide in. Time and again Shiván silently asked God to protect them.

At last they reached the river, and after a little searching they found a ford. North-east across the river they could see the town that was labelled Kapáreli on the map; a little too close for Shiván's comfort. They waited until the coast was clear, then trotted their horses across the river. On the other side they turned south on to a larger track. The light was starting to fade, and they urgently needed to find shelter. They wouldn't make it to that village—Difitari—tonight.

Danîsha was beginning to droop in the saddle when he finally spotted a rocky outcrop to the east. He guided them off the road and round the side of the outcrop. There, hidden from passing travellers, was a hollow in the lee of the rocks. They helped 'Neesh off her horse, then Perrely and Jomel made her comfortable on a soft patch of grass and snuggled down beside her while the men tethered the horses.

Shiván tied their pack horse to a bush, using a long rope to allow it to graze. Nearby, untethered, Cârin's horse cropped the grass. It had followed them, and he didn't have the heart to drive it away. He was unstrapping their rain sheet from the pack horse, when a voice spoke in his ear: "Shiván?"

His heart leapt. He dropped the strap and hurried over to the others. "Hey, everyone, it's Lannie! On the bess."

The three women sat up, their faces breaking into smiles. Gil exclaimed, "Thank the One!" Even Garset's dour expression softened.

"Are you okay, Lannie?"

"Yes, I'm fine, but—"

"That's great! Be with you in a sec." He turned to the others. "Gil, get out the blaise. Perrely, can you fetch the bellaril?—so we can all see and hear."

When the instruments were assembled they heard Lannie saying with a touch of impatience, "Are you there?"

"Yes, Lannie. You look comfortable." Gil had produced a wavering image on a cleared patch of dirt. In the dim light they could just make out Lannie lying swathed in her robe in some long grass beside a tree trunk.

"Never mind that—"

"Did you get the Ambon?" Jomel blurted.

Gil had zoomed closer, and they could see a familiar caustic look on Lannie's face. "If you'll give me half a chance, I'll tell you!"

She described the chase, and her escape. They all let out a cry of triumph when she showed them the Ambon. Then they glanced around guiltily; but the night was silent.

After that it was too dim to see anything with the blaise, and Gil put it away. Shiván considered telling Lannie about Cârin's death, but decided this was not a good way for her to hear about it. Instead he asked Lannie where she was, and she tried to describe her route; but her voice was fading in and out, and they found it hard to follow.

Gil fetched the map, and they risked snapping a firestick to provide light. Lannie tried again, but all they could work out was that she was somewhere south-east of Anlestera.

His eyes on the map, Gil told her, "Just keep heading a little south of east. You should be able to meet us at…" His finger moved between a couple of places on the map. "Um, here… At Kapá— No, at…"

Shiván took over. "Just keep going eastward, Lannie, till you come to the sea. Then…"

"Come to what?"

Shiván felt a sense of foreboding. They'd never had trouble hearing one another with the bess. "To the *sea*. Then follow the *coast road* south to *Orselm*."

"Okay. Which way are you going? Tell me some names…" Her voice faded.

Shiván replied, emphasising the names of villages on the map: Difitari, Oridenda, Gurineti, Kamenila, Lambara. After several tries she repeated them correctly. "We'll wait for you as long as we can at each village. Did you get that? … *Wait* for you. If we reach *Lambara* just outside *Orselm* we'll find somewhere to hide and wait longer."

'Neesh, Perrely and Jomel were already asleep when he said goodnight to Lannie. Garset was leaning against the rock, snoring quietly. Jomel was curled up on the ground near Gil, who sat with his arms on his knees. Shiván smiled at him, and he gave his famous half-grin. "I'll take the first watch," he murmured.

"Thanks." Shiván stretched out on the ground next to Perrely. He breathed a heartfelt *thank you* to the One before his thoughts faded into sleep.

* * *

A day had passed. Lannie sat staring at a tree trunk, depressed. Around her were the soft, evening rustles of the forest. Nearby her horse cropped grass. A few aldoret away, across a river, was a village. She hadn't dared enter it.

She hadn't made much progress today.

She'd set out at dawn, full of confidence, still following the stream. By her best guess it was headed a little south of east—the direction Shiván had suggested.

Then the problems had started. Galloping horsemen. Other travellers. Sudden detours. Hiding for long periods, heart-in-mouth, waiting for people to pass and hoofbeats to fade. If she'd covered as much as ten aldoret — seven miles — she'd be surprised.

She couldn't carry on like this. She was conspicuous in every way: alone, a foreigner, carrying the Ambon. There was no way to disguise the wretched thing. It stood out like a mediaeval lance tucked under a suburban housewife's arm.

Linking up with Shiván and the rest of the group was looking unlikely now. So the primary goal of their mission rested entirely on her: she had the Ambon. But how could she travel with it? She'd be spotted and captured in no time.

Supposing by some miracle she made it alone to Orselm, how would she enter the tunnels? She didn't know the person they were supposed to contact. Shiván had those details. And suppose she did somehow reach the Temple of Gadesh, how could she get in and raise the Ambon over the altar? Only as a suicide mission, she thought grimly; one that would end long before she reached the altar of Gadesh...

And she'd never see Shivvie, 'Neesh, Gil, Perrely, Jomel, Garset or Cârin again. She felt a pang as she thought of her friends here in Dûrion. And all of those back home... If she died here, presumably she would die on Earth as well — without ever seeing her friends and family again. Never making up with Matt. Never laughing with her brother Dale again, or visiting her dear, stuffy parents, or working out with her gym partners, or brainstorming with her work colleagues... She'd never handle design tools again, or sit at a computer, or produce a smart, catchy web page.

With a heavy heart she turned to her Creator and Father, seeking his strength and comfort. She needed him just to keep functioning these days under the Curse — and that was with the Ambon. How were Shiván and the others managing without it? She shuddered at the thought. *Dear Prince, please help them.*

As she prayed, her thoughts kept returning to the Ambon. It suddenly struck her: all day, while she'd been hiding, she'd left it lying on the ground. But to have its effect, it needed to be upright. She quickly picked it up and leant it against the tree in front of her. Then she sat down again to pray. The forest around her looked mysterious and beautiful in the waning light, the tree trunks wreathed in green leaf-shaped shadows, the grass fronds a rich, glowing emerald. It brought back that first day in Carreck Forest, when she'd longed for her watercolours to capture the subtle interplay of greens and browns.

Peace and reassurance began to colour her thoughts, along with a sense of quiet confidence. She asked the One to strengthen Shiván and the others. She laid her own situation before him, simply asking him to show her the way. She thought of the Ambon's amazing properties. Like Moses' staff in the Old Testament, when the people of Israel were fighting the Amalekites: as long as he held it up, Israel won; when he lowered it, the Amalekites started winning…

She was letting her mind wander. She resumed her prayers, thanking God for the amazing way he'd brought them this far. How, beyond all expectation, they'd defeated the Selmian cavalry yesterday. The Ambon had played a part in that, also, as Jomel and Perrely had held it up throughout the battle…

There she was, letting her thoughts drift again! Father, help me to pray straight.

You are.

I am?

Yes. I want you to think about the Ambon.

Lannie blinked. It wasn't often she had such a direct sense of God speaking to her.

Think about the Ambon. All right. Jomel had held it up at arm's length as the cavalry were bearing down on them. That amazing trumpet call had sounded, with a sudden flash of light—

Stop right there. When had she heard that trumpet call before?

When they had raised the Ambon during the war against Shambor.

Why had they done so?

To summon followers of the Light to their cause.

Because alone they could do nothing. They needed help. Garset and his 'Pure Company' had joined them thanks to the Ambon's summons. So had thousands of others. And in the end, they had overthrown Shambor.

She was alone. *She* needed help.

Raise the Ambon? Here, in the heart of the Strongholder's realm? No, that was crazy. Besides, no Lightists had come running when the girls raised it during the battle.

Maybe there weren't any Lightists in that deserted area. Maybe they *had* come running, but had reached the remote battle site too late.

Could the Ambon summon Shiván and her friends? No, they would be too far away by now. But there were other Lightists in Selmion. She knew that from what Frengor had told them before they set out. There were the 'Renegade Royalty', descendants of an ancient royal line who had secretly fought against the Strongholders for centuries. There were ordinary people who still held to their Lightist beliefs — like that poor man they'd encountered on their first evening in the country, wandering about under the curse-haze searching for his family. And, according to Frengor, there was the Renegades' network of 'agents': their eyes and ears in most of the towns and villages.

Might there be an agent in the village across the river? She doubted it. Even if there was, would he respond to the Ambon?

She could almost hear God chuckling. *There's only one way to find out.*

Lannie stood, brushed grass fragments from her tunic, and took hold of the Ambon. She clasped the two leather-lined hand grips, and positioned herself where there was a gap in the leaves above her. Then with a muttered, "In the name of the Prince!" she thrust the Ambon as high as her arms would go.

Chapter 38: *Progress to the dark city*

THE BOULDER STOOD POISED over the narrow mountain track. Behind it Shakhere had his hand raised, watching the approaching column of wagons below. Barkt squatted nearby with a sledgehammer and a metal rod, waiting for Shakhere's signal. One blow of the hammer on the rod would shatter a stone wedge — sending the boulder plunging over the cliff on to the track. That was the theory. In case the boulder stuck, half a dozen men with sweat-streaked faces and grimy clothing stood by to heave. Two of the six were true-born Grûzhack — former masters, who in times past would never have dreamt of mingling with their Grûzhileyn slaves. Shakhere was proud of them.

But it was Grûzhileyn treachery that had brought them here today. Of that he was not proud. The approaching wagons — heavily guarded by Selmian cavalry — were carrying teméyn from the Herkhept plantation. The workers there had sold out to the Selmians, accepting astronomical wages and protection for their families in return for their skills in refining teméyn.

Shakhere's fists clenched in anger. Herkhept was the only plantation still working — but its output could keep the Strongholder and his Mindbenders going long enough to lure other teméyn workers back with their money. His task force *had* to stop that caravan before it left Barazhân.

The lead wagon crept closer. Any second now —

Eyes narrowed, he measured the distance from the slow-moving wagons to their position. Not yet. If he timed it right, their boulder would destroy the lead wagon, blocking the track. If not... well, some of the Selmian cavalry would be killed, and in the confusion his force would unleash their second surprise — a trick he had learned from the Dûrians. He glanced across at a line of men hidden under the trees. Each carried a bow and arrow, and behind them pots of pitch were simmering on carefully banked fires — so that, as an added bonus, the wagons and their contents would go up in flames.

Two ex-servicemen stood with the archers, their muskets loaded and ready.

There was a sudden cry from the forest: *"Flatlanders!"* Shakhere's head snapped round. One of the sentries he'd posted burst out of the trees and pointed behind him.

The Selmians were sweeping the route for ambushes—just as his father Tal had warned.

"Fire on the flatlanders!" he yelled. The cavalrymen came into view and the two muskets roared. One of the leading Selmians fell. The musketeers started frantically reloading while the archers were lighting the pitch on their arrows and swinging their bows round... but it was too late. At any moment the enemy would be among them.

The bitter realisation hit Shakhere that it was over. He'd learned the hard way that they could not win a hand-to-hand confrontation with Selmian cavalrymen—even when they were on foot.

"Back to base!" he yelled. His task force turned and ran, the archers dropping their burning arrows. At all costs they must avoid being caught and mindbent. At least they could outrun the flatlanders.

Shakhere glanced behind, and suddenly stopped. Barkt was hammering at the wedge under the boulder! *"Barkt! No...!"* he shouted, but the overseer had signed his own death warrant. A last blow of the sledgehammer, and the boulder went crashing over the edge. The squat foreigners in tan capes had almost reached him when Barkt leapt off the cliff, following the boulder into the depths.

Half-sobbing he ran on. *Barkt, you wonderful, crazy fool! Why did you have to play the hero? What will I tell Felhis? The man she loved, the man who protected me as a child, threw himself over a cliff rather than be captured by the Selmians. And maybe snatched victory from defeat!*

Before long the Selmians gave up the chase. Shakhere and his men ran on. After a couple of hours following hidden paths through the tortuous crags and ravines of the mountains, he led his grieving yet hopeful band into the command cave of the rebels' hidden retreat. Father heard the news and tilted his head. "A costly success. If it is one." Mother wept at the news of Barkt's death.

His men dispersed to their own quarters and Shakhere threw himself on the ground beside the fire. Later he would break the news to Felhis. Tomorrow they would find out what happened to the teméyn caravan.

Someone brought Shakhere a platter of food. As he picked at it, Brakhól came up. He was wearing a blue tunic without rips or patches, which Mother had saved from better times. He stood wide-eyed and hesitant in front of Shakhere, sensing his mood. Shakhere held out an arm, and he quickly settled beside him.

"How are you, little brother?"

"I'm alright. Were the Selmin bad today?"

"Yes, they were."

"Did you beat them?"

"Not really. But maybe we hurt them."

"You're sad." He swiveled his head to look into Shakhere's face. Shakhere nodded.

Brakhól was silent for a moment. "I wish Danîsha was here. She would tell us about Prince Orrénne." He said it in Dûrian. Shakhere felt tears prick his eyelids.

Brakhól turned to look at him again, his small face alight with a new idea. "Shall I sing for you?"

"Yes, I'd like that."

"I'll sing *He's my Friend*. I'll fetch Dekhtan!"

He jumped up and ran to the entrance of one of the side caves. Shakhere watched his little brother, his heart lifting already. Dekhtan was the least likely person to have joined the rebel movement—a true-born musician from the Beauty Endeavour. But he hated the Selmians with a fervour for what they'd done to his family, and was fearless on missions. He was also a virtuoso on the *lhendift*, and he'd brought the six-stringed instrument with him. No one could take Daneesh's place, but he was the One's substitute.

Brakhól came back with the young Grûzhack in tow, complete with *lhendift*.

"Brakhól says you'd like a song?" Dekhtan said.

"Yes, we need our spirits lifted tonight."

"Well, Brakhól's the one to do that." He sat on a rock and positioned the instrument across his chest. With hands poised he looked at Brakhól.

The child nodded. Dekhtan struck a chord, and Brakhól's pure young voice filled the cave. The *lhendift* lacked the richness and deep vibrancy of Daneesh's bellaril; but Brakhól's singing more than made up for that. The command cave filled with weary, heart-hungry people as Brakhól poured out his devotion to the Prince who was his friend. Shakhere sat, eyes closed, letting the song reach down inside him and shine the One's Light into the depths of his being. Darkness fled like shadows before the sun's radiance.

The song ended. As always, he wanted it to go on and on. How could they have survived without Brakhól? Now there was a light in every face as they glanced at one another.

This was the Power that would destroy the teméyn trade.

* * *

The clear, high trumpet call rang out, and the trees around Lannie were lit up for an instant by a soft glow.

But... it was a distant sound, as though coming to her from several miles away.

Her heart sank. Last night she'd had trouble hearing Shiván in the bess. Was the Ambon also losing its power? She lowered it to the ground, still keeping it vertical.

She waited.

No one came.

Yet she found she couldn't let go of the Ambon. Its compelling summons was still ringing in her heart. Any Lightist who'd heard it would be feeling the same.

Time went by. Lannie was tiring, and knew she would soon have to sit down.

She was on the point of doing so, when she heard the faint snap of a twig in the silence of the evening. Was someone entering the forest? A few moments later there was another snap, then a distant swish of foliage and the sound of running footsteps.

Lannie stood with the Ambon, facing the direction the intruder was coming from. In the dying light her eyes were glued to the shadowy shapes of the trees and foliage in front of her. Her heart was thudding. If the Selmian Mindbenders had some way of hearing the Ambon, she and the mission might be over.

The bushes in front of her suddenly parted, and a young man burst into the glade. He wore a coarsely woven linen tunic hastily pulled on over his nightrobe, and his blue-black hair was tousled. His eyes widened when he saw the Ambon. He rushed forward, fell to his knees and grasped hold of it.

For a long moment he knelt there resting his head against the shaft. Then he looked up at her, his face filled with delight. "*Kyelarisa! Ambelu Dulurinu tematari!*" His words had the Selmian singsong cadence.

For the first time it occurred to Lannie that summoning Selmian Lightists with the Ambon might not be enough. She also had to communicate with them. Where was Jomel when she needed her?

Well, *maybe* this guy spoke Dûrian... "I'm a Restorer of the Way —
an *Atenámbar*. This is the Ambon of Sûrilane. I need help."

The young man's face clouded. *"Lina tar'isa sho."*

Obviously not.

Lannie sighed. Okay, me Jane, you Tarzan. She bent down, put an
arm under his elbow, and applied gentle pressure. He stood up. She
pointed at her chest. "Alanya." She moved her finger to his and
raised her eyebrows.

He smiled. "Kyenu."

"Chenu, I need — to find — a Renegade agent." She spoke slowly
and emphatically.

The frown was back. *"Tar'isa sho."* He grabbed her arm and pointed
in the direction he'd come. *"Isa pona! Gyelerisa a banilari, iye —"*

Not so fast, brother. "Me — find — agent: *saldon.*" When he looked
blank she repeated the Dûrian word for 'agent': *"Saldon!"*

Light dawned on his face. *"Salidu!"* He nodded vigorously. *"Aya,
aya — pona!"*

Lannie went to fetch her horse, which was standing half-asleep a
short distance away. Chenu's eyes widened when he saw the animal,
but he said nothing. Lannie followed him, leading the horse with one
hand and holding the Ambon in the other. He held branches aside
for her, a delighted grin on his face.

As they approached the edge of the forest, Lannie caught
occasional glimpses of a dim, flickering light. She wished she had her
bow and quiver at hand, but Chenu showed no alarm — in fact, he
was hurrying towards it.

They came out from under the trees to find a group of five people
approaching, one holding a lantern. They were hidden from general
view by an extension of the forest on one side and a low hill on the
other. Chenu ran to them, and there were exclamations of relief when
they recognised him. He spoke for a couple of minutes in rapid-fire
Selmian; then turned and beckoned to Alanya, holding up the lantern.

She came forward out of the shadows with her horse and the
Ambon. There were gasps from the group, quickly swept away in the
general rush to reach the Lightist emblem. As they passed under the
lantern Lannie saw briefly that these were all older folk. She anchored
the Ambon's shaft on the ground, and they clustered round it, some
kneeling to clasp it, others reaching out a hand to hold it. Most were
weeping, and several had their eyes raised heavenward, disjointed

words of praise tumbling from their lips. Lannie had a lump in her throat. That's how *she* would feel if she'd found the Ambon after suffering the curse in the Strongholder's country, with no Kindler or Hearth to turn to.

And no sooner had they found it than she would be taking it away again.

After a while an older man stood up and wiped his eyes. "*Gyela sar'enyora.*" He turned to Lannie and gestured back the way they'd come. "*Nenya ponilari?*" Lannie nodded. She'd gladly go with them.

The man laid a hand on Chenu's shoulder, and Lannie saw the likeness between them. They all set off, Chenu leading with the lantern. Lannie and the horse were surrounded by the others, all keeping as close as they could to the Ambon in her right hand.

Chenu paused when they reached a path. Once they were all on the beaten track he doused the lantern. They set off again under the faint light of the Ring of Orrénne, the spectacular circle of stars in the centre of the night sky. Neither of the moons were up, but they managed with only an occasional stumble.

After walking for about half an hour, Lannie heard the sounds of a river ahead. Everyone was silent now, and she could feel the tension in the group.

They crossed the river at a ford. On the other side was the village Lannie had been too afraid to enter earlier. Chenu's father led them to a secluded barn, where she tethered the horse for the night.

They returned to the road running through the village, and members of the group began to disperse to their homes. They glanced back longingly at the Ambon in Lannie's hand. Chenu and his parents walked silently past the closed houses; firelight showed through the cracks around the doors and shutters, and there was the occasional murmur of conversation or a sudden exclamation. Lannie was relieved when they finally reached Chenu's home, a small wattle-and-daub cottage at the other end of the village. For a while longer the Ambon was safe.

After a plain but very welcome meal in the main room, Lannie thanked her hosts—a phrase they understood, but found funny—and went to sit on a box in the corner. The Ambon stood tall and shining beside her. Under the family's curious gaze she took the bess out of her pocket, concentrated on Shiván, and quietly spoke his name.

She tried to have a conversation, but the reception was much worse than yesterday. She gathered that Shivvie was somewhere near Oridenda—the second village in the list he'd made her repeat. They'd waited a day for her in the woods near Difitari. She tried to explain the delay, but soon gave up.

She gathered that Danîsha was okay—physically and mentally— but they were struggling to keep the group together as the curse-haze bit deeper. She *had* to reach them soon. She told him about raising the Ambon and finding some local Lightists, as well as her hopes of locating a Renegade agent—and that she would use the same method to try and contact them at each village; but she couldn't tell whether he'd understood. In the end his disjointed phrases petered out altogether. With a sigh she put the bess away.

Chenu's mother led her to the only other room and showed her a straw-filled mattress on the floor. Apart from that there were two large chests and little else. She guessed it was the parents' bedroom, and tried to protest; but her hostess shook her head emphatically. She left, and Lannie subsided gratefully on to the bed, laying the Ambon beside her and her bow and quiver within reach.

The next morning she was woken before dawn. She stumbled out of the bedroom, and Chenu's mother thrust a steaming mug of chass into her hand. In the lamplight she became aware that the main room was full: besides Chenu and his father there were the three from last night, plus three new faces. Everyone beamed at her, and amid a muted babble of conversation several pointed to the bedroom and one man mimed holding a long pole. She went to fetch the Ambon, but she wasn't happy that word of it had spread.

After everyone had had a few moments to bask in the Ambon's healing influence, Chenu turned to her with a broad grin. "*Salidu!*" The Selmian for 'agent'. Her fears gave way to sudden hope as he took her to the door and she saw her horse standing ready. Chenu made repeated pointing gestures along the road that ran out of the village. "*Salidu. Difitari.*" The name of the first village in Shivvie's list.

Half an hour later as the sun was casting its first rays over the eastern hills, the whole group set off. Lannie walked safely in the midst carrying the Ambon horizontally, while one of the men led her horse.

She prayed she'd been properly understood, and that they would indeed find a Renegade agent in Difitari.

* * *

Estaron sat at his shey-nut desk in the newly-redecorated Governor's office in the Strongholder's palace. Unpleasant memories of Shambor's blackwood décor in Darthane had decided him to stick with the palace's predominant shey-nut style. The desk was new, and highly polished. He absently stroked its shiny surface. The shey-nut bookshelves on the walls were also new. He'd had four fitted — the minimum needed to house all the Selmian administrative journals Konnar had sent him. Otherwise the room was sparsely furnished, which was the way Estaron wanted it. There must be nothing to suggest the opulence of royalty.

He frowned a little as his eye fell on two of the cupboards. They were not centred on the wall. His chief steward Otaru had insisted on that, speaking airily of 'avoiding oppressive symmetry'. For the same reason the cupboards were placed slightly apart. Well, Estaron liked symmetry. He'd have them moved.

He sighed, and drummed his fingers on the empty desk. He'd received three reports from his regional representatives this morning, and he was considering how to deal with them. A mentally-competent single man had been mindbent in Orimanela, in clear contravention of his new law forbidding such arbitrary actions. In the north, a mysterious waterborne infection in the local river had caused many deaths in the coastal city of Origyendili. The fishermen of Asinora on Lake Derath were complaining that Dûrian boats were encroaching on their fishing grounds...

None of this was written down, of course. Estaron held all the facts in his head. At the end of each day he made brief notes in a personal diary which he carried with him at all times. The palace was a hotbed of intrigue, and he didn't trust any of the staff—except perhaps the impossibly stiff major-domo. He couldn't imagine Gedoriu stooping to intrigue and gossip-mongering. But he certainly didn't trust the steward Konnar had given him—greasy, grinning Otaru; nor most of the other palace servants. He didn't think Konnar was spying on him; the bond between them was too strong for that. But everyone with the slightest sliver of authority had his own agenda, and Estaron knew only too well how much damage could be caused when information fell into the wrong hands.

The door chime sounded. He plucked the answering chime at the side of his desk. His chief steward entered—just as Estaron himself had so often done when he was Shambor's secretary.

"A post rider from Orinawa, your Worthiness." Otaru's oily face wore its normal eager smile, and he kept 'washing' his clasped hands. Estaron winced: both at the title (the least grandiose of several Konnar had suggested); and at Otaru's servile mannerisms. Perhaps that made him genuine: no truly insincere person would be so obvious about it.

"Let him come in."

The rider advanced towards Estaron's desk. His clothing was travel stained, and he looked weary. In the background Otaru steepled his fingers, bowed, and exited, closing the door.

Outside the room the steward looked quickly in all directions before hurrying round a corner and down another passage until he reached a cabinet displaying ancient swords on shelves. He opened it, pulled a lever under one of the shelves, and the whole cabinet swung noiselessly aside to reveal an archway in the wall. Beyond it was a short tunnel. At the far end a door had been removed, and the backs of two bookcases could be seen. A small gap between them allowed both light and sound into the tunnel.

Otaru stepped in, gently pulled the cabinet shut, and tiptoed to a stool at the far end. He settled himself down to listen.

"...concerned about some disturbing rumours," the post rider was saying. "These have been circulating in the far north for some days now."

"What kind of rumours?" Estaron asked.

"Country people are saying that a group of foreigners has been travelling the roads. The representative in Orinawa would not waste your time with this, except that they also say these foreigners are powerful sorcerers. They are reported to have with them a magical Lightist ambon that destroys the Strongholder's troops on sight."

Estaron betrayed no emotion, but a shock ran through him.

"And *have* any of the Strongholder's troops been destroyed?"

"The representative was unable to find any evidence of this, your Worthiness."

"He checked the local garrisons?"

"Yes, sir."

"Has the representative interviewed anyone who claims to have actually seen or spoken to these foreigners?"

"No, sir. Those he interviewed were all relating the stories at second or third-hand."

Estaron was silent for a moment.

"All right. Thank you for your report. Return to me in the morning and I'll give you a reply to take to the representative in Orinawa."

The rider bowed with steepled fingers and left.

Estaron sat staring at his stark office, his mind tinged with horror at what he'd just heard.

The Restorers had entered Selmion with the Ambon; and he was now up against the worst possible dilemma.

What in the Prince's name were Shiván and the others planning to do in Selmion? Kill the Strongholder? Even they could hardly hope to succeed with such a foolhardy project.

They must have found some antidote to the Curse, to have come this far. The Ambon? He shook his head. He couldn't imagine it.

Had they actually killed some Selmian troops? It was unthinkable, but behind any rumour lay a small nugget of fact.

And what about Konnar? He must have heard the same rumours. Why hadn't he said anything?

That was as ominous as the Restorers' presence in Selmion.

Whatever Estaron did, he would betray someone.

For a long while he sat staring at the intricate whorls and curves in the grain of the shey-nut desk. Finally he decided that his only course right now was to find out as much as possible. He would ask his representative in Orinawa to track down the rumours and do all he could to find the foreigners.

If he found them… Well, he'd cross that stream when he came to it.

* * *

Shiván and his group crested a rise on the coast road… and there it was. They reined in their horses. Perrely let out a sigh, as if she'd been holding her breath. Jomel gave a small grunt of dismay. "Lord," Danîsha murmured. Garset muttered, "Prince, have mercy."

A dark grey sprawl of buildings lay on the horizon under a lowering sky.

Orselm.

Their goal, the nemesis that had haunted their dreams since leaving Stillárre. In the centre, a touch of green: the Strongholder's palace.

"We made it," Gil said flatly.

Shiván shook his head, his heart filled with foreboding. Not yet. What lay waiting for them in that city?

Closer by, the coast road ran through a small village: Lambara. Last night, looking at the map by the flickering light of a firestick, he'd decided they would find a secluded spot near Lambara this evening and tackle the problem of how to enter Orselm tomorrow. He desperately hoped Lannie would catch up with them here before they had to move on. They'd waited at each of the previous villages without success. He examined the map around Lambara, and saw what appeared to be a patch of woodland in a fold between two hills. Hidden both from Lambara and the city.

"Come on," he said, and urged his horse into motion.

They rode down the far side of the hill in silence. There were other travellers, both behind and ahead of them: this close to Orselm Shiván had abandoned any hope of having the road to themselves.

He was bone weary. The last couple of days had been a nightmare. The loss of Cârin's cheerful presence weighed heavily on him; and the curse-haze had settled deeper on his companions, making their actions more erratic — all except Danîsha, who'd been a solid rock of support. Often one of the others had wandered off the track or lingered behind, and he or 'Neesh had to bring them back. Over and again they'd repeated to them the only solution that worked: to keep their minds focused on God — moment by moment.

But two threads of brightness shone through the darkness of these days: the one was that Danîsha's wound had continued to heal; and the second was Perrely's amazing new openness.

When she wandered off and he called her or took her hand to lead her back, she came at once, often dazzling him with a smile that set his heart thudding. She was looking to him, wanting to be with him. He had to guard his responses while she was under the curse-haze.

But this afternoon they were all doing better. Perhaps his and 'Neesh's message had at last begun to sink in. He'd only once recalled a straggler — Garset, who'd stopped to stare at the sea near Kamenila. And as Gil improved, he'd taken it on himself to watch over Jomel.

Now they were approaching the village. Up ahead Shiván saw a country track winding off to the right that would take them towards the place in the hills he was aiming for. He turned on to it, and glanced back to check his 'flock': they were trotting after him, all present and correct. Perrely and Jomel were chatting together as they used to before they lost the Ambon. Praise the Prince.

Tomorrow... *how desperately he wanted to rest!* And they needed to wait for Lannie. Okay, tomorrow they would take a break in that secluded spot between the hills.

* * *

Konnar sent the last pathetic figure shambling out of his study to the cells below. *Geshu!* He lifted a hand to his mouth and began chewing the fingernails. *Three more Mindbenders dismissed for lack of teméyn, together with over twelve hundred slaves!* Only three of his personal Mindbenders left in Selmion now, plus the six with the western armies.

Three, and he'd had ten! He'd centralised all local teméyn supplies in the palace to avoid hoarding, and it still continued to dwindle at an alarming rate. The palace guard was down to a skeleton crew, and unrest was growing around the country without Mindbenders to control it. Soon he'd be reduced to relying on Bari's new City Watch and recruiting local militias to maintain order!

Fear and doubt gnawed at him. His authority here at home had never rested on so shaky a foundation. Bari had better come up to scratch as Governor of Selmion.

* * *

Lingetu, the Strongholder's chief of internal espionage, was climbing the hill to rejoin his fellow-spies at their elevated outpost. He had just finished reconnoitring the foreigners' campsite near Lambara. He smiled to himself. Such overconfidence! It was unbelievable. Here they were, within sight of Orselm, relaxing in the woods like a wealthy merchant family out for a picnic! They would soon pay the price for their presumption.

But why has his Supremacy allowed it this far? he wondered for the thousandth time. *It's completely out of character. He doesn't tolerate the slightest dissent. Anyone who steps out of line suffers instantly – and severely. Yet he's allowed these people to travel unhindered across the whole breadth of Selmion from the Dûrian border to the capital itself. And to wipe out almost two entire military units en route!*

319

It's all because of that new 'Governor of Selmion', he thought as he crested the hill. Rumour had it that he and the Strongholder had been childhood friends. Lingetu mentally shook his head. That someone in his Supremacy's position could be so swayed by sentiment was downright alarming. The whole mindbending establishment had better hope he soon came to his senses.

But now he would want Lingetu's report.

Crouching to avoid being seen against the skyline, he scuttled over to the rock that crowned the hill. With a grunted greeting to his colleagues watching the different directions, he composed himself for mindspeech.

"Strongholder."

* * *

Jomel lay on the soft, feathery bracken, staring contentedly at the late afternoon sunlight dancing between the leaves above her. Gelmion was sitting beside her, and Perrely and Danîsha were resting nearby. Today had been a wonderful day of rest. It wasn't an Anderil, but they'd treated it as one. Perrely had read from her copy of the Book, Danîsha had played her bellaril, and they'd sung muted songs and prayed together. Shiván had spent a lot of time sleeping.

Tomorrow she'd be going with him to Orselm to look for the Renegade contact Frengor had given them. Shiván had insisted on going into Orselm himself, accompanied only by her as interpreter. He didn't want to jeopardise more lives than necessary. They would trust the One to disguise his foreign shiláy.

She was proud at last to have a real part to play in their mission — something that no one else could do, because she was the only one who spoke Selmian. She would help them find their way — the address wasn't on Frengor's map — and translate when Shiván spoke to this Indoru Galida, the Renegade contact. He would put them in touch with the princes, who would give them access to the tunnels and help them fulfil their quest. It was quite exciting.

Through half-open eyes Jomel looked at the tall foreigner sitting beside her. Her feelings were mixed. On the one hand, she could never forget how he'd abused her — repeatedly — last year. On the other, she couldn't ignore how radically different he'd become in recent months. There was a kind of masculine gentleness and humility about him now.

And especially since the Ambon had left with Alanya, he'd been a tower of strength. Not demanding anything; not even saying much. Just being there, helpful and attentive. As he was right now, beside her. Several times he'd guided her back to the group when she'd been in danger of wandering off. At mealtimes and at night he always made sure she had what she needed without looking for thanks or recognition.

She needed to think about this new Gelmion.

After an early cold breakfast the next morning Jomel shrugged on her travel pouch, ready to leave with Shiván for the city. The early morning light was just starting to penetrate the leaves covering their hideaway. The others were all there to see them off.

Shiván took Perrely's hands in his. She looked up at him, undisguised love in her eyes and tears running down her cheeks. Jomel couldn't help a small pang of envy: like many another young girl, she'd once longed for a Prince Charming she could feel that way about. But her years as a temple prostitute had killed those ideals. The new Gelmion...? No. Not yet, at least.

They prayed together, then with a final wave she and Shiván set off through the trees. They were going on foot to be less conspicuous.

They soon rejoined the highway to Orselm — little more than a rutted country road by Dûrian standards. Half an hour later they were approaching the towering northern gatehouse of the city, walking in a long file of pedestrians at the side of the road. They were repeatedly spattered with mud from passing horses and carriages. The dark grey stone of the city seemed to exert its oppressive influence on all who entered; Jomel and Shiván were silent, along with most of their fellow-travellers.

They walked through the unguarded gate tunnel and into a busy cobbled street. Tall stone buildings loomed on either side. But at least there were sounds of life and commerce. Street traders hawked their wares; pedestrians shouted at coachmen and coachmen shouted back; wagon drivers cursed one another as they vied for right of way. As a city girl, Jomel felt herself coming alive again.

First they needed to ask for directions. Shiván looked at her, eyebrows raised. She nodded and set off with him in tow, heading for a trader standing beside a table piled high with fruit and vegetables. The man wore a grubby apron over a substantial paunch, and was advertising his wares with hoarse shouts of *"Melesseto! Gyilina! Kon'na!"*

"Wick Lane?" he said when she'd managed to catch his attention. He chuckled, multiple chins wobbling as his eyes roamed over their muddy garments. "And what's that worth to yer?"

Jomel reached into the small bag hanging from her neck and took out one of the Selmian silver coins Frengor had given them. She rubbed it between her fingers.

The trader's eyes widened and his smile vanished. "Oh! Right, milady. Well, you carry on down here two hunnerd paces, turn right, head up the hill, turn left at the statue of Goddess Sharn. Go down to the harbour, turn right before you reach the gates."

Jomel repeated the directions, then handed him the coin and they set off.

* * *

"Where were Governor Barilu's watchmen?" the Strongholder demanded, the tone of his mind-speech rising.

"The City Watch is very new..." Belyeru hazarded. Venturing opinions about the Governor of Selmion was risky. The Strongholder was insanely attached to the man.

"That doesn't excuse leaving the North Gate unguarded! How could he allow intruders — foreigners! — to walk into Orselm unchallenged?"

"He should not have, your Supremacy. I could order men out to arrest —"

"For the hundredth time, Belyeru, I want the Governor *to apprehend the foreign leader. Selmion is* his *domain now."*

There it was. Nothing could be done until the Strongholder realised for himself that the Lightist upstart pretending to rule Selmion could not be trusted.

* * *

Wick Lane was one of several narrow, dingy streets near the docks. They were inhabited by small craftsmen working with exotic materials brought in by the tall ships whose bare masts loomed above the rooftops. There was a salt tang in the air. As Jomel and Shiván turned into the wick-makers' alley the sea smell was banished by the scent of imported yarn and hot wax.

322

They entered one of the little shops, where a wizened old man sat cross-legged on a floor cushion. His deft fingers were braiding wax-impregnated threads into a wick that would produce a soft, long-burning light in some sea captain's cabin. Around him other strands were hanging out to dry; in the background a large pot of wax simmered over a fire. Bundles of completed wicks lined the shelves near the door. He looked up sharply as they entered.

"*Weladoru,*" Jomel said, using the polite form of address for an older man. His face softened. She went through the greeting ritual, wishing peace upon him and his family; he gave the responses in a slightly shaky tenor. Finally she said, "We are looking for Indoru Galida. Can you tell us which shop is his?"

The old man grimaced. "He's gone, has Indoru. Never seen him again after that Curse. Allus thought he were a Lightist." He spat on the floor. "His nephew's taken over now. Felinu. Not a good craftsman. The business has gone down." He inclined his head towards the docks. "Second from the end on this side."

With a sinking heart Jomel thanked him and they left the shop. Out in the alley she quietly translated the conversation for Shiván. A grim look settled on his face.

The second shop from the dock end of the street was larger than the old man's, but had an air of neglect. The window was grimy and the wall spattered with dirt. They opened the door and walked in.

A young man turned from a bubbling wax pot as they entered. He had an open, friendly face beaded with sweat. "*Reni 'ye delutereni alinu samendena*—May you and your families have peace." After Jomel gave the expected response he asked, "Can I sell you some wicks?" He took a bundle down from a shelf and dusted it off with his hand.

Jomel asked the special question Frengor had given them. "Do you have a wick for a candle that has burnt very low?"

The eagerness faded from the young man's face. He stared hard at Jomel, then at Shiván. He took a deep breath and murmured, "I have a very old wick, but the candle will have to be remade."

The correct response! "Thank you! Light enfold you," Jomel gasped.

"The One... strengthen you," Felinu answered. Jomel frowned. He should have said, "And fill you", but his face was filled with delight. Just a slip of the tongue?

Shiván realised the code had worked, and raised the young man's hand in the Dûrian high handshake, which took him by surprise.

"I've hoped so much for this!" Felinu exclaimed. "I'm not a wick-maker—" he gestured at the dusty shelves "—but the Princes have kept the shop open for just such a moment."

"So, how can we… make contact?"

"You need to see the Prince Regent. He lives in Goldsmiths' Street —the third house down from the fountain. It has a green door." He gave them detailed directions.

Goldsmiths' Street was in a different part of town, but not hard to find from the map. They turned into it, and paused to admire the marble-fronted buildings facing on to the tree-lined thoroughfare—in stark contrast to Wick Lane. The street itself was well surfaced with small, tightly packed pebble stones; halfway down it divided around a fountain. This was clearly the kind of neighbourhood where one would expect a Renegade Prince to live. They exchanged a glance of silent agreement.

"Wait here," Shiván said in a tense undertone. "I'll check the house." Jomel nodded.

Shiván walked down the near side of the street examining the doors of the mansions. He reached the fountain, crossed over, and began working his way back towards her on the opposite side. Beyond him a fancy dark blue carriage tricked out in gold was making its way up the street at a stately walking pace. It passed Shiván, blocking him from view, and she watched as it approached her, window blinds drawn. The coachman wore blue and gold livery. Even the six sinélle pulling it had gold-trimmed harnesses. There must be one large, fat goldsmith sitting behind those blinds.

The carriage creaked past. The coachman cracked his whip with a shout of *Yahaaya!* and the ponderous vehicle began gaining speed.

Jomel looked back at Shiván, and gasped.

He wasn't there.

Chapter 39: *Unexpected refuge*

IN THE MOMENT IT TOOK JOMEL to realise what had happened, the carriage rumbled past her. Instinctively she yelled and ran after it — then trailed to a stop as it pulled rapidly away. *Shiván had been captured in front of her eyes! They must have been followed.* Oh, dear Prince. She stood rooted to the spot, her heart pounding and mouth dry.

Why only Shiván? What about *her*? It made no sense.

She had to let the others know what had happened. Then another thought crashed in on her, banishing everything else. *She was now a loner as well as a foreigner in a hostile city.* She hurried back towards the north gate, constantly glancing over her shoulder, starting at sudden noises, averting her eyes if anyone looked at her.

* * *

Lannie reined her horse in at the crest of a rise on the coast road. The five Renegade agents did likewise. There on the horizon like a malignant growth lay the dark grey city of Orselm. Lannie's heart sank.

"*Oriselima*," the man at her side said. Tall, dark Ademu was the leader of the three agents who had responded to the Ambon in Oridenda. What recommended him most to Lannie was that he spoke Dûrian.

"It is the city of kings," he continued softly in that language as a couple of wagons rumbled past. She glanced at him. There was a light in his eye. "One day a king will rule again. The city will be bright, not dark. You will help this happen."

Lannie snorted. "One thing at a time, okay?" Her hand absently stroked the makeshift Ambon case strapped along the horse's flank.

The discovery of three agents at once in Oridenda had been a godsend. Chenu and his people had introduced her to Festiu, the agent in Difitari, and the man had nearly passed out from joy when he felt the Ambon's influence. He had taken her to Oridenda, where she'd raised the Ambon in the hope of attracting Shiván's group. Instead three agents had arrived, breathless — one of whom, praise the

Prince, spoke Dûrian. They, too, had been pathetically grateful for the Ambon.

From Ademu Lannie learned that he and his friends had come to Oridenda to sabotage the nearby mine, but had fallen victim to the Curse. Confused and incapacitated, they had been sheltered by the locals—who were not Lightists, but bore little goodwill towards the Strongholder.

At last, via Ademu, Lannie had been able to explain who she was and why she was here. To her surprise the agents readily accepted that she was an *Atenámbar*, a Restorer of the Way. They knew all about the prophecies and the exploits of the Restorers against Shambor in Dûrion. Her utter foreignness, and the Ambon in her hand, was all the validation they needed. In fact, she found it scary the way they hung on her every word. *Dear God, let this mission succeed!*

They'd continued along the route Shiván had given her, raising the Ambon near each village. At one of them, to her great relief, Ademu had replenished her stock of arrows from what looked like an abandoned barracks.

A fifth agent had joined them at Kamenila, but there had been no sign of Shiván's group. Lannie had kept trying the bess as well, but all she heard was the sound of the sea.

So. Now they were in sight of Orselm. One more village lay before it. Lannie sighed. "We'll raise the Ambon just beyond that place—"

"Lambara," Ademu murmured.

"Yes. And just pray the other Restorers are waiting for us."

Ademu bowed his head. "As you say, *Atémban*."

They set off again.

They had just passed through the squalor of Lambara when one of the agents in the rear spurred his horse forward and murmured urgently to Ademu in Selmian. He turned to Lannie, his face grave. "We are being watched, *Atémban*. Do not look, but Ilinu has seen men on that nearby hilltop."

"Why would they be watching us?" Lannie said sceptically.

"The local fisherfolk do not climb hills, *Atémban*. Hilltops are favoured by the Strongholder's spies. Believe me, we know these spies. They are not to be taken lightly."

"Then we must raise the Ambon quickly. We'll go round—"

"*Atémban*, no! There is no time. We must go at once to that house I spoke of, near the city…"

Lannie turned to him, her eyes hard. "Ademu, I will not abandon my friends! I *must* find them. They need the Ambon as much as you do—and this mission was given to all of us, not just me." She let her voice soften as she saw his distress. "The One will watch over us. He's brought my companions and me through worse situations than this. Come!"

She wheeled her horse off the road on to a narrow path and urged it to a near-gallop, the agents thundering after her.

They rounded the hill, and ahead was a large copse. Lannie swerved off the path and crashed in among the trees. While the others followed, she dismounted and rapidly unstrapped the Ambon case. As soon as the emblem was vertical, expressions of relief spread over the agents' faces. They surrounded her as she thrust it upward.

The clear trumpet call rang out; but ever more softly as they approached the centre of darkness in Orselm. *Please, God, wherever Shiván and his group are, let them hear it!*

Four of the agents dispersed to the edges of the copse to keep a lookout. Ademu remained to take turns holding the Ambon aloft.

No one came.

After a while short, pasty-faced Ilinu came charging back, his eyes wide. He gasped out something, and Ademu lowered the Ambon. "*Atémban*, we have to go *now*. At least ten spies are surrounding these trees. Soldiers will be here soon!"

Lannie buried her head in her hands. *Dear Prince, what do I do?*

The conviction came clearly. *Wait.*

She thrust out her hand for the Ambon. Ademu's shoulders sagged, but he gave it to her. As she lifted it up, Ademu and two of the other agents who were armed drew their swords.

The trumpet sang out again, then fell silent.

* * *

Danîsha so enjoyed the rest of that morning in the woods after Jomel and Shiván left for Orselm. The dappled sunlight through the trees, the soft grass and gentle caress of the breeze, the low murmur of conversation between Garset, Gil and Perrely, the horses browsing contentedly… all lulled her into that peaceful state halfway between waking and sleeping, where all troubles melted away and she could simply rest with her head in the lap of the Prince.

Then Jomel came stumbling into the glade alone, and her fragile peace was shattered.

Shiván – captured.

As the terrible news sank in it was all Danîsha could do to comfort the two distraught young women, while Gil and Garset anxiously tried to discuss their predicament through the curse-haze. Danîsha cried out in her heart to the Creator God for wisdom and clear thinking. *Father, where's the Ambon when we so desperately need it?*

The answer came at once: a soft, clear, electrifying trumpet-call.

Everyone froze. They turned to one another, amazement and half-doubting hope dawning on their faces.

The trumpet sounded again.

They leapt up, only one burning desire in every heart — to be where the Ambon was.

It called again — *that way!*

Danîsha grabbed her shoulder pouch and the bellaril and hurried to the horses along with the others. Perrely helped her strap the bellaril on her animal and mount, then leapt on her own horse. In a moment they were crashing through the trees and undergrowth, not following any path, just charging towards that glorious, compelling summons.

Danîsha twice almost lost her seat on the horse in the ups and downs and diversions of their tumultuous passage through the woods, but they finally burst through the undergrowth into a large copse — and there was Lannie thrusting the Ambon high, surrounded by several men on horseback whom Danîsha hadn't seen before.

In a moment they'd pushed their way through, rapidly dismounted, and were tightly packed around the Ambon, groaning with relief as their minds cleared. Perrely clasped the golden vertical rod with both hands, her eyes half closed: "At last!" Garset reached out and touched the silver circle, a smile breaking the long, dour lines of his face. Jomel was weeping, and Gil's eyes were closed, his lips moving in silent prayer. Danîsha sent up a heartfelt burst of thanks to their Father God.

"Glad to see you again too," Lannie said in the background.

"Oh! Lannie, please forgive us," Danîsha said, turning to her. "It's wonderful to see you again! *Thank you* for rescuing the Ambon!"

They hugged. "Are you all right?" Lannie asked, looking at her with concern.

"Tired from the way we charged over here to the Ambon, but otherwise I'm fine. My wound's been behaving itself."

"That's good!"

The others greeted Lannie warmly; then she looked round the little group. "Where's Shiván? And Cârin?"

There was a pregnant silence. Then Garset spoke softly. "Câr died in the battle when the Ambon was stolen. Just after you left."

"No..." Tears started in Lannie's eyes and she was silent for a moment. "And Shiván?"

"He was captured today in Orselm," Gil said. He gestured to Jomel, who told her the story in a few staccato sentences.

"Dear God." Lannie looked sick.

The men on horseback were waiting in the background, holding the reins of the newcomers' animals. Now one of them spoke urgently. "*Atémban*, we must go!"

"Yes." She took a deep breath. Turning to Danîsha and the others, she indicated the horsemen with a sweep of her hand. "These are Renegade agents — they've been guiding me."

"Oh, thank the Prince!" Perrely exclaimed.

Lannie rapidly told them the agents' names, pointing to each one. "Ademu knows a safe place. But the Strongholder's spies have surrounded us. We must leave at once."

"Right this minute?" Danîsha exclaimed.

"Yes, there's no time to lose. We've waited too long already." Lannie returned the Ambon to its case and mounted her horse. Danîsha and the others followed suit, their faces falling as the Ambon's healing influence faded.

Lannie gestured to the chief agent, Ademu. He and a colleague, Ilinu, led the group towards the southern end of the copse, while the other three agents brought up the rear.

Ademu paused where the trees ended, raising a hand. He surveyed the low hills with their patches of forest, before turning to Lannie. "We must return to the highway, *Atémban*. They will not expect us to go that way. We will ride fast."

"Right. But not too fast for Danîsha — the Lady *Atémbellar*. She's injured." Ademu looked doubtful, but bowed his head. It was clear that to the agents, Lannie was in charge. "'Neesh, come and ride beside me," she said.

"I'm okay on horseback," Danîsha said, but moved up next to her.

Ademu brought his hand down in a chopping motion. They trotted out of the copse, urging their horses to a gentle gallop as soon as they were on the path.

High-pitched whistles erupted from several points. Danîsha kept looking round, fearing any moment to see an ambush converging on them from both sides.

But no troops appeared. Strange.

They reached the road and joined the crowds hurrying to reach Orselm by nightfall, easing back to a trot. There were still no tan uniforms in sight. Danîsha looked at Lannie. "Why are they letting us go?"

Lannie turned to Ademu with raised eyebrows. The agent shrugged. "Perhaps they want to see *where* we go, and catch us later. That would be good."

"Why?"

He smiled grimly. "You will see, *Atémban.*" He placed a hand over his mouth, looking at her significantly. Lannie nodded and turned to frown at Perrely and Jomel, who were talking quietly. They fell silent. The Renegade agents had surrounded the group to weaken their shiláy. Talking Dûrian would not help.

Fifteen minutes later the great gatehouse of Orselm was looming up ahead of them. Danîsha shuddered at the ominous sight, not looking forward to entering its dark shadow. But a that moment, without warning, Ademu swung his horse to the right on to a well-made road that ran along the outside of the city wall. It headed towards a range of small hills whose crests showed the outlines of large mansions silhouetted against the setting sun.

"*Ride!*" Ademu suddenly yelled. "*Yahaaya!*" the agents responded, urging their horses to a gallop. Danîsha and the others echoed the Selmian "Giddy-up" cry, and she leant forward over the neck of her camel-horse as it leapt forward. Lannie looked back at her, and she nodded to say she was okay. Her wound was aching a little from the exertion, but that was to be expected.

Ten minutes later they reached the top of the first hill. Danîsha glanced over her shoulder and saw a cloud of dust arrowing along the road behind them. They thundered through a lush residential area, startling gatekeepers and sending servants leaping into the ditches at the side of the road.

Down into a valley, across a small stream, and up the next hill. Ademu raised a hand and pulled up at a high, solid metal gate. The top of the gate and the adjoining walls were lined with sharp spikes. Ademu leapt off his horse, fumbled for a bunch of a keys, and after trying a couple the lock creaked open and the gate swung inwards. The rest of them trotted through while Ademu closed and relocked the gate behind them. Then he led them at a gallop up a winding drive to the house itself. Behind them they heard a rumble of hoofbeats and cries as their pursuers pulled up at the gate.

The villa looked deserted. The drive and the grounds were overgrown with weeds, and white paint was visible in patches on the stone walls of the house. Ademu soon had the front door open while the rest of them tethered their horses to a rail. "Take everything you need," Ademu told them. He stood guard with drawn sword while they quickly unstrapped their packs, along with the Ambon and the bellaril, and took them into the house. The agent locked the door behind them.

Ademu issued instructions in rapid-fire Selmian. Danîsha and the others watched, bemused, as three of the agents ran down the central hallway to the back of the house, unlocked the door, and began trampling a path through the weeds towards a distant, overgrown wall. Meanwhile Ademu pulled a firestick and a jar of fireclay from his pack, rapidly daubed a joint with the clay, and broke it. He handed half the burning stick to Ilinu.

"Hurry!" He hustled them through a door on the left and down a narrow flight of stairs. At the bottom he and Ilinu lit a couple of wall lamps, and they found themselves in a basement lined with shelves containing dusty boxes and barrels.

Ademu made straight for one of the lamp holders on the far wall. He pulled and twisted it—and after a moment's silence they heard a slow, grinding noise. Memories of Carreck Manor came rushing back to Danîsha, and hope blossomed in her heart. A secret entrance, like the one to the Manor kitchen…? Sure enough, a door-shaped crack appeared in the wall next to the shelves, and a slab of masonry slowly creaked open into a black space beyond. The lamp holder righted itself.

The other three agents came down the stairs, sweeping the steps behind them with their cloaks to erase footprints. Then they doused the lamps.

With only the light of a couple of firesticks they all hurried into the darkness beyond the masonry door.

* * *

Konnar made his way to the small parlour on the second floor of the palace where he and Bari had their evening get-togethers. He was as tense as a tightly-strung bowstring. There was still no teméyn from Barazhân. Against all expectation those Grûzhileyn slaves had formed an effective army-in-hiding. They had already destroyed almost all the stored teméyn on the plantations, along with the equipment to refine it. Only one plantation was still viable; his Mindruler Randenyu was using half the army to guard it. The problem was to find Grûzhileyn with the expertise to run it...

Meanwhile, Konnar had just inspected the palace teméyn stocks. He had centralised all the individual Mindbenders' stores; but with the amount taken by the armies in Dûrion and Barazhân they now had barely a week's supply left.

Of course, it was no use saying anything to Bari about that.

He opened the white and silver-trimmed door of the parlour and entered, to find his major-domo Gedoriu laying out chass and sherili cakes on a blackwood table between two recliners. Bari lay propped up on an elbow on one of them.

"Gedoriu!" Konnar exploded. The man jumped, spilling some hot chass. "How many times have I told you not to wait on us yourself? Get out—and send someone else to wipe up that mess!" He accompanied the command with a jolt of pain.

The large man gasped, almost dropping the chass pot, and left. Konnar settled on the other recliner with a gusty sigh.

"That was a little harsh," Bari murmured.

Konnar nodded and wiped a hand over his brow. "I'm not myself, Bari. Too many disturbing... developments recently."

"I know what you mean."

There was a grim note in his friend's voice, and Konnar glanced at him sharply. For a moment he was sorely tempted to mindread him—not mindbending, just skimming the surface of his mind to see his immediate thoughts. But no. He'd promised himself long ago that he would *never*, under any circumstances, enter his best friend's mind. What Bari freely gave him in understanding and affection was something no amount of mind-power could extort.

Konnar poured the chass, as he used to in their childhood days, and they talked about small, everyday matters. But there was a constraint between them. He knew Bari felt it as well. Bari knew about the intruders, and he was doing nothing. And Bari knew that Konnar knew. A terrible anger and fear surged up in him, and he had to look away. *Geshu!* Don't destroy our friendship, Bari. It'll be the end of me.

A voice spoke in his mind: *"Strongholder."* It was his chief spy.

"Not now, Lingetu."

"Apologies, your Supremacy, but the matter is urgent."

Konnar busied himself with pouring another round of chass, keeping his face averted from Bari. *"Make it quick."*

"The foreigners have disappeared, Supremacy."

"What!!"

Hot chass splashed again over the table. Bari jerked backward to avoid it. "Holy flame!"

"Bari, I'm sorry, something urgent— We'll meet again tomorrow."

He hurried out, and entered a little-used reception room nearby.

"Lingetu, your life is on the line. What has happened?"

The man's mindvoice was nervous, as it should be. *"They rejoined the other foreigner — the one with the Lightist ambon —"*

"You found *her?"*

"Y-yes, Supremacy. We think she used the ambon to... call them."

"Go on."

"She had five Selmians with her — Renegade agents, we think."

"You think a lot, Lingetu. But you still lost them. Tell me how."

"They took the highway to Orselm, but turned off before the gate. They went to the old Chief Arbiter's residence in Kadestili."

"What, that *ancient relic? Why?"*

"We don't know, Supremacy. But they had keys for the gate and the house. They locked them after entering, and it took us some time to force an entry —"

"Forget the excuses. How could you lose them in a dead end like that?"

"They tethered their horses, and their tracks went straight through the house, out at the back, and over the wall. Some of us searched the streets and houses beyond —"

"Lingetu."

"Apologies, your Supremacy. It was a false trail. But we also guarded the house itself, and made a thorough search. Supremacy, there is no sign of them! We have turned every room upside down, including the attic and the basement, and there's no way —"

In a surge of fury Konnar squeezed his subordinate's mind. Strangled mind-screams stopped him. Bari would not call that good governance. Besides, Lingetu was a good spy. He needed him. Konnar sank on to a chair and stared unseeing into the darkened room.

The intruders would be found again. Orselm was obviously their destination, and they could do little without revealing themselves. Meanwhile he had the leader, Shiván. Soon Bari would have to make a decision. One way or the other.

* * *

The masonry door shut behind them with a thud of finality. In the darkness the two flickering firesticks gave Gil brief, shifting impressions that made him think of a mine shaft. Hard packed soil underfoot, heavy wooden beams shoring up the sides and the roof overhead; a dank, earthy smell. Being tall, he had to keep his head bent.

"Hurry!" The chief agent was beckoning them deeper into the shaft — which now took a steep turn downwards. Rotting wooden beams set in the floor provided steps. He stumbled down with the others, urged on by the three agents behind him. His head was ringing from repeated bangs against the roof beams.

After a long descent they reached the bottom. They continued for a while, almost level.

Then the head agent — Ademu, Lannie called him — signalled a halt. He and his sidekicks searched along the walls, then lit a couple of lamps, which they lifted down off their brackets. The whole scene became brighter. Yes, it *was* a mine shaft. Or a tunnel?

A *tunnel?*

Lannie anticipated him. "Does this lead into the tunnels under Orselm?"

"Yes, it does," Ademu said, surprised. "You know about them, *Atémban?*"

His question was answered by the exclamations of relief from the rest of the group. "Thanks be to the One," Danîsha sighed. She was breathing heavily, one hand over her wound.

"The tunnels are exactly what we have been hoping to find since we entered Selmion," Lannie told Ademu.

"If only Shiván had known," Perrely murmured, tears in her eyes. Jomel put an arm around her.

"The tunnel we are in," Ademu said, "is a temporary one. It was prepared for just such a situation as this. While the rest of us go on to the city tunnels, Ilinu and the other agents will prepare to demolish this one."

Gil was aghast. "You're bringing the roof down?"

Ademu shrugged, his eyes bleak. "We have no choice. Sooner or later the Strongholder's people will discover the basement entrance. We cannot allow them to follow this tunnel into the city network. That would give them access to many hidden places, including the homes of our leaders in Orselm—the princes of the Renegade Royalty. If they—and you!—are found, all will be lost. But if the tunnel collapses, they will think we died in the cave-in." He was smearing and breaking firesticks, while another agent—Ilinu—was binding the burning sticks together to form torches.

"Don't worry," he continued, "the method of destroying this tunnel was carefully set up by masons faithful to our cause like Ilinu here. He will make sure it's safe. Now we must continue to the city so that he can do his job. He and the others will start the demolition, then they will follow." He handed a torch to Lannie, another to Garset, and kept one for himself. Ilinu and the other agents had their own torches. Ademu turned and set off at a brisk pace down the tunnel.

Jomel hesitated, her eyes wide. "How do we know there won't be a real cave-in?"

Gil took her hand. "We have to trust the masons. They know what they're doing. Come!" He gently pulled her forward. She threw him a doubtful look, but followed.

As they left, Ilinu issued a volley of rapid-fire instructions to the other agents, pointing here and there at the roof, walls and floor of the tunnel.

After a while the tunnel narrowed, and in the flickering torchlight they saw that it ended in a familiar sight: a well-mortared wall with a heavy masonry door at the centre. Ademu pulled the lever beside it, and after a few creaks the door opened outwards, towards them. Gil noted with interest that it sat in a bevelled recess: the outer surface of the door was wider than the inner one.

They hurried through, and found themselves in a narrow passage whose sides, roof and floor were of mortared stone. "We are passing through the city wall of Orselm," Ademu told them.

"Thanks to the One," Danîsha panted.

She still had a hand to her side, and Gil looked at her anxiously. This had been a strenuous journey for her. "You all right, 'Neesh?"

She gave him a quick, grateful smile. "I'll manage. No, really," she added when he looked doubtful. She took her hand away from her side. "See? No blood. Just a bit sore."

"Alright. But let us know if you need help."

"Perrely's carrying the bellaril. I'll be fine."

Gil nodded, but resolved to keep an eye on her. Meanwhile Jomel was still clasping his hand.

They came out into a wider paved tunnel. "Wait here," Ademu said, and hurried back to the open masonry door. There he produced a piercing whistle with his fingers.

A few moments later there was a distant volley of muffled cracks, followed by a creaking noise, then an ominous gathering rumble. The ground began to tremble. Dust swirled towards them through the open door.

The rumble came closer, getting louder every moment. Jomel gave a low moan and her hand tightened in Gil's. Dim figures appeared in the dust beyond the door, sprinting towards them. They hurled themselves through, and Ademu pulled the lever. The heavy door began to close, grinding ponderously inward. It was three-quarters shut when the rumble of collapsing soil caught up with it. A blast of stones, earth and dust shot through the gap, followed by a shuddering crash as the door was hurled into its beveled socket. The silence that followed was almost shocking in its intensity.

When they'd all finished coughing from the dust, Ademu exclaimed hoarsely, "*Kelida elara!* We are safe under the city."

Lannie clapped him on the shoulder. "Well done, Ademu! And all of you." The other agents nodded and smiled through the dust encrusting their faces.

"*Atémban,* we must continue," Ademu said, glancing at the torches. "There is quite a distance yet to go."

"No problem with flooded tunnels?" Gil asked, remembering Frengor's description back in Stillárre.

"No, *Atémbis*, only the deeper tunnels are flooded."

Jomel gave a little sigh of relief and he smiled at her. There was a brief answering smile, then it faded and she let go of his hand.

Sadness touched Gil's heart. So much mistrust there still. Well, he couldn't blame her. How could he ever have forced himself on Jomel, holding her family to ransom? How could he have seen her as no more than a temple prostitute? Jomel—brave, beautiful, once cynical and self-serving as he had been, but now serving the Prince with all her heart? Caring, captivating, her good taste often surfacing despite their lifestyle as tramps? He knew that this new love for her was genuine and unselfish, and all he wanted was to cherish and protect her.

Well, it would take time; but he was happy to wait.

They headed off again with Ademu in the lead. After leaving the mortared rock of the wall and entering the city proper, the tunnel wound to and fro and up and down, varying in height, sometimes walled with masonry as it passed under buildings, sometimes shored up with specially-built pillars, sometimes winding through limestone riddled with natural caves. In many places there were piles of rubble in alcoves at the side—signs that cave-ins and other obstacles had been cleared. It seemed that the Renegades' masons, like Agent Ilinu, were never short of work.

Ademu advised them to keep one hand on a rope guide that had been strung through metal rings embedded in the tunnel wall. He also pointed out tiny holes in the walls in a couple of places, explaining that these were keyholes to hidden refuges if the Strongholder ever discovered the tunnels and started hunting travellers down.

They began to pass increasing numbers of side tunnels. The rope occasionally entered the side tunnel, and Ademu would warn them to pass the entrance and pick up the guide rope on the other side. They stopped several times for an Ambon-break, leaning the emblem more or less vertically against the tunnel wall and drinking in its healing influence.

The lamps they had taken from the now-collapsed tunnel under the walls were starting to flicker when Ademu finally came to a halt. Before him was a flight of steps and another door. An ordinary house door this time, such as one could find on any city street. He mounted the steps and turned to them with a broad smile.

"Welcome to the headquarters of the Renegade Royalty—which is also the Prince Regent's private home."

He reached out and plucked the door chime.

* * *

Shiván woke from a nightmare to discover it was real. He *was* in a prison cell in Orselm. That meant he *had* been hijacked by a passing coach in Goldsmiths Street. That meant… well, it looked like his part in their mission was over.

What had woken him was the clacking of the door lock in his remarkably comfortable cell. Two tough-looking characters in white tunics wearing swords came swaggering in—not unlike his escorts in the coach, who had brought him here gagged and bound. Except that they had been wearing black. From black to white… a hopeful sign? Probably not.

One of the thugs jerked a thumb upwards. Shiván regretfully threw aside the blanket and climbed off the soft mattress of his five star bed. He hadn't been so comfortable since leaving Stillárre. He'd actually fallen asleep after being thrown into prison! Was it afternoon or evening? He didn't know, but it must still be the same day. What *was* this, a detention wing for the Selmian elite? Well, the vast, beautifully-sculpted building he'd glimpsed when he arrived had looked more like a palace than a prison; maybe that was why even the lockups were palatial.

After he'd slipped on his scruffy robe and sandals, the main thug jerked his thumb towards the door. A strong believer in non-verbal communication. Shiván left his cosy bedroom with a guard in front and another behind. He felt like an oriental potentate, and wished he had the clothes to match.

The passage outside was more prison-like. Bare and functional, with doors like his own at regular intervals on either side. As they marched along, Shiván felt the light-hearted bravado slip away from him, a deep melancholy taking its place. Dear Prince, is this the end of the road for me—maybe for us all? Did Jomel escape, or was she also captured? How will the others manage without me, and without the Ambon? What about Lannie? And Perrely… His heart lurched as her winsome face flashed before him, her eyes brimming with love as he'd last seen her that morning.

But behind every thought lay another one. The thought he tried to avoid, the thought so terrifying it threatened to overwhelm him: *Will I be mindbent, and reveal everything?*

No, he wasn't going there. The ever-present spectre of despair must be held at bay at all costs. *Father, help me guard my thinking. You can get me through this.*

They marched up many stairs and along many passages. The surroundings became progressively more palatial. Shiván's heart sank further. He knew there was only one palace in Orselm, and that was the Strongholder's.

Finally they reached a door. A greasy-looking steward in a burgundy half robe rose from a chair to one side and exchanged a few words with the chief thug. They then waited while the grease-merchant plucked the door chime. When the answering chime came he left them standing while he went in and presumably announced them. Shiván found himself wondering how he was being described: A spy? A foreigner? Or even a Restorer?

Then the door opened again and his Greasiness came out. He nodded to the guards before disappearing rapidly round a corner. The two thugs marched in, Shiván between them. His heart was trying to escape his ribcage. Would he now face the Strongholder? Was this where everything ended? *Dear God, your will be done.*

A man in a blue satin half robe was sitting writing at a shey-nut desk at the far end of the room. The décor was surprisingly plain: the desk, four bookshelves and two recliners, with unadorned beige floor-cover and wall hangings. Without looking up the writer held an arm out, opening and closing his hand in the beckoning gesture. The chief thug nudged Shiván forward. He slowly approached the desk, the two heavies at his heels.

The man continued writing, his head bowed. Shiván frowned. There was something familiar about that mop of blue-black hair.

Then the writer looked up, and Shiván's own total shock was reflected in the man's face.

It was Estaron.

Chapter 40: *Privy Council*

THE DOOR OF THE PRINCE REGENT'S HOUSE was thrown open, and the first thing Jomel saw by the flickering light of the torch was a beaming face.

"Ademu!" its owner cried—a portly man in a white apron. "We never thought to see you again!" He engulfed the agent in a bear hug, almost getting set alight by his torch in the process. Then he looked down the steps at the others. "Who have you brought with you? Ilinu! Festiu! … Shaliu! Nerilu! Oh, praise the One Creator God! And the others—?" His eyes widened as he sensed the shiláy. He turned to Ademu, his voice dropping to a very audible whisper. "*Dûrians? Foreigners?*"

Ademu laughed. "All in good time, Pastenu! Are the princes here?"

The man made a face. "The Privy Council, yes. The others…? Hardly ever see them these days. But the Privies are meeting right now. I'm just making their supper. Come! They won't believe this." He beckoned them inside, holding the door wide.

Jomel was chuckling at Pastenu's irreverent nickname for the Privy Council members. "What's he saying?" Perrely hissed. She gave the others a quick summary.

They crowded into a small entrance hall. The steward, or cook, or whatever he was, closed and locked the outside door, then swivelled a wooden cover over a tube to one side of it. "Peephole." He winked. He took a lantern off a hook on the wall and led them up two flights of stairs to a familiar-looking masonry door that was standing open. They went through into a large utility cupboard containing brooms, mops and cleaning cloths. Pastenu raised a lever, closing the door, then seized Ademu's torch and unceremoniously thrust it into a bucket of water. He pointed to a heavy felt mat on the floor and wiped his feet. They followed suit. He doused the lantern and put it on a shelf.

They came out of the cupboard, blinking, into the brightness of a well-appointed corridor. Deep purple floor-cover was matched by violet wall hangings that flowed around filigree silver lamps and oval portraits of well-dressed Selmians. The corridor breathed *wealth*. Jomel gave a sigh of pleasure. A proper home again! Her mind filled with images of blackwood cutlery, delicate Marûvian porcelain and steaming baths. At the same time she felt like a smelly gutter rat invading this luxurious environment. She looked down and winced at the trail of dirty footprints they were leaving on the floor-cover, despite wiping their feet.

Pastenu hurried them through a reclining room decorated in shades of blue to a central reception hall with black and white marble floors and pillars. Up a grand staircase, to a highly-polished blackwood door. Pastenu plucked the door chime.

The door was opened almost at once by a young man with golden eyes. His powerful, athletic frame, shoulder-length blond hair and ochre half robe gave the impression of a predatory feline from the tropical plains. Pastenu bowed. "Look who's arrived, Prince Edoru!" The five agents were down on one knee, heads bent. Jomel and the others scrambled to follow suit.

"Praise be! No, no—please, up!" He reached out a hand as though to raise them physically. They scrambled to their feet again. There was a long pause as he took in the group's shiláy, and a look of wonder crossed his face. "Come in," he said at last, almost reverently. They followed him into the room, leaving the bellaril and Ambon behind with their packs on the floor of the passage.

Three men were seated at a large circular blackwood table, watching expectantly as they entered. Nearest was an older man with long, lugubrious features and bushy eyebrows, wearing a blue velvet robe. Next to him was a short, round-faced gentleman with laughter lines at the corners of his eyes and lips. Jomel saw that he bore the insignia of the printers' guild on his dark green tunic. Beside him sat a rough-looking character with a florid complexion and the matching brick red uniform of the hauliers' confederation. The room—obviously a study—had blackwood wall panelling interrupted at regular intervals by floor to ceiling bookcases. The gloomy décor was alleviated by pale gold floor-cover and four glittering light trees.

Prince Edoru drew a deep breath. "Your Highnesses, we have guests: Five of our missing agents; three Lightists from Dûrion; and—unless I'm mistaken—three Restorers of the Way."

There was a prolonged shiláy-moment as the three around the table stared at their ragged visitors. Jomel felt conviction, power and authority—especially from the old man with the long face—overlaid by a deep weariness, and thoughts blurred by the curse-haze.

"To the One Creator God be all praise and thanks," the old man murmured.

"*Lesora* — so be it," the others responded.

The master printer gave a little laugh. "Ademu, Festiu, Shaliu, Ilinu, Nerilu! What a delight to see you." The five agents almost went down on their knees again, but a raised hand from Edoru stopped them.

"Friends," Edoru said, turning to the newcomers, "allow me to introduce ourselves. We four are the Privy Council of the Renegade Royalty." Firmly banishing the servant's nickname from her mind, Jomel muttered a translation for her friends. The young prince continued, "This is the head of the Council, our Prince Regent, Sindetu Lenorida." He held a hand out toward the old man. Prince Sindetu nodded and smiled, appearing for a brief instant like a loveable grandfather.

"This is Prince Kastenu Banorida." Edoru indicated the printer, whose naturally cheerful face broke into a smile of welcome. "Then we have Prince Tindoru Kyiletida." The choleric haulier made do with a gruff "Good t'see you."

"And I, as you know, am Edoru Marida."

Jomel made a formal curtsey. "Peace be upon your houses, great ones."

Kastenu and Edoru laughed, and Sindetu's smile reappeared. "A courtly response from one who knows our ways."

Jomel felt herself blushing under the grime; she translated for the others, and saw an appreciative twinkle in Gelmion's eye.

The old man switched to Dûrian. "Please, friends, be seated." With both hands he indicated the vacant chairs around the table. Without being told the five agents bowed and left the room.

As they all found chairs, Prince Sindetu turned to Alanya, the group leader. "Forgive our lack of courtesy in not allowing you time to freshen up. We hope you will understand how anxious we are to learn who you are and hear your news."

"No problem, if you can put up with us."

"Oh, we can put up with you!" said Kastenu the printer. He translated for Tindoru, who gave a bark of laughter. Jomel found it fascinating that Tindoru obviously did not move in the same educated circles as the other three; yet here he was, a working man, sitting as an equal in the highest council of the Renegade Royalty.

Sindetu looked from Alanya to Gelmion to Danîsha. "Is Edoru right, that you are three of the renowned Restorers of the Way?"

Alanya's "Yes, I'm Alanya" chimed in with Gelmion and 'Neesh's "Yes." Kastenu's translation for Tindoru rumbled in the background.

Sindetu looked at Gelmion. "I would guess you are... Gelmion. Am I right?"

He smiled and nodded.

"And you must be Danîsha."

"Yes."

The Prince Regent's eyes went back to Alanya. "So where is the Lord Shiván?"

"With your permission, before I answer that, your Highness...?" Alanya paused in the act of rising from her chair. Sindetu frowned, but waved a hand in acceptance.

Alanya went out into the passage. A few moments later she came back in and walked towards them, holding the Ambon upright before her.

Relief filled Jomel's mind as the Ambon's healing influence swept over her. But her reaction was nothing compared to its effect on the princes.

"*Kelida elara!*" Prince Edoru's chair toppled to the floor as he leapt up, lips parted in amazement. Sindetu slowly rose as well, a look of sheer delight wiping away the mournful lines of his face. Kastenu shook his head, his gaze riveted on the Ambon, tears starting in his eyes. Tindoru sank back in his chair, eyes closed, muttering "Orrénne, Orrénne, Orrénne..."

The Prince Regent was the first to recover. He looked ten years younger. "*Ambelu Ansulurinu* — the Ambon of Sûrilane! You've brought it *here! Amu ela'sora* — the One be praised!"

Edoru was still wide-eyed. "It's — the *Ambon* that does this? That clears our minds — lets us think again?"

Alanya nodded. "It was only with the Ambon's help that we got here. And the Ambon will break the Curse. But first, your Highnesses, can the agents — and your steward — be allowed to return?"

Sindetu's eyebrows rose. "Is their contribution needed? This is a private council."

"Their well-being is needed, your Highness. It's the Ambon that enabled your agents to bring us here. Without it they may fall victim to the curse-haze again."

"Forgive me, I should have realised. Yes, we can trust them. Edoru…?" The young prince went to the door, and before long the five agents entered. Their faces cleared as they saw the Ambon leaning against the wall. The servant Pastenu followed. He uttered a startled exclamation, half-ran towards it, then apologised profusely to the princes. Jomel struggled to keep her face straight. The steward and the agents lined up on either side of the Ambon and bowed.

The Prince Regent nodded and turned back to Alanya. "You said the Ambon will break the Curse?" Kastenu pitched his translation for Tindoru a little louder so the new arrivals could hear.

Alanya turned to Perrely. "You'll do a better job of repeating what Frengor and Bishop Harlon said to us."

Jomel looked anxiously at her cousin. Her eyes were red-rimmed and her face drawn; she'd hardly had time to come to terms with Shiván's disappearance. But she rose to the occasion.

"Your Highnesses. Bishop Harlon and Visionary Frengor came to the conclusion that the Curse has ushered in the Great Darkness spoken of in *Visions*, section seventeen." There were nods and murmurs of agreement. "But they linked this with the second part of the Ambon prophecy in *The Return of the Prince*, section thirty-six: *they will raise the Rod of Truth over the altar of darkness, and release my captive people.* We believe the Curse will be broken and the Darkness will end when the Ambon of Sûrilane is lifted up over the altar of Gadesh here in Orselm."

There was a gasp from one of the agents, followed by a stunned silence.

To Jomel's apprehension she saw anger gathering on Prince Tindoru's face.

"Have you come all this way to mock us?" he burst out. "Raise the Ambon over the… That's madness!"

"Peace, Tindoru," the Regent growled. But his brows were knitted. "The prophecy *could* have that interpretation. Do you agree, Kastenu? Edoru?"

The printer shrugged his shoulders. "It could, certainly, but…" The young athlete shook his head dubiously.

"It's impossible!" Tindoru roared.

"I would hesitate to call anything impossible where these *Atenámbare* are concerned. Remember, they did overthrow Shambor — against all the odds. Reserve judgment, my friend."

Tindoru snorted.

The Prince Regent turned back to Alanya. "And how do you intend to do this, *Atémban?*"

"That's… what we wanted to discuss with you."

Kastenu translated her answer. The red-faced haulier slapped the table and turned to stare challengingly at Sindetu.

Jomel's heart sank. This whole trip suddenly seemed hopelessly naïve.

The Regent sighed. "We accept that the prophecies you quote could be interpreted that way. But we feel your mission… lacks some essential planning. Perhaps you have not fully appreciated how impossible it would be even to enter the Temple of Gadesh, let alone to raise the Ambon of Sûrilane over the altar."

There was a dangerous glint in Alanya's eye, and as she opened her mouth to speak Jomel prayed desperately that she wouldn't alienate the only people who could help them. But Gelmion forestalled her.

"Your Highnesses, we believe in the One Creator God. For him, nothing is impossible. We did not defeat Shambor or start a revolution in Barazhân by our own clever planning. The *Creator* did these things. We were simply the tools in his hand. If he intends us to raise the Ambon over the altar of Gadesh in the Strongholder's own city, then *it will happen.*"

In the heavy silence that followed Jomel felt her remaining antipathy towards Gelmion warring with admiration for the new man he now was. In a few simple words he had turned the princes' doubts inside out. His quiet strength gave her a feeling of safety.

Edoru's face relaxed. He and Kastenu nodded. Tindoru snorted.

A small smile touched Sindetu's lips. "You have spoken the truth, *Atémbis.* We do not reject this outright. Rest assured that we will give it very serious consideration."

* * *

Estaron's mouth went dry at the sight of Shيván standing before him. A 'dissident', the Strongholder's messenger had said; no mention of the foreign shiláy that radiated from him like a powerful scent. That silence was Konnar's rebuke.

"Estaron! What are you doing here?" the young man gasped in Dûrian. Then his face hardened. "Oh, I get it. The Strongholder's a better boss, is he? Higher pay, more job security?"

Estaron's reply was automatic as he tried to grapple with the situation. "I'm my own master. In case you didn't know, you're appearing before the Governor of Selmion."

"Oh, my. I'm so *sorry*, your Loftiness." Shiván made an ornate bow as the two guards looked on approvingly. Estaron's lips tightened.

"What are you and your companions doing in Selmion? With the Ambon of Sûrilane as well, by all accounts! Are you crazy?"

Shiván blinked. "My companions? I'm a loner, I—"

"Shiván, we don't have time for that. Your life hangs by a hair. Did you honestly imagine you and your friends had got this far without being seen? The Strongholder has been aware of you all along. If it weren't that he allows *me* full authority in Selmion, you would be dead by now."

The young man swallowed and fell silent. Then he said in a tired voice, "Okay. Well, if you're interested, we came to break the Curse of Futility. But it doesn't look like we'll succeed."

"Oh? And how did you plan to do that?"

"It's not exactly relevant now, is it?"

Seeing the resignation in Shiván's eyes, Estaron felt his anger evaporate. After a moment he said quietly, "I'm sorry about the Curse. I had nothing to do with that."

"Oh, you're *sorry*? That's great. Tell that to the thousands of Dûrians lying in rags in the gutter, who've lost their homes—their relatives—their livelihoods!"

"I can hardly imagine how devastating it has been. If I could lift it myself, I would."

Shiván took a deep breath. "Estaron, I don't know how you've ended up in your present position. But if you're really sorry about the Curse—and if you're really the boss in Selmion—can't you do something? Plead with your pal the Strongholder... Or help us! Keep me in prison if you like, but don't arrest the others. At least give them a chance! You're still a Lightist, aren't you? You care about people's sufferings. I can't believe you would just sit back and do nothing."

If only, Estaron thought, his heart wrenched by Shiván's pleading. But Shiván had no idea of the cleft stick Estaron was in. Maybe he'd already compromised himself by the sympathetic tone of his recent comments—which the guards would have picked up, even though they didn't speak Dûrian. And he couldn't risk talking to Shiván alone. Konnar would hear of it and draw his own conclusions.

In fact, Estaron thought, he faced an impossible dilemma. It was obvious that Konnar had thrown Shiván into his lap as a test of loyalty. How could he avoid handing the Restorer over to Konnar — or, at the very least, putting him on trial for subversion? Even that Konnar would regard as stalling for time. He'd had promised to protect Estaron's friends — if they offered no resistance. Brazenly entering Selmion with the Ambon of Sûrilane he would certainly regard as resistance: even as an act of war. All they would deserve in his eyes was summary execution.

With an aching heart he hardened his expression. "There *is* nothing I can do, Shiván. You and your companions have brought this on yourselves, and you must face the consequences. *Ney li silmend* — May the Light be with you." He looked at the guards and added in Selmian, "Take him back to his cell."

"And may the Light show you a few things about yourself!" was Shiván's parting shot as they pulled him towards the door.

As soon as it had closed Estaron buried his head in his hands.

* * *

Gil felt rested and energised. Last night after hot baths and a sumptuous meal, they'd slept on comfortable beds; and this morning he'd enjoyed a long, uninterrupted time with the Creator while the others slept in. Relaxing in God's presence beside the Ambon had brought a deep sense of peace.

Their meeting with the Renegade Privy Council was to continue today — there were still many things to be sorted out. The servant Pastenu had laid out a magnificent breakfast featuring various pulses served up in interesting ways, a wide array of cheeses, flatbreads with sweet preserves, and other things the ladies exclaimed over, much to the cook's delight.

While they were eating they heard the other three Council members arrive, and as soon as they were ready Pastenu took them upstairs and announced them at the study door. Lannie entered with the Ambon, and the Renegade princes once again exclaimed with heartfelt relief as they felt the One's healing flow into them and clarify their minds.

Prince Sindetu called the meeting to order, speaking in Dûrian while printer Kastenu translated for the haulier Tindoru and the agents, who with Pastenu were lined up against the wall.

Sindetu's sharp eyes engaged Lannie, 'Neesh, Gil and their companions one by one. "Friends, until now we have been blighted by the Curse. Our network of agents has broken down, and most of our supporters have been betrayed or become useless. All our operations against the Strongholder—our sabotage of his teméyn supplies, of essential installations like mines and armouries—have ground to a halt. The enemy has penetrated every layer of our security almost to the inner circle itself, which you see here in this room.

"But now that you have brought the Ambon and restored these agents to us, we can start rebuilding what has been lost. We cannot thank you enough. This will give us an advantage that will take the Strongholder by surprise!" The other two princes drummed their hands on the table, while those against the wall slapped their thighs. Gil suppressed a smile at their exuberant applause.

"But first, please tell us: where is Shiván *Aténnelor*, the Overguardian?"

Lannie came straight to the point. "He was captured yesterday, here in Orselm."

All the Selmians froze. A deathly silence fell.

"The *Aténnelor* was *captured*?" Kastenu's eyes were round with shock.

"We... tried to contact you," Jomel blurted. She told them what had happened, her eyes wide with alarm. "I'm so afraid they'll arrest the young man we spoke to, and find out about *you* —"

"Calm yourself, Lady Jomel," the Regent said. "Since the Curse we have not had an agent in Wick Lane. Indoru Galida disappeared. The person you met must have been a spy of the Strongholder's."

Gil's eyebrows rose. That would explain a lot.

"But we are concerned about the Overguardian. We cannot allow him to be mindbent and executed by the Strongholder."

"Executed!" Jomel exclaimed.

Perrely was looking at the Regent with wide, red-rimmed eyes. "Please— We *must* rescue him! *Anything* you can do..."

Compassion touched Sindetu's face. He looked around the table. "Are we all agreed that our first order of business must be to rescue the *Aténnelor* before he is executed?"

Haulier Tindoru growled an emphatic response. "We won't leave the Overguardian in the Strongholder's filthy hands—no way!"

"But how can we rescue him?" Lannie said, frowning.

Sindetu smiled. "We have an agent in the palace—one of the few we've kept in touch with. Gedoriu is our source of inside information. He comes to us via the tunnels."

Gil was amazed. "How has your agent kept his secret?"

"Gedoriu is... an unusual person," the Regent responded. "He has a responsible position: he's the Strongholder's major-domo—but he is not mindbent. He comes across as efficient, but unimaginative and unambitious. The Strongholder takes him for granted. Yet the truth is that he's a strong-minded loner, like yourselves; and this is what has enabled him to continue functioning as an agent under the Curse. He's been keeping us informed about our Heir, Prince Nomariu, who contacted us through Gedoriu when he first arrived."

Lannie put Gil's reaction into words. "Your Heir's not in the Strongholder's *palace*, surely?"

Sindetu sighed. "Sadly, yes. You know him, in fact. He was Secretary to the Bishop Suffragan of Dûrion—Estaron don Geldor."

Six voices spoke in unison. "*Estaron!*"

"Yes, that is the name our Heir used in Dûrion. His true name is Prince Nomariu Tarenida a KariLanta; although, like all of us, he had another everyday name when he lived here. But for many years now he and his family have been based in Dûrion for safety. Alas, that safety vanished when the Strongholder invaded Dûrion earlier this year. Nomariu's father Tarenu was Heir until then; but he and his wife, Princess Selinai, took their own lives rather than be mindbent when the Strongholder captured Astenar. And now..." The mournful lines of his face deepened. "He has also captured Prince Nomariu—your Estaron."

Gil and the others sat for a moment in stunned silence.

"Is he mindbent?" Gil asked.

"Apparently not. If he were, we would all be dead by now." Sindetu heaved a sigh. "Incredible as it may seem, he and the present Strongholder were childhood friends. He has been appointed Governor of Selmion—a position created specially for him."

Prince Tindoru hawked and spat over his shoulder, to Sindetu's obvious distaste. "He's decided to sell out his heritage and be the Strongholder's puppet in this country, instead of our rightful King."

"Now, Tindoru, we don't know that. He might have had no other option."

"Yes, and *guruneto* might fly," the other rumbled.

Gil shook his head. Estaron, a traitor? It didn't fit the personality of the man he remembered.

"In any case," the Regent said, "we do not yet know if he can be trusted. Gedoriu was here yesterday, before you arrived. He told us that Nomariu — Estaron — has captured an important foreign prisoner. *Very* foreign, he said. This can only be the *Aténnelor*."

"Shiván is in *Estaron*'s hands?" Perrely gasped. "But surely, that's good... I mean, Estaron knows Shiván well. He wouldn't... he *couldn't* do anything..."

"My lady, much as it pains me to say it, we cannot assume that. He *could* do anything."

Gil saw Perrely's iron restraint slipping. Her face began to crumple, and with a muttered "Excuse me" she hurried from the room. Jomel followed her.

Sindetu sighed. "A pity Lady Perrely couldn't have waited a little longer. She would have heard more encouraging news about the prospects of rescuing her... betrothed?" He looked at them with raised eyebrows.

"Not yet," Lannie said.

"Ah. Well then, of rescuing her intended via the tunnels."

"Oh! Could that really be done?" Danîsha said.

"We'll need to discuss the feasibility with Gedoriu," Sindetu replied.

"Our map shows a tunnel from the palace," 'Neesh commented hopefully.

"Yes, indeed, there is. Gedoriu said that the Royal Guard has been reduced to a bare minimum in the palace, due to the shortage of teméyn. There are few of them to spare for guarding the prisoners. Add to that the tunnel you mentioned — about which the Strongholder knows nothing — and there is at least a good possibility that this could be accomplished."

"Oh, that is such a relief!" Gil and the others murmured their agreement.

After some further discussion about Renegade matters, the meeting adjourned. Ademu took the Restorers' party via the tunnels to a large 'safe house' nearby which had been prepared for them.

The chatter during the hot meal the agents prepared was cheerful, everyone talking as if Shiván's rescue was a foregone conclusion.

Afterwards as he lay in bed Gil stared at the ceiling. *Please God, make it actually happen.* He sensed that his prayer had not fallen on deaf ears. Then he smiled at himself. Here he was, Dr. Gilbert Denbigh, senior lecturer in linguistics, doing what? *Praying!* For whom? For the one student who'd always annoyed him the most. Yet it was real, and he meant every word.

———————————————

Chapter 41: *Desperate protection*

GWARGIF SAT WITH HUNCHED SHOULDERS in the front room of the farmhouse. Outside the early summer day was drawing to a close. The Dorbian commander heaved a deep sigh. The encroaching darkness was all too reminiscent of what was happening to the Legion.

Grey shapes loped past the windows from time to time. Eighty-six warriors of the Legion were guarding this vital storage depot of food for Stillárre. Stores of grain, fruit and preserved meat had been laboriously gathered with Dûrian help from abandoned farms for miles around. They could not afford to lose it now.

"You're sure it was tonight that Hmengiz was planning to attack, Gorlekh?" Gwargif asked the grizzled subordinate sitting beside him.

Gorlekh snorted an affirmative. "Our scout overheard Warriorleader Hmengiz. They are hungry; and tonight there is no moon."

Gwargif nodded, then shook his head as if to clear it. "Hmengiz. Of all the Warriorleaders, that *he* should succumb to the Curse... Our greatest fighter. He saved my life at Carlis. He carried *Hrarborgh* Shiván back to the city."

"I know, High Commander. And he has taken his whole clan with him." There was a note of despair in Gorlekh's voice. "Where will it end, sir? Over three hundred of our warriors have turned to the darkness. The same number of those who remain are kept busy hunting them and defending food supplies. If the Selmians attacked now, only two thousand six hundred — half the Legion — could be mustered to defend the city."

Gwargif looked at his faithful lieutenant. "The one thing we must not do, Gorlekh, is to lose hope. The Shining One fights with us. He fights, too, with our Father of Warriors, Shiván, who *will* overcome the Curse. Remember that the Shining One led me to the Warriors of Light last year. Remember that *he* brought the Legion here. He will enable us to fulfil his purposes."

Gorlekh gave a subdued snort of agreement and dropped his eyes.

* * *

The defenders sent the reverters packing—and still hungry. The storage depot was saved. Gwargif could only hope the scouts would continue to discover the reverters' targets before they attacked.

But today his business was with the Selmians, who were advancing on Stillárre via the southern highway. The town of Hillane straddled the Stillárre River, and the Selmians had taken the southern half. Now they were attempting to cross the bridge to North Hillane, and the Legion was there to stop them.

With a mighty roar the Dorbians burst out of the ruined buildings where they were hiding. Gwargif's grey form was in the forefront as they leapt at the Selmian horses, sending them careening into those behind. In moments the well-ordered column on the bridge became a scene of chaos. Riders were thrown, horses crashed into one another, and many were forced into the swiftly-flowing river.

When the last Selmian north of the river had been despatched, Gwargif squatted on his haunches and let out a howl of victory. The thousand Dorbian warriors in the task force joined him, their voices echoing across the water to the defeated Selmians. Once more they had been thrown back. Once more the forces of Light had triumphed.

Gwargif stared across the river, a weariness in his bones. How much longer?

* * *

"His Supremacy wishes to see you, your Worthiness."

Estaron's heart sank. Major-domo Gedoriu looked resplendent in his white and silver livery. This was a formal summons.

"Tell him I'll come at once."

"In his study, sir."

"Very well."

Gedoriu withdrew.

Estaron sighed. He knew the reason for this summons: Shiván. He tidied the papers on his desk. Then he stood and straightened his shoulders.

When Gedoriu showed him into the Strongholder's study, Konnar's head was bent over a document on his desk. He did not look up. Estaron waited a moment, then settled himself on one of the recliners. He wasn't going to stand shifting from leg to leg like some lackey.

"When you're ready, Konnar." There was no response.

Suddenly Konnar's head snapped up. At the top of his voice he shouted, "How *dare* you allow this enemy into Orselm?"

Estaron couldn't help himself. He jumped. Konnar's face was suffused, his eyes like the gleaming points of twin daggers.

"I—"

"Where were your watchmen on the North Gate? Why was it left to *me* to arrest him?"

"Konnar, if you'll allow me—"

"No, I will not allow you. *You* have allowed seven enemies of the state to travel freely through Selmion right up to the gates of Orselm. *And now you've let their leader stroll into the city unchallenged!*" His voice rose to a crescendo, his eyes blazing.

Estaron was appalled at Konnar's fury. He'd never seen his friend like this. "There was a reason—"

"Do you know that the rest of that group have vanished?"

"What!"

"Of course you don't, you've left them free to do what they like. Now they've disappeared without trace. They are probably with the Renegades, plotting to overthrow us."

"I don't have the resources you do, Konnar! I *was* aware they were in Selmion, and I have been making enquiries—"

"Yes, for three days," Konnar scoffed. "You heard about them almost a week ago, and *that* was five days after they entered the country."

"How...?" Anger flared in Estaron. "You've had that toad Otaru spying on me!"

Konnar leaned forward, menace in his hunched shoulders and tight face. "Yes, and I'll do more than that if *you* don't do your job!"

There was a tense moment of silence.

Estaron rose from the recliner. "In that case, I resign. You said I would have independent authority: 'my own decisions, without reference to you or anyone else'. Those were your exact words. If you're going back on that, I cannot continue." He turned towards the door, his mind a tight knot of anger, sorrow and apprehension.

"Stop! Did I say you could leave?"

Estaron paused and looked back at Konnar. "Oh, so you're going to force me now? Make me just another slave of the Strongholder's?"

They stood, eyes locked, breathing hard.

Then the anger faded from Konnar's face. He looked away. After a long pause he muttered, "We can't... let it go this way."

He came out from behind the desk and lay on a recliner. Estaron accepted the unspoken invitation and settled on another, facing him.

"*Why*, Bari?" Konnar's eyes were still hard. "Why did you let them get so far without doing anything?"

"I was certain that sooner or later one or more of them would be brought to me. I do have a network of informants, Konnar. Then I would have found out about their whole group and their purpose in coming."

"And when were you planning to let *me* in on this?"

"I assumed you already knew about them. You have far more sources of information. Why didn't *you* mention it to *me*?"

A ghost of a smile touched Konnar's lips. "We didn't trust each other."

Estaron nodded. "Well, as I'm sure you know, I've found out from Shiván why they're here, and there's no direct threat to you or me. The Restorers have come merely to practise some Lightist mysticism with the ambon they've brought with them, hoping to lift the Curse of Futility. You know as well as I do how likely *that* is to succeed. Practising religious rites is not an offence in Selmion; but because of the war, my intention was to imprison Shiván and his friends until our victory is complete. This sudden disappearance of the rest of the group is as much a surprise to me as to you."

"'Practising religious rites?'" Scorn dripped from Konnar's words. "Come, Bari, you're not that naïve. They're here to destroy us. *How*, exactly, were they planning to lift the Curse?"

"That I don't know. Assuming I have your undertaking to respect my authority as Governor —" He gave Konnar a hard look. "— I will see Shiván again and find out. And if they're here to destroy us, I'll take appropriate steps."

"And if he refuses to tell you?"

"He'll tell me." Estaron hoped he sounded more confident than he felt.

"With a little... persuasion."

"I'll get the information without torture."

Konnar stared at him, unconvinced. Then he appeared to make up his mind. He stood up, and Estaron followed suit.

The sharp points were back in Konnar's eyes. "Listen to me, Bari. This so-called Overguardian's companions must be found; and they must be appropriately dealt with. I'll allow you one week — no longer. If you feel unable to abide by that…"

His voice trailed off. Impulsively he moved forward and clasped Estaron in his arms, holding him tight for a long moment.

Then, gripping Estaron's shoulders and staring into his face, he said with a quiver in his voice, "You're my only friend, Bari. Don't let me down."

* * *

Estaron sat in his office staring at the beige floor-cover with unseeing eyes. At any moment Shiván would be brought in again. Would the young man tell him how they had planned to lift the Curse? Estaron was far from sure about that.

And if not? He knew that he himself could never order Shiván tortured or executed. But Konnar would. Estaron wondered how he could live with himself if that happened.

The door chime sounded. Estaron plucked the answering chime, and his steward Otaru entered. "The prisoner, Worthiness." There was a superior smirk on the toad's face. Estaron nodded curtly. That would soon disappear.

Shiván was brought in by two prison guards as before. There were dark circles under his eyes. Estaron stood and came round the desk. Too much depended on this interview to observe protocol. Or to risk being overheard.

"Follow me," he told the guards. They glanced at one another, but fell in behind him with Shiván as he led the way out of his office.

A little way down the passage Otaru came trotting after them. "Worthiness — the prisoner — are you not interviewing him?" There was anxiety now on the greasy face.

"Yes, Otaru. In my private quarters." He spoke in Dûrian.

"Oh! But, your Worthiness… That is hardly proper —"

Estaron allowed himself a grim smile. "I will decide what is proper, Otaru."

"But the Strongholder —"

"I'm sure you will tell him exactly what has happened." He turned and left the toad standing.

Two of Estaron's own guards flanked the only entrance to his quarters. He trusted them. Surprisingly, it was that stuffed shirt Gedoriu, Konnar's major-domo, who had brought them to him. "These men are reliable, your Worthiness," he had murmured. Estaron had tested the men's shiláyet and and found both honesty and integrity — rare qualities in the palace. There was also a faint hint of something else: could it be that they were secret Lightists? If so, they were coping remarkably well under the Curse. At any rate, they were the best to be found in this nest of intrigue.

He turned to the prison guards. "You may leave now." They stared at him in amazement. "Go! My guards will take over from here." With doubtful glances they left.

When they were out of earshot Estaron said in an undertone to his own men, "Do not allow Otaru in, whatever reason he gives." They saluted with hands to their chests. He opened the door and ushered Shiván into the apartment.

The young man's head swiveled as he took in the luxurious appointments, the elegant shey-nut furniture and the white-and-silver décor. "My, my. Done well for yourself, haven't you?"

Estaron sighed. He led Shiván into the small reclining room and pointed to one of the long chairs. "Make yourself comfortable, Shiván. Would you like anything to eat or drink?"

"Oh, no, the service down below is quite adequate, thank you." He stretched out on a recliner and stared challengingly at Estaron. "What's with all the special treatment? You have a favour to ask?"

Estaron settled himself on an elbow facing Shiván. "Shiván, I'm bargaining with the Strongholder for your life and that of your companions. As long as you're under my protection, you're safe. But if my enquiries about you fail to satisfy him, he'll take over. That will mean torture at best, mindbending and execution at worst."

The young man shrugged. "I'll take my chances."

"Please, Shiván." Estaron injected into his voice all the earnest entreaty he could muster. "I don't blame you for not trusting me. I know it must look bad from your point of view. But believe me when I say that I did not accept this position to benefit from it materially. Look at me!" He gestured at the plain blue tunic he wore. "Remember my office, where *I* was able to choose the décor.

Is this the outward appearance of someone scrambling for wealth and status?"

Shiván's eyebrows rose. He was silent for a moment. "I have to admit... it isn't. So why *did* you accept the position?"

"Because the Strongholder turned out to be my cousin — and my best friend as a child. There was good in him then, and I believe there still is now, hidden under all the layers of evil. I hoped I could reawaken those good impulses by being alongside him — as a constant reminder of our friendship and the high ideals we once had. He's a lonely man, Shiván, and I know he values me as his only friend in this den of self-seeking sycophants."

Shiván stared at him incredulously. "You're hoping to reform the *Strongholder?*"

"I know it sounds ridiculous. You'd have to understand the nature of our friendship to appreciate that there's at least a slim chance of success. In any case, it was the only option that offered any hope. I was brought here against my will, and if I had refused this position I would have been imprisoned or executed."

"So you're not mindbent? You accepted this job freely?"

"Yes."

"But how do I know if that's the truth?" Shiván muttered, staring at Estaron with narrowed eyes. "This could be a clever deception by the Strongholder himself, to trick me into giving the information he wants."

"Why would he do that, when he could simply mindbend you himself?"

"Hmmm. Point taken."

He sat staring at Estaron, who tried not to hold his breath. So much depended on Shiván's response.

"Okay, let's assume I believe you. What does the big boss want to know?"

"Exactly how you planned to lift the Curse of Futility; and whether this included killing or overthrowing him." Seeing the scepticism in Shiván's eyes Estaron added, "I need to persuade him that you are here solely to perform some mystical Lightist rite involving the Ambon, in order to end the Curse. If I can have your word that you had no intention of *directly* challenging his rule — and a rough idea of what you were planning to do with the Ambon — I think I can persuade him to allow you and the others, if they're captured, to be imprisoned. Not mindbent or executed. That's the best I could offer right now. Later... we'll see."

There was a lengthy pause. Finally Shiván said quietly, "We weren't planning to attack the Strongholder directly. Our main aim was to lift the Curse." He fell silent.

"Using the Ambon?" Estaron prompted.

"Yes."

"How?"

Shiván slowly shook his head. "I'm sorry, Estaron. You've persuaded me you're sincere, and in a very difficult position. But I don't trust the Strongholder, and I don't trust your relationship with him. I dare not tell you the details of our plan."

Estaron's heart plummeted. "Think carefully, Shiván. I can reveal as much or as little of it as I feel will satisfy the Strongholder. But if I can't tell him anything, you'll end up telling him everything."

Shiván shook his head again. "It's not the kind of thing where you can tell some and not all of it. I'm sorry."

"Mindbending may be preceded by torture."

"I'll have to risk that."

Estaron heaved a deep sigh. He stood. "This will have severe consequences for us all. May the One protect us."

"He's the only one who can." Shiván rose from the recliner. Estaron grasped his hand and raised it in the high handshake. Then he took him to the door and handed him over to the guards.

* * *

This time the Selmians didn't cross the bridge. Nor did they come on horseback. Gwargif was first alerted to their presence by a howl from one of his sentries, abruptly cut off. Before he could organise a proper defence two hundred or more cavalrymen were charging them on foot—from behind, in the direction of Stillárre. They poured into the streets and buildings of North Hillane like a dirty, tan-coloured flood, sabres flashing as they rose and fell.

Dozens died in the opening minutes. Gwargif howled the retreat. He and the stalwarts around him leapt at their attackers and broke through into an alley that took them out into the western countryside. More Selmians were fanning out across the fields to cut them off, and it was only after a bloody battle that they made it to the Stillárre road. There Gwargif rallied the remnant of the task force—about five hundred and fifty—and they took their stand facing the cavalrymen.

Gwargif's heart fell as, beyond the massed Selmians—about three hundred of them, he guessed—he saw many Dorbians slinking out of the village and running off into the empty farmlands. Every defeat added to the ranks of the reverters: those Dorbians who had succumbed to the curse and abandoned the Light.

He looked round at the warriors gathered behind him. Weariness and defeat were written on many faces. No, he couldn't launch a counterattack with forces like these.

His whole being ached with shame as he turned and silently made his way through the ranks. Today an indelible stain would appear on the proud record of the Dorbian Legion: they had turned away in the face of an enemy they outnumbered. Once more he howled the retreat. The weary remnant of the Legion followed him as he set off at a rapid pace towards Jern, the last defensible village south of Stillárre.

A roar of derision from the cavalrymen rose up behind them. But the Selmians didn't pursue them. They had secured the bridge, and now their full force could cross.

Gwargif would try to rally the Legion to make another stand at Jern. If the Selmians were victorious there, nothing would stand between them and Stillárre itself. And Stillárre could not survive a siege for more than a couple of days.

* * *

In the days following the Renegade Privy Council meeting, Lannie took part with the others in some intense discussions with the Renegade Princes and their palace agent Gedoriu. Together they planned a rescue mission: not only for Shiván, but also for the Renegade Heir, Prince Nomariu—alias Estaron, the so-called Governor of Selmion. Gedoriu explained that if Shiván escaped while in Estaron's custody, Estaron would face the Strongholder's wrath, and might not survive. Lannie and the other Restorers understood the reasoning, though they were unhappy about doubling the risk. But they agreed that Gedoriu's plan stood the best chance of success.

Today it was happening, and Lannie was in the hot spot as the Restorers' representative. Ademu was leading the rescue party through the tunnels to the palace, holding a shuttered lantern aloft.

Lannie followed with agents Festiu and Nerilu, who carried a second lantern. Gedoriu had given them disguises: Lannie was dressed in plain white as a palace servant, complete with a little white cap that made her look ridiculous; while the three agents looked resplendent in white and gold-trimmed uniforms of the Royal Guard.

As they passed through well-paved tunnels with no sign of the flooding Frengor had mentioned in Stillárre, Lannie was very aware of the bow and quiver slung over her shoulder. Ademu and Festiu were carrying swords. Lannie prayed it wouldn't come to a fight: that could be disastrous. Gedoriu had said he did not expect trouble. She hoped he was right.

After many twists and turns the tunnel they were in widened into a stone-built passage. It ran straight for a long distance, with no side tunnels or alcoves. Their footsteps echoed back at them from the bare stone walls. Ademu brought them to a halt. "Tread softly," he murmured. They continued more slowly, trying to reduce the sound.

Finally up ahead Lannie saw an archway. It was filled in with a stone slab. Another masonry door? As they drew closer she noticed an emblem engraved in the wall above the arch: a running horse set against what looked like stylised waves of the sea.

When they reached the arch Ademu turned to face them. "This is the entrance to the palace," he said quietly. He pointed to the carving above the arch. "And that is the ancient emblem of the Selmian royal house, which we are pledged to restore." Festiu and Nerilu stared at the emblem with hungry eyes. "From now on, we had better keep silent until we meet with Gedoriu."

Lannie took the bess from her pocket. "Let me just see if I can contact Perrely. I promised her I'd try before we went in." Ademu nodded.

She held the turquoise shell to her ear with both hands, concentrating on the fair-haired girl. But all she heard was the sound of her own blood pumping, like the distant roar of the ocean. After a moment she shrugged and returned it to her pocket. "Didn't think it would work."

Ademu reached to the right-hand side of the arch and pulled a lever. The stone slab filling the archway began to open soundlessly towards them. They all moved back a pace.

Inside the arch was the last thing Lannie expected: a pile of wooden boxes blocking the opening. Ademu reached up and pulled the top one towards him—they all had convenient hand-holds cut into their outward sides. Festiu joined him, passing the empty boxes to Lannie and Nerilu. The barrier was soon cleared, revealing another surprise: the inside of a large, now-empty storage cupboard.

Ademu led the way into the cupboard, which accommodated all four of them with ease. It appeared to be a permanent structure, anchored to the wall.

He stood listening for a moment, then cracked the door open and peered out in both directions. "No sign of Gedoriu and the Heir yet. We must wait."

They waited. One or two people walked by, and Ademu looked through after they'd passed. Still no Gedoriu or Estaron.

They waited some more.

It was getting horribly stuffy in the cupboard. They heard more footsteps, and Lannie—who was bored stiff with waiting—whispered, "Let me look!"

She peeped out after the footsteps had gone slowly by—and what she saw struck her like a thunderbolt.

"Good grief!" she exclaimed in English, much louder than she'd intended.

Chapter 42: *Escape and capture*

SHIVÁN SAT ON THE BED in his five-star prison cell with his head buried in his hands. Two days had passed since his last meeting with Estaron. Two days in which he'd had nothing to do and too much to think about.

Had he been right in refusing to tell Estaron how they intended to use the Ambon?

Maybe the Strongholder would just have laughed on hearing that they were hoping to raise it over the Altar of Gadesh. Estaron could have sold it as a silly, impractical Lightist idea that they could never carry out. Had he denied himself and his friends the option of life—albeit imprisoned—over the death of mind or body? Had he in fact betrayed their entire mission, which would utterly fail if the Strongholder mindbent him?

Estaron's words haunted him: "If I can't tell him anything, you'll end up telling him everything."

His blood ran cold at the thought of mindbending. What would it be like to have someone else in your mind? To have no control over your own body? Especially if the controller were someone as utterly evil as the Strongholder. Lannie knew, and Gil. They'd both had Shambor in their minds. And still shuddered at the memory.

No. That could *not* happen. No way. It was simply not an option. Apart from anything else, there was Perrely…

Could he ask to see Estaron again, say he'd changed his mind? Great idea, but it wouldn't fly. The guards who brought his meals spoke no Dûrian, and completely ignored him anyway.

In any case, he wasn't convinced he'd been wrong to clam up about the Ambon. His first instinct, that the Strongholder would know exactly what was meant by raising it over the Altar of Gadesh, could be right. Or their plan to enter the sacred Temple might be seen as a threat. And knowing their intended destination would almost certainly result in increased security, making their job a lot harder, if not impossible.

He stood and began pacing between the door and the far wall. Ten steps each way.

One thought kept reverberating in his mind: *I can't sit waiting to be mindbent. I have to get out of here.*

Impossible. Why waste time thinking about it?

Totally inconceivable.

Or was it?

He reached into the pocket of his robe and pulled out his small King James Bible with its orange and black tortoiseshell cover. It had stayed there during the kidnapping, and had been a great comfort in the long, empty hours since. He sat on the edge of the bed and opened it towards the end, at the book of Acts. He began paging through, and uttered a satisfied "Ah!" when he came to chapter twelve. Here it was.

He read slowly through verses one to nineteen. Then he looked up and stared unseeing at the blank wall facing him. If God could do it for Peter, why not for him? Peter had been bound with two chains, had a soldier on either side of him, and two more at the entrance to his cell. Now *there* was an impossible situation! Yet the chains had fallen off his wrists and the guards had seen nothing as he calmly walked out of prison.

Why wait? Shiván put the book back in his pocket, raised his arms and looked upward in the Dûrian manner. After a long pause he said softly, "Creator God. Father. You know I need to get out of here. Please… let it happen."

He lowered his arms. There was no point saying more: God knew what he needed.

He looked at the door. He remembered the key turning in the lock and the bolt on the outside being shot home after his last meal was delivered.

He stood and tightened his robe around him. He walked to the door. His hand hovered above the lever for a long moment. Then he grasped it and pulled downward.

The door opened.

Shiván gasped as he stumbled out into the empty corridor. No guards! He barely managed to stifle a whoop of joy. *Thank you, God!*

With great caution he tiptoed past the other cells, going the way he'd gone twice before to see Estaron. After rounding several corners without meeting a soul, he saw up ahead the left-hand turn toward the guard station and the main entrance to the prison area. Crunch time. There would definitely be some guards *here*. Would the One get him past them as well?

The slight scuffing of his sandals on the bare stone floor assaulted his ears like the loud *whoosh–whoosh* of someone walking through long grass. They must have heard him! Were they standing there, waiting to grab and beat him up? He reached the corner and with infinite caution put an eye around it.

Only one guard was there, and he was leaning back in his chair, fast asleep. *God, you're the greatest!*

He tiptoed past the guard towards the main gate. The keys were lying on the guard's table, but he'd never got the hang of those slim, complex slivers of metal; and it would make too much noise trying them out till he found the right one. He went up to the gate and turned the handle.

It opened.

Silently thanking the One a third time and asking him to continue guiding his steps, he set off, trying to remember the various passages and flights of stairs he'd followed to reach Estaron's office. He met no one en route. But after a while he found himself in a less plush area with bare floors and utilitarian doors and fittings. He didn't remember that — everywhere he'd gone before had looked like a five-star hotel. *Lord, have I missed a turning?*

Up ahead there was a large cupboard against the left-hand wall. Beyond that was another corner. He walked slowly and softly towards the corner, poised to dash back and hide in the cupboard if he heard anyone coming. Then he jumped a couple of inches when the cupboard said "Good grief!".

Whirling around, he could hardly believe who was peering out of the cupboard door wearing a dainty white cap. *Lannie?*

"Shiván! How did you get here?" she exclaimed.

He felt himself grinning all over his face as he replied, "Lannie, I can honestly say, the One brought me! I like the headgear, by the way."

Scowling she snapped, "Come inside before anyone else appears!"

She stood back, and he slipped through the door. He was surprised to find three others there. In rapid whispers Lannie introduced him to the Renegade agents, and his heart was filled with awe and gratitude to the living God when he heard they had come to rescue him. They in turn could not get over their amazement at how the One had brought him out of the prison and right to the hidden entrance of the tunnel.

They discussed what to do, and decided that Ademu and Festiu would continue waiting for Estaron and the palace agent, while Lannie and Nerilu took Shiván back to the Renegade safe house.

Half an hour later they were there. Great excitement greeted Shiván's arrival, and he had to tell and retell his story. But he had eyes for only one person.

* * *

Perrely sat beside Shiván in the reclining room. The Ambon stood against the chimney breast spreading its healing influence. Their friends had tactfully left them to themselves. Now Shiván was back Perrely didn't want to let go of him. Their hands lay clasped on the recliner between them. Dim afternoon light shone through the closed window hangings.

"I was afraid I would never see you again."

"Me too."

"I kept thinking of all the things I wanted to say to you. It was terrible, feeling I might have lost the chance."

Shiván's hand tightened around hers, and warmth flowed into her.

"Most of all, I wanted to tell you what Danîsha said to me when we thought she was dying."

He turned to look at her. She could dimly see his face.

"She told me what you said to her in Stillárre. That you would always be there for me. That you would never go back to your own sky, even if you could. That you'd never marry anyone else. She also showed me — that I was wrong about God's call to singleness." Perrely heard the quiver in her own voice. "She said it was only for a time. To teach me obedience. She said it was like — Who was Eyber-, um... Eyberram?"

She saw Shiván's eyebrows shoot up and she smiled. "Abraham?" he said.

"That was the name. Danîsha said it was like Eyberram and his son. People in your Book."

"Oh. She must have meant the time when the One told Abraham to sacrifice his son Isaac."

Perrely was horrified. "To do a human sacrifice? Of his own *son*?"

"That's right. But don't worry — it has a happy ending. You want to hear the story?"

"Of course!"

"Well, old Abraham had always obeyed the One, but one day God decided to test how far his obedience went. So he told Abraham to sacrifice his only son to him. Now you have to realise, this son was very special: Abraham and his wife Sarah had prayed for a son for many years—and finally God had given them Isaac. Now he was telling Abraham, basically, to kill him."

"Did he *do* that?"

"He took the young boy to a mountain to make the sacrifice. They had wood and burning coals for the fire. As they walked up the mountain, the son—Isaac—asked his father where the animal was for the sacrifice. Abraham told him that God would provide one. At the top they built an altar of loose stones and arranged the wood on it. Then Abraham tied up his son Isaac and put him on the altar, on top of the wood."

Perrely was aghast. "I can't believe this is in your Book. It sounds like something from the Cult of Gadesh!"

"Ah, but wait for the ending... Abraham took a knife, and raised it to kill his son. Our Book doesn't say what they felt, but it must have been terrible—the boy screaming, Abraham weeping... Then at the last minute the One called out to Abraham and told him to stop. He said he now knew Abraham would always obey him, because he'd even been willing to sacrifice his own son."

There was a moment's silence.

"That was quite a test."

"It sure was."

Perrely thought about the story. Finally she said softly, "So the One was testing me, to see if I was willing to give you up—as Eyberram was willing to give up his son. Danísha said I've passed the test. So now he's giving you back to me."

There was a crooked grin on Shiván's face. She smiled back, and Shiván reached out a finger to stroke her cheek. "That's the best news I've heard in a hundred years."

He leaned back and slipped an arm round her. She nestled against his shoulder.

* * *

Governor Barilu had retired to his private apartment for the night. Steward Otaru, as was his habit, had slipped along behind to make sure that it *was* his apartment he went to. Now, on the way back, he stopped at the sound of rapid footsteps approaching along a side passage. Someone visiting the Governor, on a matter of some urgency? Who would that be, at this time of the evening?

Otaru looked around quickly and darted into a utility cupboard, leaving the door slightly ajar. He peered through the crack as the visitor passed.

Gedoriu!

Now *that* was interesting.

When the Strongholder's major-domo turned the next corner, Otaru left the cupboard and scuttled up the nearest staircase to the apartment above the Governor's. These rooms were empty, but work had been done in them just yesterday—to his specifications. He had been mortified by his failure to find out what passed between the Governor and the foreign prisoner the other day, and had taken immediate steps to put matters right.

He hurried to the corner of one room, where a chair had been placed next to a wooden tube rising from the floor. The end of the tube had a small, flexible trumpet-arrangement attached to it. Its lower end came out in a cupboard in the Governor's reclining room, immediately below.

Otaru pulled the chair up to the tube and put the trumpet to his ear.

* * *

Estaron was lying on a recliner reading the Book when one of his guards came in to announce a visitor.

"Gedoriu! This is a surprise."

"Pardon my arriving unannounced, your Worthiness, but something urgent has come up."

"What is it? Take a seat."

"Thank you, sir, but there isn't time. I have been looking for a moment to speak to you all day, but... no matter." There was an intensity in the man's face that Estaron hadn't seen before. Gedoriu stood for a moment, gathering his thoughts. Then he spoke in a low voice.

"Your Highness, you are the Heir of the Renegade Royalty."

Estaron blinked. It was a while since anyone had called him 'your Highness'. "True. That has been acknowledged publicly."

"Then you will understand that as an agent of the Renegade Princes, I cannot allow your life to come into danger."

Estaron sat bolt upright. "Gedoriu! *You*—a Renegade agent?"

"Yes, your Highness. You are the first person outside of Renegade headquarters to know this."

A lightness touched Estaron's heart. Not alone any more. Then he frowned. "How is my life in danger?"

Gedoriu cleared his throat. "The Overguardian is being rescued from prison as we speak, sir."

"What!" Estaron stared wide-eyed at Gedoriu. A muffled sound from the nearby cupboard went unnoticed. "How —?"

"I arranged it, your Highness, with help from the other Restorers and some of our agents. There is a tunnel. But sir —"

"The other Restorers are alive? Praise the One!"

"Yes, sir. But, if I may suggest— There's very little time. We are already overdue for our rendezvous with the rescue party. Please come with me, sir."

"You mean— leave the palace?"

"Yes, your Highness. It is too dangerous for you to stay here. When the Strongholder hears that the Overguardian has escaped…"

Estaron stared at Gedoriu as the implications crashed in on him. Yes, when Konnar heard, he would jump to the conclusion that his old friend had betrayed him. Estaron could deny it, blame Gedoriu… But the security of this particular prisoner was his responsibility.

On the other hand… Leaving with Gedoriu would be the ultimate betrayal. It would mean the end of all his hopes of recalling Konnar to the high ideals they had once shared—which he was convinced were still there, deeply buried. Konnar would interpret his departure as a denial of the most precious thing in both of their lives—their friendship. His heart ached at the thought.

Yet… Once Konnar heard of Shiván's escape, how could Estaron convince him he had not been involved? Would he be in any frame of mind to listen to reason? Recent experience suggested not. This could be the final bag in the wagon that tipped it over. Visions of Konnar's contorted features and hard, unyielding eyes rose before him. They might be friends, but Konnar was still the Strongholder.

"Your Highness…?"

"Yes." He heaved a shuddering sigh. "You're right, Gedoriu. I'll come with you."

It didn't take him long to collect a few things and hurry with Gedoriu out of the apartment, leaving his guards at the door to allay suspicions and to tell any casual visitors that he was indisposed.

* * *

Gedoriu led them at a rapid pace down several flights of stairs and along passages unknown to Estaron until they reached the servants' area of the palace. Hardly anyone was about.

Suddenly behind them came the thudding of boots. They stopped, looking at one another in alarm. "Hurry!" Gedoriu muttered.

They ran down a long passage. Puffing with exertion, Gedoriu led them into a side passage. As Estaron rounded the corner he heard a shout behind them — "*There they are!*" The passage turned again up ahead; there were a few doors on either side and a sturdy wooden cupboard on the right. Gedoriu stopped in front of the cupboard and gave a quick double knock. The door opened a crack as the pursuing footsteps came rapidly nearer.

When whoever was inside got a good look at Gedoriu, the door opened wide. Gedoriu stood aside and Estaron scrambled in. He saw two men — more Renegade agents? One of them reached up and did something near the ceiling. A faint vibration could be felt, and to Estaron's amazement the back of the cupboard swung slowly open. He had a brief glimpse of what looked like a tunnel before Gedoriu joined them, closing the cupboard door, and they were engulfed in blackness. "Go through, go through! Save the Heir!" Gedoriu exclaimed.

But at that moment the door was wrenched open. Hands grabbed Estaron from behind. His head whipped round, and he had a fleeting impression of Royal Guards in their white and silver uniforms before someone seized him by the legs and he toppled forward. One of his would-be rescuers grabbed his arms, and he became the rope in a tug-of-war. He jerked his legs and tried to kick, to no avail. Despairingly he felt the hands holding his arms losing their grip. One final yank, and he was dragged out of the cupboard.

"Escape! Warn the princes!" Gedoriu shouted before he, too, was roughly manhandled back into the passage they'd come from.

When Estaron regained his feet he found himself looking into the smug face of Otaru. "I think a little visit to the Strongholder is called for — don't you, your *Worthiness*?"

Chapter 43: *Through the tunnels*

"COME BACK TO THE LIGHT, Hmengiz," Gwargif growled softly. "You will not be punished."

The two groups of Dorbians stood facing one another in the Stillárre alley. Hmengiz—First Warrior of the Legion, the champion who had carried *Hrarborgh* Shiván on his back—crouched snarling against the end wall of the narrow street. With him were two of his lieutenants and three half-starved followers; all Hmengiz had left of the eight hundred warriors of his clan who had marched proudly with him from Dorbai. They, like Gwargif and the nine faithful with him, were panting from the chase through Stillárre.

"Come back," Gwargif repeated. "Resist the darkness. We have food. We need you."

Doubt hovered in Hmengiz' eyes. Then they hardened, and with a roar he launched himself at Gwargif, the other reverters close behind.

Gwargif jumped aside, and his companions leapt on Hmengiz as he landed. Gwargif left the darkened Dorbians to his companions. They would have little difficulty sending them packing in their weakened state; and there were other urgent matters demanding his attention in the chaos that was now Stillárre.

With a heavy heart he trotted back to the Westgate Road, where groups of frantic people were clashing in their attempts to move in opposite directions: some entering the city to take refuge from the advancing Selmians; others leaving it to escape the dark Dorbians within the walls—his own warriors, falling into darkness by the dozens every day now. The shame was almost too much to bear. *Hrarborgh* Shiván had charged him with protecting the city from outside enemies; and he could not even protect it from his own people. Elsewhere in the city every surviving Dûrian citizen was locked indoors to keep out the reverters who roamed the streets.

Dodging the running battles in the Westgate Road and evading a half-crazed Dorbian who leapt at him from an alley, Gwargif entered the gatehouse and trotted up the stairs to the wall. He had gathered his faithful remnant here and at the Domicile, making forays into the city to curb the reverters' excesses.

The wall was still intact for almost its whole length: only at the docks in the east had the Grûzhack cannon destroyed it; and the

Selmians were not approaching from that side. Even if they did, they would need a flotilla of boats to cross the River Carreck—and the Grû-zhack had used up the entire local supply.

He looked out over the countryside west of Stillárre with its deserted fields and small patches of woodland. In the distance was a grey and tan haze: the Selmian army. He'd learned from his scouts that they were cutting down trees to build ladders and other siege equipment. After the Legion abandoned Hillane, the Selmians had made rapid progress up the south-western highway.

It would not be long now.

* * *

The same thought was in Frengor's mind as he knelt in prayer with Bishops Harlon and Mâron, Ongaret, and a few of the priests in the Domicile's Fraternity Room. Their days were numbered. In the corridor outside, guarding the door, were the eight remaining soldiers of the Dûrian army. In the streets Dorbian fought Dorbian; west of the city the Selmians were preparing to swarm over the walls.

Bishop Harlon looked frail and weary; he would not long survive their inevitable defeat. In that he was fortunate: better to depart this life and be with the Prince than to live in mindbent torment at the Strongholder's whim…

No! That was the Curse speaking. There was still their one final hope: Shiván and the Restorers of the Way. The strangers and loners the One Creator God had sent to rebuild the broken path and restore his Way… to raise the Rod of Truth above the altar of darkness, and release his captive people.

"Father God," he prayed, "Show everyone that darkness cannot overcome your Light. Protect the Overguardian and Restorers. Do the impossible. Bring them to the Temple of Gadesh in Orselm. Let them raise your sign over the altar of darkness. Fulfil your prophecy. Have mercy on your captive people…"

Murmurs of agreement filled the gap as his voice trailed off.

* * *

In the Renegades' safe house the door was thrown open with a crash, shattering Shiván and Perrely's moment of peace. Three figures burst into the reclining room. "Wake the house!" an elderly man in a

372

scruffy robe exclaimed. His companions, equally dishevelled, began shouting "Wake up! Wake up!"

Shiván and Perrely leapt to their feet. "Who are you?" Shiván demanded, his arms loose, ready to lash out.

The old man jumped back, startled: he hadn't seen them sitting on the recliner. There was a gasp from Perrely. "Prince Sindetu!"

"Lady Perrely!" he exclaimed. With his wild hair he hardly looked like a prince to Shiván.

"Yes, it's me. This is Shiván—the rescue was a success! But what are you—"

"No, my dear, the rescue was not a success. Overguardian, I am glad to meet you, but there's no time to talk now. You must leave this house immediately."

"What's happened?" Perrely gasped. Shiván squeezed her hand, which was clasping his tightly. By now other members of the household had arrived.

"After Shiván escaped, Gedoriu and Prince Nomariu—your Estaron—came running to the tunnel entrance where Ademu and Festiu were waiting. But they had been discovered, and the Royal Guard were right behind them. They were both captured as they tried to enter the tunnel. Ademu and Festiu got away and warned me. The Strongholder's men will already be in the tunnels—and they lead to my house and to this one. You must go *now!*"

There was a cry of alarm from Jomel and a hubbub of anxious questions. Shiván felt a lead weight descend on his heart. Out of the frying pan... He raised his voice to be heard. "Where can we go?"

"Ademu will take you to another safe house only he knows of." Sindetu glanced at the dishevelled agent, who had entered with him. "Using the tunnels will be quickest and safest: there are hiding places en route. If you hurry you can reach one of them while the Strongholder's men are searching my house. Festiu is standing watch in the tunnel leading here.

"Ademu, you must take whatever food, lamps and digging equipment are stored here. Find an exit from the tunnel system near your safe house and open it if necessary. Here is an up-to-date map." He handed the agent a leather document tube.

Ademu bowed and hurried off, calling out instructions to the other agents.

"What about you—and the other princes?" Gil asked.

"Nomariu's guards will warn the others. Pastenu and I—" he glanced at a large man standing beside him—"will follow our prearranged escape route to the north. We must leave now." He took a deep breath. "Farewell, my friends. I wish I could have stayed and worked with you to see the breaking of the Curse. But now… we are all in the One's care."

He raised a hand and began intoning the priestly blessing. With a lump in his throat Shiván joined the others, repeating the Dûrian words so similar to those in the Bible: "*The One bless us and keep us. The One make his Light shine upon us, and be gracious to us. The One smile upon us, and give us peace.*"

Without another word the prince turned to leave. His companion Pastenu looked at them, his face working. He said something in Selmian, and Jomel hurried forward and embraced him. The big man wiped his eyes, sniffed, nodded to them all, and shambled out.

"My lords—ladies—we are ready," Ademu said. He and the other four agents who had been staying in the house with them had reappeared laden with bags, pots, firesticks and fireclay, buckets, a small pick and a couple of shovels.

The Dûrian party scattered quickly to gather their belongings and fill their water pouches; after which the larger items were distributed among the whole group. A few minutes later they were descending the underground stairs with Ademu and Gil holding lanterns aloft.

As they entered the tunnel, a man came running towards them— Agent Festiu, whom Sindetu had left as a lookout. "The Strongholder's men are coming!" He dashed through the door they had just left—heading for the streets to warn the other princes, Shiván guessed.

They broke into an awkward run with Ademu in the lead. Perrely had an arm round Danîsha to steady her. Ademu suddenly swerved right, and they followed him into a side tunnel. A hundred yards down he inserted a key into an almost-invisible keyhole in the right wall and a hidden door opened. As soon as everyone had crowded into the emergency refuge, Ademu closed the door and extinguished his lantern. Gil did likewise.

They waited in the darkness, hardly daring to breathe.

After what felt like an eternity Shiván heard the sound of pounding feet from the main tunnel. Soon afterwards came an exclamation and the buzz of voices; they'd found the house entrance. Metal rasped as blades were drawn. Then the clatter of shoes on wooden stairs, cut off when the door closed.

Great. They were stranded in tunnels swarming with the Strongholder's guards, with only the hope that they could dig their own exit to Ademu's safe house...

* * *

By the time Estaron and Gedoriu were brought before Konnar, the toad Otaru had obviously been whispering in the Strongholder's ear. Both men stood between a pair of palace guards with their hands bound behind their backs.

Estaron gazed sadly at his old friend. The Strongholder sat behind his desk, his face devoid of expression, eyes flat. The fact that his attention was focused on Gedoriu afforded little comfort. The long silence could only mean that he was mindreading his former major-domo. The large man was sweating, his face contorted in agony, grunts and whimpers of pain escaping his lips.

Finally it ended. Gedoriu gave a piercing cry and collapsed convulsing on the floor. "Take him away," Konnar said curtly. "He'll be doing a lot more of that before he dies." The guards dragged him out.

The Strongholder turned a cold gaze on Estaron. "And you. What do you have to say?"

Estaron swallowed. "Only that I couldn't trust you not to blame me, Konnar. Even though I had nothing to do with Shiván's escape."

"So you decided to run away."

The pain Estaron had felt since Gedoriu first suggested escaping clenched a hard first round his heart. "I think our agreement has been... weakening for some time, Konnar. When this latest thing came up, I just... couldn't believe any more that we would work it out."

"You gave up on me."

Estaron hung his head at the hurt behind his friend's words.

"When Gedoriu came to you, you could have arrested him. You could have brought him to me. At *least* you could have refused to go with him, and informed me. But no—" His voice rose in a sudden crescendo. *"You ran away to join the Renegades!"*

The half-scream was accompanied by a bolt of pure pain. Estaron would have crumpled to the floor if the guards had not grabbed his arms. He sagged between them, his brain a raging inferno of agony. Konnar had never before used his mental powers on him. *Never.*

The Strongholder came out from behind his desk to stand over Estaron. He was quivering with rage. "You *want* the Renegades and these—*Restorers*—" he spat out the word "—to defeat me and make you King, don't you? You wouldn't accept the title under me—oh, no. You want to rule on your own!"

"No..." Estaron croaked.

"*No?* Shall I mindbend you and find out the truth? *Shall I?* Is that what you want?"

Estaron laboriously struggled to his feet, still supported by the guards. "I have— never— lied to you— Konnar. I never— will."

"I raised you higher than anyone else. I passed over all my senior Mindbenders. I gave you a position second only to myself. And how did you repay me? You *betrayed me!* You *ran away!* You *joined my enemies!*"

Each exclamation was accompanied by jolt of pain, and Estaron lost his footing again. Staring up at his friend's contorted face, he could no longer see the boy who had once been his bosom companion.

He painfully straightened his knees and forced himself upright. "Mindbend me, then. If that's— what it'll take to make you— believe me."

The fury slowly faded from the Strongholder's face and the turmoil of his feelings showed. He bowed his head and stood chewing his fingernails. Beyond all logic Estaron's heart went out to his friend. Those fingernails had always been the first to suffer when Konnar was confused or unhappy.

Konnar's head snapped up, eyes hard again. "Can you swear loyalty to me, Bari? Can you swear, on the name of your God, that you will always give priority to *my* interests, and the interests of my Stronghold, over foreign interests—over *Lightist* interests? Can you swear that—now?"

Estaron stared at his friend, despair rising in his heart. There it was. Out in the open. The fatal difference between them.

Konnar's face twisted bitterly. "I thought not!" He turned to the guards. "Lock him in the escaped prisoner's cell."

"Konnar—"

"*Get away from me!*"

* * *

They remained in the hidden room off the tunnels for what seemed like a couple of days, but must have been seven or eight hours, Lannie reckoned. At first there were periodic outbreaks of distant shouting or the slapping of feet running by; but these gradually became fewer and further between. Nevertheless to Lannie's annoyance Ademu insisted the twelve of them continue waiting in the small, unfurnished space. *Dear God, you know I'm not good at this sort of thing. Help me to be patient!*

The small lantern was lit for the moment, and Lannie's eyes ranged over the group. Garset was staring at the ceiling, his fingers tapping the floor. The agents sat stiff and tense, ready to leap up if there were any trouble. Shiván and Perrely were huddled together — no surprises there. Jomel was sitting next to Gil, not quite holding his hand. The silly girl should make up her mind. Everyone could see they were becoming an item. *Rather her than me,* she thought; then rebuked herself.

'Neesh was the only one who seemed fully at peace, wedged into a corner and dropping off to sleep with one arm round the bellaril. She, at least, was benefitting from the rest.

So they waited, as the room grew stuffier and their combined body odour more pronounced. There was no danger of suffocation, though: Lannie had noted the metal grilles on opposing walls through which the smoke of their lamps slowly drifted when they at last relit them.

"They must have given up, Ademu," she hissed. "There's been no sound for ages now." He shook his head and held up a hand. To her disgust a few minutes later there was a further flurry of calls and footfalls. Ademu snuffed out the lamp; but the sounds were from the main tunnel some distance away, and what little light might have been visible round the edges of their tightly-fitting door went unnoticed.

Another long wait in the dark followed until Ademu broke a firestick and relit his lamp. He signalled to Gil, who followed suit with the second lamp.

"So! What are we going to do when we finally get there?" Lannie demanded. "It seemed like Sindetu was saying there's no entrance to your safe house from the tunnels. We're going to have to *dig* one." She gestured at the pick and shovels resting against the wall between Garset and Agent Shaliu. Next to her the Ambon stood upright, for which she was profoundly grateful.

"Prince Sindetu" — there was a subtle rebuke in the faint emphasis Ademu placed on the Regent's title — "wanted us to have the equipment in case we need it. Most of the old access doors to the tunnels have been blocked off. Some just with a layer of plaster; others bricked over. We must be prepared to break through. The same will be true if we eventually hope to gain access to the Temple of Gadesh from the tunnels."

Jomel gave a little moan and Gil murmured something to her.

"But why is there no entrance to your safe house from the tunnels? The house here has one. Surely that would be the most obvious requirement for a safe house!"

Ademu shook his head. "No, *Atémban*. That would lead the Strongholder's searchers directly to all the safe houses if the tunnels were discovered — as they have been now. The nearby safe house is an exception especially for the Prince Regent, if his identity became known and his house was entered from the street. The other safe houses are meant for this kind of emergency, and they have no connection to the tunnels. Only one agent knows the location of each."

"Oh. I see."

"But there is a way out of the tunnels near to this safe house of yours?" Garset asked.

"Yes, Lord Marshal." He cleared his throat. "You will understand if I do not give further details at this point."

Garset nodded slowly and silence fell again. Yes, Lannie thought grimly, they understood. If they had a run-in with the Strongholder's guards before reaching the safe house, some of them might be captured. Not knowing anything about its location could save the lives of those who escaped.

* * *

Gil was relieved when they left the hidden chamber in the early hours of the morning. They'd spent long enough there, and tempers were fraying.

They followed Ademu on a roundabout route through many small tunnels that went deeper underground and then rose again to basement level. In places they had to make detours to avoid flooding. For safety they kept their hands on the guide ropes strung along the walls of most of the tunnels.

Once they heard distant voices and froze; but the danger passed, and now they were walking along a wide, paved tunnel—obviously in an affluent area. The walls varied between limestone, earth shored up with timbers, and masonry walls set at slightly differing angles to the tunnel's direction. These were the basements of city houses—their only hope of finding an exit.

"Last stretch," Shiván said. "Now we can start looking for a way out—hey, Ademu?"

"Yes, Overguardian. This is the difficult part." There was a smatter of rueful laughter.

"How right you are. Can you now tell us what we're looking for?"

"Yes, my lord. We need to find the old City Provost's residence. That's how it's marked on the map; but it now belongs to a wealthy merchant."

"And we have to break in without disturbing him."

"Yes, my lord."

"And then get out into the streets so we can walk a short distance to the safe house."

"Yes, my Lord."

"Shiván."

"Yes, Lord Shiván."

Gil laughed with the others. The Renegade agents could not bring themselves to share the Restorers' informality.

They walked slowly down the tunnel with Gil and Ademu holding their lanterns close to each basement wall, looking for an ancient entryway that might have been bricked up or otherwise closed.

In the end they almost missed it. They had finished checking one particular wall and were moving on when Gil noticed a small cluster of hollows and ridges just above eye level. When they looked closer and held the lantern at a particular angle, Ademu gave a sudden exclamation. "This was the emblem of the city of Orselm! But it's been defaced." The others followed his finger as he traced the broken outline of a hook-shaped anchor against the wavy lines of the sea. "This must be the City Provost's house."

They stared at the blank limestone wall below the emblem. Then Ilinu the mason bent and pointed at what looked like a small groove running vertically down the limestone. It was a gap that had been filled with mortar. Holding the lamps close they were able to trace the outline of a rectangular doorway below the anchor-and-sea emblem.

Ilinu said something in Selmian, his eyes gleaming in the lamplight.

"He says, 'This will only take a moment,'" Ademu translated, smiling. The stonemason suited word to action and began tapping away at the righthand groove with a chisel and mallet from his pack.

Before long Ilinu's gentle tapping had opened up a clear outline of the door. He pulled a short crowbar from his bag and after a few harder smacks, as expected, a heavy masonry door stood revealed. Ilinu looked at Shiván and gestured to a small recess on the right. In it was a familiar-looking lever.

Shiván took a deep breath. "This is it, folks. Let's hope no one's heard us." He grasped the lever and pulled.

Nothing happened.

He pulled harder. There was a creak somewhere in the mechanism, but the door remained closed.

Ilinu lunged forward to stop Shiván as he tensed to pull again. Prising Shiván's hand off the lever, he returned it to the upright position. Then he rummaged in his pack and brought out a small earthenware jar. He poured a little of the contents into the slot where the lever fitted, worked it to and fro for a few moments, then stood back. Shiván pulled the lever all the way down.

With a long, low rumble and some protesting creaks, the door ground halfway open. A stale, dusty smell drifted out into the tunnel.

Gil and Garset stood ready with swords drawn as Ademu shone the lamp into the opening. But there was nothing to see: just an empty room two or three paces deep and perhaps six wide. A flight of stone steps rose steeply in one corner.

"Right, folks, remember what we discussed." Shiván spoke softly. "Through the house and out into the streets without disturbing anyone. If we have to, we'll hide till the coast is clear." He took a breath. "Ademu and the agents will lead. If we meet anyone, they'll do the talking; there'll be no fighting except in an absolute emergency. Everyone clear on that?" Ademu finished translating for the agents, and there were murmurs of assent.

"Up we go, then." He gestured to Ademu, who entered the room with the other four agents. Garset went next, followed by Perrely, Shiván, Jomel and Danîsha, while Gil and Lannie formed the rearguard. They pulled the masonry door almost shut, so it would not be conspicuous from the outer tunnels, but could be reopened if they needed to re-enter.

Ademu had just set foot on the stairs when Ilinu grabbed his arm. Excitement gleamed in the short mason's eyes. Ademu followed him to the inside wall of the room, holding up his lamp. As the light fell on the wall the clear outline of a doorway appeared, filled in with roughly set stones and mortar. "Light be praised!" Ademu exclaimed.

Lannie frowned. "What? Why?"

The agents stared at her. But Gil shared her surprise, and from their confused expressions it seemed that others did too.

"Why are we happy to find *another* doorway to break through?" Lannie spoke slowly and carefully for those slower on the uptake. "Why not just go up the stairs?" she added sweetly. Gil stifled a smile.

Ademu grunted. Was that impatience? "Because, *Atémban*, the stairs will lead us to the main living areas of the house, where there will be another closed entrance and any noise we make breaking through that will most likely be heard. But this doorway will lead into the rest of the basement."

"And that will that help us... how?"

The agent looked puzzled.

"I think what Alanya is trying to say," Gil interposed, "is that we'll have to go upstairs anyway at some point, whether from here or from the rest of the basement. How else will we get out into the street?"

Ademu's face cleared. "Oh! No, my lord — and lady: the basements of all these great houses have sunken street entrances, to allow delivery of goods not for immediate use. We'll be able to exit to the street without even entering the house."

"Ah! Then, as you say, Light be praised!"

Lannie nodded, looking grudgingly relieved.

Ilinu went to work. A few well-placed strokes with a chisel and careful application of the crowbar demolished the rough fill blocking the doorway, revealing a simple internal door behind. It was locked, but a bundle of slim skeleton keys produced a satisfying click. After that it took a few grunts and shoves to break through the paint and thin plaster that had hidden the door on the other side. Ilinu raised a hand for silence, then gently cracked the door open.

* * *

The cell door banged shut, followed by the *thwack* of the bolt and the rattle of the key. Estaron sank down on the bed and buried his face in his hands. What little hope he'd had of restoring the relationship with his old friend had just died.

He'd fought despair most of his life. Burdened with the Curse of Futility, he'd made his own hope when there was none. But now there was none left in him to make. The story of his life would be one of unrealised ideals and unreached goals.

Tears filled his eyes as he stared at the bare flagstones of the prison floor. Not for himself: he'd never been one to indulge in self-pity. But for the thousands of ordinary Selmians whose last light in the darkness was now extinguished. The futility of his own story would be repeated in the Renegade Royalty. They would dwindle into oblivion, and he would be their epitaph.

Teméyn was flowing again from Barazhân. Konnar would achieve the absolute rule he had always craved. There would be no Bari beside him to rein in his excesses and promote 'good governance'. The lands would enter a long age of despair.

* * *

Some obstacle was preventing the door from opening more than about an inch. Ademu brought the lamp up closer, and through the crack a number of objects appeared at different heights. Peering over Ademu's shoulder, Danîsha finally made them out to be items standing on shelves that had been fixed across the doorway: a roll of fabric, a jar, a wooden box, and various other containers.

Ilinu began levering the shelves away from the wall, producing a series of crashes and thuds. Danîsha glanced up at the solid stone ceiling, grateful that little noise would escape into the house above. The mason soon had the door open, and they all made their way into a large underground storeroom, climbing over the broken shelves and their shattered contents. Danîsha was still clutching her bellaril, and Lannie was carrying the Ambon in its makeshift case. Scattered around the room was a collection of typical basement debris: old furniture, packing cases with long-forgotten goods, broken children's toys.

There was another door opposite the first, which Ilinu unlocked and locked again when they were all through, hiding the broken shelves. The next room was larger, and had a flight of stone stairs in the far corner. Haunches of meat hung from large hooks in the ceiling, eliciting a grunt of disgust from Perrely. There were a couple of empty wooden tables in the centre of the room, and the walls were lined with shelves laden with boxes and jars containing cheese, preserves, dried meat, and other non-perishables.

"Here's the street exit," Ademu called softly. He was standing by a more substantial door with a small window next to it. Ilinu did his magic with the skeleton keys, once again locking the door after they'd all passed through. At last they were out in the open! A flight of steps led up from the basement door to street level. Even though it was an unattractive little alley, Danîsha stared up at the sky, and rejoiced in the fresh air moving against her cheek.

But when they reached a larger road the danger of their situation drove out other thoughts. Ademu went on ahead, and almost at once came hurrying back. "Palace guards," he snapped. "Heading this way. Quick, back to the basement!"

They ran back along the alley and down the steps to the basement door. Ademu held up his hand and they waited breathlessly in the small area below street level. After a while Ademu went back up to check.

He returned a few minutes later and beckoned to them to join him at the top of the stairs. "The guards have passed," he murmured, "but they could be one of several patrols on the lookout for us. When we get out into the street we'll walk briskly, but not fast enough to attract attention. If you see any soldiers in white and silver tunics, let me know."

Danîsha's heart was in her mouth as they walked rapidly down the wide street, with the Selmians on the outside. She and Alanya were in the middle, surrounded by bodies, carrying the bellaril and the Ambon. The street was a commercial thoroughfare with shops on both sides, people and vehicles travelling to and fro. Lilting Selmian accents filled the air. Thanks be to the One, they saw no white and silver uniforms.

After several twists and turns they reached a large house set back from the road. Ademu took them down an alley to the rear entrance, where he produced keys and began opening locks. Soon they were all sitting in the kitchen with a kettle on the stove for chass. The Ambon was propped upright in a corner. Danîsha heaved a sigh of relief at the same moment as Perrely. They both laughed.

After allowing themselves to unwind for a while, they began exploring the house, taking care not to show themselves at the windows. It was not a mansion, like Prince Sindetu's, but there were four bedrooms upstairs; and, in addition to various smaller chambers, downstairs boasted a dining room and two reclining rooms—the first large enough to accommodate ten or twelve around a wide fireplace; the second a smaller, more intimate parlour. The furniture was basic; and there were few decorations on the walls.

Danîsha and the girls managed to rustle up a basic midmeal using dry food the agents had brought from the other safe house—an uninteresting mush brightened up with nuts and dried fruit.

When they had finished the agents rose from the table in a body. Ademu turned to Shiván. "Excuse us, my lord."

"Where are you going?" Shiván asked in surprise.

"To buy supplies," Ademu replied. "We need more food, lamp oil, and other things. We also want to hear the latest news: especially, to pick up any rumours about our princes."

"Of course—thank you. I hope the news is good. Watch out for those palace guards!"

With a smile and a nod Ademu and his colleagues left.

The night before had been a long one. By unspoken agreement the Dûrians and foreigners stretched out on beds and recliners and made up for lost time. Before she dropped off Danîsha's thoughts drifted back to her cosy cottage near Birmingham. How wonderful it would have been to welcome the group there, rather than in this impersonal safe house! She felt a pang of longing for her little home. And for Tim, Rose, Maureen, the grandchildren... Would she ever see them again? *Please, dear Lord.* He had assured her they were all right during that ride together after she was wounded; but would she be with them again one day? Still, he was looking after them, and that was all that mattered. Her wound was so much better now...

A couple of hours later they gathered again in the kitchen, yawning and rubbing their eyes.

Suddenly the door was thrown open and the agents burst in. One look at them was enough to wipe the smile off everyone's face.

"We have heard some bad news, Overguardian," Ademu said, shock in his eyes, his mouth a hard line. Danîsha's mouth went dry. What now?

"Oh, no. The princes…?"

"Much worse than that, my lord. Our Heir—Prince Nomariu—who was captured when you escaped…" He paused, struggling to continue.

"Estaron! Yes? Tell us what you've heard!"

"A proclamation was made yesterday. The Heir is to be publicly dismembered and sacrificed to the Worldruler. It will take place in the Temple of Gadesh."

"*No!*" Danîsha exclaimed. Perrely's hands flew to her mouth.

"When?" Shiván demanded.

"Tomorrow morning."

Chapter 44: *Impossible predicaments*

"WHY ARE WE RUNNING AWAY, SHAKHERE?"

"Because—the bad men—have found our cave," Shakhere panted as he ran up the mountain path with Brakhól clinging to his back. Behind him he could hear the slap-slap of many Grûzhack sandals. Mother and Father were up ahead somewhere; his patrol was with the others in the middle; and Dekhtan the *lhendift* player was leading the rearguard. Shakhere hoped for Brakhól's sake that he survived.

"Why don't we fight the bad men?" Brakhól asked.

Shakhere dodged a patch of ice lying in the shadow of a rock. "Because there are—too many of them. And they can reach—our old cave too easily."

"Is the new cave better?"

"Yes. It's higher up. We can—see a long way, and—shoot the enemy before they get close."

Suddenly a Selmian soldier reared up out of nowhere in front of Shakhere. At the same moment he tripped and sprawled to the ground, losing his hold on Brakhól. There was a terrified scream from the child as Shakhere rolled desperately to avoid a sword that slashed down at him.

Then he and his companions were fighting for their lives, crippled by waves of terror that crashed over them, only fading as his brother's screams grew more distant.

One thought kept ringing in Shakhere's mind like a death knell: *They've got Brakhól!*

* * *

When the gasps died down in the Orselm safe house, Ademu continued. He spoke to Shakere, his voice trembling with urgency. Danîsha listened in growing dismay.

"Overguardian, we have to rescue him. The death of the Heir..." He paused, searching for words, then spread his arms in despair. "It will mean the end of the Selmian monarchy. The end of the Renegade Royalty. Of everything we have worked towards for centuries."

"We understand, Ademu. Estaron is also our friend." He broke off, staring into the middle distance. "The execution will take place in the Temple of Gadesh, you say?"

"Yes, my lord."

"No, Shiván!" Lannie exclaimed. He shot her a glance and continued.

"So our original goal, to raise the Ambon over the altar of Gadesh, takes us to the exact place where they're planning to execute Estaron. I'd say that was more than a coincidence."

"Shiván, don't be a fool!" Lannie hissed in English. "You'll get us all killed. Then we won't achieve either goal!"

Danîsha felt desperately torn. On the one hand, Lannie was right: trying to rescue Estaron on top of the already-impossible task of raising the Ambon over the altar sounded like a sure path to suicide. But on the other hand... they were Estaron's only hope. The grisly alternative — dismemberment — turned her stomach.

"Lannie," Gil said. "I think you're forgetting something."

"Oh, really? What, like the fact that we'll be welcomed with open arms if we show up for the execution?"

"No. The fact that we're liable to die anyway."

Lannie's mouth opened and closed, her eyes blazing. But before she could fire a sizzling retort, Shiván had turned back to Ademu. "If we can reach the Temple through the tunnels tonight, would that be our best chance to rescue Estaron — by breaking in unexpectedly during the ceremony? Or is there another way we could get to him?"

Ademu shook his head reluctantly. "There is no other way, *Aténnelor*." He translated the Overguardian's response for his colleagues.

Danîsha's heart sank, and there was an outbreak of alarmed comment from both the Dûrians and Selmians. Lannie overrode them in fiery English. "What, so we come crashing in with guns blazing like the US Marines, raise the Ambon over the altar and rescue our friend, in the teeth of a thousand Mindbenders? Get *real*, Shiván!"

Shivvie flashed her his cheekiest grin. "I think you're leaving something out."

"Oh, you too? What?"

"We'll also have to kill the Strongholder if we want to get Estaron out alive."

* * *

Konnar sat at the shey-nut desk in his study, chewing his fingernails. He'd given orders that he was not to be disturbed. His face had been a cold mask as he'd spoken to Otaru, but inwardly he was a maelstrom of desperate emotions.

He'd done what he had to do, surely! What his Mindbenders had been urging him to do for weeks. He'd lanced the suppurating boil that was poisoning his life. Bari could not continue to live. He was untrustworthy; he'd *betrayed* him. He'd refused the oath of allegiance.

Besides, everything Bari stood for ran counter to what he, the Strongholder, could still achieve: absolute rule over the entire Dûrai area. A goal all his predecessors had striven for and none had attained. He, Konnaru Galenida, the youngest person ever to become Strongholder, would attain this. And with the power of the Curse of Futility he would go on to conquer all the surrounding nations — Khrellárre, Gilléck, the Gnarthrog empire; even distant Anricar, Emilaze…

All the lands under Malane a single Stronghold! Just imagine it.

If only Bari could see what a power for good that would be! Suddenly the desire to talk with his old friend was overwhelming.

But he'd cut Bari out of his life. He'd condemned him to a sacrificial death. Dismemberment in the Temple of Gadesh tomorrow morning.

It tied in with the desperate situation he found himself in. The teméyn was almost gone — the caravan from Barazhân that they'd pinned their hopes on had been destroyed by those Gadeshu-cursed Grûzhileyn. Mindbending was breaking down; his last three Mindbenders had had to lay off all their own subordinates. Law and order was collapsing across the country. Yet still he hoped to snatch the prize, if he could last out until more teméyn was dispatched from their only functioning plantation, and the others were restored to normal operation.

Bari's death would be his great sacrificial offering to Gadeshu. He'd lost Bari for himself, so he was offering him to the Worldruler, to regain his favour.

He was doing what? *Offering* Bari *as a sacrifice? The only true friend he'd ever had? What was he thinking?* Pictures of him and Bari together rose up in his mind: running in the woods as children; sitting in their little hideaway when they were older, drawing up sweeping plans to impose 'good governance' on the world; sternly dispensing justice when they found younger kids fighting; Bari leaping to his defence when older kids called him a freak...

The Strongholder buried his head in his hands.

* * *

By mid-morning in Stillárre the Selmians were at each of the three gates of the city, raising ladders and setting up battering rams. As fast as the ladders reached the parapet the Dorbians threw them down — but the Selmian archers were taking a terrible toll. At the Westgate Gwargif sent packs of his best fighters out of the sally doors beside the gate to attack those setting up the battering ram: time and again the great iron-tipped tree trunk was sent crashing from its supports, and the famous Selmian cavalry fled, their horses bolting at his warriors' feral scent.

But it couldn't last. By noon messengers from the other gates reported rapidly-mounting losses; and by mid-afternoon a sad remnant of the Eastgate garrison came limping in: the Selmians had gained the wall, and any moment now the gate would give way to their ram. To avoid getting caught between Selmians inside the city and those outside — and being cut off from the Domicile and those he was sworn to protect — Gwargif gave the order he had long dreaded: "_Abandon the wall! Back to the Domicile._"

Now, ironically, the reverters inside the city came to their rescue: mindlessly attacking all in their path, they slowed the Selmian advance with street battles while Gwargif and the few who had survived the wall made their way along side alleys to the Domicile.

There he deployed his faithful remnant along the streets at the front and back of the building. Futile; but honour demanded it. Maybe one day epic songs would be sung in Dorbai about the Legion's last stand in far off Doorin, where they died holding darkness at bay to the very end.

The light was fading by the time the tan and grey-caped Selmians reached the Domicile. From his position at the top of the steps leading to the entrance portico, Gwargif snarled defiance at the cavalry commander who stood smiling — without his horse — at the nearby intersection.

The commander gave an order, and the Selmians began settling down for the night, breaking into houses and shops for sleeping quarters, but leaving unmounted cavalrymen   and archers guarding every exit from the street.

It would be a long night; but the end would come quickly tomorrow.

Chapter 45: *Prince on trial*

THE DISCUSSION WAS HEATED, on Lannie's side, and anguished on the other; but Gil knew they could only reach one conclusion: they had to try and rescue Estaron, even if (as Lannie argued) it jeopardised their main goal of raising the Ambon over the Altar of Gadesh. When they prayed about it, the fight went out of Lannie. It was clear to them all that this was what God wanted them to do.

Leaving the fresh food they had bought for the others to prepare, Ademu and the other agents went out again immediately to gather further information about the execution. They returned an hour later looking grim. News on the street was that the former Governor of Selmion was to be sacrificed at dawn. That didn't leave much time to find their way through the tunnels to the Temple of Gadesh and force an entry. Gil's heart sank. He silently asked the Creator God to do something special to make it happen.

While waiting for traffic on the streets to ease off, they ate the fragrant bean-and-vegetable stew 'Neesh and Perrely had cooked. Then they cleaned up and packed before gathering round the map to plot their route. It didn't *look* too far, Gil thought: but maps had a nasty habit of making you think a distant goal was just around the corner.

He brought out Frengor's map and compared it with Ademu's more up-to-date version. It was mostly the same, though some smaller tunnels were missing and the names of the buildings to which the tunnels connected were often different. On Frengor's map the Temple of Gadesh was an unnamed, dotted rectangle. Ademu shook his head. "That was three hundred years ago, in the time of the Dûrian Founders. They destroyed the Temple of Gadesh. It was rebuilt when a new Strongholder seized power seventy years later."

A nail-biting couple of hours followed until Agents Festiu and Nerilu reported that the streets were clear. Then at last, in the dark, they left the safe house. Between them they carried their shoulder pouches; the bags with Ilinu's picks and shovels; and small backpacks found in the house containing other items that might come in useful, like extra lamp oil, firesticks and fireclay, and a sturdy length of rope. There were no travellers to be seen in the dim street, but they took no chances, walking bunched together as before with the Ambon and bellaril carried horizontally in the middle.

Jomel glanced backward longingly at the safe house, and Gil gave her a reassuring grin. In return he received a small, hesitant smile that warmed his heart. It would take time, he knew; but he believed the One wanted him to wait—and he would.

They made it without incident to the basement entrance of the Provost's mansion. Ilinu used his skeleton keys, and Garset and Gil entered with drawn swords, Garset holding his lamp aloft. But as expected, the basement was empty. They made their way into the other room, locking both doors behind them. After climbing over the fallen shelves and surrounding debris, they entered the walled-off space beyond. Facing them was the masonry door to the tunnels— pulled almost shut, as they'd left it.

Garset gently pushed the door open while Lannie and Gil stood behind him with weapons drawn. "All clear," he called softly; and the party filed through.

They were back in the tunnels.

* * *

Estaron had not slept. It must be getting towards dawn now; soon the guards would come to take him to the Temple of Gadesh—and the end of his story.

He could not help it: his heart continued to cling to the faint hope that the Renegades would still break him out—impossible though his mind told him that was. They had organised the first rescue attempt; but Gedoriu had been involved in that, and Gedoriu was... no longer available.

It was easy now to bitterly regret accepting Konnar's deceptive offer of joint rule. But what else could he have done? To have loitered around the palace doing nothing would have been a living death. Yet the affection he and Konnar felt for each other was genuine; he was convinced of that, and also that there was some good left in his old friend, though deeply buried. For instance, despite the death sentence, Konnar had not mindbent him—or even tried to mind*read* him. That spoke of some lingering regard for their old friendship.

Could Konnar still be persuaded to relent, even to follow a more benevolent path—once his immediate anger had abated? Estaron didn't know, but he desperately hoped so. If only Konnar would visit him again before the execution, even if just to gloat; that would give one last chance to appeal to their friendship…

But, failing those slender hopes, he could only pray that the One Creator God would give him the strength to face the same ghastly death his Son had suffered.

* * *

The guards came while his arms were still raised in prayer. They seized him roughly and bound his hands behind his back, hitting him when he did not respond quickly enough. Then they dragged him, stumbling to keep up, to a covered cart at the back of the palace, threw him into it and tied his legs. As the cart trundled through the streets of Orselm he was grateful at least that Konnar had not exposed him to public ridicule.

At the Temple he was marched through the auditorium to the front left, where he was thrust against a vertical sacrificial frame—a sturdy wooden board, braced at the back, and studded with leather straps and iron manacles. It stood in a wide, shallow stone basin: presumably to catch the blood. He shuddered. The guards bound him loosely at the neck, and tightly at the armpits, wrists, chest, thighs and ankles. He could barely move any part of his body except his head. Thankfully they'd left him still wearing his blue tunic.

He looked around him.

At the front centre was the altar, and in its fire trough he could see broken pieces of what looked like wooden ambons—looted from Dûrian Hearths, no doubt. The wood was gleaming with oil to get it burning quickly. Between the altar and Estaron was a table with knives, chisels, pincers, saws and other instruments. Estaron averted his eyes, his bile rising, and swallowed against the restraint of the band around his neck. His pulse quickened, and he found himself panting until he took a few deep breaths to steady himself.

He remembered the last time he had been here: when the Curse of Futility had been cast. It was hard to believe now that Konnar was not the personification of evil he had appeared to be in that dreadful ceremony. But Estaron resolutely reminded himself that there was still good in his childhood friend; he had seen it. Despite all the evil influences surrounding him, there was something deep inside Konnar that wanted to do what was right. He cried out to the Creator God to awaken that tiny flame this morning and let him see the reality of what he was setting out to do.

His confidence was shaken a few moments later when a procession of six chained *Gorelenye* were led into the Temple by Borendu — the Mindbender he'd labelled Skull-face. *Konnar had broken his word!* He had kept back some of those poor, abused children, who were supposed to be in foster homes: six of the older ones, including Tomaru with the scar on his face, whose broadcast agony could kill at a range of over eight aldoret. Skull-face gave Estaron a sardonic smile as he passed. He heard the *Gorelenye* being shackled somewhere behind him.

Oh, Konnar. Is there any hope for you at all?

The temple gradually filled with priests and Initiates of Gadesh — the more important ones at the front and centre, lesser dignitaries towards the back. Estaron noticed that there were considerably fewer than when the Curse was cast; and besides Belyeru and Skull-face there was only one other Mindbender: Menaru, the efficient head of the Customs service. The promised teméyn from Barazhân had clearly not come in yet. How ironic, that he was being executed just before the final collapse of mindbending.

At last a fanfare rang out and Konnar made his grand entrance in the Strongholder's black and silver regalia, proceeding to the front where he took up his position beside the altar. His face was tight, and he avoided looking at Estaron. Irrationally Estaron's heart went out to his old friend. It was obvious he wasn't finding this easy.

Konnar held up a hand, and complete silence fell. "Fellow servants of Great Gadesh, welcome to this special sacrifice. Today we are offering to the Worldruler..." His voice broke off and he looked down for a moment. "We are offering to the W-Worldruler someone I th-thought I could trust, but who has b-b-betrayed me — " There was another pause, and Estaron thought his heart would break. This was not the Strongholder; this was his childhood best friend, falling back into his stammer as he forced out words his whole being revolted against.

With an effort Konnar continued. "B-Barilu, formerly G-G-Governor of Selmion and s-supposed 'Heir' of the R-Renegade Royalty." At last his eyes turned to Estaron, who took in his contorted features and tormented eyes. He returned his old friend's look, silently pleading for their old friendship. Konnar turned away.

"T-today the last remaining offshoot of a d-decayed and rotten royal elite that has p-polluted Selmion for centuries will be c-c-cut down and burnt." There were cries of approval from scattered members of the congregation. Estaron saw Belyeru looking around, before turning back and fixing him with a basilisk stare. Konnar's chief Mindbender must have orchestrated this—maybe even written the speech.

Konnar drew courage from the responses. "Selmian forces now control the whole of Dûrion—they have entered Stillárre and are at this very moment destroying the last opposition!" Estaron felt tears prick his eyes. The shouts were louder now, accompanied by the drumming of hands on thighs. "After this nothing will prevent the recapture of the so-called Dûrian 'Overguardian' whom Barilu so treacherously allowed to escape, and of his foreign rabble." More drumming of hands. "Selmion has defeated the mighty Grûzhack— we control teméyn-production—nothing can stop us!"

The thunder of approval was deafening.

* * *

Jomel watched as Agent Ilinu closed the masonry door to the former Provost's mansion behind them. Then they all squatted on the paved floor of the tunnel to look at Ademu's map. Two of the agents held up the lamps, while Ademu moved his finger along the map murmuring "We turn here... then here...," reminding them of the route they'd follow to the Temple of Gadesh. Jomel shivered and moved closer to Gelmion. She'd seen enough of the Stillárre temple to last her a lifetime; she had no desire at all to see this one.

"Okay, folks," Shiván declared. "The sooner we get going, the better." He stood, and everyone followed suit. "Garset, you and I will go in front with Ademu. Ilinu and Shaliu, follow us. Lannie, you're next with your bow. Perrely and Jomel, you can carry the Ambon in the middle. Then Danîsha and Nerilu. Gil, you guard the rear with Festiu. Okay? Good. *Felleneynor!* Let's go!"

They arranged themselves in the order Shiván had listed, Jomel joining Perrely in the centre, each holding one end of the horizontal Ambon. Jomel wished it could be upright, so they could benefit from its clarifying effect; she hoped they'd stop fairly often for Ambon breaks…

They set off, most of them keeping one hand on the guide rope along the tunnel's wall. Jomel glanced behind at the receding masonry door. Their hours of safety had been so few since leaving Stillárre; and now they were deliberately walking into the worst danger imaginable. Immediately behind her was Danîsha with her bellaril—*that* would be important when they reached the Temple. The old lady was doing well, though she still occasionally grimaced with pain. Jomel admired her courage.

With Danîsha was Agent Nerilu, holding up the rear lantern; then at the very back came Gelmion and Agent Festiu with their swords. Festiu was quite accomplished with the weapon, though not as good as Gelmion. Ademu was also a reasonable swordsman, which was why Shiván had positioned him in the front with himself and Garset. *Father, please look after us!*

At first they made reasonable progress—though it wasn't rapid, as they had to avoid going too fast for Danîsha and stopped fairly frequently to check the map. An hour and four different tunnels later everyone was feeling dazed. They stopped for an Ambon break in one of the hidden refuges the Renegades had built into the tunnel system. Perrely placed the Ambon upright in a corner, and Jomel relaxed against the wall with a sigh of relief as its healing washed over her.

Shiván only allowed them a short rest and then they were off again. They had just entered a wider tunnel when he suddenly raised a hand and they all stopped. His sharp *Hssst!* cut off questions and exclamations. Then Jomel heard it: a distant slap of approaching shoes on the tunnel floor behind them. After a hurried glance at the map Ademu pointed ahead, and they trotted to a side tunnel. Danîsha was breathing heavily as she tried to keep up; with a quick glance Jomel saw that Agent Nerilu was carrying the bellaril for her, the lantern in his other hand.

They turned down the other tunnel and waited a moment, but the feet kept coming closer, accompanied now by the occasional faint echo of spoken commands. One of Jomel's hands was tightly clenched on the horizontal rod of the Ambon; the other was on her heart.

Shiván gestured forward with another *Hsst*, and they continued down the tunnel, walking as quietly as they could. After rounding a bend they stopped for Ademu to consult the map; then started forward again. The sounds faded, but Jomel's heart kept thumping. The Stronghholder was hunting them...

Ademu led them from one tunnel to another, but it was not long before they heard noises behind them again — more rapidly this time. They began trotting, but had to keep stopping for Danîsha to catch her breath. The sounds behind them eventually faded, and they took a hurried Ambon break.

They had barely started off once more when Shiván and Garset stopped abruptly, and those behind almost cannoned into one another. Jomel heard the sounds of feet approaching from the front this time. They all began turning to go back the way they'd come, when there was a noise from the side tunnel right next to Jomel, and a man in a white tunic suddenly came charging out at her. With a scream she let go of the Ambon and jumped back into Danîsha. She had a brief glimpse of Perrely leaping the opposite way and the Ambon case falling to the floor with a muffled thud. Then she and Danîsha collapsed in a tangle while Nerilu leapt away holding the bellaril and the lantern.

Gelmion and Festiu rushed forward with swords drawn, and she covered her head and cowered away from the clash of weapons. After what seemed like an age she felt Gelmion pulling at her shoulder and shouting "Jomel, we must go!" She scrambled to her feet. Festiu was helping Danîsha up while Nerilu still held the bellaril and lantern. Gelmion had turned and was driving a white-clad soldier back with his longsword. Then the soldier was attacked from behind, and Gelmion broke free and dashed towards them. "*Run!* Take that other tunnel!" He grabbed the lantern from Nerilu and led the way.

They ran as fast as they could, the two agents supporting Danîsha, then swerved into a tunnel on the right that they'd passed earlier. Gelmion led them another hundred paces to a third tunnel that branched left, and let them pass into it while he stood guard, longsword drawn, at the entrance. A long moment passed, then another. Sounds of fighting could still be heard, receding as the battle moved away from them.

Finally Gelmion rejoined them in the tunnel. "Are we safe?" Jomel blurted out. Danîsha was sitting against the tunnel wall, her face grey even in the yellow light of the lantern Gelmion was holding.

"For the moment, maybe," Gelmion said. "But... we're on our own."

He paused, his eyes bleak. "And the Strongholder will soon have the Ambon."

Chapter 46: *In deep water*

BRAKHÓL SCREAMED, his mind and body overwhelmed with pain. In the moments when he could think he was paralysed by fear that his old life had returned, and he'd never be free again. But the only way he could be free was if Shakhere came. And Shakhere couldn't come if he and his warriors were stopped by Brakhól's pain. So he tried not to scream too much, and in the moments between the pain he cried out words of strength and hope.

Then his thoughts would be swept away by the agony as they cut him again and again, whipped him, tore out his fingernails, and it hurt, oh it hurt…

Daddy, help! Daddy, it hurts! Daddy, send Shakhere! Shakhere, come — Daddy will help you! Shakhere, be strong! Daddy, help Shakhere! Aaaaaah…! Daddy! Help me help me help me help Shakhere help…!

* * *

Shakhere and three companions — all followers of the flatlanders' God — stood at a hidden side-entrance to the new cave system where he and the remaining rebels had taken refuge after yesterday's ambush and the capture of Brakhól. Father and Mother had survived, but not Dekhtan the *lhendift* player; and many others had died on the mountain path.

The survivors were now holding off a second Selmian attack from a strong position at the wide mouth of the new caves, firing down on the climbing Selmians with their muskets. But the Selmians were still gaining, because every Grûzhack warrior was weeping as he fired his musket; the volleys were ragged, and many shots went astray. They could barely keep up the defence, because beyond the Selmian troops Brakhól was screaming. If it weren't for the brief moments between his screams when courage flowed back into them, they would have given up long ago.

Deep in the cave system fresh warriors waited, their ears plugged to block out Brakhól's screams — though they could not block out the pain that tore at their hearts. As men collapsed at the front entrance overwhelmed by the child's agony, those in waiting came forward to take their place. But they could not continue much longer.

Slipping out of the side entrance, Shakhere and his companions made their way along narrow paths hopefully unknown to the Selmians, to reach the place where Brakhól was being tortured and rescue him. That would only provide a temporary respite until they were killed and Brakhól recaptured; but it might—just *might*—be enough to allow a full-scale attack from the caves that might—just *might*—prevent the enemy from resuming Brakhól's torture. If the great Creator God intervened for them, the rest of their troops might even succeed in rescuing Brakhól a second time. They could only hope and trust in the One they had learned to call their Father.

But then there was a shout from up ahead: a Selmian lookout had spotted them! The next moment five or six other soldiers in tan uniforms appeared, and Shakhere and his friends were running back to the caves. Not only had their attempt to rescue Brakhól failed, but they would now need to guard the side-entrance as well.

Father — Creator God — we're finished. Unless you do something. Save us! Save Brakhól. Only you can do it.

* * *

In the tunnels under Orselm, Perrely leapt away from the intruders who suddenly burst in beside her. She felt the Ambon case slip out of her hand and made a grab for it, but white-caped soldiers were pushing in between her and Jomel. Alanya yelled at her to get down, and she huddled against the wall as the fierce-faced Restorer loosed an arrow at the flickering shapes of the intruders, barely visible in the light from the lantern Agent Shaliu was holding aloft behind her. There was a cry, and one of the shapes stumbled to the floor, blocking the others.

In the other direction there were shouts and the clash of swords. Perrely's heart leapt into her mouth. Shiván, Garset and Ademu must be fighting the group they'd first heard! Alanya shot again into the group behind them, and one or two of them turned and began coming towards them. Shiván was calling something from the front. "Perrely, this way!" Alanya shouted, holding out her hand. Perrely grabbed it.

"But… Jomel and Danîsha! The Ambon!" she cried out as Alanya yanked her to her feet. "There are too many for us!" the red-haired Restorer exclaimed.

Moments later she was running down a side tunnel after Alanya, who had grabbed the lantern from Shaliu. Behind her she heard Garset shouting and others in the group following, while the clash of swords continued. *Jomel! Poor Mâra! Where are they? Did they pick up the Ambon?*

They rounded several corners in the downward-sloping tunnel, then stopped and waited for the others to catch up, Alanya with her bow at the ready. Agent Ilinu came trotting round the corner first, carrying his inseparable bag; followed by Ademu, Garset, and finally Shiván. Ademu was breathing heavily, with blood staining the side of his tunic; and Shiván was limping. "You're hurt!" she exclaimed, and hurried towards them.

"We'll survive," he said with a brief smile. "None of us could see enough to do any serious damage. But they're after us. We must keep going!"

"But the Ambon! And Mâra and Jomel...!" Perrely exclaimed in despair.

He shook his head sadly. "There's nothing we can do now." Sounds of pursuing feet came from behind them. "*Felleneynor!*"

Alanya passed the lantern to Shiván and they ran on, the feet behind relentlessly following. Were they gaining on them? Perrely felt the curse-haze dulling her senses, and pleaded silently with the One for clarity—for herself and all of them. As the tunnel began to slope even more steeply downwards Alanya almost lost her footing. She cried out, then exclaimed, "Why doesn't this tunnel have a rope to hold on to?"

"It is not one we normally use," Ademu gasped. "We need to get out of it, *Aténnelor!*"

"Why? No side tunnels," Shiván said between breaths.

"We must—find one. Because I think this goes—to the deepest part. Where the tunnels are—flooded."

Perrely's heart sank. Alanya muttered an Inglish expletive that sounded like 'Osheet'.

* * *

"After them!" the Royal Guard patrol leader shouted. But a young recruit was blocking the way, holding something.

"What do we do with this, sir?"

"Get out— What? Where did you find that?"

"It was in a case on the floor, sir. They must have dropped it."

"Let me have a look. Daniu, hold that lamp higher!"

The patrol leader examined the strange object: a tall, golden rod with the two halves of a silver circle joined to it at one end. It looked like a piece of Lightist paraphernalia. "Where's Orinu when we need him?" he muttered. Orinu had been their mindbent link with headquarters, but like so many others he had recently been 'retired' for lack of teméyn.

Geshu! They couldn't carry this thing with them. Should he send off two men he couldn't afford, who would probably lose their way in these cursed tunnels, to take it back to the palace?

"Miliaru!" came a call from further along the tunnel—Ranelu, leader of the other patrol. "You waiting for the Strongholder to strike you dead? Get after them, man!" There were sounds of Ranelu's patrol charging down a side tunnel after their lot.

Benorisa! No, this looked too important. They'd all be mindread on their return by that creep Belyeru—and he couldn't risk Belyeru deciding he'd been negligent.

He quickly dispatched his two most intelligent men (which wasn't saying much) back to the palace with the rod-thing. If they got lost it wasn't his fault.

"Right! Daniu, to the front with the lantern. Now chase those Lightist vermin, you fat lumps of *gurunu* dung!"

* * *

Gil squatted next to Danîsha and Jomel on the tunnel floor. 'Neesh was looking all-in. The lantern showed an ominous dark red stain on her tunic. *Dear God, help us to know what to do.*

"We only have a few minutes," he said. Jomel translated into Selmian for the agents. "Danîsha is in trouble: it looks like her wound has reopened. We've lost the Ambon: I saw it in the hands of one of the soldiers. They will be coming after us at any moment. But Danîsha needs time to rest…"

Young, dark-haired Nerilu interrupted with a rapid volley of Selmian. As he spoke Jomel gave a little cry of delight, and Festiu was nodding. Nerilu had always struck Gil as quick-witted. What had he come up with?

Jomel explained, her eyes bright. "Nerilu says he knows this area of the tunnels. He says, why don't he and Festiu lead the soldiers away from here? He knows another tunnel nearby where they can easily double back without being noticed. Then the soldiers will keep on chasing nothing, while we—"

"—go a different way," Gil completed. "Nerilu, that's brilliant!" Accelerating footsteps made themselves heard from the main tunnel. "Go! Do it!"

Nerilu and Festiu ran out of the side tunnel making as much clatter as they could, and before long a group of white-caped soldiers went thudding past. "Creator God, keep our friends safe," Gil whispered; Jomel nodded solemnly.

As the sounds of the chase dwindled Gil and Jomel tended to Danîsha, removing her blood-soaked bandage and cleaning the seeping wound as best they could with water from Jomel's gourd. 'Neesh groaned and thanked them. They tore strips from their own tunics to replace the bandage, binding them firmly in place. With a sigh Danîsha relaxed against the wall of the tunnel, and Gil and Jomel sat quietly, letting her rest.

After a while Jomel relaxed too, leaning her head against Gil's shoulder. His heart warmed—maybe the day would still come when she could forgive him. He knew his love for her was genuine, and his longing was to slowly and gradually make up, if possible, for the abominable way he had treated her last year. But that was in the One's hands—and hers.

After about half an hour Nerilu and Festiu slipped back into their tunnel, reporting with grim humour that their pursuers were running down into the deepest part of the tunnel system—which was flooded. "There's a very narrow side passage right near the top of that tunnel," Nerilu said. "You can't see it if you don't know it's there. We dodged into that, and let them carry on. It gets quite steep, and there's no rope guide. It sounded from the shouts as though they were sliding down." They all chuckled—except Danîsha, who seemed miraculously to have dozed off.

Gil took out Frengor's map and with Nerilu's help worked out where they were. There was tacit agreement among them that their only option was to continue to the Temple. First, they had nowhere else to go; second, that was where the others would head to; and third, if 'Neesh recovered sufficiently, she and the bellaril might still have a crucial rôle to play.

The two of them plotted the best route to the Temple from their current position. Nerilu pointed out a few places nearby where the ancient map wasn't accurate; they could only hope there weren't too many errors beyond that, where Nerilu's personal knowledge ended.

Gil and the agents kept guard at the mouth of their side tunnel for another three quarters of an hour while Danîsha continued to doze. Gil saw the anxious glances the others cast at him, but he felt an inner peace about allowing 'Neesh to rest. God knew she needed it, and he would keep them safe.

She finally stirred, levered herself off the wall and asked what was happening.

"Nothing, 'Neesh," Gil said. "The soldiers have gone, and you've been resting."

"What! How long—? We need to go!" She tried to rise, and Jomel and Festiu leapt to her assistance.

"Only if you're ready."

"Of course I'm ready!" She glared at him.

He smiled at her mock indignation. "Alright. Slowly, then. Nerilu, lead the way."

Jomel translated and the young agent smiled. He took the lamp and led them back to the main tunnel.

* * *

Shiván and those behind him kept running and scrambling and sometimes sliding lower and lower as the tunnel descended, spurred on by the sounds of their pursuers. Finally Ademu's fear was realised: Shiván rounded a corner and skidded to a stop as his lamp showed the floor of the tunnel disappearing into a long, narrow black lake. Behind them the Strongholder's men were catching up. There was no choice.

"Into the water! Lannie—hold them off if you can!"

With cries of dismay—and shock at the bitterly cold water—they waded in. Glancing back, Shiván saw Lannie standing to one side where she had a good view of the tunnel behind. She was nocking an arrow to her bowstring.

The water quickly got deeper, and everything slowed down as they waded against the water's resistance. It had reached Shiván's thighs when he heard the first *twang* of Lannie's bow. Their pursuers had just come round the bend in the tunnel and the leading soldier was holding a lamp. "Oh, well done, Lannie!" he exclaimed as the lamp-holder cried out and collapsed into the water, the light abruptly extinguished.

They themselves, however, were still lit up by Shiván's lamp. Soon he was holding it over his head as the water reached his midriff. Not far ahead the roof of the tunnel disappeared under the water. Behind him the shorter Selmians and Dûrians were half-wading, half-swimming: he had glimpses of Ilinu and Shaliu helping Perrely and Garset, and he chided himself for forgetting that the land-locked Dûrians didn't know how to swim.

He called a halt, but now the bowmen behind them had found their weapons and were shooting at the light. An arrow glanced off the lantern housing, breaking a pane, and another whizzed over his head. Then the arrows abruptly stopped as sounds and a flickering light came from further up the tunnel, beyond their immediate attackers. There was a medley of cries and the splashes of bodies hitting water. *The soldiers were being attacked from behind!*

"To me, everyone!" he called. Beside him Ademu repeated the command in Selmian. The agent was shivering, the water up to his chest, holding a leather tube above his head. The map! *Oh Lord, please protect it – and the lamp I'll soon have to put out... We need them!*

Ilinu arrived with Perrely in tow, and she clutched on to Shiván. "Shiván, where... How can we escape?" she gasped, looking up at him with pleading eyes. His heart sank. She wouldn't like what he had in mind. He was saved from having to answer when Agent Shaliu and Garset reached them, spluttering; and finally Alanya swam up almost casually, the bow over her shoulder with the quiver and back pouch making her look like some rare aquatic monster.

"Praise God we're all here!" he exclaimed. There were mutters of agreement, with many anxious glances back towards the soldiers. "What I want to do is —"

He was interrupted by a whizzing sound and a cry from Shaliu. "Under water!" Shiván shouted, plunging under himself with Perrely. There was a hiss and the crack of suddenly-cooled glass as the lamp went out.

They resurfaced in the dark, coughing and spluttering. There were a few more whizzes and splashes, but no hits. "*Hsst!*" Shiván warned. Good archers could also target sounds. Then he murmured softly, "Shaliu?"

There was a whisper of Selmian and Ademu breathed in Shiván's ear, "Only his arm. Not serious."

A hand came groping against Shiván's chest. "Ilinu will look after the map," Ademu murmured. "And the lamp." Shiván gave them to him.

As their eyes adjusted to the darkness they could dimly see one another—and behind them the soldiers, lit up by a new lamp, their archers peering into the gloom and firing random shots. None found their mark, though, and the shooting soon stopped. They were wasting arrows, dazzled by their own light.

Nearby Shiván could make out Ademu holding Ilinu's bag while the stonemason wrapped cloths around the lamp and map. Good thinking!

"Ademu," he murmured, holding Perrely tightly against him. No, she would not like this. "That length of rope. Does Ilinu still have it?"

Ademu nodded.

"Can I have it, please?"

Looking puzzled, Ademu pulled the coil of rope from the stonemason's bag. Shiván took it. He'd seen it in the safe house: it was about forty metres long, strong but light, and would do just nicely.

"Shiván, what...?" Perrely whispered.

"A way of getting us out of here—I hope. You'll see. Don't worry, I know what I'm doing."

The others had crowded close. Shiván handed one end of the rope to Ademu. "Tie this around your waist—tightly—and hold on to it. Garset?" He was the heaviest, apart from himself. "Hold on to Ademu and make sure he doesn't lose his footing."

He took a breath and looked at the others. This would take a lot of faith on their part, but it was the only plan he could come up with. He'd unravelled the rope, and now let go of Perrely. He started tying the other end of the rope around his own waist.

"When I get where I'm going, I'll tug on the rope. One tug means I have to come back and you must start pulling. Two tugs means you must all follow me one by one. I'll be holding the other end of the rope."

"Shiván!" Perrely exclaimed.

An arrow whizzed by. "I'd better go. The One protect us all."

He took a deep breath, plunged underwater, and began swimming along the submerged tunnel. He dimly heard Perrely's muted scream.

"Shiván! No!"

Chapter 47: *Into the Temple of Gadesh*

THE WATER WAS PITCH-BLACK, completely still, and icy cold. It seemed to drag Shiván's sodden clothing down towards the tunnel floor. *Start swimming. You've managed a hundred and fifty seconds before. Stop at a hundred. Ademu will pull you back…*

He swam blindly through the water-filled tunnel with long, careful strokes, feeling the floor sloping downward. The rope trailed behind him.

Sixty-seven, sixty-eight, sixty-nine… The pressure was building in his lungs. He felt the floor. Was it level again? He stroked up to the roof with a hand raised — it was still submerged.

The weight of rock and dark water pressed down on him. The curse-haze darkened his thoughts, and he felt himself slipping towards the old despair. A long, watery coffin… Panic flooded him. *No! Fight, swim, count!* Eighty-one, eighty-two, eighty-three… The ceiling had to lift, he had to find air.

A hundred. No! He couldn't turn back. He had to succeed. *Go on!*

Hundred and ten, hundred and eleven, hundred and twelve, hundred and thirteen… His lungs felt as though they might burst at any moment. He had to turn back. *No!* He had to go on!

He trailed his hand on the floor — it was rising! Up to the roof… Oh, God, yes, a shallow gap above the water. He tried to get his nose into it, to breathe, but there wasn't enough room. He pushed on, touching the roof intermittently. It sank underwater again. *No…!* Panic threatened to engulf him. Just a little further…

He pulled himself forward and downward. This was his last chance.

Hundred and twenty-five, twenty-six, twenty-seven… The rope jerked taut behind him, slackened, then tightened again. There was a single tug. He'd reached the end of his rope — literally. Desperately he surged upward, and his raised hand broke the surface of the water. No roof, as far as he could reach! He pushed himself upright, and with indescribable relief gulped in the damp, musty air. *I made it!*

Thank you, Lord.

He lost his balance for a moment, then found his footing on what felt like a flight of stairs. His head and shoulders were out of the water.

He tugged twice on the rope. There was a delay, then two tugs in return. *Dear God, we're not out of this yet. Please help the others to get through!*

A violent tug on the rope jerked him off the step he was standing on. Someone was coming, pulling themselves along. He struggled to regain his footing, and braced himself against a slight outcropping on the tunnel wall. There were more jerks, then the rope suddenly went still. What now? Was he or she in trouble? He was just about to swim down and find out when the jerking resumed. Oh! He was on a flight of stairs, higher than Ademu, who was anchoring the rope at the other end. The rope must be flush against the roof at some point, hard to get a grip of—probably that bit where it went underwater again.

There was a last jerk, a splash, and he heard someone just in front of him gasping for breath. *"Kelida elara!"* It was Ilinu. Shiván reached out a hand, and encountered a sodden, canvas-covered lump. Ilinu's ever-present bag! He managed to find the handles and took it from the stonemason, who continued to gasp for a moment. Then he took the bag back, said something in Selmian, and started moving up the stairs. Shiván hoped he could get the lamp relit.

Shiván tugged twice on the rope, and received the answering signal. After more jerking and the agonising interval of stillness, Agent Shaliu made it. He took up a position beside Shiván and grasped the rope with both hands.

The next set of jerks on the rope were more frequent and not as violent. Perrely? The moment of stillness came—and stretched on. Shiván's heart leapt into his mouth. *She couldn't swim!* He rapidly untied the rope from round his waist, gave it to Shaliu, and plunged into the water.

Keeping a hand on the rope he stroked down to where it tightened against the roof. Then he waited a few seconds, totally still in the blackness. *There!* A current of water washed against him from his lower right. He plunged towards it, and something struck his arm. A moment later a pair of hands was clutching him in a vice-like grip. He kicked off the floor and soon the two of them were gasping for breath on the stairs.

"Shiván!" Perrely gasped.

"I'm here."

She held on to him, the gasps turning to sobs. He stroked her wet hair. Moments later Lannie arrived, stroking smoothly upwards.

Her first words were, "Well done, Shivvie! Sorry, I lost her when she let go of the rope. I hope my bowstring is still dry..."

Shiván gently disengaged himself from Perrely and took his place beside Shaliu. Another two tugs on the rope. After some mighty jerks and violent currents in the water Garset arrived on the stairs coughing and spluttering, immediately followed by another good swimmer, Ademu. As Ademu stood upright on the steps a dim yellow light from further up the tunnel illuminated the scene. Shiván gave a whoop of joy. "Ilinu's relit the lamp!" There were exclamations of relief all round.

As soon as Garset and Ademu had caught their breath they all climbed the stairs out of the water, and found Ilinu sitting on the dry tunnel floor holding up the lantern to examine the contents of his bag. Shaliu took the lamp and they squatted down beside him.

"How did you get the lamp going again?" Lannie asked. Ademu translated. Ilinu gave a quick reply while rummaging through his bag, and Ademu told them he'd brought spare lamp oil, extra glass panels, and a couple of new wicks from the first safe house.

"Wow. A man who believes in being prepared."

"How about your bowstring, Lannie?" Shiván asked.

She gave a lopsided grin. "It's more or less dry. I wrapped it inside every bit of cloth I had in my back pouch. Luckily the enemy bowmen decided to stop wasting arrows on us, so I had time."

"No sign of them trying to follow?"

"No. The last I saw, they were hurrying back up the tunnel."

Ilinu had taken the leather map roll out of his bag and was prising the round cap off one end with Ademu hovering beside him. He removed the cap and handed the roll to Ademu. With infinite care the agent eased the heavy paper out of its case. He held it up to the light and gave a grunt of relief. The lines of the map were clear except at the two ends, where a little water had seeped through the caps. Even there the damage was minimal.

"We need to thank the One!" Shiván said. "We're all safe, we have light, the map is okay, and Alanya's bowstring is dry."

"And we need to thank you, *Aténnelor*," Garset said. "Without your quick thinking this mission would have been over." There were murmurs of agreement. Shiván grinned. "I think it was God's idea." He raised his hands in prayer, and, wet and shivering, they thanked the One Creator God.

They sat silent for a few moments, everyone busy with their own thoughts. Shiván was happy that they had come through the latest crisis — and that Perrely's hand was in his, her head resting against his shoulder.

"We lost the Ambon," Perrely murmured. "But maybe Gelmion and Jomel managed to pick it up ..." Her words lacked conviction.

"The Strongholder's men have probably got it," Lannie muttered. "In which case our main mission in Selmian has failed."

Ademu said quietly, "We still need to rescue the Heir."

"Yes," Shiván declared, doing his best to strike a positive note. "That must now be our goal. And we can be sure Gelmion and Danîsha will head for the Temple. That's what we agreed. Let's pray that we'll meet them there. Then at least we'll have the bellaril."

They prayed along the lines he had suggested, then plotted their route to the Temple on Ademu's map.

"*Felleneynor!*" They struggled to their feet and began trudging wearily up the tunnel.

* * *

Konnar knew Belyeru had orchestrated the applause that filled the Temple auditorium, but he was glad of it. Condemning his best friend — his only friend — to die was a pain so deep that he needed all the help he could get to go through with it. With only three active Mindbenders left in Selmion, such artificial support was all he had.

As the applause died down he nodded to Mindbender Belyeru, who turned and gave a signal. The great doors at the other end of the auditorium opened. A rhythmic chant began and a column of figures entered, silhouetted against the light. A tall emblem was being carried at the front.

"And entering the Temple now," Konnar declared, "is a symbol of our imminent victory!" He looked at Bari and saw the horror spread over his face as he recognised the Ambon. It gave him no pleasure, but this was what divided them — this cursed Lightist religion with its high-minded scruples and unrealistic idealism. Bari needed to understand that.

All heads turned to watch the procession. "Yes! What you see is none other than the Ambon of Sûrilane! The Lightists' most treasured relic, captured last night!" Applause broke out again — spontaneously this time. "This symbol of Lightist dominance is now in our hands,

411

and those who arrogantly brought it to Selmion thinking they could use it against us—those so-called 'Restorers of the Way'—will soon appear before you here in the Temple, either dead or alive. Lightism will be destroyed once and for all! It started centuries ago with Prince Orrénne, sacrificed right here on this altar; it will end today on the same altar with the sacrifice of the last prince of his line!" The drumming of hands on thighs redoubled.

Bari's head was sunk as low as it would go against the neck restraint and his eyes were closed, sorrow written in every line of his face. Konnar's heart lurched, and he clamped down viciously on it. He would grieve later; right now he had to do what needed to be done.

He nodded to Mindbender Borendu and the torture of the *Gorelenye* began. As the children's cries and whimpers arose Konnar watched Bari carefully. He had given Borendu strict instructions that the torture was to be low-key, not enough to overwhelm Bari: for the sacrifice to be valid he had to remain conscious as long as possible. Bari's eyes squeezed tighter and a tear trickled down one cheek; but he gave no sign of passing out.

As the torture proceeded the congregation gave worship to Gadesh in low murmurs, the volume gradually rising. When the moment was right Konnar held up a hand and the voices died away while the torture continued.

"Prepare the victim."

The executioner, dressed in the traditional plain black hooded robe, was standing at the instrument table. He took a knife and with slow, ponderous dignity approached the sacrificial frame. Bari's eyes opened and widened at the sight of the large black figure standing before him. He allowed Bari to see the knife, then started cutting off Bari's outer robe. He took his time, but cut carelessly, often slicing through both robe and tunic into Bari's flesh. Konnar felt each cry and cut as though it was his own flesh, and had to restrain himself from telling the man to be more careful. When the robe was finally removed, Estaron' tunic was scored with bloodstains. The executioner cut off his shoes in a similar cavalier manner.

"Light the altar fire." Konnar could hear the quiver in his voice. *Was he really doing this? Ordering his only friend to be slaughtered and burnt?* A couple of acolytes processed out of an anteroom carrying lighted torches. They climbed the altar steps and thrust the torches into the oil-soaked wooden ambon fragments, waiting until it was all burning.

A long moment passed before Konnar could bring himself to utter the fateful words: "Let the s-s-sacrifice b-begin."

A priest came up, spread his arms wide, and intoned a flowery ritual prayer to Worldruler Gadesh. Konnar heard the words dimly as if through a mist. "...accept the life offered to you now... Take his body parts, offered one by one... compensation for this man's scorn and rejection of your devoted Strongholder..."

When he at last finished a choir of Temple acolytes filed in and stood behind the altar. They took a while to prepare themselves before the leader sang a single note. Then they all joined in with the sacrificial anthem. After each of the many stanzas the congregation joined in with the responses. Konnar had always enjoyed the sense of anticipation aroused by the eerie, two-part song with its gradual crescendo; now it filled him with dread. Tradition demanded that the anthem build up slowly to a particular point, at which the executioner would begin the procedure. Konnar clasped both hands tightly behind his back to stop himself from chewing his fingernails.

At last the high point was reached and the executioner stepped forward. He took a pair of pincers from the instrument table and held them up, announcing in a deep voice that carried over the anthem and the cries of the *Gorelenye*: "The sacrifice begins. We start with the lower extremities. *Let him no longer walk!*"

He went down on one knee before Bari and twisted his left foot outward so that it could be seen, while still leaving the ankle bound. Holding the foot firmly with his left hand, he forced one jaw of the opened pincers between the smallest and second-smallest toes. Konnar couldn't help himself: he looked away, barely managing to avoid screwing his eyes up.

The pincers closed: and Bari screamed.

* * *

Shiván stopped. He didn't know how much further he could go. He looked behind him, holding up the lamp. Garset was plodding doggedly along, his head down, his whole bearing that of a man at the end of his tether. Behind him Perrely glanced up, her face wan in the dim lamplight. She tried to smile, but her lips barely moved. Garset saw Shiván had stopped and sank down to the floor, resting his head on his knees. Perrely joined him. Some distance behind them Shiván could make out Ilinu stumbling along, bent over as if his bag carried the whole weight of the world. In the distance Lannie was haranguing Ademu and Shaliu, trying to keep them moving.

Something in Shiván's tired memory stirred. This was more than their wet, heavy clothes hampering each step. He had seen this before. When? Where?

It had started maybe a quarter of an hour ago, though it felt much longer. They'd escaped the third patrol since the submerged tunnel, and after consulting Ademu's map they'd set out on what they hoped would be the last diversion before reaching the Temple of Gadesh. Then, gradually, a great weariness had descended on them. They'd thought it was the curse-haze, becoming worse the longer they were separated from the Ambon and the closer they came to the temple...

But no. This was far more than the curse-haze. His own thoughts ground to a halt, and as the others all settled on the floor in various postures of defeat he struggled to keep trusting and thinking. This was... like... that other time and place. They had been marching. Marching into darkness.

Yea, though I walk through the valley of the shadow of death, I will fear no evil: for thou art with me... Thou art with me. He'd continually repeated those words from the twenty-third psalm. It was what had saved him from the despair all around him...

He suddenly sat up straight. *That was it!* Brakhól—the Child of Despair! Last year—Shambor's ambush that Gil had led them into, when their army was wiped out... He, Garset and a small remnant had barely escaped. *This was the same despair that had numbed their thoughts and deprived them of all will to fight.*

"Lannie!" he croaked. "Lannie, do you remember... the Child of Despair?"

She looked at him, dark circles under her eyes. Then light dawned in them. "The ambush. This is the same!" At the same moment Garset exclaimed, "Yes!"

The others stared at them, uncomprehending. Shiván explained, "We have felt this before. It comes from a Child of Despair. A Mindbender must be torturing one somewhere..."

"Of course—the *Gorelenye!* They use them in Gadeshite rituals..." Ademu said. He explained in Selmian to the other agents.

"'*Them*'—more than one?" Shiván said. "Dear God. Anyway, it means the Temple can't be far away. "Come on! We're almost there."

They pushed on, fighting the almost physical waves of darkness that would have driven them to their knees in defeat. Somehow knowing what it was gave them the will to resist, to throw all they had into one last, desperate drive to reach their goal.

Finally Shiván stopped, Ademu beside him. Shiván rested his hand on a brick wall that formed the left side of the tunnel they had just entered. "This is it," he declared wearily. "The basement of the Temple of Gadesh."

The others crowded round. Lannie surveyed the wall. "No sign of a door."

"Let Ilinu do his thing."

The stonemason had already taken the lamp and was moving along the wall, examining the gaps between the bricks. At last he straightened up and said something to Ademu.

"He says there is no door," Ademu translated. "We'll have to break through the wall."

"Well, that's wonderful," Lannie muttered in English. "Why don't we just walk in from the street and ask if we can join them?"

Garset grunted and sat on the floor. Shaliu followed suit. Perrely was leaning against Shiván and uttered a low moan.

"Come on, people, don't give up when we're right here!" Shiván said. "We know our chances of success are low. Gelmion, Danîsha and the others are not with us, and if we want to rescue Estaron we can't wait for them. That means we don't have the bellaril. We don't have the Ambon. We'll be facing the Strongholder and his Mindbenders—*and* these Children of Despair. But we have one thing they don't have: *God is with us*. The Book says, 'Even if we walk through the deepest darkness, we need fear no evil. *He* is with us, and his rod of protection is over us.'

"He brought us here! Whoever would have thought, a month ago, that we could reach the Temple of Gadesh in Orselm without being captured? It seemed totally impossible—but we've done it! We can't stop now. Maybe we'll be heard as we break in—or maybe God will block their ears. But we can't just sit here and give up!"

They were all looking at him. "Good pep talk, coach," Lannie muttered with a crooked grin.

Garset pushed himself to his feet and held out an open hand to Ilinu. After a moment the stonemason placed the haft of the pick in it, and showed Garset where to attack the wall. Shiván and the three agents took turns as well, and to their relief the ancient mortar crumbled under the pick's assault. Soon there was a hole big enough for them to squeeze through.

Shiván went in first, with the lamp in one hand and the Blade in the other. Garset followed with his own sword drawn. There was no one there. Above them they could faintly hear a confused medley of singing and shrill cries of pain—the Children of Despair.

Shiván put his head back through the hole and beckoned to the others. Perrely came first, and gave a little whimper of horror when she saw the basement's contents: besides cupboards and shelves filled with books and cult artefacts, there was a rack, thumbscrews, a table littered with nameless instruments of torture—and a pile of skeletons. She clutched Shiván's hand, and he could feel her trembling. She had suffered from the same kind of instruments in Shambor's torture chamber.

As soon as everyone was inside Shiván led them to a flight of stairs against the far wall. There was no time to lose.

At the top of the stairs was a small landing and a wooden door. The singing and cries of pain came from beyond that. "The first thing I'm going to do," Lannie muttered, "is to shoot whoever's torturing those children."

"Agreed," Shiván replied softly, looking round the group. All except Garset nodded.

"Shouldn't she shoot the Strongholder first? Then it's all over."

They looked at one another. He had a point—didn't he? It was so hard to think with the children's unremitting despair battering the mind.

But trust Lannie to have it all worked out. "Only if I have a clear shot right away. Otherwise, if I miss, I've revealed our presence for nothing. But the children sound quite close. If I shoot their Mindbender, we'll all be able to think again."

There were nods all round. Logical or not, they'd go with that. Shiván took a deep breath. "Well, this is it, folks. Once we go through this door, there's no turning back, whether we live or die. It's either that or complete failure. Are you with me?" There were nods and muttered yesses. "Then let's pray."

Quietly they committed themselves and whatever awaited them through the door to the One Creator God.

"Children of Despair first, then the Strongholder, then Estaron," Shiván murmured when they'd finished. He added with an ironic grin, "If we free Estaron without killing the Strongholder—and if we're still alive—we'll escape this way to the tunnels."

He gestured to Ilinu, who carefully tried the door. It was locked. Out came the skeleton keys—but this time they didn't work. Perrely let out a groan and Lannie a sharp sigh of frustration. Shiván closed his eyes. Half a dozen times those keys had let them through locked doors—did they have to fail *now*, at the most crucial one? *Dear Prince, please help us!*

Ilinu was feeling around the hinges and the frame. Shiván, Lannie and Garset stood in a semicircle behind him with their weapons ready, while Perrely and the other two agents waited on either side of the door. Ilinu took out his crowbar and gently fitted it between the lock and the frame. He shot a questioning look at Shiván. With another silent plea to the One, Shiván nodded. Ilinu leaned back on the crowbar and the door creaked. They all froze.

The sounds from within the Temple continued unchanged. After a brief pause Ilinu braced himself, then pulled back hard. There was a loud crack and the door flew inwards. Ilinu and his crowbar dropped to the floor while Shiván tensed, ready to leap over him...

...only to be faced with an empty room and another closed door. He, Lannie and Garset let out tensed breaths. They exchanged tired grins at the sudden anticlimax. Then they all entered the room, which appeared to be a vestry or chamber for the priests to prepare in. On the walls were bookshelves full of volumes with unreadable titles and pegs from which sets of grey robes hung. The singing and the cries were louder in here. "Steady," Shiván murmured as they all felt the waves of despair washing over them. "Remember, the One is with us."

They clustered round the inner door while Ilinu gently tested the handle. It wasn't locked. Shiván held up a hand and they listened. The singing was a little quicker and louder, and the pathetic cries of the Children of Despair continued. Shiván very cautiously opened the door a short way and peered through the crack. The volume of sound increased.

He found himself looking into the main sanctuary of the Temple. The anteroom they were in was at the front, to one side. Some distance away on the left, as he peered round the doorframe, was the altar with a fire burning on it. Beyond the fire, visible through the wavering flames, a man in a fancy black and silver outfit was standing: had to be the Strongholder. *Not a good shot for Lannie.* Shiván shivered at the thought of the power that figure embodied, which they would soon be confronting. In the background he could just glimpse the auditorium where rows of spectators were sitting.

Shiván looked to the right, and his heart lurched as he saw six Children of Despair chained to benches just near their door. A grey-robed man had a small girl's hand grasped in his. A knife glinted, and her high-pitched scream struck Shiván like a blow.

Between the children and the altar was a table with instruments of torture. A large guy in a plain black robe was standing beside it. Beyond and to his right was a vertical wooden frame with many holes through which leather straps, metal bands and chains passed. Estaron must be tied to the other side of that.

Shiván was relieved that their anteroom was mostly hidden from the spectators.

He stood aside and let the others have a look. After Lannie had done so she breathed in his ear, "Strongholder no go. Shooting the children's Mindbender first." Shiván nodded.

Perrely took a brief glance into the Temple and came back to Shiván. He was glad to see a grim determination in her face as she clasped his hand. They had agreed that she would stand by to help with Estaron if they managed to free him. His heart clenched at the thought of Perrely in danger, but all their fighters—himself, Garset, Lannie and Ademu— would be looking out for her; and the other two agents, Ilinu and Shaliu, would be standing by as well.

Shaliu and Ademu were peering through the door when a deep voice spoke, overriding the singing and the cries of the children. All three agents uttered exclamations of dismay and Ademu turned toward them: "The execution is starting!"

They had barely unsheathed their weapons and gathered at the door, Lannie in the lead, when Estaron's scream of agony pierced them.

"I'm going in!" Lannie cried, and opened the door.

* * *

Gil glanced anxiously at Danîsha in the flickering lamplight as they made their slow way through the tunnels. Her breathing was rapid and shallow, her face tight with pain. She had an arm over Jomel's shoulders, and the younger woman shot him a pleading look.

He nodded. "Let's take a break."

"Can't— afford to," Danîsha said. "May already be— too late."

"We won't be any use if you're too done in to play the bellaril, 'Neesh."

Nerilu led them to a side passage where Gil and Jomel eased Danîsha down to the floor. Festiu stood with sword drawn at the entrance. He said something in Selmian and Jomel translated: "He thinks we've lost the last patrol."

"I hope so," Gil muttered grimly. Twice now they'd had to run, and that had cost Danîsha dearly. They had also walked twice as far as necessary with all the backtracks when Frengor's ancient map had led them astray.

Jomel's eyes grew wide at the sight of 'Neesh's blood-soaked bandage. She undid it and gently cleaned the wound, which had opened further. Danîsha ground her teeth and moaned softly. Gil would have given his entire annual salary for morphine and a doctor right now. Nerilu tore a strip off his tunic and they re-bandaged the wound.

"Right. We'd better—" Gil broke off as a mind-numbing darkness descended on him. He'd been getting up, but subsided suddenly to the floor. Jomel gave a little cry. Nerilu grunted, and Festiu slumped against the wall, his sword drooping downwards.

It was no use. They would never make it to the Temple. Even to try was laughable. What had they been thinking? It would all end down here. 'Neesh wouldn't last much longer. The Strongholder's white-coats would catch them, and they would either die or spend the rest of their miserable lives as his mindbent playthings.

The future grew bleaker by the moment as they sat in silence, bereft of will.

Finally Jomel spoke. "We must go on. They're torturing a Child of Despair. Remember last year? The ambush?"

What was she talking about?

"It was different for you, Gil. You weren't— You hadn't—"

Memory returned. The long march to Stillárre, when he had been a traitor leading them into Shambor's ambush. This is what it had felt like? And Shiván and Jomel had withstood it and rescued Bra-khól? That was... amazing.

Then they *could* go on. But what had been almost impossible would now require a miracle.

"You're right. Explain to the agents."

Jomel did so, while Gil told 'Neesh, who had not been part of the ambush.

Then they gently helped Danîsha to her feet and slowly and stumblingly resumed their journey. With despair whispering defeat at every step, Gil could only keep calling out in his heart to the One Creator God, now his Father: *Help us, dear God, please help us.* As if wading through water in a nightmare they pressed on towards their impossible goal: the Temple of Gadesh.

* * *

Perrely and the others followed Alanya as she slipped quietly through the anteroom door. All eyes in the Temple were on the wooden execution frame, from which groans of agony could be heard. Perrely moved a little way along the wall, leaving Shiván and the fighters room to move when the time came. Heart in mouth she watched Alanya raise her bow and draw a calming breath as she took aim at the Mindbender torturing the children. She loosed the arrow, and it hit him in the neck. With a grunt the Mindbender collapsed to the floor, hidden by the execution frame from the audience's view.

The children's cries immediately diminished, and Perrely let out a sigh of relief as the weight of despair that they'd all been labouring under eased. She suppressed an impulse to run and help those poor, injured children.

Alanya turned her bow at once toward the Strongholder—but Perrely could see that the intermittent image through the flames made too doubtful a target. The red-haired Restorer swung back towards the large, black-robed executioner, who was facing the audience brandishing... was that a *toe?* Perrely felt sick. Then Alanya's arrow sprouted from his back. He shouted and half-turned, then stumbled to the ground. With practised speed she whipped another arrow from the quiver. Then it all started happening.

Shiván, Garset and the agents immediately sprinted to the execution frame while Lannie leapt on to a nearby empty pedestal. Perrely moved next to the pedestal, Jomel alongside her. Among the audience mouths opened in shock and there were scattered shouts. The Strongholder was still shrouded by the flames. A grey-clad

Mindbender in the front row leapt forward and Lannie shot him in the chest. Shiván and Garset had their swords drawn while the agents were busy at the torture frame, cutting Estaron free.

Now people began surging toward Shiván's group around the frame. Lannie's bow sang twice in rapid succession and the crowd paused. Ilinu and Shaliu appeared with Estaron between them, limping toward the benches where the Children of Despair were shackled. Estaron's face was a ghastly white, his tunic scored with bloody slashes, a bleeding stump where his left small toe had been. Perrely's heart went out to him.

Meanwhile Shiván, Garset and Ademu were making for the Strongholder with weapons drawn, but knife-wielding Temple staff interposed themselves and hand-to-hand fighting broke out. Perrely was amazed: the Strongholder just stood there, and no other Mindbenders appeared to strike them down. She glanced up, and saw Alanya swing her bow towards the Strongholder. Perrely looked around to see if anyone had noticed, and something on the near wall caught her eye. She focused on it... and could hardly believe what she saw.

There, leaning against the wall of the Temple of Gadesh, was the Ambon of Sûrilane.

She cried out—she couldn't help herself, her heart soaring in triumph: *God was with them!* A volley of pungent English floated down from the pedestal, and Perrely realised she'd made Alanya miss her shot at the Strongholder. Two angry eyes stared down at her. She pointed at the Ambon, and the eyes widened in amazement. Beside her Jomel also followed Perrely's gaze and gasped in delight.

Perrely started sidling along the wall towards the Ambon, Jomel following her. Not far away Shiván, Garset and Ademu were breaking through the cordon around the Strongholder. *Was victory already in their grasp?*

Then, suddenly, she froze. She couldn't move. Panic seized her. With her peripheral vision she could see that the three men had also stopped moving, their sword arms hanging limp by their sides. That clatter behind her had to be Alanya's bow falling to the floor.

The Strongholder gave a command in a strong, calm voice and the spectators and Temple staff returned to their seats. Perrely and the rest of their group remained motionless. Despair engulfed her. *So* close! If only Alanya had shot the Strongholder... if only she hadn't distracted her...

The Strongholder made a triumphant declaration in Selmian to the audience which was greeted with laughter and applause. Then, after a moment of silence, he spoke again in thickly-accented Dûrian.

"Did you really think you could just break in here and kill the Strongholder? Did you imagine a few swords and a bow could destroy *me*? What arrogance! What stupidity! Before you die you will learn to respect my power."

Pain entered Perrely's body from the top of her head and moved slowly downwards. She screamed, and heard the others screaming as well. She writhed in agony as burning knives attacked every nerve in her body. She gasped for breath, screamed, and gasped again. She had never imagined such pain was possible. It surpassed even Shambor's torture last year.

Somewhere at the back of her mind a thought flashed briefly and died: *Now Shiván and I will never be together.*

Chapter 48: *Path to the Altar*

FRENGOR STARED DOWN AT THE BATTLE from an upper window in the Domicile. For over an hour now the Dorbians had been holding the Selmians at bay; but they could not do so indefinitely. Gwargif's warriors were worn out, wounded, and too few.

Time and again the Selmians attacked the portico, and time and again the Dorbians drove them back. But each time it was a fresh cohort of Selmians; while each time two or three more Dorbians were added to the grey bodies littering the street.

Behind Frengor in the Fraternity Room, Mâron was giving Bishop Harlon a sip of water. The old bishop of Dûrion sat grey-faced at the oval table. The combination of the curse-haze and the agony of watching the city being slowly destroyed was proving too much for him. Perhaps it would be best if he passed into the Light before the end. Frengor could not bear to think of Harlon mindbent.

There was a roar from below, and Frengor saw Gwargif again leading the attack against the latest incursion of Selmians. He leapt at a cavalry officer, and a sabre flashed in the morning light. Frengor's cry of distress blended with howls from the Dorbians as Gwargif's great grey-white body crashed to the ground. His lieutenants seized him and dragged him towards the portico as warriors all around turned on the Selmians with a roar of fury that shook the avenue.

But now there was no one to call the retreat. Driven beyond restraint the Dorbians tore into the Selmians, scattering death left and right. They drove them relentlessly back toward the intersection — but Frengor's heart leapt into his mouth as he saw more Selmians pouring towards them from the opposite end of the avenue. They would be cut off from the Domicile! He wanted to shout out, to call them back — but could only watch, helpless, as the grey mass of Dorbians was surrounded and slowly cut to pieces in the street below.

He turned to Harlon and Mâron. "Gwargif has fallen. It won't be long now."

The Bishop of Dûrion nodded. "Help me up." Mâron did so, and at a further gesture assisted him into his red, gold-trimmed robe of office. The three of them walked slowly to the door. Frengor opened it, and the last patrol of the Dûrian army snapped smartly to attention.

"Your Radiance," their commander said. "Speak the word and —"

"No, Fallenor," Harlon responded wearily. "We will all die soon enough. Escort us to the entrance hall. We will meet our conquerors with dignity."

They descended the stairs slowly. In the marble-paved entrance hall a cluster of Dorbians and travelling priests surrounded Gwargif's body, while only four Dorbians stood in the doorway, their bodies stiff and hackles raised. From outside the clamour of battle was fading. Brother Ongaret hurried towards them.

"Your Radiance— Your Wisdom—we don't know if he will live..."

"It's in the One's hands, Ongaret," Frengor replied, placing a hand on the younger man's shoulder.

Harlon raised his voice so all could hear. "We will wait here for what will come. There will be no fighting. Is that understood?"

One of Gwargif's lieutenants looked up from Gwargif's body and stared for a long moment at the Bishop of Dûrion. Then he turned and barked a command at the door guards. They relaxed and moved inside, dejection in every line of their bodies.

Mâron, Harlon and Frengor took their stand facing the door. The Dûrian soldiers lined up behind them. Ongaret and a group of priests stood on one side, while on the other the Dorbians clustered protectively over their commander's body.

They did not have long to wait.

The sounds of battle died away save for the distant whimpers and cries of the wounded. There was a clatter of booted feet on the outer steps and a grey-robed Selmian Mindbender swaggered in, followed by various lackeys and the Selmian cavalry commander.

The Mindbender surveyed them for a long moment. Then he shook his head.

"Pitiful! Here stands all that is left of the great Dûrian nation. A red Bishop, a blue Suffragan, and a purple Visionary. Much good your fancy colours will do you, now that your Dorbian dogs have failed." A low growl rose from the Dorbian lieutenant's throat. The Mindbender smiled. "Down, doggie! You'd be dead before you reached me."

Harlon spoke. "You have won. We surrender. Your mocking is unseemly."

The Mindbender laughed. "'Unseemly', old man? You'll soon discover a whole new meaning for the word 'unseemly'." He craned his neck theatrically to look behind them. "And what have we here? Why, I do believe it's the Dûrian army! All one, two, three, four, five, six, seven, *eight* of them." His lackeys chuckled.

He suddenly straightened and dropped all pretence of humour. "His Supremacy the Strongholder now rules Dûrion, as he also rules Selmion, Barazhân, Marûvin, Pandiar and Thrinar. All enemy leaders will be mindbent and put to endless suffering as an object lesson to their former citizens." Ice formed around Frengor's heart.

The Mindbender took a step toward the Bishop, an evil smile spreading over his face.

"Starting with you, your Unseemliness."

* * *

With difficulty Konnar had overcome the conflicting emotions that paralysed him as he watched Bari being set free. Bari had betrayed him: he had to die. But Konnar would instruct the assistant executioner not to drag it out.

However he had no such compunction about the Restorer scum. Putting them to death slowly would be a pleasure. He drenched their defenceless minds with pain and relished their helpless screams: Shiván their upstart leader and his two swordsman writhing as they stood in front of him, their blades lying useless on the floor; that woman archer on the pedestal, twisted in agony; the young woman who'd thought she could snatch the Ambon, rigid against the Temple wall; and the two obvious Renegades on the *Gorelenye* benches beside Bari, stretched out in pain. Let them suffer! He did not look at Bari.

But wait... This couldn't be all of them. There were four Restorers. Only two here had that obnoxious foreign stench in their shiláy — Shiván and the woman archer. Where were the other — ?

At that moment the most appalling sound Konnar had ever heard broke through his victims' screams. A vicious Lightist music crashed into his mind, scattering his thoughts, breaking his barriers. Visions of innocent childhood days with Bari flared before him, accusing, condemning, revealing every dark desire and evil thought. He cried out, barely able to keep his prisoners immobile, his control slipping. *This was impossible!*

Dimly he saw an old lady settling on to the *Gorelenye* benches near Bari. She was playing a bellaril. With her was a tall foreigner, a young woman, and two more Renegades.

He fought back with every fibre of his mental power, and with unheard-of difficulty could just hold on to the swordsmen and the archer. But the others broke free. Free of *him*, the most powerful Strongholder since the foundation of the Cult of Gadesh!

As the music battered down his defences he saw the tall foreigner draw a longsword and come striding towards him. By a supreme effort he stopped him. But now the young woman had taken hold of the Ambon and was raising it—

A high, clear trumpet call filled the Temple and shattered the last of Konnar's control. He collapsed to the ground, clutching his head in a vain attempt to ward off that terrible purity.

* * *

Danîsha was at the end of her strength. That final nightmare in the tunnels, fighting despair, pain and loss of blood, had almost finished her. The despair had lifted in the nick of time, reviving her just enough to reach the Temple and struggle up the stairs. Then as she heard the screams of her friends she cried out to the living God, took the bellaril from Festiu, put the strap over her shoulder, and started playing.

And supernatural strength poured into her.

Knowing that God was literally holding her up she walked into that place of darkness. The first faces she saw were those of six children chained to benches. Two were twisted in revulsion, but hope was dawning in the four younger ones. Then she saw Estaron, looking up at her in amazement and delight. Gil and Jomel helped her on to the bench beside him.

She continued to play as she looked around. There were Shiván, Garset and Ademu—apparently paralysed, but no longer screaming. Beyond them were rows of unconscious spectators sprawled on or off the benches. Near the altar stood a figure in black and silver staring at her with burning eyes, his face twisted in pain, forehead slick with sweat. That had to be the Strongholder. A shiver of fear touched her that he had not succumbed to the bellaril. Gil drew his longsword and headed towards him—then suddenly stopped. The Strongholder was still exercising his power. But they were all in the hands of God now.

Her heart lifted as she saw Lannie on a nearby pedestal, also unmoving but silent, her eyes closed and her face peaceful. Beyond her was Perrely, reaching for... the Ambon! Joy filled her. *Thank you, Father!* Jomel ran towards Perrely.

Perrely raised the Ambon high and its glorious trumpet call rang out.

The Strongholder collapsed.

* * *

Estaron could hardly believe how rapidly events unfolded. At one moment he was in the process of dismemberment; the next the Restorers arrived, he was cut free and helped to this bench, Danîsha started playing the bellaril—Perrely raised the Ambon—and Konnar lay collapsed on the floor.

The Renegade agents now clustered around him and tried to help him up from the bench. "You must leave, Highness," one urged. "While you can," another added. A third placed his palm under Estaron's elbow.

But Konnar was lying on the floor. Already Shiván had recovered and Gelmion was handing him his sword. "No!" He stood with difficulty, favouring his mutilated left foot. "I must go to him—"

"Highness, no! This way—" They tried to pull him towards the anteroom, and he almost fell.

"Let go of me!" He jerked himself free and started limping toward the group beside the altar.

* * *

Konnar couldn't remember ever feeling so weak. The mind-numbing music continued to beat on his brain, eroding his mental energies. At least the Ambon had fallen silent. What had possessed him to bring the wretched object to the Temple? Well, he and Belyeru obviously hadn't known its full potential. But Belyeru was dead—shot by that cursed archer. He had only two Mindbenders to support him now; and they were incapacitated by the bellaril. *He had to silence it!*

He also had to protect himself. The swordsmen were recovering. He extended his shaky powers to his armed opponents and the bellarist—and failed. *Geshu take them!* Very well. One at a time...

From his position on the floor he looked at the old lady, and with a great effort managed to freeze her. The bellaril fell silent. Now his supporters would recover. He had to get up and rouse them —

* * *

"I've never been so glad to see you!" Shiván gasped as Gil picked up the Blade from the floor and handed it to him. Shiván felt like a pile of wet clothes that had been through the wringer.

Suddenly the strengthening music of the bellaril stopped. 'Neesh was sitting still, the instrument clasped in her hands, her eyes wide.

"Watch out! The Strongholder —!" Ademu called out.

Shiván turned to see the Strongholder pushing himself slowly up off the floor. He leapt forward and seized him by the scruff of his black robe. He raised the Blade and was about to plunge it into his ribs when there was a hoarse shout behind him.

"Shiván, no! Don't kill him!"

Estaron! What the…?

The delay was fatal.

* * *

There was a growing roar of outrage as the audience came to and took in what was happening. Konnar jerked himself free of Shiván's grip and scrambled away. Again he tried to exert his power over the swordsmen and failed. But now his people were free of the bellaril's grip. He was snatched to safety by a crowd of supporters and Temple staff.

He reached out to his last remaining Mindbenders and found a void. *Gadeshu, no!* Then it would be a hand-to-hand battle, but he had the numbers.

"Kill them all!" he screamed.

* * *

Lannie's relief when 'Neesh started playing the bellaril had known no bounds. As soon as she'd managed to untwist her aching body she'd leapt to the floor and recovered her bow and quiver. Back on the pedestal she looked for the Strongholder, but he'd disappeared on the other side of the altar. Instead she'd put one of her dwindling supply of arrows into a frozen grey-robed figure in the front row who looked like a Mindbender.

Then the bellaril stopped. She whirled to look at Danîsha, and saw her sitting motionless. The Strongholder! She turned back, saw Shiván with the Blade raised — then heard Estaron's shout. *Was the man crazy?*

By then it was too late. The spectators were coming to life. The Strongholder appeared briefly and was immediately surrounded by his minions. He screamed *"Kill them all!"* and knife-wielding Gadeshites began running up towards them. They were in a fight for their lives, and badly outnumbered. *Dear God, help us!*

She found it hard to use her bow for fear of hitting a friend. She cried out as she saw Garset fall to the ground with a knife in his back. She loosed off an arrow at his attacker, but missed. Shiván, Ademu and Gelmion continued fighting furiously, keeping the crowd from sweeping in towards her and Danîsha. Estaron had subsided on to a bench, his head in his hands. *I'll have some strong words to say to him when this is over.*

She turned, and saw Perrely and Jomel with the Ambon at the wall of the Temple, accompanied by three of the agents, trying to reach the altar against a press of Temple staff. At least one of the agents knew how to use a sword, and was keeping their opponents at bay. Lannie shot a grey-robed figure running up behind them.

Then a hand grabbed her arm and she was fighting off an attacker with a knife. Fortunately her sword — even without much skill — reached him first.

* * *

Jomel looked up and saw the Ambon sagging. "Perrely, keep it raised! Let me help you!" She clasped the lower handgrip and together they thrust the Ambon higher. The trumpet call rang out, thrilling them with its stirring encouragement. Their opponents fell back, fear on their faces.

"That's it! Keep pushing it upward!"

They surged forward, making their way towards the steps at the rear of the altar. The agents slashed at any who stood in their way.

"Again!" The trumpet call rang out. But the crowd opposing them was getting thicker, and they could hardly move. More grey-robed Temple staff appeared with knives, pushing to the front of the fray, and the agents were being overwhelmed. Jomel screamed as Festiu fell and a man in grey leapt toward her, his knife gleaming red in the light of the altar fire. The man collapsed with an arrow in his back. *Alanya! Praise the One.*

Then there was a commotion from the rear, and Jomel's heart leapt as she saw Gelmion hacking his way toward them. The great longsword rose and fell and people tripped over one another trying to get out of the way.

* * *

Perrely exclaimed in relief as Gelmion with his sword and Alanya with her bow cleared a way for them to the altar steps. Then she almost lost her footing as a Temple servant grabbed Jomel, ripping her hands from the Ambon. Perrely cried out as Jomel wrestled with him, screaming. She thrust the Ambon as high as she could, and the trumpet sounded. She couldn't see what was happening to Jomel — but Gelmion would take care of her.

The altar steps lay ahead, the fire warm on her face.

Side-stepping two grey-robed figures who threw themselves at her and hit the ground hard, Perrely leapt up the altar steps. She stood for a moment before the barbaric fire intended for Estaron's body parts, its heat threatening to set her clothes and flesh alight.

Then she thrust the Ambon of Sûrilane high in the air over the altar of darkness.

_____

Chapter 49: *The Ambon of Sûrilane*

THERE WAS A SEARING BURST OF LIGHT and a deafening trumpet blast. Her hands burning, Perrely released the Ambon and staggered back down the steps as the altar fire roared into new life. A great column of flame rose upward. The iron flue above turned cherry-red, then broke apart and fell as molten metal into the fire. The flame reached the roof and set the ridge beam on fire. A blackened hole rapidly appeared above the altar through which the column of fire soared into the sky over Orselm. Inside, at the centre of the flame, a blindingly-white shape began to form:

A great, glowing Ambon.

The spectators and Temple staff reeled back, many collapsing under the impact of the One's power. The eyes of all who remained standing were riveted on the shining symbol of Prince Orrénne, who had died on this very altar. A great weight rolled off the Restorers and their friends, and Shiván gave a whoop of joy: *the Curse was lifted!*

* * *

The first to move was Estaron. After the initial overwhelming joy, an aching pain flooded his heart.

Konnar.

He limped to the instrument table and took a knife. Then he walked towards the Strongholder who stood gasping among his closest subordinates, his face white as a sheet.

* * *

Shiván also ran towards the Strongholder. The ruler of the Cult of Gadesh needed to be dealt with. He might have suffered a major defeat here, but he still controlled Mindbenders and Mindrulers in many lands. Glancing behind he saw Gil and Ademu following.

As he approached, the man in black and silver screamed, *"You will die for this! All of you!"* His eyes narrowed and Shiván faltered at the sheer hate in his face, expecting any moment to be frozen in place.

But nothing happened.

* * *

Konnar's mind threatened to close down. Never in his worst nightmares had he imagined anything like this. His power was gone, his defences shattered.

It was over.

Everything he had dreamed of—all his plans for world government—consumed in the towering flames of that cursed Ambon.

* * *

Shiván pushed through the Strongholder's slack-faced companions and raised the Blade. But at that moment a hoarse voice came from behind him.

"Shiván, stand aside! This is between the Strongholder and me."

He turned and saw Estaron limping up, a knife in his hand. He was pale, his tunic criss-crossed with blood, but determination filled every line of his face. It came to Shiván that this was the rightful King of Selmion. He stood aside.

Estaron walked up to the Strongholder, seized him, and put a knife to his throat.

Shiván stared at the two men: Estaron, pain and anger suffusing his features; the Strongholder riveted by his gaze like a rabbit caught in a car's headlights.

Shiván started pushing back those nearby. Gil and Ademu did likewise. Then they stood around the pair with swords drawn.

Stillness rippled out among the Strongholder's hundreds of followers as they saw their master at knife-point. All were rooted to the spot, oblivious of the crackling fire spreading through the roof above them.

* * *

Konnar was the first to break the silence.

"B-Bari, what are you d-doing? Bari, we're f-friends... I never m-m-meant it to happen this way—"

There were tears in Estaron's eyes. "No, Konnar. You meant to sacrifice me and seize world power, didn't you?"

"I— I wanted to s-stop, Bari. When your f-f-friends started c-cutting you free I was g-glad! Listen, we c-could still make our v-vision come true. This was all a m-mistake—"

"I kept hoping for that, Konnar." Estaron heard his voice break and felt a warm dampness on his cheeks. "Right up to the last minute, I kept hoping. That's why I stopped Shiván from killing you. But then, Konnar— then you said, '*Kill them all!*' And you repeated it a few moments ago."

He paused to ease the pain in his heart.

"You would have seen me killed with all my friends, wouldn't you? And you'd have gone on to extend your Curse of Futility over every nation under Malane."

"N-no, Bari, I w-wouldn't— I d-didn't want that—"

"You've never lied to me Konnar. Don't start now."

"I—" He fell silent, fear and pleading in his eyes.

"I thought so. I kept hoping there was still good in you, something of the old Konnar I knew as a boy. But I see now there isn't. You're no longer the person who was once my best friend. You don't really want to do good; you just want power for yourself. You are evil through and through."

Desperation filled the Strongholder's face. "B-Bari—"

Suddenly, like a cornered thief, Konnar's hand shot downward and a knife appeared in it. He started to lunge at Estaron, but he was too late. With a rapid motion Estaron slit his friend's throat.

He allowed the body to fall to the floor then sank down beside it, a hand on the narrow shoulder, weeping.

* * *

All the Strongholder's slaves in the sanctuary froze. A wail of terror rose from the unmindbent spectators and Temple staff, who turned and fled towards the main doors.

But now the ridge beam of the Temple roof—unsupported at the front end—sagged inward with a deep, protesting *creak*. Herding the Gadeshite stragglers out into the street the Restorers and Renegades quickly left the building, supporting Danîsha and carrying Garset with them.

They watched from a safe distance as the Temple of Gadesh slowly collapsed. Silence engulfed the city as the pillar of flame reached up into the sky—at its centre a brilliant white Ambon.

Chapter 50: *Mindbending ended*

AT THE FRONT ENTRANCE of the Grûzhack rebels' cave system the musket men standing in the rear line struggled to reload while those on one knee in the front fired. The volley was even more ragged than usual. Three warriors slumped to the ground, one hit by a Selmian arrow, the others overcome by the black despair of Brakhól's unending screams. Replacements from the deeper caves came running to take over as more arrows rained down.

Tal stood holding his wife as sobs racked her body. Shakhere fought the darkness in his mind as he shouted hoarse orders to other wounded and soul-weary warriors. Selmians were already in the tunnel from the side entrance. It was only a matter of time. He shuddered as a piercing scream of Brakhól's shredded his heart.

Then suddenly the screaming stopped. The oncoming Selmian troops faltered, and there was a long moment of eerie silence. A vast weight rolled off Shakhere's mind, and strength, courage and joy surged up within him like an unstoppable tide. *Why were they cowering in the caves? They could demolish these flatlanders!*

Pointing out of the front entrance he yelled, "*Charge!*" Faces alive with the fire of battle roared their eager response and dozens of feet thundered down on the milling enemy soldiers. In the side tunnel Grûzhack war cries and Selmian screams showed that there, too, the tide had turned.

Shakhere followed the charge from the front entrance, and exulted as he and his warriors cut through the leading enemy soldiers like a knife through soft fat. Left and right they felled men, and some tumbled screaming from the mountain path to the depths below. Their own access of new energy seemed matched by a corresponding loss among the enemy.

They pushed on towards where Shakhere guessed Brakhól must be held, and now the enemy was running before them, scrambling into the bushes to get out of their way. *Why was Brakhól silent? Why wasn't he either being tortured or crying out for help?*

Then, as suddenly as the tide had turned, something else happened. Enemy soldiers in headlong flight sprawled to the ground and lay still. Others who were standing froze where they stood. In an instant not a single Selmian was moving.

The Grûzhack faltered to a stop. What was happening? Then it dawned on Shakhere: *Daneesh, Gelmin and their friends have succeeded! They have defeated the Strongholder!* He gave a shout of triumph—then remembered Brakhól. His brother had stopped screaming before this happened. *Is he alright? Why isn't he calling for help? Have they killed him?*

Heart in his mouth, Shakhere sprinted towards the place where he believed Brakhól had to be. *Dear Creator God, let him be alive! We haven't won if we've lost Brakhól!*

In a clearing beside the path Shakhere found his brother. He lay naked and covered in blood, his neck, wrists, waist and ankles pegged with straps into the hard ground. Sprawled beside him were two grey-cloaked figures, their faces frozen in a rictus of horror. Instruments of torture lay scattered about. Around the clearing, standing and fallen, were six frozen Selmian soldiers.

Brakhól did not move as Shakhere approached. He cried out in horror and grief, and comrades rushed to his aid; only to stand, bereft, their voices rising in sorrow, at the sight of the pathetic figure lying on the ground.

Shakhere walked forward slowly and knelt beside Brakhól, tears flowing freely. His fingers traced the lines of that innocent face, the eyes now closed, the lips silent that had transformed a nation. They touched the criss-crossing wounds on his chest, picked up a flaccid arm and held the limp hand. He was on the point of collapsing in grief when he felt a small movement in his brother's wrist.

He grasped the wrist with two fingers. Yes, there it was! A pulse—very faint, but regular. "He's alive!"

Brakhól's eyes fluttered open and slowly focused on his brother. He spoke in a faint whisper. "Shakhere. I knew you would come. I asked Daddy."

* * *

In the Stillárre Domicile the Selmian Mindbender advanced menacingly on Bishop Harlon. "Think your last free thoughts, old man."

His eyes narrowed as he focused on his victim. Frengor's heart plummeted, remembering the time he himself had briefly been mindbent by Shambor. He watched with dread, waiting for his old friend's face to harden as the Mindbender took over his thoughts.

But... something strange was happening. He became aware of a growing hubbub in the street outside and a sudden lightness in his own heart — the feeling of a great weight removed. He looked around, and saw his own amazement dawning on his companions' faces. The air was vibrant with light: a huge waterfall of light cascading from the ceiling, streaming through the windows, bouncing off the floor tiles, shining inside him, scattering the heavy cloud in his mind.

It hit them all at the same moment and there was an outburst of unbelieving, delighted cries: *The Restorers have succeeded! The Curse is broken!*

The Mindbender stared at them in shock, staggering backwards and raising one arm as if to ward off a blow.

A tremendous relief and an almost overwhelming surge of new energy swept into the Dûrians in the entrance hall. At the same moment a volley of joyful barks broke out among the Dorbians surrounding Gwargif as their commander struggled to his feet. His chest was soaked with blood, but his hackles were up and triumph was in his eyes. "Light!! *Ligrrrht!*" he barked. "Light has returned!"

He launched himself at the Mindbender and with one savage rip tore his throat out. The Mindbender collapsed to the floor. Behind him his slaves' eyes lost focus and their faces fell slack.

The Selmian cavalry commander stared in horror before dashing out to rally his troops. Gwargif barked a command at his subordinates and they charged after him. The Bishops' Dûrian bodyguard needed no prompting to follow.

Outside there was an increasing uproar. Frengor, Mâron and Harlon hurried to the Domicile steps, where they saw the cavalry commander sprawled unmoving, a Dorbian leaping off his back. Crowds of ordinary Stillárre citizens were surging into the street, cheering and attacking the leaderless Selmian troops with anything they could find. Dark Dorbians were being beaten, cowering but not defending themselves as their minds lightened and they realised what was happening. Many rejoined their comrades in the Legion as they charged after the fleeing enemy. The few wounded Selmians remaining in the street were in danger of being trampled.

The Bishop ordered one of the priests to ring the huge bell in the tower above the Domicile entrance, and as the clear, deep sound rang out the frenzied citizens turned their attention to the steps. A roar of delight broke out as people recognised the Bishop in his red robe of office.

"Citizens of Dûrion," Harlon cried out, his voice strong and clear. "The One Creator God has done a miracle today!" When the cheers died down he continued. "Through his servants the Restorers of the Way he has broken the Curse that nearly destroyed us. The Restorers have raised the Ambon of Sûrilane over the altar of darkness in Orselm, and not only are *we* free, but mindbending is ended in all the lands!" There was another prolonged burst of cheering.

"So let us not needlessly punish these Selmian soldiers who tried to capture our city: *they failed!* Those who sent them here have been utterly defeated, and all these troops can do is to return to a homeland that will be completely different now."

This was not quite so well received, and mutters of discontent rumbled. But no one dared contradict the Bishop.

"We will see them on their way!" Harlon called out in a ringing voice. "You, citizens of Stillárre, and our Dorbian brothers—to whom we owe more than we can ever repay—escort them out of our city. See them off! Let them return to their homeland as dishonoured and unwelcome guests!"

Now there were cries of approval. Frengor nodded, smiling at the Bishop's wisdom. To declare a guest unwelcome and dismiss him from your home was the ultimate social disgrace, both in Dûrion and Selmion.

Then the citizens of Stillárre, along with the Dorbians—reverters and true—and the Dûrian army swelled by deserters released from the Curse, joined in driving the Selmians out of the city. Frengor and the bishops followed them to the western walls, where a great cry of triumph arose as their enemies were seen scattering in all directions.

Frengor turned to Harlon as they stood on the wall above Stillárre's Westgate. "Free at last, against all hope! Praise to the One Creator God."

The old bishop's face was aglow and his eyes bright. "And to his Restorers of the Way! How they did it..." His voice trailed off.

"In his strength alone."

Harlon nodded, and his expression sobered. "And now... to rebuild. So much has been destroyed."

The two men stared out over the ruined countryside: neglected farms; untended crops choked with weeds; broken wagons in ditches;

unburied bodies of soldiers and civilians. Yet among them survivors were emerging, greeting one another with joy, dancing in sheer delight as the Light swept away their darkness.

"A new Dûrion will arise," Frengor said softly. "A cleansed nation. The One has restored his Way."

Epilogue: *The Way restored*

"CLOSING IN FIVE MINUTES!" Denise called. Children—and a few adults—began to straggle up to the desk with items to check out, or requests for final printouts. The community library was busy on Saturday mornings, with school children researching projects, adults looking up family ancestry documents and other online information, and many using library computers or the free wifi to access eBooks, digital magazines, online music libraries and other internet resources. Some even came to borrow good, old-fashioned printed books.

A young teenage girl plopped a book called *The History of Our Bible* in front of her—probably for a school project. The cover showed the title page of a seventeenth century King James Bible. Denise's thoughts shot immediately back to Dûrion and Shiván's precious Bible: an Authorised Version just like this one, in a tortoiseshell cover, which he'd carried with him all across Dûrion and Selmion. How precious that book had been in times of trouble! Here a Bible like that would be under glass in a museum, never opened, much less read for the unchanging truth it contained. She smiled at the girl as she scanned the book's barcode, a pang of longing in her heart for the wildness and reality of Dûrion.

She'd only been home ten days, but already she was sorely missing her friends under that other sky, whom she'd lived with and cared about and battled alongside for over a year to restore the Way of the One. It was a great joy to be home with her family and friends again, but they didn't even know she'd been away: she'd arrived back the morning after she'd fallen asleep fully clothed all those months ago by Dûrian time. Here no time had passed at all: she was still struggling to get her head round that.

There was Lannie, of course: it had been good to meet in church last Sunday, both of them with their hair properly done and dressed in the familiar style of this world—no more Dûrian shifts or robes! They'd shared knowing smiles and exchanged a few words about how they were settling back in. Poor Lannie had been rather dispirited: she'd been trying to contact her former fiancé Matt, but without success.

Denise dealt with the last customer, then did the closing up rounds with her colleague. She pulled on her winter jacket, gloves and hat before climbing on to her bike and cycling down the high street to her favourite café, where she always had Saturday lunch with her younger daughter, Maureen. Maureen arrived, and they enjoyed traditional fish and chips while she regaled Denise with the latest ups and downs of her life as a hairdresser—and especially the latest young man looming on the horizon.

After lunch she headed back to her little cottage on the outskirts of town, where she had a short rest before getting changed to go out again. Her pulse quickened as she drove her ancient VW on to the motorway and started following the signs to Oxfordshire.

The autumn countryside flowed by, and at last she passed the faded sign reading 'Leston'. A few more bends, and there it was: the so-called 'Round Church' on the village green. It was painted creamy white with a grey slate roof; and towards the north end rose the unusual circular tower after which it was named. This was where it had all begun, thirteen months—or eleven days—ago! Now the circle would be closing.

Denise was excited to see two cars in the parking area: a sleek black sports model and a silver—… she wasn't good at cars, but it had to be a BMW. She parked her faded blue VW beside it. Then, hardly able to wait, she hurried into the church.

The sound of voices came to her as she entered the surprisingly modern nave, with its dark blue carpeting, white walls, and warm light from the ochre glass in the windows. Chairs were arranged in circles around low tables, and along the south wall was a counter with a coffee machine, a kettle, mugs and cups. Beyond it the door to a small kitchen stood open. At the other end of the nave was the base of the circular tower, which contained several rows of chairs set in a three-quarter-circle facing the communion rail and altar in the chancel beyond. On the wall above the altar, which had once been graced by the Ambon of Sûrilane disguised as an Irish cross, a very similar reproduction now hung.

But Denise's eyes were riveted on the group of people talking and laughing around one of the tables. The tall figure with black hair was unmistakeable—Gil! Then that unruly blond thatch—Shiván! She cried out in delight. They all turned her way, and she recognised the other two: Lannie and… oh, heaven be praised, *Perrely!*

The four at the table leapt up, and soon she was enclosed in loving arms, weeping for joy as greetings and exclamations flew to and fro in two different languages.

At last they escorted Danîsha — as she was again in this company — to the table and sat her down in a comfortable chair. "I would go and get some chass for you," Perrely said, "but here they only have this horrible 'coffee' and 'tea'!" Her face was beaming. Married life was doing her good.

"My dear, the joy of seeing you and hearing good, honest Dûrian again is all I need!"

"I'll get you a drink, 'Neesh," Lannie said. "Tea or coffee?"

"Tea, please — black, not too strong, no sugar."

"Coming up," she said with a bright smile.

Hmmm, Danîsha thought. *Good news on the Matt front?*

As Lannie left, Danîsha looked round at the others, delight in her heart. "It was wonderful to hear you'd arrived! *Thank you* for arranging to meet here, which is so appropriate. How much time has gone by in Dûrion since we left? It's only been ten days here."

"About five months," Gil said, and Shiván nodded.

"Oh, my. Five months! What's been happening? Tell me everything, I've been missing Dûrion and all of you so much!"

"Well," Gil said, "we heard recently that the last private caches of teméyn have been destroyed in Selmion; and the same has been reported from Marûvin, Pandiar and Thrinar."

"That's good news," Danîsha declared fervently.

"Yes, it is. Also, all the former Mindbenders in Selmion and other countries have recovered from mindlock during this past month, and most have been brought to justice. A large group escaped, though, and took ship from Calardane to some unknown destination."

"Oh! Can they still cause trouble, do you think?"

"Not without teméyn," Shiván said.

"Well, we hope not," Gil added grimly.

Lannie put Danîsha's tea down on the table in front of her, and rejoined the circle.

"Thank you, my dear."

"I hope they're treating the Mindbenders they captured fairly," Lannie said. "I had my work cut out in Dûrion after Shambor's fall. A lot of people wanted revenge, but I always tried to distinguish between what they only did because they were required to by a higher power, and what they did out of their own autonomy."

"In Selmion they're being tried personally by King Nomariu—our friend Estaron—and he's a stickler for justice." Gil looked at Shiván. "One of the best things you did in Selmion was to crown that man!" Shiván laughed and nodded. Danîsha's thoughts flashed back to the glorious coronation ceremony they'd all attended in Orselm, where Shiván had placed the ancient crown of Selmion on Estaron's head.

"Selmion's being transformed," Gil continued; "they're even sending finances, food and other supplies to Dûrion, Barazhân and other countries for reconstruction after the Curse."

"But how are the ordinary people being helped?" Danîsha asked. "There are no Hearths at all in Selmion. Is Frengor doing anything?"

"Yes, a lot!" Shiván said. "He was telling us the other day that his priests are building simple wayside chapels throughout the country. A large group of them, led by Brother Ongaret, are working on this, as well as travelling the roads helping people in trouble and generally spreading the Light. They're doing the same in Dûrion. Apparently they've had a huge influx of novices, and they're putting them to good use."

"That's wonderful! The people of Selmion and Dûrion have a lot to thank Frengor and his priests for."

"You can say that again."

"And what about the reconstruction in Dûrion?" Lannie asked. "When 'Neesh and I left Garset had recovered from his wound and was getting the Dûrian army together again, but there was still a lot of lawlessness in the countryside and some of the towns. Has that improved now?"

Shiván nodded. "Yes. It's been helped a lot by something Mâron started a couple of months ago. He called for town and village gatherings to be held across the country. Even if only a few residents are left, they have to get together and reaffirm the authority of the surviving Elders or elect new ones. A senior figure appointed by Mâron attends, with an army patrol in case of trouble. He's been to many of the bigger gatherings himself, and Gil and I went to some as well. People are so relieved to see order returning to their lives that in most places they throw themselves into the process: all we do is to start the ball rolling."

Perrely frowned. "'Ball rolling'? What ball is this?" There were chuckles all round.

"Perrely's been learning English," Shيván said, flashing the boyish grin that had often lightened their dark moments in Dûrion. "She's doing quite well. You've understood some of what we've been saying, haven't you, love?"

"Yass, a leetle. Just dawn't start talking about thee–... uh... thee-aw-lijy!"

"Theology!" Gil laughed. "Shivvie and I got going on that the last time the four of us were together, and Perrely and Jomel weren't amused."

Danîsha smiled. It was good to see this serious academic who had been her mission partner in Barazhân so happy and relaxed; and it was truly wonderful that despite their past history, the One had brought him and Jomel together. Pictures flashed across her mind of their spectacular double wedding in Darthane Cathedral together with Shيván and Perrely. Bishop Mâron had led the joint ceremony and she had played the bellaril and Brakhól had sung while all of Darthane rejoiced.

Meanwhile Gil was reassuring Perrely. "Don't worry, there'll be no more talk of theology now, unless the Reverend here gets us going on transubstantiation..."

"'Reverend'?" Danîsha queried, staring at Shيván. "Are you actually—...?"

"No, no, that's just Gil's joke. He calls me that privately in Dûrion. But I'm no Reverend here, yet."

"This 'dual pastorate' thing is so confusing!" Danîsha exclaimed. "You were inducted as Kindler of Sûrilane before Lannie and I left, but you say you're not Vicar of Leston yet? When will the change actually take place? When will you—and Perrely?—start switching between Sûrilane and Leston?"

Shيván shrugged. "We don't know, 'Neesh, but it won't be for a year or two yet."

"*That* long?"

"Yes. I need to complete my degree and then do some theological studies. Remember that for us, events in Dûrion are a year ahead of where we are here. This end still needs to catch up! So when the time's ripe Father Martin will introduce me to the church council as a candidate to take his place."

"Oh, these terrible time differences! So, if you're accepted, will you and Perrely *both* be coming here?"

"We wish! But I'm afraid not, 'Neesh. The One has made that clear—though it's also commonsense. To live in the UK Perrely would need a mountain of paperwork she doesn't have. So we'll do as Mâron and Shindorel did—I'll be a bachelor vicar here, with my secret wife hidden in Dûrion. But never fear: we're praying she'll often be able to visit—maybe as my exotic cousin, or something!"

"And Gil, how about you?" Danîsha asked, turning to him. "Has Darthane University reopened? Do you have a post there?"

"Yes, Bishop Harlon saw to that. I've ended up as High Preceptor of Languages—their equivalent of Professor and Head of Department."

"Oh, that's wonderful! That was always what you wanted, wasn't it?"

"Yes. It's rather humbling that although I cheated here—plagiarised a colleague's work—God still gave me 'the desire of my heart' in a different place."

"Sounds like you enjoy it." He smiled and nodded. "And Jomel? How is she? I take it she wasn't keen on coming to a different sky?"

"No, she said the sky in Selmion was different enough to last her a lifetime!"

They all laughed.

"She has something else to keep her in Dûrion now, though." He paused. "We've adopted a son."

Danîsha and Lannie's exclamations clashed. *"What!"* "You don't say!" Shiván and Perrely were grinning.

"Yes. One of Estaron's first concerns as King was for those Children of Despair that we rescued from the Temple of Gadesh. Well, you know Jomel is the eldest in a large family, and she's pretty experienced at looking after children. Also, she speaks Selmian fluently. So, soon after you two left, we went to Selmion and met one of those children. His name's Tomaru. He's about ten years old and a powerful emotional telepath. He suffered a lot as a Child of Despair, and he's often... not easy to deal with. But Jomel is doing wonders with him."

"I can imagine she would," Lannie murmured.

"That's marvellous!" Danîsha exclaimed. "I'm so happy for you both—and for Tomaru."

She turned to Perrely. "And what about your Anna?" Her mind went back to the little five-year-old waif who, when the Curse fell in Stillárre, had attached herself to Shiván, thinking he was her father. "She's still with you? No one's come to claim her?"

Perrely responded in Dûrian. "No, her parents must both have died under the Curse. So she's truly our daughter now. We're so happy to have her!" Her face was radiant.

"Light be praised!" It did Danîsha's heart good to hear that both couples had a child, albeit an adopted one. With no prospect of children the normal way, this was clearly the One's gentle blessing on their lives together.

"What about you two?" Shiván said, looking from Danîsha to Lannie. "How are you settling in back home again?"

"Oh, it's business as usual for me," Danîsha said. "I have a part-time job at the local library, and otherwise I keep busy with church activities, visiting elderly shut-ins, keeping in touch with family, friends and former students... All quite tame after Dûrion!" As the words came out they sounded unbelievably dull. *Lord, is this my future now?*

"How about you, Lannie?"

Lannie smiled and shrugged. "The same, really. Trying to get my head back into my old job. Going to church again. Umm... And that's about it."

"Oh, no," Gil was shaking his head. "I'm not letting you get away with that. What about Matt? Have you been in touch with him again?"

Lannie looked away. Was she *blushing?* "Oh, um, just one phonecall." She fell silent.

Gil's "*And...?*" clashed with Shivvie's "Tell us!"

"Oh, all right." Lannie grinned at them. "I'll tell you." She paused, collecting her thoughts. "I learnt a few things in Dûrion. One is that human conflicts are never simple right-and-wrong issues. Before Dûrion, I never thought I was in the wrong. It was like that with Matt. I was prepared to admit my reactions had been over the top, but not that I'd been wrong. But I realised in Dûrion that I *had* been wrong — many times. So when I got through to Matt I grovelled. I told him it had mainly been my fault — which is true — and that I really wanted to change, and to put things right between us." She paused, and a smile puckered her lips. "He was speechless." They all laughed as Shiván translated for Perrely.

"So he's agreed to meet me next week, and we'll see if we can get together again."

"Lannie, that's fantastic!" Shiván exclaimed. "We're really happy for you." Perrely and Gil nodded. "Me too, my dear," Danîsha said, patting her hand.

Lannie heaved a sigh, her eyes sparkling. Then she glanced around the church. "By the way, where's Father Martin? I thought he'd be here."

"Oh, didn't you know?" Danîsha replied. "When I phoned they told me he was away on a trip to America."

"No, really? That's a shame. I wanted to tell him about Matt. He's the one who said I should learn to listen and not make black-and-white judgments—here, in this church."

"We all owe a lot to Father Martin," Gil murmured.

"Actually, he's taken a year's post as a visiting lecturer at an American university," Shiván said.

"A *year?*" Lannie exclaimed. "Lecturing? As an Anglican clergyman?"

"You're forgetting he also has a PhD in linguistics," Gil said. "He's well respected in the field."

"Oh. Right. Then I suppose we can allow him to go off lecturing."

Gil turned to Shiván. "Where are you and Perrely staying?"

"At the village inn," Perrely replied in her accented English.

Shiván laughed. "I made her learn that. Yes, we're bedding down at the inn for a night or two. It's not the Hilton, the beds are lumpy and the food's basic, but hey! We've survived on worse in Dûrion and Selmion!"

"That we have," Danîsha murmured, her eyes losing focus as her thoughts went back. "All those nights in forests and caves, sleeping on the hard ground…"

"Or hard Domicile mattresses," Gil put in. They laughed.

Danîsha said dreamily, "Talking of the Domicile, and Stillárre—and the Dorbians, who guarded it right to the end—wasn't that a sad but wonderful day, when they finally left to go back to their home in the far north? I find myself often thinking of that. We owe them so much."

There was a chorus of agreement from the others. They fell silent as their thoughts went back…

* * *

It was a bright summer day towards the end of Mallerând when the entire city of Stillárre, with the Bishops, Restorers, Frengor and the travelling priests, gathered at the Eastgate to bid farewell to the Dorbian Legion. Of the five thousand who had set out from Dorbai almost a year ago, only one thousand seven hundred and eleven remained. That number included many who had rejoined their comrades after reverting to darkness under the Curse. They were gathered now in a long column of shaggy, grey-white warriors on the Berûvis road: many wounded, some with missing limbs, all with deep-set eyes that had endured the horrors of war and darkness.

In one of his last public appearances before handing the reins of government to Bishop Mâron, old Bishop Harlon expressed the unending gratitude of the Dûrian nation to their allies from the north who had so sacrificially spent themselves in guarding the defenceless and fighting alongside the Restorers to rebuild the Way of the One.

When he had finished Gwargif stepped forward – with a slight limp, though he was largely recovered from the wounds he had suffered in defence of the city.

"Shining One call us," he said, "and we come. We fight for Light and for Father of Warriors. Now Light is come and darkness is ended! We go home!*" There was a roar from the Dorbian ranks that swelled into a drawn-out howl of approval, with every wolf-like head raised to the sky.*

Gwargif rose on his hind legs and, placing his fore paws gently on the Bishop's shoulders, licked his brow. "Shining One light your days, great Heart of Doorin people." He gave a similar farewell to Bishop Mâron – 'Leader in the Way'; Frengor – 'Finder of Light'; Gil – 'Father of Seeing'; and Lannie – 'Lady of Hearing'.

*Then he reared up in front of Shiván. "*Hrarborgh *– Father of Warriors! You lead, we follow, and Shining One give victory! We go home now, we tell children and children's children that we fight for* Hrarborgh *in Doorin! Is story is told to end of days in Dorbai!" A full-throated roar of acclaim rose from the Dorbian ranks as Shiván embraced his faithful friend.*

*Finally he came to Danîsha. "*Mylendel *– Lady of Song," he said softly, licking her gently on the forehead and both cheeks. Danîsha's tears flowed as she put her arms around her friend and protector, remembering how he had cared for her in those darkest days after her friends were slaughtered at Carreck Manor. For a long moment they stood together. Then Gwargif disengaged and went down to all fours.*

He raised his head in a howl of farewell and all the Dorbians joined him. Then he cried something in his own language and barks of delight accompanied him as he trotted through the ranks to the head of the column. Another command, and the Dorbians began their long walk home. At the slow pace allowed by the wounded, the journey would take the better part of two months.

But now, as they left, the highway was lined for many aldoret with cheering Dûrians showering them with flowers, thanks and good wishes.

* * *

Danîsha broke the spell of memory. "Has there been any word from Gwargif? He promised to send a message with one of their 'out-runners' after they reached home."

"Yes!" Shiván said. "He did. A young Dorbian warrior arrived in Stillárre a week ago. The new Gate Wardens escorted him to the Domicile, and fortunately Frengor was there. Frengor wrote down what he said word for word." He reached down to a backpack under his chair and pulled out a hard-sided folder. In it was a thick sheet of paper mostly covered with the flowing Dûrian script, which he handed to Danîsha.

Danîsha took it eagerly, but her heart plummeted as she squinted at it. "Oh dear. Frengor has very fancy handwriting. I don't think I can read this. Perrely, can you?"

Perrely took the sheet and began reading the Dûrian—haltingly, because Frengor had indeed written it exactly as he heard it:

"Mylendel, is all Dorbi warriors is now back to Dorbai. Is big happiness here, is people is sing, dance, eat for a week. Even families of dead warriors is happy because they have praise till end of days in Dorbai. Me, is so happy with Hishray and eight pups..."

Danîsha laughed delightedly. "Eight! He had five when he first came to Carreck Manor. Hishray must have had triplets after his last visit home!"

Perrely continued. *"We now rest, get better, tell stories about Doorin war and Father of Warriors and Warrior of Song and Warrior of Hearing and Warrior of Sight and Warrior of Prayer. But yesterday we have big meeting. Big thing happen. Ba- Ban-"* Perrely struggled to read the word. "Bankhez... Do you know what that is, Danîsha?"

"Oh! Yes, that's the name of their leader. It means 'Great Father', I think."

"Bankhez *is leave. Is very tired. Elders choose new Father. New* Bankhez *is me, Gwargif.*"

There were exclamations of surprise all round. Danîsha was thrilled. "Oh, that's wonderful! Gwargif will make a great leader!"

"*Is ask you, Mylendel, and all Warriors of Light, is pray for me. Is big work. Is need help from Shining One. You stay now with Shining One. His Light shine everywhere. Send words back with warrior.*"

Shiván added, "That Dorbian warrior is waiting for your return message, 'Neesh—he's staying in one of the disused barracks in the city. He won't leave till he has words from you."

"Then I'll write some for you to take back." She heaved a sigh of happiness. "That's made my day! As well as seeing all of you, of course," she added hastily. Her friends laughed.

They all refreshed their coffee and tea cups—Perrely risked some weak black tea and sugar, pulling a face when she tasted it. As they settled back around the table Danîsha asked, "What's the news from Barazhân? Is the new desegregated society working? I hope Shakhere's father Tal is still holding them all together."

"As far as I can see he's making an excellent Overmaster," Gil said. "It counts for a lot that he was unanimously elected by *all* the family heads—both Grûzhack and Grûzhileyn."

"And there's no danger of any secret teméyn production?" Lannie asked.

Gil shook his head. "Nope. As you know, they destroyed the one remaining plantation that the Strongholder was guarding; and with it the last of the plants from that special strain that have been produced only by grafting for as far as records go back. That means it would take many decades—maybe centuries—for an equivalent strain to be developed."

"Thank God for that," Lannie muttered.

"And what about Brakhól and Shakhere and Mistil?" Danîsha asked eagerly. "How are they doing? Is Brakhól still singing?"

"Oh yes! His singing is so much in demand that they've had to limit it for his own good. He has a whole orchestra to back him up now from the Beauty Endeavour—but it still doesn't sound as good as the bellaril!"

Danîsha smiled and shook her head, thinking nostalgically of those amazing meetings in Kharzil, when she and Brakhól and the One

Creator God would reduce a packed hall of unemotional Grûzhack to tears.

"Tal told me worship of the Grûzhack goddess Makhril is now in terminal decline, and people everywhere want to learn about the flatlanders' God. And to hear Brakhól!

"Speaking of which… we have something else that I think will make your day, 'Neesh." Gil nodded to Shiván, who pulled a second paper from his hard-sided folder and handed it to her.

She stared at it. At first she only saw a crudely drawn circle in black ink with a smaller circle inside, and various other marks. Then suddenly it resolved into a face: a childish Grûzhack face with down-turned eyes and a large, wide-open mouth.

"Brakhól!" she gasped. "Did *he* draw this?"

The three from Dûrion laughed. "Yes, he did!" Gil told her. "The last time I was in Barazhân I told them I believed the One would be sending me to see you, and Brakhól *had* to give you something. So he drew this picture. It's him, singing — for you."

Danîsha stroked the edges of the picture as the tears gathered in her eyes and trickled down her cheeks. That blessed child. A prayer welled up in her heart that God would keep him from pride and self-will, and make him truly a prophet to his own people.

* * *

They talked long into the evening, enjoying a basic pub meal together at the village inn. Danîsha was glad they'd see each other again at the morning service, which they'd all be attending; but discussing events on a distant planet would not be an option there. She was able to get a room for the night at the inn, steeling herself to endure the lumpy mattress. Gil and Lannie drove home to their respective flats in London and Birmingham — it was okay for them, with their fast cars!

She paused, sighing, as she prepared for bed. This had been wonderful reunion. When would she see these dear friends again? And all the others who hadn't come — Jomel, Garset, old Bishop Harlon, Frengor, Gwargif… and of course, Brakhól. A longing for their faces and voices filled her.

Dear Father, maybe one more visit to Dûrion? If it's what you want.

Did you enjoy this book?

In the new world of publishing, word of mouth is often the most important way a story finds its readers. If you enjoyed this book, it would be fantastic if you would consider **rating** *it and leaving a* **review**. *You can do so at your local* **Amazon** *site. Thank you so much!*

If you haven't read the previous books in this series, now's the time!

Four unlikely strangers suddenly find themselves in an unknown country on an unknown world, their ears assaulted by the clash of swords on armour and the whizz of arrows...

Captured, enslaved, barely escaping, betrayed by one of their own, they are pursued across the country from one precarious refuge to the next by Mindruler Shambor dom Beldet.

Can the God they call upon overcome even the Mindruler's unimaginable powers? Are they themselves the long-awaited 'Restorers of the Way', who will set his tormented subjects free?

The Restorers of the Way have seriously inconvenienced Dûrion's despotic ruler, Shambor dom Beldet. News of their achievement spreads, and thousands rally to their cause. But Shambor's response is devastating.

Inexperienced and outnumbered, how can the 'strangers and loners' from Earth, with their Dûrian friends, prevail against an enemy who not only controls the resources of a nation, but also wields deadly powers of mental and spiritual oppression?

Their only hope is to rely on the greatest Power of all...

Both books can be found at your local Amazon store!

Visit *The Mindrulers* online!

*For news about upcoming releases, special offers,
author's comments and background insights, do visit:*

https://www.facebook.com/pg/TheMindrulers/.

*And for fascinating details, pictures, full-colour maps,
descriptions of the Dûrian people and how they live,
notes on the Dûrian language, and a wealth of
information about the world of Malane,
come and see us at:*

https://www.themindrulers.com/.